SPARTAN HEART

JENNIFER ESTEP

SPARTAN HEART

SPARTAN HEART

A MYTHOS ACADEMY NOVEL

JENNIFER ESTEP

To all the fans of the Mythos Academy series who wanted more stories, this one is for you.

To my mom, my grandma, and Andre—for everything.

CHAPTER ONE

The first day of school is always the worst.

A new school year means new classes, new books, new professors, new projects to prepare and papers to write. Plus, you have to decide what you're going to wear and how you're going to act and what kind of person you're going to be—and be seen as—until school breaks for the summer several long, distant, dreary months in the future. There's so much freaking *pressure* to get every little thing right starting from that very first day. And that's just for regular kids.

That pressure is turned up to extremes at Mythos Academy.

"Are you excited for the first day of school?" a light, happy voice asked.

I stuffed one last textbook into my dark green messenger bag, then slid it over to one side of the kitchen table. I looked up to find Rachel Maddox, my aunt, smiling at me. "Not really."

Instead of being put off by my sour, surly tone, Aunt Rachel's smile widened. "Well, you should be excited. It's a brand-new school year and a brand-new start for us.

Everything's going to be great, Rory. You'll see."

"You mean like all the other kids, professors, and workers suddenly forgetting that my parents were Reapers of Chaos and all the horrible things they did?" I snorted. "Not bloody likely."

Aunt Rachel's warm smile vanished like a candle flame being snuffed out by a cold wind. She dropped her gaze from mine and turned back to the stove, flipping the blackberry pancakes that she was making special for my first day of school. And hers too, since she worked as a chef in the Mythos dining hall.

I winced, guilt churning in my stomach. Aunt Rachel was twenty-seven, only ten years older than me, since I had turned seventeen a few days ago. She had always been more of a big sister to me than an aunt—at least until my parents were murdered last year.

My mom and dad, Rebecca and Tyson Forseti, hadn't been brave, strong, noble Spartan warriors like I'd thought. The two of them had secretly been Reapers, working with others to bring Loki, the evil Norse god of chaos, back here to the mortal realm. And my parents hadn't been your average, run-of-the-mill Reaper bad guys. Oh, no. They had been Reaper *assassins*, the worst of the worst, responsible for killing dozens and dozens of innocent people.

I had been absolutely horrified when I'd learned the truth about them, especially since the whole time, all my years growing up, I had never realized what kind of evil warriors—what kind of evil *people*—they truly were.

My parents had fooled me as easily as they had everyone else, leaving behind a deep, jagged wound that just wouldn't heal. Even now, a year after their deaths, their betrayal still coated my heart like a cold frost, freezing out all my previous love for them.

Sometimes I couldn't feel anything but that cold numbing me from the inside out. Other times, I was so angry at my parents for all their lies that I half expected red-hot steam to spew out of my ears like I was a cartoon character. In those moments, I wanted to lash out at everyone and everything around me. I just wanted to *hurt* someone or something the same way my parents had hurt me, especially since I was still dealing with the consequences of all their evil actions. Maybe I also wanted to lash out because I was a Spartan, and fighting was what we were naturally hardwired to do. If only dealing with my emotions were as easy as battling Reapers.

I didn't know which was worse, not feeling anything or feeling way too much. Or maybe it was going back and forth between the two extremes. Either way, the cold numbness and hot anger had been my constant companions ever since the day I found out about my parents.

But I wasn't the only one who'd been devastated by the truth. So had Aunt Rachel, who had always looked up to her big sister, Rebecca. Aunt Rachel had been hurt just as badly as I had been, but she'd stepped up and taken me in anyway, despite all the horrible things my parents had done. She had even put her dreams of going to culinary school in Paris on hold so she could stay here in Colorado and take care of me. Aunt Rachel had been so good to me this past year, and she did her absolute best to protect me.

I didn't mean to snap at Aunt Rachel. Really, I didn't. That was my hot anger boiling up through the icy numbness and getting the best of me. Sometimes, though, it was hard to even *look* at her, since she had the same long, glossy black hair, green eyes, and pretty features that my mom had. The same black hair and green eyes that I had as well and the same features that haunted me every time I looked in the mirror.

More than once, I had thought about dyeing my hair neon-pink or wearing violet contacts so I wouldn't look so much like my mom anymore. Who wanted to be the daughter of notorious Reaper assassins? Much less look exactly like one of them? Nobody, that's who.

But that was me, Rory Forseti, and this was my life, like it or not.

I didn't want to be like my parents, and not being like them meant not snapping at Aunt Rachel the way my mom had done so many times over the years, especially in the weeks right before she died. Or at least, trying to make things better when I did snap at Aunt Rachel. So I forced myself to sit up straight and plastered a smile on my face.

"I'm sorry," I said. "I'm just a little…nervous. I'm sure you're right. This is my second year at Mythos, so it's bound to be easier. Besides, Loki has been defeated, so everyone can finally relax and get on with their lives without worrying about him or Reapers or mythological monsters anymore."

Aunt Rachel turned back to me, a smile spreading across her face again. "Exactly! And everyone knows how much you helped Gwen and her friends defeat Loki at the Battle of Mythos Academy. They know that you're a good person, Rory. A hero, just like Gwen is."

My dad, Tyson, and Gwen's dad, Tyr, were brothers, which made Gwen my first cousin. Gwen Frost was kind of a big deal in the Mythos Academy world these days. Okay, okay, so she was more than just a big deal. She was like a freaking *princess* now. Since, you know, she'd found a way to trap Loki and keep everyone safe from the evil god forever.

Several months ago, Loki and his Reapers of Chaos had stormed onto the Mythos Academy campus in Cypress Mountain, North Carolina, in one last, desperate attempt to recover an ancient artifact that would restore Loki to full health so he could enslave us all. But Gwen had beaten the god, tricked him into almost killing her, so that she could sacrifice herself to trap him and save us.

If I closed my eyes, I could still see Gwen lying on the floor of the Library of Antiquities, looking deathly pale, bleeding out from the stab wound she'd inflicted on herself with Vic, her talking sword, in order to stop Loki from taking control of her body, her mind, and her powerful psychometry magic. But Gwen had pulled through, thanks to some help from her friends and Nike, the Greek goddess of victory. Gwen truly was Nike's Champion, the person who worked for the goddess in this realm, in every sense of the word.

And now she was everyone else's Champion too—the hero of all heroes.

In an instant, Gwen had gone from just another Gypsy girl to an outright celebrity. Gwen had told me that every time she walked across campus or worked at her job in the Library of Antiquities or even went out for coffee with her boyfriend, Logan Quinn, people were always staring at her and whispering about her. I'd seen it for myself when I visited her over the summer. Now everyone treated Gwen like she was royalty instead of a regular student. Some of the other kids—adults too—would even come up and ask her for autographs and pictures. Gwen hated all the attention, and she just wanted to get on with her life.

I knew the feeling, even if my life was as dark as hers was golden.

The fake smile slipped from my face, and I slumped in my chair.

Aunt Rachel slid a stack of pancakes onto a plate and set it on the table in front of me. "Rory? What are you thinking about?"

I picked up my fork and forced myself to smile at her again. "How great these pancakes look and smell."

She grinned back at me and sat down at the table with her own plate of pancakes. "Thanks. I used the wild blackberries we picked when we visited the gryphons at the ruins a few days ago."

I nodded. The Eir Ruins were located on top of the mountain that loomed over Snowline Ridge. Named for Eir, the Norse goddess of healing, the ruins were a magical place, always full of blooming wildflowers and green herbs, no matter how cold and snowy the Colorado weather was. Even better, the ruins were home to the Eir gryphons that Aunt Rachel and I had befriended several months ago.

I loved hanging out with the gryphons, who were like the pets I'd never had. If, you know, pets were enormous mythological creatures who could eat you if they really wanted to. And I especially loved riding on the gryphons' backs as they soared around the mountaintop and over the evergreen forests below.

"Maybe we can go to the ruins this weekend," Aunt Rachel said. "After we're both settled into our routines for the new school year."

This time when I smiled at her, my expression was genuine. "I'd love that."

She reached over, grabbed my hand, and gently squeezed my fingers. "I have a good feeling about today. You'll see, Rory. Everything's going to be great. For both of us."

I didn't know about that, but her cheerful voice and happy expression made a tiny bit of hope spark to life in my chest. I squeezed her hand back. "Of course it will."

We ate our pancakes, along with the bacon, scrambled eggs, and cheesy hash browns that Aunt Rachel had also whipped up for breakfast. She was a terrific chef, and everything was delicious, especially the light, fluffy, golden pancakes. Aunt Rachel had also made some blackberry syrup, which added even more sweet yet tart flavor to the pancakes.

The good food lifted my mood, and by the time we finished breakfast, I was feeling really hopeful about starting school. So I grabbed my messenger bag from the table, slung the strap across my chest, and left.

Aunt Rachel and I lived in a small stone cottage nestled in a stand of pine trees on the outskirts of the academy. I stepped onto one of the ash-gray cobblestone paths and walked across the lush, green, landscaped lawns, past the student dorms, and up the hills, heading to the main part of campus.

It wasn't quite eight o'clock yet, but the sun was shining brightly in the clear blue September sky, further lifting my mood. We were so high up on the mountain that the air was still cool, and I stuck my hands into the pockets of my forest-green leather jacket to keep them warm. It didn't take me long to climb the last and steepest hill and reach the main quad.

Mythos Academies were located all around the world, from the one here in Snowline Ridge, Colorado, and the one in Cypress Mountain, North Carolina, to those in London, England; Frankfurt, Germany; Saint Petersburg, Russia; and beyond. But all the campuses looked more or less the same, and each one featured a quad that served as the heart of the academy.

Five buildings made of dark, almost black stone ringed the grassy quad in front of me—math-science, English-history, a dining hall, a gym, and a library. These same five buildings were arranged in the same starlike pattern at every Mythos Academy, including the North Carolina campus where Gwen went to school and where the final battle with Loki had taken place.

But plenty of differences existed among the various academies. The buildings at Gwen's school resembled old, creepy Gothic castles, while the ones here were shaped like enormous cabins, made of heavy boulders and thick logs that had been fitted together. Wide windows were set into all the buildings to take advantage of the spectacular views of the pine trees that covered the grounds and the high, craggy mountain that loomed over the campus.

But the things I liked best about the quad were the statues of mythological creatures perched on top of, around, and beside all the buildings. Nemean prowlers, Fenrir wolves, Eir gryphons. All those creatures and more looked out over the quad, their gray stone eyes seeming to follow the students as they moved in and out of the buildings.

Most of the other kids didn't care what the buildings looked like, and they completely ignored the statues, but I enjoyed the rustic feel of everything, and I especially loved seeing the mythological creatures. They might be frozen in place, but I knew they were only a few seconds and a little bit of magic away from breaking free from their stone moorings and leaping down to the ground to protect the students, just as they had during the battle at the North Carolina academy.

I nodded at the Fenrir wolf statue sitting on the steps closest to me. The wolf studied me for a moment, before one of its stone eyes slid down in a slow, sly wink. I grinned back at it, then drew in a deep breath, letting the cool air seep deep down into my lungs.

To everyone else, this was just another Mythos Academy, but a sense of wildness, of freedom, existed here that I'd never experienced while visiting any of the other academies. I could see it in the shadows that pooled around the statues, smell it in the crisp, clear air, and hear it in the sharp, whistling wind that ruffled my ponytail.

It felt like home to me.

Since this was the first day of school, the quad was packed, and practically everyone had a coffee in one hand and a phone in the other. All sorts of mythological warriors attended Mythos Academy, but the majority of the guys were Romans and Vikings, while the girls were mostly Amazons and Valkyries. Bright, colorful sparks of magic flashed in the air around many of the kids, especially the Valkyries. For some reason, Valkyries almost continuously gave off magic, and showers of sparks streamed out of their fingertips with every gesture they made and every text they sent.

Each kid, each warrior, had their own skills, powers, and magic—everything from enhanced senses to being able to summon up lightning to the ability to heal other people. But in general, Romans and Amazons were superquick, while Vikings and Valkyries were superstrong.

I was none of those things.

I was a Spartan, like my parents, and it was another way I didn't fit in with everyone else, since Spartans were rare—and very, very dangerous. Almost all the other kids were carrying at least one weapon, whether it was a sword or dagger belted to their waist, a staff propped up on the bench beside them, or even a bow and a quiver full of arrows peeking up out of their gym bag.

But I didn't have any weapons. I didn't *need* them, since I could pick up any object and automatically know how to kill someone with it.

Seriously. I could kill someone with a toothpick if I wanted to. A plastic fork, a paper clip, an ink pen. Whatever was handy. Not that I would ever actually do that, as it would be difficult, even for me, especially when it would be much easier to take away my enemy's sword and use their own weapon against them. But if I had to, I could defend myself with whatever was lying around, no matter how small and innocuous it might be.

I didn't know how it worked for other Spartans, how their magic manifested itself, but anytime I was in a fight, I could see what the other person was going to do before they did it. How they were going to move their feet, how they were going to shift their weight, even how hard they were going to swing their sword at me. It was like we were both part of the same movie, only I was three steps ahead of the other person.

And the same thing happened when it came to weapons, whether it was a traditional sword or something as flimsy as a toothpick. As soon as I touched a sword, I could tell how well made it was, how balanced, how strong, and I intuitively adjusted my feet, my grip, and my swings to maximize the damage I could do with the weapon. Ditto for the toothpick, the plastic fork, the paper clip, the ink pen, and anything else I could get my hands on.

And it wasn't just that I instinctively knew how to hurt people. Something about my Spartan blood made it seem *natural*, like it was something that I was *supposed* to do.

Holding a sword or a staff or drawing back a bowstring seemed as right and easy as breathing to me.

Sometimes that scared me a little.

I didn't want to be like my parents. I didn't want to hurt innocent people. I didn't want to be a bad person.

I didn't want to be a Reaper.

I wanted to be…well, I wasn't quite sure yet. I wanted to do something with my life the way Gwen had. I wanted to do something important. Something that mattered. Something that would aid other people.

And maybe, just maybe, something that would help make up for all my parents' mistakes.

But I couldn't do any of that standing here, so I took a deep breath, squared my shoulders, and stepped out onto the main quad.

"Here goes nothing," I muttered.

I walked along one of the cobblestone paths, winding my way toward the English-history building, since that's where myth-history was, my first class of the day. I loved myth-history and learning about all the gods, goddesses, warriors, and creatures, and I wondered what new things the professor would talk about this year, especially given the recent battle and Loki's imprisonment—

"Look!" a voice hissed. "It's Rory Forseti!"

I was halfway across the quad when I heard my name.

I froze and looked over to my right, dreading what I would see. Sure enough, a group of Valkyries wearing designer boots, jeans, and matching plaid jackets were gathered around one of the iron benches that dotted the quad. They were all quite pretty, with perfect hair and makeup, and their phones and purses were even more expensive than their clothes.

Dezi, Harley, Kylie… I recognized several of the girls,

since they were all second-year students like me. None of them had liked me when we started school last fall, and they had outright hated me after it came out that my parents were Reapers.

The Valkyries realized that I was staring at them. But instead of turning away and pretending they hadn't said my name, they all pointed at me, making pink, green, and blue sparks of magic crackle in the air around them. My heart sank. I knew what was coming next.

"I can't believe she came back here this year."

"Did she really think that just because she helped out in North Carolina, we would forget what her parents did? Or what they were?"

"They were Reapers, through and through, and rotten to the core. And she's probably even worse than they were…"

The snarky comments went on and on, each one sharper, crueler, and more vicious and hurtful than the last. Even worse, the Valkyries' loud voices drowned out everyone else's conversations, causing the other students to turn and stare at me as well. In less than a minute, I was the center of everyone's attention, and they were all talking, texting, and whispering about me.

All I could do was stand there frozen in place with my mouth gaping open, looking like a clueless fool. I'd actually gotten my hopes up. I'd actually thought that this year would be different, better, normal. That I'd done enough good things to change everyone's opinions of me. But I'd been wrong—dead wrong.

I was such a freaking *idiot*.

Of course the other kids wouldn't forget that my parents were Reapers—not for one lousy second. How could they when Reapers had terrorized them all for so long? When they had lived in fear of Reapers their whole lives? When

Reapers had killed their friends and family members for generations on end? One battle wasn't going to change all of that history, all of that bad blood, all of that fear, anger, and hate.

Nothing could *ever* change that.

But the worst part was that I had hoped it would. I had hoped for the fresh start that Aunt Rachel had said we would have. I had wanted it more than *anything*.

My first class hadn't even started yet, and my school year was already ruined, soaked in blood and burned to ash by my parents' evil actions, like so many other things in my life.

In many ways, my feelings about Mythos Academy mirrored those about my parents. I loved so many things about the academy—the scenery, the statues, the sense of being home—just as I had loved my mom's quiet strength and my dad's unending patience. But part of me also hated the academy, especially all the other students knowing about my Reaper parents. Sometimes I felt like I had a big red bull's-eye strapped to my chest, one that gave all the other kids permission to mock me.

The cruel comments, snarky whispers, and hateful stares continued. A hot, embarrassed blush flooded my cheeks, and my anger bubbled up to the surface again. But I knew from past experience that there was no point in fighting back against the other kids. It would only make me even more of a target than I already was. Besides, they had just as much right to their anger as I had to mine. So I gritted my teeth, ducked my head, and hurried forward, determined to get inside the English-history building as quickly as possible—

A shoulder slammed into mine, making me stagger to one side of the cobblestone path.

"Watch it!" I snapped.

"Why don't you watch it?" a low voice growled right back at me.

Normally, I would have kept on going, since this wasn't the first time someone had accidentally-on-purpose rammed into me while I was walking across the quad, thinking that it was hilarious to pick on the girl with the dead Reaper parents. All the taunts, whispers, and stares had filled me with a familiar, sickening mixture of guilt, shame, and embarrassment, but those emotions quickly morphed into a cold, hard knot of anger in my chest. Dirty looks and whispers were one thing, but actually plowing into me was something else, especially when I was already struggling with my emotions.

Once again, I felt that need to lash out, and I decided to give in to it, since my day was already ruined. Someone wanted to mess with me? Well, I was tired of taking everyone else's crap, and I could give as good as I got.

I whirled around to confront the person who'd run into me and realized that it wasn't one of the snotty Valkyrie girls like I'd expected. It was a guy—and he was *gorgeous*.

Seriously, he was tall and muscled and just plain gorgeous in his black boots, black jeans, dark gray henley, and black leather jacket. Rich honey highlights ran through his dark blond hair, which stuck up at odd angles, as though he constantly ran his fingers through it, but the slightly messy, unkempt look totally suited him. He had the kind of great cheekbones, perfect straight nose, and strong jaw that you'd see on a movie star. But his eyes…his eyes were simply *amazing*—a light, bright, piercing gray. I'd never seen eyes like that before, and I tried to figure out what their color reminded me of. Rain-soaked clouds, maybe, or the gleaming edge of a freshly sharpened sword…

The guy glared at me, breaking the spell. I blinked and forced myself to ignore how cute he was. Instead, I studied him again, and I realized I'd never seen him before. Last year, after all that mess with my parents had happened, I had made it a point to know every single student at the academy, especially the ones I should avoid. But this guy? He was new.

Oh, I was sure there was a perfectly logical explanation. Lots of students transferred from one academy to another, especially at the start of the school year and especially at the start of this school year, since the North Carolina academy was still undergoing repairs from the earlier battle.

Still, I kept studying the guy, this time trying to figure out what kind of warrior he was. He couldn't be a Roman, since his magic would have made him fast enough to avoid running into me. My gaze dropped to the black duffel bag dangling from his hand. The bag's long, distinctive shape was meant to hold a battle ax, and a couple of smaller axes were hooked to the outside of the bag as well. So he was a Viking. They were the only warriors who used axes like that. No wonder he'd almost knocked me down. His Viking strength would have let him knock me into next week if he'd wanted. Maybe he hadn't slammed into me on purpose after all.

The guy's eyes narrowed. "What are you staring at?"

Embarrassment spurted through me that he had caught me gaping at him. But I ignored the fresh, hot blush stinging my cheeks, crossed my arms over my chest, and glared back at him.

"What are *you* staring at?" I snapped. "I was walking along, minding my own business, when *bam!* You plowed right into me. And now you're not even apologizing for almost knocking me down."

Anger sparked in his eyes, turning them a darker storm-cloud gray, which, of course, only made him look that much more handsome. "I didn't plow into you. You weren't watching where you were going. If anyone should be apologizing, it's you, cupcake."

My arms dropped to my sides, and my hands clenched into fists. "You did not just call me *cupcake*."

He arched an eyebrow. "What? You don't like that nickname? Well, it's true. Look at you, with your designer clothes and expensive bag and perky little ponytail. You're a cute little cupcake of a warrior, just like the rest of the girls here."

More anger surged through my body, and I stepped up so that I was standing inches away from him. "I am a *Spartan*," I hissed. "One who is perfectly capable of kicking your ass, right here, right now, Viking."

He arched his eyebrow at me again. "A threat? Aw, that's so cute. Maybe some other time. Right now, I've got to get to class, and so do you. Unless you want to be late on the first day of school."

"I—"

I started to snap back at him, but a series of bells rang out across the quad, cutting me off and signaling that we had five minutes to get to class.

"And that's my cue to leave. Later, cupcake." The Viking snapped his hand up to his forehead in a mock salute. He hefted his bag onto his shoulder, making all the small battle axes hooked to the outside *clank-clank-clank* together, and moved past me.

"But—"

I whirled around, but he was moving fast, heading for the gym on the opposite side of the quad. He was already out of earshot, unless I wanted to scream insults at him. I was still so angry that I opened my mouth to let loose, but then I realized that everyone was staring at me again, including the Valkyries who'd been mocking me earlier. The girls all rolled their eyes and snickered, adding to my humiliation. Everyone had seen my confrontation with the Viking, and they were already gossiping about it.

Great. Just great. I had wanted things to be different this year, but I was right back where I'd started, with everyone talking about me, the supposed Reaper girl in their midst. And it was all *his* fault.

I glared at the Viking's back, but there was nothing I could do about him now. So I sighed, turned around, and trudged across the quad toward the English-history building.

As I walked along, one thought kept running through my mind. I had been absolutely right before.

The first day of school is always the worst.

Especially at Mythos Academy.

CHAPTER TWO

The rest of my day didn't get any better.

I suffered through all my morning classes, painfully aware that everyone was talking and texting about my confrontation with the Viking. I slumped down in my seat, keeping my gaze on my books, but I could still hear the other kids whispering about me. Well, at least they weren't talking about my parents being Reapers anymore. I didn't know if that was better or worse, but at least my misery was new and different—for today, anyway. The other students would remember my Reaper parents soon enough.

Lunchtime rolled around, and I trooped over to the dining hall with the other kids, all of whom kept a healthy distance from yours truly. Apparently, talking about me behind my back was just fine, but actually walking beside me on the cobblestone path was not. I gritted my teeth and plodded on toward the dining hall. I wasn't hungry—not in the slightest—but I had to show up for lunch, or Aunt Rachel would start worrying.

I stepped into the dining hall, which looked exactly the same as it had last school year, right down to the open-air garden in the center of the room. Instead of pretty flowers, this garden featured evergreen trees that grew between dense boulder formations and perfumed the air with their sharp, tangy sap. A narrow creek curled through the garden and over to a tower of boulders, where it dropped down and created a small waterfall and a pool at the base of the rocks. Gray stone statues of bears, rabbits, ducks, and other animals ringed the pool, along with one of Coyote Trickster, the Native American god. Two more statues, both of them Eir gryphons, perched on the rocks at the top of the waterfall, as though they were keeping watch and protecting the animals below.

Lion bodies, eagle heads, broad wings, long tails. The two statues looked just like the real gryphons that lived in a cavern near the Eir Ruins. I stared at their stone faces a moment, getting my anger under control, then grabbed a plastic tray and got in line to get some lunch.

Unlike that of your typical school cafeteria, the dining-hall food was upscale all the way, in keeping with the wealth and expensive tastes of the students, professors, and other workers. No rubbery chicken nuggets, plastic cups of lumpy applesauce, or paper cartons of sour milk here. Instead, the chefs chopped, grilled, and whipped up everything from crisp garden salads to honey-apricot-glazed chicken to Parmesan-garlic mashed potatoes.

I breathed in, enjoying the delicious aromas and curls of steam that wisped through the air. Maybe Aunt Rachel's cooking had spoiled me, but I loved all the fancy food, and I didn't understand why Gwen always wanted to have plain old boring pizza and cheeseburgers. Gourmet was where it was at, baby.

Aunt Rachel was working the end of the lunch line today, dishing up sundaes made with vanilla-bean ice cream, warm chocolate sauce, and fresh sliced strawberries. My stomach rumbled in anticipation. Spartans didn't have many weaknesses, but dessert was definitely one of mine. I had a massive sweet tooth, and sundaes were one of my favorite treats. I might not have been hungry before, but I could always eat ice cream.

Aunt Rachel knew all about my sugar addiction, and she fixed me an extra-large sundae with lots of chocolate sauce and strawberries, along with chopped toasted almonds sprinkled on top for some nutty crunch. She slid the sundae dish onto my tray, and I admired it. The dessert was almost too pretty to eat. Almost.

"How's your first day going?" she asked.

I forced myself to smile. "Great. Just great. Except for all the homework."

She frowned. "Homework already? On the first day?"

"Oh, yeah."

That part was definitely true. My myth-history professor had already assigned us a lengthy term paper, and we had to have an outline ready for approval next week, which meant that I would be spending some time in the library this afternoon, tracking down reference books.

"How about you?" I asked. "How's your day going?"

Aunt Rachel smiled, but it seemed she was clenching her jaw to hold the expression in place. "Oh, great. Just great. Just…getting back into the groove of things."

Unlike my parents, Aunt Rachel was a terrible liar, and I could tell that her day had been as bad as mine. I wondered if the other chefs had gossiped about her behind her back like all the kids had done with me. Probably.

But I forced myself to smile. She would be disappointed that things weren't any better for me, and I wasn't going to make her day any worse than it already was. "I've got to hit the library after classes and get started on a paper, so I'll see you tonight at home. Okay?"

"Sure," Aunt Rachel said. "Sounds good. I'll fix us a special late-night snack to celebrate our first day."

"Great."

I nodded and smiled at her again, as though everything was fine and I really was having a terrific day. Then I dropped my head, moved past her, and paid for my food at the cash register. I stuffed my change into my jeans pocket, grabbed my tray, and turned to face a new dilemma.

Where to sit.

Since this was the first day of school, the dining hall was packed, just like the quad had been this morning, and I didn't see any empty tables. I didn't even see any empty seats. At least, none at a table where I thought I could sit and eat in peace without everyone else muttering snarky comments about me. Of course, I could always go outside and eat on the dining-hall steps. I had done that almost every single day last year, no matter how cold and snowy it was outside. Being by myself was better than being with people who hated me.

I started to head outside to find a quiet, deserted spot, but then I realized that Aunt Rachel was still watching me from her place at the end of the lunch line. If I left the dining hall, she would realize that something was wrong, so I clenched my jaw and forced myself to walk past the tables, searching for a seat, any seat, where I could sit for a minute until she went back to work and I could get up and sneak outside—

A shoulder rammed into mine, almost making me drop my tray. I whirled around, ready to snap at the person who'd run into me, but the words died on my lips.

Lance Fuller stood in front of me.

The Roman warrior was six feet tall, with broad, muscled shoulders. His eyes were an intense blue against his tan skin, and his wavy black hair gleamed like polished jet under the lights. In addition to his poster-boy looks, he radiated confidence, and with good reason. Lance Fuller was, quite simply, *the guy* at Mythos Academy—smart, rich, handsome, charming, popular. He was the guy all the other guys wished they could be and the one all the girls wanted to be with.

Including me.

I'd had a massive, massive crush on Lance ever since the first time I saw him walking across the quad last year. And to my amazement, he had seemed to like me too. We'd had a couple of classes together last year, and he was always volunteering to be my lab partner in chemistry or to work with me on other projects. He had even started asking what movies and music I liked, as though he was thinking about asking me out. But then all the bad stuff with my parents had happened, and my dreams of dating Lance had vanished like a cloud of smoke.

Lance realized that he'd run into me, and he actually smiled, revealing the two perfect dimples in his cheeks. "Hey, Rory. I'm so sorry. I didn't see you standing there. How's your first day back?"

It took me a moment to quit staring and answer him. "Um, fine. How are you?"

"Good." His smile widened. "Really good now."

My heart picked up speed and started pounding in my chest. Unlike all the other kids, Lance didn't mock or berate me for what my parents had done. All last year, he had still waved at me whenever he saw me walking across the quad, and he had even talked to me a few times too. His kindness had made me like him that much more.

"Hey, Lance!" Kylie, a cute Valkyrie with sleek blond hair, called out. "Over here! We saved you a seat!"

But Lance kept staring at me, his face still crinkled in that adorable smile. "Maybe I'll see you around this week."

My heart beat even faster. "Sure, that would be great."

Lance winked at me, then moved off to sit with his friends. I watched him go, wishing that I could join his table, but of course, Kylie shot daggers at me with her eyes, clearly telling me that I was not welcome. So I sighed and moved on, still searching for an empty seat.

And I finally found one—at the Viking's table.

He was sitting at a table in the corner, and he wasn't alone. A beautiful girl with perfect blond curls perched next to him, leaning in close so she could whisper to him and hang on to his every word in return. I snorted. Of course he had a girlfriend. Gorgeous guys like him *always* had a girlfriend. Sometimes two or three at once.

But theirs was the only table with an empty seat, so I headed in that direction. I didn't even ask if I could sit with them. There was no point in it, since they would tell me no. So I marched over, plopped my tray down, and scooted the empty seat as far away from the two of them as I could get and still be sitting at the same table.

I dropped into the chair across from them, and they both practically jumped out of their seats. I had startled them out of what seemed to be a very private, very intense conversation. The Viking frowned, recognizing me from before, but the girl smiled and nodded at me. She had to be a new student, like the Viking was. No Mythos kid who knew anything about me or my parents would ever give me such a warm welcome.

"Hey," she said. "What's your name?"

I sighed, not wanting to make any sort of polite chitchat

with them, but it would be totally rude not to answer her. "Rory."

The girl smiled at me again. "Hi, Rory. I'm Amanda, and this is Ian."

So that was the Viking's name. I grunted in response, and so did he. Amanda looked back and forth between the two of us, wondering what was going on, but I didn't say anything else, and neither did Ian.

I put my head down and reached for my tray. Instead of digging into my salad, chicken, and mashed potatoes, I grabbed my sundae, sank my spoon into the melting ice cream, and shoveled it into my mouth as fast as possible without choking or getting brain freeze. The sundae was delicious, a perfect mix of vanilla, chocolate, and strawberry, but I still wanted to eat it and leave as soon as I could.

Especially since the happy couple looked so cozy.

Ian leaned over and murmured in Amanda's ear. Her blue gaze locked with mine, and her eyes widened with surprise. My heart sank. I knew that look. I had seen it a hundred times before. Ian had told her about my Reaper parents.

Amanda wet her lips, glanced away from me, and scooted her chair even closer to the Viking's. I rolled my eyes. As if I was going to attack them in the middle of the dining hall in front of the entire school. Please. My parents might have been Reapers, but they weren't *stupid*—and neither was I.

I thought they might start whispering about me, like some of the kids at the surrounding tables were doing, but the two of them ignored me. Like totally ignored me. They didn't even look at me. Instead, Ian pulled out his phone and thumbed through some screens until he found the one he wanted. Then he and Amanda both bent over the phone, their heads close together, completely absorbed in whatever they were staring at.

For a moment, disappointment filled me. I had been looking forward to snarling some insults at the Viking, since he had gotten the better of me on the quad this morning, but I got over it. Being ignored was much better than being gossiped about, and besides, I still had more than half of my sundae left. So I tuned them out just like they had done to me and focused on my food again, eating much more slowly and taking the time to enjoy every single delicious bite of ice cream.

Sadly, it was the nicest, quietest lunch I'd had in the dining hall since before everyone learned the truth about my parents.

CHAPTER THREE

Ian and Amanda were still staring at his phone when I finished my food, got to my feet, and grabbed my tray. I expected them to keep ignoring me, but Amanda looked up and waved at me.

"It was nice meeting you," she called out in a warm voice.

"Yeah. You too." My tone was far less genuine and much more surly than hers.

Ian opened his mouth like he was going to make some snarky remark and call me *cupcake* again, but I stared him down, and he apparently thought better of it. Chicken. I rolled my eyes, turned away, and left the dining hall.

But once again, the rest of my day didn't get any better.

More classes, more homework, more kids gossiping about me.

Even gym class, my second-favorite class after myth-history, was a total bust. Coach Wanda, one of the few teachers who had always treated me fairly, even after the ugly revelations about my parents, had been replaced. Our new teacher was a man in his early thirties, with black hair, dark brown eyes, and a charcoal-gray tracksuit that highlighted his lean frame. A silver whistle hung around his neck, and a clipboard dangled from his hand.

"My name is Coach Takeda," he said.

I eyed him, wondering what kind of warrior he was. Not a Roman or a Viking, since he didn't seem to be either exceptionally quick or strong, but he gave off an air of quiet, controlled power. Probably a Samurai, given his perfectly straight posture and the way he was holding that clipboard like it was a sword that he was about to brandish at us.

Takeda stabbed his clipboard toward the far end of the gym, where a series of orange cones had been set up in elaborate patterns. "We're going to start with some agility drills."

"Agility drills?" I muttered to myself, since no one else would talk to me. "Really? What's the point of that?"

I hadn't spoken all that loudly, but of course Takeda heard me. He looked at me, his face perfectly calm and devoid of any emotion.

"Do you have a problem with agility drills, Miss..." He ran his finger down the sheet on his clipboard. "Forseti?"

I sighed, knowing what was coming next. "No, sir."

Takeda gave me a thin smile. "Good. Then you can run laps around the gym while the rest of us get started. Ten laps should be enough to stretch out your legs. Perhaps then you'll look a little more fondly on my agility drills."

Of course, all the other kids thought my punishment was absolutely hysterical, and they all started snickering. At least, until Takeda turned his gaze to them. He didn't do or say anything, just kept staring at them with that same calm expression he'd given me, but it was plenty intimidating. One by one, all the other kids shut up, lest they be forced to run laps with me.

Takeda made a shooing motion with his hand. "If you would be so kind as to start running, Miss Forseti."

I sighed again, but I had no choice but to shuffle forward and do as he commanded. Takeda was right. By the time I got done running all those laps, I wished I had kept my mouth shut and gone along with his stupid agility drills. They would have been far less tiring.

Gym was my last class of the day, but I was so sweaty from running laps that I ducked into the locker room and took a shower before changing back into my regular clothes. I texted Aunt Rachel and told her I was heading over to the library to grab a snack and get started on my homework. She texted me back, saying she was still working in the dining hall, prepping for tomorrow's meals, and she'd see me at home later tonight.

I left the gym and walked across the quad to the Library of Antiquities, which soared five stories into the air, making it the tallest building on campus. The center section of the library was a large square tower, with three attached wings sticking out from it like the spokes on a wheel. Two stone gryphons perched on boulders on the sides of the main steps, and I stopped and nodded at each one of them.

I wanted to be polite, since I had seen what statues like these could do at the North Carolina academy, but looking at the gryphons also delayed my going inside the building for another moment. Thanks to my parents, the Library of Antiquities was something else I had a love-hate relationship with at the academy. So I focused on the gryphons and tried to ignore the hurt and loss stabbing through my heart and the sick dread churning in my stomach. The same emotions assaulted me every time I went into the library.

Just like the Fenrir wolf earlier, these two statues winked back at me, almost as if they could sense my turbulent feelings and were trying to comfort me. I nodded at them both again, then let out a long, tense breath and headed into the library.

I walked down a hallway and stepped through a set of open double doors into the main space. A wide aisle ran from the doors all the way over to a long checkout counter in the center of the library. Wooden study tables were clustered in the open spaces in front of and behind the counter, while a large silver coffee cart was parked off to the side. Shadow-filled stacks spread throughout the rest of the first floor, each tall shelf housing hundreds of books. Glass display cases also gleamed here and there among the aisles in the stacks.

The library had been chiseled out of the same lovely dark stone as all the other campus buildings, although in here, you could see the thick exposed logs that made up many of the walls and supports for the upper floors. Colorful rugs decorated with a variety of Native American symbols and gods, including Coyote Trickster, covered the floor, looking like runes that had been carved into the stone. Overhead, the ceilings of the three outer wings all flowed into the square ceiling of the center tower.

Gwen always claimed that frescoes were painted on the library ceilings, showing people, weapons, artifacts, and battles. But to me, the ceilings—especially the tower ceiling—looked like they were made of bright bits of stained glass that had been stitched together with silver thread. Sapphire-blue, emerald-green, ruby-red, opal-white, amethyst-purple. All the different jewel-toned colors and delicate shapes reminded me of the wildflowers at the Eir Ruins.

Before my parents died, I had loved to sneak off into the stacks, find a quiet spot, and lie down on the floor, using my messenger bag as a pillow so I could study the ceiling to my heart's content. Sometimes, if I had stared at them long enough, the stained-glass shapes seemed to move, like a phantom breeze was blowing over the wildflowers and making their petals slowly sway back and forth. Watching the flowers had soothed and given me a sense of peace. I still thought the ceiling was beautiful, but my enjoyment of it had greatly diminished, given all the other dark, ugly things that had happened in here.

Besides the ceiling, the library's other most impressive feature was the enormous stone fireplace that was close to the checkout counter. It was more than thirty feet wide and made of the same blackish boulders as the rest of the structure. Given that it was September, no flames crackled behind the tall iron grates, but it was still the busiest part of the library. Overstuffed chairs and couches flanked the freestanding fireplace, front and back, and every single seat was taken. Now that classes were over with, students had flocked here to catch up on all the juicy gossip, as if they hadn't already been texting about it all day long.

I stood in the doorway, studying everything. I had always loved books and artifacts and history, and the Library of Antiquities was full of those things. The library used to be my favorite place on campus, and I had spent hours wandering the aisles, finding books to read, and examining the artifacts on display. There was always something new and wonderful to discover.

But now I was torn, just like I was about so many other things at the academy. On one hand, I still loved the library. The quiet stacks, the interesting artifacts, even the faint musty scent of paper that filled the air. But on the other hand, I hated the library for one simple reason.

My parents had been murdered here.

I stared at a spot in front of the checkout counter. That's where Covington, the former head librarian, had stabbed my parents in the back, and that's where they had been lying when I raced into the library that awful, awful day. I didn't get vibes off objects, not like Gwen did with her psychometry magic, but the memories were so strong that they rose up in my mind and blotted out everything else.

In an instant, all I could see was my mom and dad crumpled on the floor, their eyes open wide with shock and pain. All I could hear was the faint whisper of their black Reaper cloaks fluttering back and forth in the air-conditioning, looking like death shrouds draped over their bodies. All I could smell was the coppery stench of their blood oozing across the floor, staining the stone a sickening scarlet...

A Roman guy hurried past me, and his backpack accidentally clipped my shoulder. The faint nudge snapped me out of my trance, and the images faded away, although not the pain they left behind.

Nothing *ever* took away that heartache.

These same memories haunted me every single time I set foot in here. And I wondered, like I always did, if I could really go over, sit down at a study table, open my books, and pretend everything was fine. That my parents hadn't died a few feet away.

More hurt and loss stabbed through my heart, while more of that sick dread twisted my stomach. Not for the first time, I wanted to whirl around, run out the door, and never set foot in the library again, but I forced myself to take in slow, deep breaths and hold my ground. I couldn't avoid the library, not even for a few days, given the massive amounts of homework my professors dished out on a weekly basis. Besides, Covington and my parents had already taken so much from me. They weren't taking the library too. I wouldn't *let* them take that too. So I pushed the memories back down to the bottom of my brain, squared my shoulders, and strode forward.

"What's *she* doing here?" A snide voice caught my ear.

I glanced over at the fireplace, and I realized that all the other kids were staring at me again.

"Isn't it bad enough that we have to sit through classes with her?" Kylie, the blond Valkyrie from lunch, continued. "Does she have to come to the library too?"

In an instant, everyone started whispering about me, and once again, I wanted to turn around, leave the library, and never come back. But Spartans never ran away from a fight, not even one like this that I could never, ever win, so I gritted my teeth and walked down the center aisle, as though I didn't hear any of the cruel taunts. Besides, I really did need to do some research and get started on my term-paper outline. I took pride in getting good grades, and I wasn't going to flunk my first myth-history assignment of the semester because of some stupid gossip.

So I went over to one of the computer stations close to the checkout counter, typed in the titles of the books the professor had given us as starting points, and printed out their locations. But the other students had beaten me to them, and all the copies of the first few books on the list had already been checked out. Still, I trudged from one side of the library to the other, trying to find something that would help me. Every time I left the stacks and walked by the fireplace, a fresh round of whispers rippled through the groups of kids, but I ignored the harsh murmurs and marched on.

Since all the books on the first floor were already gone, I pushed through a door, climbed the stairs, and stepped out onto the second floor. Like all the other Libraries of Antiquities, the second floor featured a balcony that wrapped all the way around the library, boasting a pantheon of statues of the gods and goddesses of all the cultures of the world, everything from Greek to Norse to Egyptian and all the others in between.

Zeus, the ruler of the Greek gods, with his lightning bolt clutched in his hand. Odin, the ruler of the Norse gods, with his two ravens perched on his shoulders. Bastet, the Egyptian cat goddess, with her claw-tipped fingers. I moved past those deities and dozens more. Just like the stone gryphons outside, these statues also studied me, although none of them gave me a friendly wink or an encouraging smile. But I didn't mind their silent scrutiny. At least I couldn't hear their thoughts about me, whatever they might be.

All the other students were lounging around the fireplace, so it was much quieter up here, and I was the only one on this floor. I sighed with relief. Now that no one was watching me, maybe I could relax and focus on my homework. Besides, up here, I didn't have to keep walking by the spot where I had seen my parents' bodies.

A few minutes later, I finally found one of the myth-history books on my list and slid it out of its spot on the shelf along one of the walls. I grabbed a couple of other volumes, enough to get started on my outline, and headed toward the exit so that I could go downstairs, check out the books, and take them home.

I was almost to the door when a bright gleam of metal caught my eye.

A glass display case sat at the end of one of the bookcases along the wall. The case was one of hundreds in the Library of Antiquities, which got its name from all the, well, antiquities that were housed inside. Weapons, armor, jewelry, clothing, and more were displayed throughout the library, all of them used and worn by gods, goddesses, warriors, and creatures over the centuries, many of them possessing magical powers and properties.

I had spent a lot of time in the library over the past year, and I didn't remember seeing this case before. Curious, I walked over and peered through the glass.

A silver sword that glimmered like it had been freshly polished lay on a bed of dark green velvet inside the case, along with a black leather scabbard. I glanced around, but I didn't spot an identification card inside the case or a metal plaque attached to the outside that would tell me whom the weapon had belonged to, what battles she had fought with it, and what magic it might have.

Swords were a dime a dozen in the library, and I had started to turn away from it when another gleam of metal caught my eye. I stepped forward, peered through the glass again, and took a closer look at the sword.

Was that...a face...engraved in the metal?

For a moment, I thought my eyes were playing tricks on me, but they weren't. A round bulge of an eye, a pointed cheekbone, a sharp, hooked nose, a curved chin. All those things joined on the sword's hilt to form a face—a woman's face, judging from her heart-shaped lips and the delicate eyebrow etched into the metal. Surprise jolted through me, and I held my breath, wondering if the sword's eye might pop open and the woman inside the metal might look up or maybe even talk to me.

Nothing happened.

The sword didn't talk, blink, yawn—nothing. It was like the weapon was, well, just a weapon, albeit one with a very pretty face. Disappointment filled me. Gwen had a talking sword named Vic, who was totally bloodthirsty. Ever since I'd met Vic, I had thought it would be so cool to have a talking sword of my own, but of course, something that amazing could never happen to me.

Sometimes I felt like nothing good *ever* happened to me.

Sighing, I hoisted the heavy library books a little higher into the crook of my elbow, turned away from the sword, and looked up—and found myself staring at a goddess.

I was standing directly across from Sigyn, the Norse goddess of devotion and the former wife of Loki. Unlike all the other statues, who were standing proud, straight, and tall, Sigyn had her head bowed, and her hair trailed over her shoulders, almost as if she were trying to hide her face behind the long locks. And her expression…it was so sad and mournful and full of regret that it made my own heart ache in response.

Loki had tricked Sigyn into freeing him from the prison the other gods had placed him in long ago, and countless people had suffered—*died*—because of her mistake. Gwen had told me about Sigyn, how she'd masqueraded as Raven, an old woman who did odd jobs around the North Carolina academy, and how she'd spent years watching over the students there and shielding them from all the evil things the Reapers did on Loki's behalf. Sigyn seemed to be one of the few goddesses, perhaps even the only goddess, who fought her own battles here in the mortal realm, instead of asking a Champion to do it for her.

I admired the goddess for trying to make things right, for trying to clean up the mess she'd made, for trying to help and protect the people who'd been hurt by her mistake. Those were some of the reasons I'd decided to write my term paper on her.

But the main reason was that I knew exactly how she felt.

I had trusted my parents, believed in them, *loved* them, and they'd still done all these horrible things. My parents had always told me to help people, to be a good warrior, to fight against the Reapers, when they had done the exact opposite. I just didn't understand *why* my mom and dad had been Reapers, why they had thought it was okay to bring pain, death, destruction, and suffering to so many innocent people. I felt like I didn't know them at all—that I'd *never* known who they truly were.

And now they were dead, murdered, and I would never know the answers to my questions. Why my parents had been Reapers, why they had tried to leave the group, what kind of future they had really wanted for me. Not knowing made me sadder than anything else. All the questions, all the doubts, had cracked deep down into my heart, splintering away my love and respect for my parents and leaving this jagged, hollow crater behind, this aching emptiness that I could never fill, no matter what I did—

The door to the stairs banged open. I whirled around, expecting an attack, but a Valkyrie and a Roman stumbled through the opening, giggling like crazy. They lurched to a stop, and the Valkyrie looped her arms around the Roman's neck, stood on her tiptoes, and pressed a loud, smacking kiss to his lips. Gold sparks of magic streamed out of her fingertips and flashed in the air all around them, making them look like a fairy-tale couple experiencing true love's kiss.

I rolled my eyes. More like true lust's kiss. In addition to being a place to hang out and gossip, the library was also a popular spot for kids to make out. Couples would often sneak away from the fireplace and the study tables, find a shadowy spot back in the stacks, and play tonsil hockey for hours on end. These two must have had the bright idea to come up to the second floor, where it was even darker and more private.

I had zero desire to witness their make-out session, and I was a little annoyed that they had interrupted my peace and quiet. So I loudly cleared my throat, letting the Valkyrie and the Roman know they weren't alone. The two of them yelped in surprise and jerked apart, their heads snapping in my direction.

"Isn't it a little early to be sucking face?" I sniped. "It's still the first day of school. Usually, people don't start hooking up until at least day two."

The Valkyrie slapped her hands on her hips, gold sparks of magic hissing all around her fingertips. "Well, at least I have someone to make out with. You, Rory Forseti? You'd be lucky to get a prowler to kiss you. C'mon. Let's get out of here."

She grabbed the guy's hand, and they both turned around, went back through the door, and clomped down the stairs. I grimaced, trying not to let the Valkyrie's words get to me, but she was right. Everybody hated me, guys included. I didn't have any friends here, much less an actual boyfriend, and I never would.

An arrow of hurt shot through my heart, but I ignored the sting, went over to the balcony railing, and looked down. On the first floor below, kids laughed, talked, and texted in the chairs by the fireplace, while others stood in line in front of the coffee cart, nibbling on cinnamon rolls, cheese Danish, and other pastries while they waited for their espressos and cappuccinos. A few truly dedicated students hunched over their laptops and textbooks at the study tables, concentrating on their homework. They all looked so relaxed and carefree. The tension, worry, and threat of Loki and his Reapers had finally been lifted, and everyone was happier than they had ever been.

Everyone except me.

Now that I had the reference books for my term paper, I should go downstairs, check them out, and leave the library. But the second I set foot on the first floor, all the kids would start watching me again like they had before. My breath escaped in a long, weary sigh. I couldn't take any more harsh, accusing glares. Not right now, anyway.

I would much rather stay up here by myself than listen to the other students' snarky whispers and cruel snickers. So I set my books aside and plopped down on the floor in front of Sigyn's statue.

"I guess it's just you and me now," I said.

I stared up at Sigyn, hoping that she would open her eyes, nod her head, or give me some other indication that she knew what I was going through. That she would give me some small sign of hope, friendship, or at least encouragement like the animal statues outside had with their winks earlier. But Sigyn remained utterly still, her face frozen in the same sorrowful expression as before. I waited one minute, then two, then three, but the goddess didn't respond, so I sighed again as I cracked open the first reference book and pulled a pen and a notepad out of my messenger bag.

The first day wasn't even over yet, but I could already tell it was going to be a long, long school year.

Chapter Four

The first reference book was very dry, long-winded, and boring, and so were all the others. I tried to concentrate and take notes, really I did, but after a while, the words swam together before my eyes, and my pen and notepad slowly slipped from my hands...

I must have fallen asleep, because the next thing I knew, I was sprawled against Sigyn's statue, my face mashed up against the cold, smooth white marble.

I gently peeled my face off the stone, yawned, and sat up. The lights were still on, but the library was eerily silent. I pulled my phone out of my jeans pocket and checked the time. Just after nine o'clock, which meant the library had closed a few minutes ago. I slid my phone back into my pocket and peered down at the first floor through the stone slats in the balcony railing.

All the kids who'd been sitting in the chairs and couches around the fireplace were gone, along with the ones who'd been at the study tables. The coffee cart had been closed up, and I didn't even see a librarian at the checkout counter, shelving a few last books before leaving. But I wasn't worried. This wasn't the first time I'd been in here alone at night.

In the weeks after my parents were murdered, I had spent hours and hours in the library. Maybe it was weird and morbid, since this was where they had died, but roaming through the stacks and looking at the books and artifacts actually made me feel a little closer to my parents. But I hadn't been wandering around aimlessly—I had been searching for clues.

My parents had had so many secrets, and part of me had hoped that they'd left something behind in the library for me to find, since this was the last place they'd been. A letter, a diary, an artifact. Something, *anything*, that would answer my questions about why they had done all those horrible things.

I hadn't found anything, not here at the library or at our old house, not so much as a scribbled note, but that didn't keep me from looking, from hoping, even to this day. Maybe I wasn't weird and morbid. Maybe I was just foolish for thinking that my parents were anything other than the evil Reapers they appeared to be.

The other reason I had spent so much time in the library was that it was the one place on campus where I could find a quiet spot away from prying eyes and sit and think about everything that had happened. Sometimes, when the other kids' stares and whispers got to be too much, I would play hooky from class and hide in the stacks until I felt I could face everyone again.

Ever since Loki and the Reapers were defeated, the librarians had gotten really lax when it came to security, and they didn't roam through the stacks and check on the books and artifacts nearly as much as they used to. Plus, one of the side doors had a flimsy lock that was easy to jiggle open with a paper clip, so I could come and go as I pleased without anyone even knowing I was in here.

Since it was so quiet, I wondered what had woken me up. Probably some faint noise, like a book falling off a shelf—

Something moved in the stacks on the first floor.

A black blob detached itself from the wall and crept through a pool of shadows before stopping at the end of one of the aisles. For a moment, I wondered if I was only imagining the inky shape, but then it moved again, sidling over to a glass display case, and I realized it was a person—wearing a black Reaper cloak.

My breath caught in my throat. A Reaper? In the library? They were all supposed to be either dead, in prison, or in hiding. So what was a Reaper doing here?

I studied the figure. Despite the black cloak that covered the Reaper from head to toe, I got the impression that it was a guy, judging from his tall frame and broad shoulders. My suspicion was confirmed a second later, when the Reaper reached out and started fiddling with the display case. Those were definitely a guy's hands. I squinted at the Reaper, but the hood of his cloak covered his head and cast his face in shadow, and I couldn't make out his features.

My gaze dropped to the display case, but the Reaper was blocking my view, and all I could see was a glimmer of gold. I thought back, trying to remember what artifact was in that particular case. Not a weapon or a piece of armor but something to do with some...creature, although I couldn't remember anything more specific. But it didn't matter. The Reaper wouldn't be stealing that artifact or any others.

The Reapers had already taken far too much, especially from me. They weren't getting anything else.

I got to my feet, tiptoed forward, and scanned the first floor below in case the Reaper had brought some friends with him—

Clack-clack. Clack-clack.

The sound of footsteps whispered up from the first floor. The Reaper froze. Yeah, me too. Especially since the footsteps were coming from the opposite side of the library.

Someone else was in here.

I eased forward a little more and looked to my right toward the center aisle. A second later, Amanda, the girl from the dining hall, slipped out of the stacks on that side of the library. She was dressed in jeans and a T-shirt, just like at lunch, and her black leather boots tapped softly against the floor as she walked. She wasn't wearing a black Reaper cloak, but she was carrying a long staff, a weapon usually preferred by Amazons.

Amanda crept forward, both hands clutched around her staff, ready to use her speed to whip up the weapon and bring it crashing down on someone's head. She moved slowly and cautiously, glancing around as though she was searching for something—or someone.

My eyes narrowed. Was she looking for the Reaper? Had she come here to stop him? I glanced back at the Reaper, but he'd gotten over his surprise and was now using a dagger to try to force open the lock on the display case. The more I looked at the Reaper, the more his tall frame and broad shoulders reminded me of Ian, the Viking that Amanda had been so cozy with at lunch. Maybe she was his lookout, making sure the library was clear so he could steal that artifact.

My hands clenched into fists. Well, I didn't care what they were doing. Neither one of them was leaving with any artifacts. Not as long as I was here to stop them. Amanda might have a staff, and the Reaper might have a dagger, but I was a Spartan, and I could take both of them down with my bare hands if I had to.

But first things first. I had to text Aunt Rachel and tell her what was going on. Otherwise, I would probably get blamed for Amanda and the Reaper breaking into the library. Aunt Rachel would believe me. She was the *only* one who would believe me.

So I pulled my phone out of my jeans pocket and entered my message.

Aunt Rachel texted me back almost immediately. I'm on my way! DO NOT try to fight the Reapers by yourself!

I frowned. Of course I was going to stop the Reapers. I was a Spartan, and that was what we did. I had started to text her back when my phone lit up with another message.

I mean it! DON'T DO IT! Stay where you are! Stay safe!

I sighed. Aunt Rachel didn't often tell me what to do, but the capital letters and the exclamation points told me she meant business. I still felt bad about snapping at her this morning, so I decided to do as she asked and keep watch on the Reapers instead of going downstairs and confronting them. Besides, I could always follow the Reapers if they left the library before she got here.

I texted her back. Okay. I'll stay on the balcony.

I had just hit send when a soft noise caught my attention. I frowned. Was that…humming?

Bum. Da-bum-bum. Bum.

Yep, that was definitely humming, and it sounded like it was coming from this floor. This night kept getting stranger and stranger. How many people were in here? Had the librarians even bothered to lock the doors when they left?

I made sure that my text went through, then slid my phone into my jeans pocket and glanced back down at the first floor. Amanda was tiptoeing around the fireplace and peering at the chairs and couches, like she thought someone might be hiding under one of them, while the Reaper was still trying to open the display case on the opposite side of the library. Neither one of them seemed to be in a hurry, which gave me enough time to try to figure out where that weird humming was coming from. I had to protect my own back first. I didn't need another Reaper sneaking up and attacking me from behind.

So I tilted my head, listening. The humming sounded like it was coming from behind me. I turned to the side and realized that a display case was standing directly across from me—the case with the silver sword that I had been looking at earlier.

A bit of uneasiness rippled through me. This was getting really weird, even by Mythos standards. My gaze flicked back and forth between the first floor and the display case. I should keep an eye on the Reapers, but I also wanted to know who—or what—was making that noise. Aunt Rachel had told me not to confront the Reapers, but she hadn't said anything about checking out strange sounds on this floor.

So I pushed my worry aside and crept forward. The closer I got to the display case, the louder the humming became and the more the light, trilling babbles sharpened into distinct words.

"Aye, this case will do quite nicely," a high, lilting, almost singsong voice murmured. "Look how clear and shiny the glass is. No one's put their grubby hands on this case in ages. Perfect. Absolutely perfect! I wonder if the librarians use antibacterial window cleaner. I certainly hope so. I wouldn't want to catch a cold. 'Tis a bit drafty up here…"

I frowned again. Antibacterial window cleaner? Was that even a real thing?

"And I even have a balcony view. It's terrific being able to look out and see so much of the library," the voice continued. "Aye! This is *so* much better than being stuck in that moldy storage room for another decade. This will do quite nicely…"

The longer I listened to the voice, the more I realized that it belonged to a woman, one with a lovely Irish accent.

That uneasiness welled up in me again, along with an eerie sense of déjà vu. This sounded almost exactly like a story Gwen had once told me. So much so that I glanced over my shoulder at Sigyn's statue, but the goddess was as still and stone-faced as before, and so were all the other statues around her.

That feminine voice kept chattering away in that lilting Irish accent, talking about the view, the balcony, and more. My curiosity propelled me forward, and I crept closer to the display case. And closer still…and closer still…

I looked down at the case and the same sword I had seen before, the one with the woman's face inlaid in the hilt. Eyebrow, cheekbone, nose, lips, chin. The sword's features were the same as before, with one notable difference.

Her eye was now wide open.

It was a beautiful color, a deep, dark green that gleamed under the lights, as though a polished emerald had been set into the sword's hilt, instead of an actual eye. But it *was* an eye, and it swiveled left and right, admiring the so-called balcony view, and the sword's lips twitched as it—*she*—started happily humming and talking to herself again.

"Aye! This is *so* much better than being stuck on the shelf next to that grumpy battle ax. All he ever did was reminisce about chopping off people's heads. Why, he about talked my bloody ear off, he did, and I only have one of them to start with. What a crotchety old blade he was…"

The sword kept babbling to herself, completely unaware that I was standing right next to her. So I did what anyone would do in this situation. I rapped my knuckles on the glass like I was knocking on a fishbowl.

The voice immediately cut off, and the eye swiveled around to me. The sword looked at me, and I stared right back at her. I knew that I should go back over to the balcony and see what the Reapers were doing, but I couldn't tear my gaze away from the sword. Her strong features, her intense green eye, her sharp silver blade. She was one of the most beautiful swords I had ever seen, a metallic work of art, and I itched to open the case and pick her up. The urge was so strong that I had to curl my hands into fists to keep from reaching for the case.

I shouldn't have been so mesmerized. It wasn't like I'd never seen a talking sword before. I'd had plenty of conversations with Vic, Gwen's weapon. Vic loved crowing about how awesome he was and how many Reapers he'd helped cut down over the years. He was so proud of his battle prowess that I sometimes thought he should have been a Spartan's weapon instead of Gwen's. Not that I was jealous of her or anything. Okay, okay, so maybe I was a teeny, tiny bit jealous. I mean, c'mon. Gwen had a talking sword. How freaking *cool* was that?

But now that I was face to face with another talking sword, I couldn't even form a coherent sentence.

"You—you—you—" I sputtered, but I couldn't get out the words that were stuck in my throat.

The sword's eye widened. "What are you doing here? The library is supposed to be closed for the night."

Her incredulous tone finally snapped me out of my fangirl stupor. "Of course the library is closed for the night. I fell asleep studying and just woke up a few minutes ago."

I didn't think it was possible, but her eye widened even

more. If it grew any bigger, it was liable to pop right off her face.

"Oh, no," the sword whispered. "No, no, no. This can't be happening. I just got taken out of storage by that nice old lady this morning! And put in this shiny new case! No. Oh, no, no, no…"

She repeated those same words over and over again, as if my looking at her was the worst thing that could have possibly happened. This was not going the way I'd expected. Not at all. Vic might be bloodthirsty, but this sword seemed downright paranoid.

I softly rapped my knuckles on the glass again, trying to interrupt her chatter and get her to quiet down. I didn't need the Reapers on the first floor to hear her and realize that someone else was in the library and spying on them. "It's no big deal. You're not the first talking sword I've seen, and you probably won't be the last. Everything's cool."

Her green eye narrowed. "Wait a second. What other talking swords have you seen? Where? Are they here in the library?"

"Um, no. His name is Vic, and he's with my cousin, Gwen, in North Carolina. He's her sword. Or she's his Champion. Or however that really works."

"Vic? That old blowhard?" The sword scoffed. "He's a braggart. Likes to make promises that his blade can't keep. I can't believe he's still around. I would have thought someone would have cleaved him in two by now. Or melted him down for scrap metal. Or…"

Instead of quieting down like I had hoped, she revved right back up again, listing all the things she thought would have happened to Vic by now. As far as incessant talking went, I thought she could give the other sword a run for his money, but I kept that to myself.

As fascinating as the sword was, I really needed to get back to watching the Reapers, so I rapped my knuckles on the glass a third time, interrupting her rant. "Anyway, it was nice meeting you, um…"

"Babs," the sword said. "You can call me Babs."

"Okay, Babs. My name is Rory. I've gotta go now, but I'll see you around—"

A scream tore through the air, cutting me off.

Before I had time to blink, another scream sounded, echoing through the library. I winced at the sharp, screeching howls, and my breath caught in my throat.

Those weren't human screams.

The scream came a third time, and I rushed over to the balcony railing. Down below, Amanda was standing in the open space in front of the checkout counter, her staff up and at the ready. In front of her was a large…*creature*. I didn't know what else to call it.

In many ways, the creature reminded me of a Nemean prowler—pantherlike body, burning red eyes, midnight-black fur shot through with crimson strands. But its paws were much bigger than a normal prowler's, as if they belonged to some larger creature and had been glued onto this one by accident. Its razor-sharp claws were longer than my fingers and gleamed a glossy crimson, as though each claw had been dipped in blood. As the creature padded back and forth, it left smoking paw prints behind on the stone floor.

But the truly terrifying part was its head. Oh, the creature had the pantherlike head of a Nemean prowler, but its teeth were much longer and sharper than a regular prowler's and gleamed like jagged rows of diamonds in its mouth. Enormous black ram's horns sprouted up from the creature's head, each curled into a tight, hard knot with a daggerlike point on the end, while a scorpion's stinger tipped its long black tail.

The crimson claws, the jagged teeth, the horns, the stinger. It looked like someone had taken bits and pieces of various mythological creatures and mashed them all together to create this one truly terrifying being.

The creature hissed at Amanda, and noxious clouds of black smoke spewed out of its mouth. Of course it could breathe smoke. Because all those claws, teeth, and horns didn't make it dangerous enough already.

Amanda scrambled around a study table, putting it between her and the creature, but the creature hissed at her again, and black smoke washed over the top of the table, charring the wood the same way the creature's paws were scorching the floor. So not only did the smoke stink of sulfur, but it also had some sort of burning, caustic property.

I stood there, frozen in place, my mouth gaping in shock. I had seen a lot of bad things, especially during the final battle with Loki, but I had never encountered a creature like this before. No, not a creature, a *monster*, in every sense of the word, a twisted, evil thing right out of every warrior's deepest, darkest nightmare.

"Chimera," Babs whispered, still sitting in the glass case behind me. "That's a Typhon chimera."

I kept staring at the monster. Chimeras were the stuff of fairy tales, even to Spartans like me. I had thought they were just a legend, just, well, a *myth*. Some scary old story that warrior parents told their kids in order to get them to behave, the way regular mortals made up tales about spooky bogeymen for their own children.

But I had been wrong—very, very wrong.

The chimera hissed out another cloud of black smoke,

further charring the table between it and Amanda. A grim look filled her face, and she gripped her staff tighter, shifting the weapon into an attack position. The chimera crouched down, and its tail lashed back and forth over its head, the stinger on the end pointed at Amanda, as it got ready to leap over the table and launch itself at her.

"I have to help her," I muttered. "No way can she kill that thing on her own."

I still didn't know what Amanda was doing in the library, but she had been nice to me at lunch and had treated me like an actual person instead of a villain like all the other kids did. I wasn't going to let her get clawed to death, even if she might be a Reaper.

"Are you crazy?" Babs hissed. "You need to get out of here. Run! Go! Now! While you still can!"

The sword babbled on and on about how I needed to leave and save myself, but I ignored her frantic words and scanned the rest of the library below. My gaze cut to the left, but the Reaper was gone, along with whatever artifact had been in that display case he'd broken into. So he hadn't been working with Amanda after all. Otherwise, the two of them would have left the library together. So what was Amanda doing here? Had she been trying to stop him from stealing?

Frustration filled me. I should have gone downstairs and confronted the Reaper the moment I saw him, instead of waiting up here like Aunt Rachel had asked me to. Now Amanda was in danger. But I could fix that. I could save her from that chimera.

I looked at first one case, then another, searching for a ranged weapon to use against the chimera. A spear, maybe, or a bow and a quiver full of arrows. I had zero desire to get close enough to the creature to stab it with a sword—

Babs sucked in a startled breath. "Watch out!"

A shadow moved across the floor, springing toward me. That and Babs's cry were all the warning I had, but my Spartan instincts kicked in, and I whirled around and threw myself forward, sliding across the slick stone floor. My left shoulder slammed into the bottom of Babs's display case, rattling the entire thing and making the sword shriek in surprise. Pain jolted through my shoulder, and I grunted at the hard, bruising impact.

Behind me, I heard the *scrape-scrape-scrape-scrape* of claws against stone, and I knew what was coming next. I grabbed the top of the case and pulled myself up and onto my feet.

Babs's green eye widened. "Look out!"

I pushed off the case, whirled around, and threw myself down and forward again, doing another slide across the floor and going back in the opposite direction. And not a moment too soon.

Crash!

Something slammed into the spot where I'd been standing, shattering the glass display case and sending Babs flying. Emerald-green sparks shot out from the sword's blade and hilt as she tumbled end over end along the floor. I hit Sigyn's statue with my left shoulder and bounced off. More pain radiated from my shoulder, but I ignored it, gritted my teeth, scrambled onto my feet, and whipped around to face this new danger.

A Typhon chimera stood in front of me, its teeth bared, black smoke dripping from the corners of its mouth. The monster's eyes burned a bright crimson, and its black tail snaked back and forth in the air above its head, the scorpion's stinger on the end pointed at me like an arrow seeking a target.

I stared at the creature, studying every single thing about it, from the way its crimson claws dug into the floor to the ripple of the muscles in its broad, powerful back to its long, sinuous strides as it paced back and forth in front of me. My Spartan instincts took over, and that movie started unspooling in my head as I thought about and discarded various plans of attack.

I had to stay away from the chimera's teeth and claws, or the fight would be over in seconds. The same thing went for that stinger attached to its tail, and forget about bashing it in the head. Those ram's horns were much too hard for that.

I had to go for one of the chimera's weak spots, like its stomach. If I could get underneath the creature, then I could cut open its belly. I didn't know if that would be enough to kill it, but it would be a good start.

Another inhuman scream ripped through the air, and I glanced over the balcony railing. Down below, Amanda was running around, putting more and more study tables between herself and the first chimera, which was yelling out its frustration at not having killed her yet. The Amazon would have to take care of herself right now.

I couldn't help her if I was dead.

I looked at the creature again, which was still stalking back and forth in front of me. My gaze moved past the chimera, and I scanned the balcony for something I could use as a weapon. I could try to topple one of the statues on top of it, but I doubted I had the necessary strength to move the heavy stone, and the chimera could easily claw me to death while I tried. The flimsy ink pens in my messenger bag wouldn't even scratch through the creature's thick fur and skin. Even the heavy reference book I'd been reading earlier wouldn't so much as stun the monster if I threw it at the chimera's face.

That left me with only one option: Babs.

The sword was lying off to my right, closer to the chimera than to me. Her eye frantically swiveled around as she looked from me to the creature and back again.

"Hey, Babs!" I called out. "I hope whoever put you in that case remembered to sharpen your blade."

"Oh, no!" she called out. "Don't you even *think* about using me!"

"Sorry. Not a lot of other weapons lying around here."

"Why?" she wailed. "Why does this always happen to me? All I want is a nice, quiet life in a museum somewhere. Is that too much to ask? Is it?"

The chimera grew tired of waiting for me to run, and it hissed and sprang through the air, its claws outstretched, ready to pin me to the ground and rip me to pieces. I darted forward, running straight at it.

At the last possible moment, I threw myself headfirst, diving across the floor for the third time. The slick stone helped me slide right on past the creature, which hit Sigyn's statue and bounced off, much the same way I had done earlier.

As I slid, I stretched my hand out toward Babs's gleaming silver hilt. The sword's eye widened.

"No!" she yelled. "You don't know what you're doing! Don't pick me up! Don't pick me up! Don't pick me up!"

I frowned. What kind of talking sword didn't want you to use her in battle? But I didn't have time to puzzle it out. My hand closed over the sword's hilt, right over her mouth, muffling her frantic cries.

The chimera bellowed out a loud scream that made the hair stand up on my arms. I knew what was coming next. I flipped over so that I was lying on my back on the floor and snapped up the point of the sword. A shadow fell over me, blotting out the overhead lights, and all I could see were the chimera's crimson claws, zooming toward my throat—

Crunch.

The chimera landed beside me just as I shoved the sword upward—straight into the creature's stomach.

The chimera threw back its head, snarling and screaming with pain, and it stretched a giant paw up, as though it were going to swipe it down and lay my throat open with its claws. I gritted my teeth, locked both hands around the sword's hilt, and shoved the weapon even deeper into the creature's belly. The chimera might kill me with its claws, but I was taking it with me the way a true Spartan would—

Poof!

Just before the chimera's claws would have cut into me, the creature dissolved into a cloud of smoke. I coughed and coughed, trying to get the sulfur stench out of my lungs, and waved my hand in front of my face, trying to clear away the smoke, which stung my skin with its intense heat.

Babs slipped from my hand and clattered to the floor. The second the sword stopped rattling around, her eye snapped open, as though she had it shut tight during the fight with the chimera.

"Okay, that wasn't so bad." Her high, nervous tone made her Irish accent far more pronounced. "At least there was no blood to dirty up my blade. Now, if you'll just do me a favor and find me a new display case, we can forget that this whole thing ever happened…"

Babs babbled on and on about how all she'd ever wanted was to live in a case with a nice view, but I tuned her out, got to my feet, and lurched over to the balcony.

Down on the first floor, Amanda was still running circles around the other chimera, which taking great pleasure in leaping from table to table and swatting at her like a cat playing with a mouse. It wouldn't be long before the creature moved in for the kill. Amanda knew it too, and she was trying to get to the exit doors. But every time she moved toward the main aisle, the chimera would leap onto the table in front of her, cut her off, and force her back to the center of the library. Amanda swung her staff at the chimera over and over again, landing several solid hits, but she couldn't do enough damage to slip past the monster.

She was dead—if I didn't save her.

I had already killed one chimera. I could kill another one. Even more than that, I *wanted* to do it. My Spartan instincts screamed at me to wade back into the fight, to hack and slash until all my enemies were dead, dead, dead.

The chimera leaped closer and closer to Amanda. In seconds, it would launch itself at her one final time, knock her to the ground, and tear her throat open with its teeth. I didn't have time to run over to the door and rush down the stairs, and there was only one other way to get down to the first floor. I looked over the balcony railing, judging where I was in the library and the distance down to the ground. This was going to hurt, but there was no other way. But first, I still needed a weapon, so I whipped around and sprinted over to where I'd dropped Babs.

"Oh, no! Not again! Don't pick me up!" Babs yelled. "Don't pick me up! Don't pick me up—"

Too late. Once again, I ignored her frantic cries and scooped the sword up off the floor. Then I ran forward, took hold of the stone railing, and leaped up and over the side of the balcony.

For an instant, I had the weightless sensation of free-falling, but all too quickly, the ground rushed up to meet me. Or in this case, a library table.

My boots slammed into the top of the table, and the

jarring impact shot all the way up my legs, spread out into my hips, and wrapped around my back. I lost my balance, staggered forward, and fell off the table, landing hard on my left side on the floor. A low groan escaped my lips, but I pushed the pain away and scrambled back onto my feet, ready to stab this chimera the same way I had the one upstairs.

But I was too late.

Amanda lashed out with her staff, but the chimera was faster, and it avoided the blow and slammed her to the floor. The creature raised its paw, then swiped it down, raking its claws all the way across Amanda's stomach. She screamed and beat at the creature with her staff, but the chimera grinned back at her. More of that noxious black smoke boiled out of the creature's mouth and dripped onto the horrible wounds in her stomach, adding to her agony. The coppery stink of her blood mixed with the smoke's sulfur fumes.

The chimera drew its claws back for another strike.

"Hey!" I screamed. "Pick on someone your own size!"

It was a stupid, cliché thing to say, since the chimera was even longer than I was tall, but my shout got the creature's attention. It hopped over Amanda and stalked toward me.

I shook off my hard landing and subsequent fall and slowly started twirling the sword around in my hand, getting a feel for the weapon, since I hadn't had a chance to do that earlier when I'd been battling the first chimera.

Strong, durable, lightweight, perfectly balanced, with a razor-sharp blade. The sword truly was a beautiful weapon, and I couldn't have asked for anything better. Well, maybe something a little more cooperative. All the while, I could feel Babs's lips moving under my palm, and I could still hear her babbling at me.

floor and shouts filling the air. Out of the corner of my eye, I saw Ian, the Viking, race into the library, a large battle ax clutched in his hand. His eyes widened when he saw the chimera, and he headed in my direction. But Amanda let out another loud, bloody cough, and he stopped, obviously torn. I waved my hand, telling him to help her instead.

I had this under control.

The Viking jerked his head at me in what I assumed was a *thank you*, then went over to the other girl, still keeping an eye on me and the chimera the whole time.

"Help!" he said in a sharp voice. "I need some help in here! Amanda's down! Repeat, Amanda's down!"

I didn't know who he was talking to, since we seemed to be the only three people in the library. It didn't matter right now anyway, so I tuned him out and focused on the chimera.

The chimera snarled at me again, and I twirled my sword around in my hand, thinking about the quickest and easiest way I could kill the creature. It was leaning on its right side, given the gash I had put in its left flank, and it would overcompensate for its injury. The chimera would move that way, and I could turn the other way and raise my sword at the same time. The images filled my mind, and I could see exactly how the fight would go in three, two, one...

The chimera leaped at me exactly the way I'd thought it would. I wrapped both hands around my sword, pivoted to the side, and snapped up my weapon. This time, I drove the blade straight through its heart. The chimera screamed, then—

Poof!

It disappeared in a shower of smoke. I coughed, lurched away from the hot, stinging wisps, and looked over at the others.

Ian was crouching down by Amanda's side, his hands on her stomach, trying to use his Viking strength to stop the bleeding. But her wounds were too deep, and she had already lost too much blood. Ian wasn't going to be able to save her. From the grim set of his lips, he knew it too, although he kept murmuring words of encouragement, telling her to hold on and that help was on the way.

I hobbled over to them, even though every movement made more and more pain spiral out through my blistered fingers, burned skin, and bruised, battered body. Ian looked up as I staggered to a stop beside them.

His gray eyes narrowed. "You're bleeding."

I looked down. Blood had soaked into my T-shirt sleeve. I pulled the tattered fabric away from my right arm and peered at the long gashes that ran from my shoulder all the way down to my elbow. The chimera had clawed me as I'd killed it. Weird. I hadn't even felt it strike me, and I should have, given how much blood was pouring out of the deep, ugly wounds. Or maybe that was because the hot, throbbing, pulsing feel of the burns on my skin was so much more painful.

But I forced the pain away, let go of my shirt sleeve, and dropped—well, more like fell—to my knees beside Amanda. "It's nothing. Just a few scratches."

Ian raised his eyebrows, knowing that I was lying, but he turned back to the other girl. "The others will be here any second. Hang on, Amanda. Just hang on."

She looked up at him, pain and tears shimmering in her eyes. "I tried..." she rasped. "But I couldn't find him... Whatever he took... I think he summoned...the chimeras with it..."

She coughed, causing more blood to bubble up out of her lips and trickle down her face. She shuddered out a breath, and her head lolled to one side. Amanda stared at me for a moment, and then her eyes went dark, distant, and blank.

Dead—she was dead.

"Amanda?" Ian said. "Amanda!"

He started shaking her, but of course it was far too late for that. He knew it too, and after a few seconds, he stopped, his face pinching tight with grief. This time, Ian shuddered out a breath and ran a hand through his blond hair. Then he reached out, gently closed Amanda's eyes, and bowed his head.

The gentle, respectful motion of one warrior saluting a fallen comrade made my heart ache. Tears stung my eyes, but I blinked them away. At least I thought I did, but Ian's and Amanda's faces blurred together, and white spots winked on and off in front of my eyes. A second later, my sword slipped from my hand and clattered to the floor. All the strength left my body, and I flopped down to the floor as well.

My face was right next to Babs's, and the sword's features twisted into a stricken expression.

"Don't die!" she said. "You can't die! Not so soon! It's not time yet!"

I opened my mouth to tell her that I didn't have a choice, given how badly the chimera had clawed and burned me, but the words got stuck in my throat, and the library started spinning around and around. One very troubling, ironic thought popped into my mind.

A talking sword and a dead girl in the library.

This was how it had all started for Gwen.

Chapter Five

I lay on the floor, staring up at the library tower ceiling. All those bits of stained glass glimmered even brighter than before, and I could have sworn that an invisible breeze was gusting over the wildflowers, making their petals sway back and forth and back and forth…

I blinked, and from one instant to the next, everything changed.

Instead of lying on the library floor, I was now standing in the middle of an enormous open-air courtyard. Flowers, vines, and trees stretched out in all directions, each one more colorful than the last. The vibrant blues, greens, reds, whites, and purples made it seem as though I were standing on a jeweled carpet instead of in a garden, and a crisp, clean scent blanketed the air, like fragrant flowers mixed with fresh snow.

A small stream snaked through the wildflowers, leading into a broken stone fountain before trickling out the other side. Cracked walls and crumbled heaps of stone ringed the courtyard, separating it from several nearby buildings that had collapsed in on themselves. The walls might be broken, but I could still make out the bears, rabbits, foxes, songbirds, and gryphons that had been carved into the stones.

Wildflowers, rocky ruins, animal carvings. I knew exactly where I was: the Eir Ruins on top of Snowline Ridge Mountain. But why? And how had I gotten here from the library?

I looked down. My clothes were still torn and bloody, but the burns and blisters on my hand had vanished, and my skin was smooth and whole again. The claw marks on my right arm were also gone. Someone had healed me. But who? Ian and his mysterious friends? Why would they help me?

I moved my arm back and forth and flexed my fingers, but everything worked the way it was supposed to, and I didn't feel the slightest twinge of pain. Good. That was good.

What wasn't so good was this weird dream that I was in—if it even *was* a dream.

This reminded me of another story Gwen had told me, about how Nike, the Greek goddess of victory, always seemed to appear to her in a strange dream realm, which was like a mirror image of the real world. I frowned. But what would Nike want with me? Gwen was her Champion, not me—

"Hello, Rory," a soft voice called out behind me.

I whirled around. I wasn't quite sure who I was expecting, but Nike wasn't here.

Another goddess was.

I could tell she was a goddess by the way she moved, as if she were floating along instead of actually walking on the ground like we mere mortals did. Her footsteps didn't disturb the wildflowers, didn't rustle so much as a single petal or snap the smallest stem. Her long white gown rippled as though it were made of sheets of snowflakes that were swirling around her body. Her hair trailed down her shoulders in thick, black waves, and her eyes were even blacker, making her skin seem as white and luminous as a pearl in comparison.

The only things that marred her beauty were the old, faded scars that crisscrossed her hands and crept up her arms, but they somehow suited her. Despite her lovely features, she radiated sorrow, as though she had seen so many bad things that she could never, ever forget them, despite all the good things still left in the world.

I knew exactly who she was, especially since I'd been staring at her statue in the library earlier: Sigyn, the Norse goddess of devotion.

Sigyn stopped in front of me. "Hello, Rory."

I bowed my head, wondering if I should curtsy and if I could do that without tripping and doing a face-plant into the flowers. Did you curtsy to a goddess? Gwen had never really explained that part of things to me.

"Um, hi." My voice was barely above a whisper.

Sigyn nodded at my hoarse greeting. Then she gestured at the garden around us. "Will you walk with me?"

"Um, sure."

I didn't really think I had a choice, but I wanted to walk with her. I wanted to know what was going on and why I was here...wherever *here* really was.

So I stepped up beside the goddess, and the two of us slowly meandered around the courtyard. Maybe I should have curtsied after all, because it seemed like every single one of the wildflowers bowed its brightly colored head to Sigyn as she passed them. I bit my lip, wondering if it was too late to curtsy. Probably. Besides, if the goddess knew anything about me, then she knew I definitely wasn't the prim, proper, curtsying type.

"I'm sure you're wondering why we're here, in Eir's courtyard," Sigyn finally said.

"The thought had crossed my mind."

Sigyn looked at me out of the corner of her eye, and I winced.

"Sorry. Was that too snarky?"

She let out a small, pleased laugh. "On the contrary. I enjoy your honesty. It's refreshing after so many lies from so many people over the years."

A shadow passed over her face, dimming her beauty, and another wave of sorrow radiated off her, as cold as a cloud of snow kissing my cheeks. Somehow I knew that she was talking about Loki and how he had betrayed her. My heart ached for her—and for myself too. My parents had lied to me my entire life, and I didn't know how to let go of my anger at them.

"Well, I hate liars too," I said. "Just as much as you do."

The goddess nodded, and we walked on. It took me a minute to work up the courage to ask her the question that was burning in my mind.

"So…why *am* I here?"

Sigyn eyed me again. "Gwendolyn Frost didn't tell you?"

I shrugged. "Not exactly. Gwen has told me lots of stories about her meetings with Nike…and you. How she finally realized that you were masquerading as that old woman, Raven, all this time. Gwen said that you had…plans for me. Or something like that."

I had been more than a little skeptical when Gwen had told me that Sigyn seemed interested in me. But here I was, face to face with the goddess and talking with Sigyn the same way Gwen talked to Nike. So why was I here? As far as I knew, Sigyn took care of her own problems by wandering around the academies in her Raven disguise. Besides, she was a freaking *goddess*. What did she need me for? Unless...

My breath caught in my throat. Sigyn didn't...she couldn't...she wasn't going to ask me to be her *Champion*, was she?

No—no way.

As soon as the thought occurred to me, I realized how ridiculous it was. For one thing, I had never even heard of Sigyn having a Champion. Sure, the goddess had brought me here to this weird dreamscape and was talking to me, but there could be any number of reasons for that. Maybe she had been wandering around the library as Raven and had seen the chimera claw me. Maybe she had brought me here to help me. Maybe she had healed me so she could ask me to do something for her in return. Or maybe she just felt sorry for me. But she wouldn't ask me to be her Champion.

Not me, Rory Forseti, the daughter of notorious Reaper assassins. I wasn't worthy to be anyone's Champion, especially not hers, given how horribly Loki had betrayed her. Even if Sigyn suddenly decided that she did want a Champion, I was probably the very last person she would ask.

The goddess must have seen the questions and confusion on my face, because she spoke again. "I had hoped that I was wrong and that things wouldn't turn out the way they have. That it wouldn't come to this. But unfortunately, evil never quite dies, no matter how hard you try to kill it."

"What do you mean?" A terrible thought occurred to me. "Loki...he's not *free*, is he? He hasn't found some way to escape that prison Gwen put him in?"

Sigyn shook her head. "No, no, nothing like that. Loki is still trapped in the realm of the gods, where he will remain for all time." She paused. "But a new danger threatens not only mythological warriors but the entire mortal world if it is left unchecked."

"What new threat? And why are you talking to me about it?"

"Because you're the only one who can stop it...if you choose to do so." Her voice was soft, but her words made a chill slither down my spine.

I frowned. "Why wouldn't I want to stop some evil threat?"

"Because of what it might cost you in the end, Rory Forseti." Sigyn stared at me, her eyes like two midnight-black pools in her pale, beautiful face. "What price are you willing to pay to protect the ones you love? That's the question you have to answer for yourself."

I frowned again. Gwen had told me that Nike always talked in riddles, but I had never thought Sigyn would too. Then again, what did I know about the goddess and what she wanted with me? So far, she hadn't told me anything important. Nothing specific about this threat or how I could stop it or why she thought I should be the one to face down this new evil.

"I don't ask this of you lightly," Sigyn continued. "It's your choice, Rory. Everything is *always* your choice. Remember that. But if you decide to fight, know that I gave you a proper weapon to help you in the days and battles ahead."

A weapon? What weapon? The answer came to me a moment later. Babs—she had to be talking about Babs.

Something the sword had said popped into my mind. My eyes narrowed. "Wait a second. *You* were the nice old lady who took Babs out of storage and put her on display in the library?"

Sigyn nodded. "Yes, I did that as Raven."

"But why? Why would you do that?"

She shrugged. "Because Babs needed a fresh start, and so do you. Besides, with this threat, you're going to need all the help you can get, and talking swords can be quite useful." Her mouth curved into a faint grin. "Especially the ones who truly love to talk, like Babs does."

So Sigyn had given me a sword and was asking me to use it to battle some vague new threat. I had heard of situations like this, where the gods asked something of mortals, but I had always thought they were stories out of myth-history books. Well, except for Gwen, of course. But I had never thought that a goddess would ask me to help her with anything.

I didn't know whether to be honored or frightened. Not all of those myth-history stories ended well for the mortals. Sometimes death wasn't the worst thing that happened to those who wanted to be heroes.

But the one thought that kept running through my mind was *why me?* Out of all the warriors out there, why had Sigyn asked me to help her? What could I do that someone else couldn't?

I opened my mouth to ask her that question and the dozen others that popped into my mind, including where those creepy chimeras in the library had come from, but Sigyn tilted her head to the side, as though she were listening to something very faint and far away.

"Unfortunately, our time together is at an end," she murmured. "Fight well, Rory Forseti. More lives depend on it than you know."

The goddess reached out and touched my hand. Her fingers felt as cold as ice against my skin, making me shiver, and I felt a wave of...*something* wash over me.

I wasn't quite sure what it was, but it made me feel strong and powerful, like I could keep on fighting, despite all the wounds I'd suffered in the library.

Sigyn smiled at me, dropped her hand from mine, and stepped back. Her elegant gown swirled around her again, like a snowstorm increasing its intensity, and the fabric glowed with such a brilliant silvery light that I had to shut my eyes against it. When I finally opened them again, the light and the goddess were gone.

And so was I.

CHAPTER SIX

My eyes snapped open, and I sat up with a startled gasp.

Instead of being in the courtyard of the Eir Ruins or even back in the library, I found myself lying in a hospital bed. I glanced around the room, which was full of medical equipment, along with a monitor that hooked into the clip on my finger and steadily *beep-beep-beeped* out my heart rate.

I looked down at my hand, but all my burns and blisters were gone, replaced by whole, healthy skin. The deep, ugly gashes in my arm had vanished as well, and I was wearing a fresh white T-shirt and a pair of matching pajama pants. Someone had healed me and cleaned me up, and I seemed to be in some sort of infirmary. I looked around again. This wasn't the regular school infirmary. The walls there were painted a soft blue, not made of dark gray stone like these.

Where was I?

Worry tightened my stomach, and I ripped off the finger clip, threw back the covers, and surged to my feet, determined to figure out where I was and what was going on—

Someone cleared her throat, and I whirled around in that direction.

Babs, the talking sword from the library, was propped up in a chair in the corner. I couldn't see the sword's blade, since it was encased in a black leather scabbard, but she stared at me with her emerald-green eye.

The sword was here, with me, which meant that I hadn't imagined my talk with Sigyn. The goddess really had given me a weapon and wanted me to fight some great evil. Once again, I didn't know whether to be honored or frightened.

"Rory, right?" Babs said in her Irish accent. "That's what everyone kept calling you when they brought you in here."

"Who is everyone?"

She shrugged. Well, as much as she could shrug with half a face. "I don't know. I've never seen them before."

Well, that didn't tell me anything. I glanced around the infirmary again. I spotted my clothes lying on another chair in the opposite corner, so I walked over to them.

I picked up my green T-shirt, which was ruined, given all the blood and gashes in the fabric, so I wadded it up and threw it into a nearby trash can. My jeans, socks, and boots were all still in one piece, if a bit bloody, so I left the white T-shirt on and slid back into the rest of my regular clothes. I held up my green leather jacket, examining it with a critical eye. I had taken it off in the library earlier, and it had survived the chimera attack unscathed. I shrugged into it as well.

Babs looked at me the whole time. The sword opened and closed her mouth half a dozen times, as though she wanted to ask me something. Finally, she worked up her nerve.

"Are you a Valkyrie?" she asked in a hopeful voice.

I snorted and waved my hand around, but of course nothing happened. "Do I look like I have princess-pink sparks of magic streaming out of my fingertips? Of course I'm not a Valkyrie."

Her face fell, as though she was disappointed, but she perked right back up again a second later. "So you're an Amazon, then? A nice, quiet Amazon who just happened to be studying late in the library when those chimeras attacked?"

"Oh, I was studying in the library, but I'm not an Amazon either." I lifted my chin. "I'm a Spartan."

Her green eye widened with shock. "A Spartan? No! No! You *can't* be a Spartan!" Her voice dissolved into a bitter wail.

I slapped my hands on my hips. "And what, exactly, is wrong with me being a Spartan?"

She winced at my sharp tone. "Well, nothing, on the face of it. It's just…"

"What?"

She sighed. "Spartans have a tendency to be exceptionally reckless. Always charging into battle without thinking things through. Always taking on more enemies than any sane warrior would ever dream of. Always believing that your fighting skills and killer instincts are going to be enough for you to win, no matter how badly the odds are stacked against you."

"Why do you have a problem with that?" I asked. "Because that's what Spartans *do*. We fight the battles that others don't or can't. That's why we're the best warriors in the Mythos world."

Babs sighed again. "Yes, yes, and you die at an exceptionally alarming rate because of it. Which doesn't work out so well for me."

I frowned. "What does *that* mean? What does Spartans dying have to do with you? What kind of sword are you, anyway? What kind of sword doesn't want to be picked up and used in battle?"

Babs's mouth opened and closed and opened and closed again.

"Well?" I demanded.

So far, all I had were a whole lot of questions and no answers. Somebody needed to tell me what was going on, even if that somebody was a talking sword.

Babs sighed for a third time. "Never mind. Forget that I said anything. It doesn't matter anyway. It never does in the end."

She was talking in riddles like Sigyn had, but since I didn't know who or what might be waiting outside this room, I went over, grabbed the scabbard, and hooked it to my black leather belt. Then I practiced pulling the sword out of the scabbard, getting a feel for the weapon like I had in the library earlier.

Babs's hilt fit perfectly in my fingers, like she had been made just for me. Her nose hooked over my hand, forming a sort of wrist guard, with her eye clearly visible above. Sure, it was a little odd, feeling Babs's lips against my palm, but I quickly grew used to it. Once I was sure that I could pull out the sword and use it with ease, I slid Babs back into her scabbard, opened the door, and left the infirmary.

I stepped into a stone hallway. No windows were set into the walls, and the cool, still air gave me the impression that I was deep underground. Instead of regular lights, the ceiling featured smooth stones that cast out a warm, golden glow. Each stone was shaped like a different mythological creature, from Nemean prowlers to Fenrir wolves to Eir gryphons. Not only that, but each stone seemed to burn a little brighter as I passed below it, almost as if the creatures were following me down the hallway. I shivered, dropped my hand to Babs's hilt, and walked on.

A few twists and turns later, the hallway opened up into an enormous square room with more corridors branching off it. A long rectangular table squatted in the center of the area, with all the seats turned to face several monitors hanging on one of the walls. Several desks were spread throughout the room, each one seeming to have a different purpose and personality.

One desk boasted a high-end laptop, two keyboards, and three monitors. Several small foam footballs, soccer balls, and tennis balls emblazoned with various sports team logos and autographs were nestled among the computer equipment.

Tools, wires, daggers, arrows, and odd pieces of metal covered a second desk, along with a blowtorch and several pairs of goggles and gloves. Scissors, fabric swatches, rolls of ribbons, and small boxes full of sparkly plastic jewels also sat on the desk, as though whoever worked there made either really cool weapons or really cool clothes, or both, depending on their mood.

A battle ax was laid out on a third desk, surrounded by daggers, short swords, and other weapons. Several history books about ancient battles, warriors, creatures, and artifacts were neatly stacked in one corner, with colored sticky notes marking certain sections for easy reference.

A fourth and final desk was completely empty.

My gaze moved to the back half of the room, which featured several rows of floor-to-ceiling shelves. Books crowded together on many of the shelves, old, thick, worn-out tomes that looked like they hadn't been cracked open in years, given the dust coating them. Several shelves also housed armor and weapons, everything from gold gauntlets to bows boasting silver strings to bronze-tipped spears that were taller than I was. Other objects were on the shelves as well, including jeweled necklaces, crystal figurines, and small stone statues.

All put together, the room was an odd mix of modern high-tech gear and ancient artifacts.

As much as I would have liked to wander around and look at all the computers, tools, and weapons, I still had no idea where I was or who had brought me here, and I wanted to leave before they came back. So I stepped deeper into the room and peered down the various hallways, searching for a way out—

A loud *bang* sounded in the distance, as though someone had thrown open a door and it had slammed into a wall. The sharp noise was quickly followed by an even louder voice.

"Absolutely not," the voice said, drawing closer and closer. "I don't want her on the team."

Since I didn't know who or what was coming my way, I ducked into the shadows behind the closest shelf and peered around a couple of silver jewelry boxes.

Footsteps scuffed against the floor, and Ian stormed into the room, followed by a man who was much calmer and walking far more slowly: Coach Takeda.

My eyes narrowed. What was he doing here? What was going on?

What *was* this place?

Two other kids who looked about my age—seventeen or so—entered the room behind Ian and Takeda. One of them was a petite girl with beautiful mocha skin, hazel eyes, and wavy black hair that brushed the tops of her shoulders. She wore a bright blue crop top, black leggings, and black ankle boots with chunky heels. A blue-plaid designer bag that was big enough to double as a suitcase dangled from her left arm.

The girl went over to the desk covered with tools. She nudged a couple of hammers aside to make room for her enormous purse, then plopped down in the chair. She rooted around inside her purse for several seconds before pulling out a large notebook and an ink pen, which she set off to one side on the desk. Then she picked up a piece of wire and started bending it with her bare hands. Pale blue sparks of magic shot out of her fingertips and flickered in the air all around her. So she was a Valkyrie.

The other kid—a guy—sat down at the computer desk and flipped on all three of the monitors. He was a couple of inches under six feet tall, with a runner's thin build and lean muscles. His dark brown hair was cut short, and the light from the monitors made his dark brown eyes and bronze skin gleam. He wore black jeans, along with a gray T-shirt that read *Bigtime Barracudas*, a popular football team in Bigtime, New York.

He hit the power button on the laptop, then leaned back in his chair and propped his black running shoes up on the desk. While he waited for the laptop to boot up, the guy pulled out a candy bar from one of the desk drawers, ripped off the wrapper, and sank his teeth into the chocolate. He grunted with happiness. A guy after my own sugar-addict heart.

He gulped down the candy bar, then dropped his feet and scooted his chair closer to the desk. With one hand, he typed on the laptop. With the other, he typed on another keyboard, his gaze sweeping back and forth between the laptop and the other three monitors the whole time. So he was a Roman. They were the only guys who could multitask that quickly.

Takeda moved over to the long table in the middle of the

room. He crossed his arms over his chest, but his face remained as calm and blank as it was in gym class. Ian stalked the length of the room, from the guy with the laptop, across the wide open space in front of the wall monitors, over to where the girl with the tools was sitting on the opposite side of the room, and back again.

"No," Ian repeated. "I don't want her on the team."

"You saw what she did to those chimeras," Takeda said. "She killed both of them all by herself. Not many Spartans could do that. Not many warriors could do that, period."

I blinked. I supposed I shouldn't be surprised that they were talking about me, given how strange this entire day had been. Chimeras in the library, meeting with Sigyn, and now this…whatever *this* was. What sort of team were they talking about? And why did Takeda want me to join it? Somehow I didn't think it had anything to do with sports.

"So she's a good fighter. So what?" Ian said. "You've read her file. You know about her parents. You know they were Reapers. And not regular Reapers but Reaper *assassins*. Rebecca and Tyson Forseti were responsible for the deaths of dozens of people, including several members of the Protectorate."

My heart clenched, and my stomach twisted with guilt, shame, and embarrassment. Every word he said was like a dagger stabbing into my gut—because they were all *true*. The sick feeling in my stomach intensified, and for a moment, I thought I was going to vomit. But I swallowed down the hot, sour bile rising in my throat and focused on that cold frost coating my heart, letting the chill numb my turbulent emotions.

"All of that is true," Takeda said. "But perhaps you shouldn't be so quick to judge Miss Forseti, especially not based on the sins of her Reaper parents."

His soft, chiding words made Ian jerk to a stop, and something very similar to my own guilt, shame, and embarrassment flashed in the Viking's gray eyes. But he shook off the emotions and started pacing again.

"Forget about Rory Forseti for a second," Ian said. "Amanda Ersa was only on the team for two days. She didn't even have time to unpack any of her stuff."

He looked over at the empty desk against the wall. So did the guy with the laptop and the girl with the tools. Sadness filled all three of their faces.

"We might not have known Amanda all that well, but she was still one of us," Ian said. "She hasn't been dead three hours yet, and you're already talking about replacing her with someone else."

"I feel Amanda's loss just as deeply as you all do," Takeda said. "More so, because she was my responsibility."

His voice was as soft and calm as before, but I could hear the regret rippling through his words. Like all warriors, Takeda had seen his share of death, but that didn't make it any easier to deal with, especially not when the victim was a teenage girl.

The Roman guy sighed, quit typing, and pushed his laptop away. He asked the inevitable question. "But?"

Takeda squared his shoulders. "But the mission comes first, before any of us. You know that. You all know that, along with the risks. This is what you signed up for, Mateo. You too, Zoe."

Zoe snorted. "Speak for yourself."

Takeda stared at her, his face still that calm, emotionless mask. Zoe scowled and crossed her arms over her chest, causing more blue sparks of magic to shimmer in the air around her.

"Well, I agree with Ian," Mateo said. "Amanda might not have been here long, but she was still our friend."

"She was your friend," Zoe muttered. "She didn't like me."

Mateo shook his head. "She liked you just fine."

Zoe snorted again. "No, she didn't. Amanda knew that I wasn't nearly as gung-ho about this little operation as she was." She slouched down in her seat. "Coming here wasn't my idea, remember?"

"It doesn't matter whose idea it was," Ian growled. "Only that Amanda is dead. You were supposed to watch out for her."

"I *did* watch out for her!" Zoe snapped back. "I used my lockpick gun to open that library door so we could go inside like we planned. It's not my fault that I had to leave her, run around the building, and let you in through another door. I'm not a magician. I can't be in two places at once. Besides, Amanda is the one who decided to forget about the plan and head into the library all by herself without waiting for backup."

Ian's lips pressed together into a tight, thin line. Takeda remained expressionless, while Mateo looked back and forth between everyone.

"And let's face facts," Zoe snapped again. "I'm not a great warrior. Even if I had been there, I couldn't have done anything to save Amanda. Not against a freaking *chimera*. I didn't even think those things were *real*."

She threw her hands up into the air, and blue sparks streaked out of her fingers like fireworks exploding over and over again. Valkyries always gave off more magic when they were upset or emotional. Zoe shot an angry glare at Ian, then one at Takeda, as though the two of them were responsible for her being here. Maybe they were. Still, I couldn't help but wonder what all of them were up to and why Takeda thought I should be part of it.

But I didn't want to stick around and find out.

Once again, I glanced around the room, wondering which hallway might lead to an exit, but I didn't have any better idea than before. Besides, I couldn't leave my hiding spot without them seeing me. They had gone to a lot of trouble to bring me here and heal me, and they probably wouldn't let me leave without a fight. I had no doubt that I could take out Zoe and Mateo, but I wasn't so sure about Ian, since his Viking battle ax was lying on that desk, along with all those other weapons. Not to mention Takeda. Who knew what fighting skills and magic the Samurai might have?

I might be a Spartan, but I wasn't reckless, and I was in no hurry to die, no matter what Babs claimed. Part of being a warrior was knowing when to fight—and now was not that time. Not when I was outnumbered four to one and had no idea how to escape. Besides, the other warriors couldn't stay down here forever. I'd wait for them to leave and then slip away quietly.

"It doesn't matter who was supposed to be where," Takeda said. "We can't change what happened to Amanda or the fact that our mission isn't over. Now that the Reaper has an artifact, the situation is even more dangerous, and we could use Rory Forseti on our side."

Ian's face hardened. "We don't need her."

Takeda stared at him. "If Rory had been working with us tonight, if she'd had some advance warning, if she'd known what was really going on, she might have been able to save Amanda."

Ian's lips pressed together again, and he didn't say anything else. Neither did Takeda. Zoe kept glaring at the two of them, while Mateo drummed his fingers on his keyboard. Hello, dysfunctional dynamic. Whoever these people were, they might be on the same side, but they were most definitely not a team.

Takeda was the adult and obviously the boss, given his air of command and authority. Mateo seemed to be a computer guru, and Ian was definitely a fighter like me. But what did Zoe do with all those tools? And why were the four of them here? What artifact had the Reaper stolen from the Library of Antiquities?

More and more questions swirled around in my mind, but I had no way to get any answers. At least, not without revealing myself to them, which was something I didn't want to do—

"I want to see my niece right now!" a familiar voice called out.

My heart lifted. Aunt Rachel was here.

A low voice murmured something to her in response, although I couldn't make out the words. More footsteps scuffed against the floor, and Aunt Rachel stormed into the room. She glanced around, stalked over to Takeda, and slapped her hands on her hips.

"I want to see Rory right now!" she demanded.

"Ah, Ms. Maddox," Takeda said in that same annoyingly calm voice. "I've been expecting you."

She moved even closer to him, anger staining her cheeks a bright red. Aunt Rachel didn't often get mad, but when she did, watch out. If I had been Takeda, I would have stepped away from her, but he didn't know her like I did.

"Maybe you didn't hear me before." Her was voice lower and more dangerous this time. "I want to see Rory *right now*. And if I find out that you have harmed one single hair on her head, then I will break you into pieces."

Takeda's face remained blank, but he did step back and

bow his head to her. "Follow me, and I'll take you to your niece."

"Um," Mateo said. "One small problem. Rory's not in her room."

He hit a few buttons on his laptop, and a picture of the empty infirmary room popped up on one of the monitors on the wall.

Aunt Rachel whirled back around to Takeda. "Where is my niece?"

I winced at her sharp, demanding tone, the one that always told me I was in serious trouble. Aunt Rachel was about to blow. I had to stop her before she did something she might regret, so I stepped out from behind the shelves and walked forward where everyone could see me.

"I'm right here," I called out.

Startled, everyone turned in my direction. Aunt Rachel ran over and swallowed me up in a tight hug, which I returned with one that was equally fierce.

"I was so worried about you," she whispered in my ear. "I got your text and rushed over to the library, but when I got there, the place was surrounded by the Protectorate, and they wouldn't let me inside. I tried texting you again, but you didn't answer me, and I thought—I thought—" Her voice choked off, and her arms tightened around me, telling me how worried she had been.

Guilt rippled through me. With everything that had been going on, I hadn't even thought to check my phone after I'd woken up in the infirmary.

"I'm fine," I whispered back. "They healed me, and I'm fine. Despite the chimeras."

Aunt Rachel drew back, her green eyes wide. "Chimeras? What chimeras? I thought you were going to stay on the balcony, where it was safe!"

"I did stay on the balcony. At least until the chimeras showed up. They attacked me and killed Amanda, another girl, one of them." I waved my hand at the others.

Aunt Rachel stared at me a second longer, then whirled around to Takeda again. "Chimeras? Typhon chimeras? In the Library of Antiquities? You told me that Rory had been attacked by a Nemean prowler."

Takeda shrugged. "Well, chimeras are part prowler. I didn't want to worry you any more than necessary. And as you can see, Rory is perfectly fine." He paused. "In fact, I was just discussing her future with the rest of my team."

Ian started shaking his head *no-no-no*, still not wanting me to be part of this mysterious group. Mateo looked from Takeda to Aunt Rachel and back again, his fingers tapping out a nervous, uneven pattern on his keyboard. Zoe leaned back in her chair and grinned, entertained by all the drama.

Aunt Rachel stabbed her finger at Takeda. "If you think for one second that my niece is going to be part of—of—of whatever *this* is, then you have another think coming, mister. Rory is coming home with me where she belongs."

"We all know that there is only one place where Spartans truly belong: on the battlefield," another voice cut into the conversation.

For the third time, footsteps sounded, and a shadowy figure appeared in the hallway. The shadow grew closer and closer, morphing into a tall, thin man wearing a gray cloak with a symbol stitched on it in white thread, a hand holding a set of balanced scales.

Blond hair, blue eyes, a sword belted to his waist. I recognized him. I had fought side by side with him during the Battle of Mythos Academy.

Linus Quinn, the head of the Protectorate.

CHAPTER SEVEN

L inus Quinn strode into the middle of the room, his gray cloak swirling around his body.

He shook hands with Takeda, eyed Ian and the other kids, and nodded to Aunt Rachel. Then he turned and studied me from head to toe. Linus's blue eyes lingered on the sword hooked to my belt, but after a moment, he nodded to me as well.

"Hello, Miss Forseti," he said. "You're looking well. All things considered."

"Mr. Quinn." I nodded back at him, then crossed my arms over my chest. "You mean the fact that a chimera killed a girl and almost clawed me to death? Yeah, that was a great surprise for the first day of school. I thought the Library of Antiquities was supposed to be a safe place now, but I see that it's just as dangerous as ever."

Linus winced a bit at my snarky tone, but he couldn't deny the truth of my words.

"What's going on?" I asked. "Where are we? Who are these people? And what does everyone want with me?"

Linus's lips curved up into a small smile. "I see that you have the same sarcastic attitude as your cousin Gwen."

I shrugged. "It must run in the Forseti and Frost families."

Zoe leaned forward, her face creasing in confusion. "Wait a second. Gwen? As in Gwen Frost? *She's* related to Gwen Frost?"

"Yeah," I said. "So what?"

The Valkyrie's hazel eyes lit up with admiration. "So Gwen Frost is a *hero*. Like the greatest hero *ever*."

I sighed. Zoe wasn't the first person to have this sort of reaction when she found out that I was related to Gwen. I loved my cousin, really, I did, but I wouldn't have minded if she had been just a little *less* heroic. It was a lot to live up to. Since, you know, Gwen had basically saved the entire world.

Mateo stared at me with a similarly incredulous hero-worship expression, but Ian snorted. Seemed he wasn't a Gwen Frost fan. His loss.

"Rory is a hero in her own right," Linus said. "She and her aunt were both instrumental in helping Miss Frost and the Protectorate defeat Loki and his Reapers. They helped save us all, and you should treat them with the proper amount of respect."

He gave Ian a pointed look, and the Viking actually winced a bit.

Linus stared at Ian a moment longer, making sure that the Viking got his point, then gestured at the table in the center of the room. "Let's all have a seat, and I'll bring Miss Forseti and Ms. Maddox up to speed."

Aunt Rachel glared at Takeda one more time, but she pulled out a chair and sat down at the table. I took the chair next to her, with Ian sitting across from me. Zoe and Mateo left their desks, moved over, and plopped down beside Ian. Takeda took the seat at the head of the table, but Linus remained standing.

Mateo grabbed what looked like a TV remote from the center of the table and handed it to Linus, who hit a series of buttons on the device. A second later, photos began appearing on the monitors on the wall.

Images of the Battle of Mythos Academy.

My heart clenched as shot after shot of the North Carolina academy popped up on the screens. The grounds, the main quad, the inside of the Library of Antiquities. All littered with dented weapons, shattered statues, and bloody bodies.

So many bodies.

Reapers and Protectorate members lay crumpled next to each other on the ground. Their torn black and gray cloaks were draped over their bodies like makeshift shrouds, while their swords, staffs, and spears were stuck point-first in the grass like crude crosses marking where they had fallen. But they weren't the only ones who had died. So had kids, professors, and other people who worked at the academy, and their bodies littered the quad like broken dolls, along with those of the Eir gryphons and other creatures that had taken part in the battle.

The photos took me right back there to that awful day. In an instant, the briefing room vanished, and I was in the midst of the fight. Yells and screams echoed from one side of the quad to the other and back again, along with the violent, continued *clash-clash-clash* of weapons crashing into each other. I was yelling too, swinging my sword at Reaper after Reaper, cutting down as many of them as I could, even though they just kept coming and coming and coming...

Aunt Rachel reached over and grabbed my hand, pulling me out of my memories. No doubt the same ones darkened her own thoughts. I squeezed her hand back, grateful that she was here. We might be Spartans, but that had been a battle unlike any other, and I would never, ever forget it—and all the people and creatures who had died so that we all might finally be free of Loki.

Linus hit some more buttons, and the battle scenes faded away, replaced by shots of people moving around the quad, cleaning up the destruction. Gwen appeared in several of the photos, hauling away debris with the help of Logan Quinn, her boyfriend and Linus's son. Gwen's other friends, including Daphne Cruz and Carson Callahan, also showed up on the screens, along with Professor Aurora Metis, Gwen's mentor, and Nickamedes, the head librarian at the North Carolina academy.

Seeing them all again made my heart squeeze tight with longing. They were my friends too—my only friends—and I missed them all terribly. More than once, I had thought about transferring to the North Carolina academy, but Aunt Rachel's job was here, and I didn't want to leave her. Besides, I had foolishly thought that things would be better, that the other kids might give me a chance—a real chance—after I had fought alongside Gwen and the others. But of course things hadn't worked out that way, not at all.

"As you all know, the North Carolina academy was decimated by the final battle with Loki and his Reapers of Chaos," Linus said. "A lot of progress was made over the summer, and the school year started as usual, but the cleanup still continues at the academy."

"So what?" Aunt Rachel asked. "Rory and I know how damaged the academy was. We were there, remember?"

"Yes, I remember," Linus said. "And your bravery was one of the reasons we were able to win, along with the help of the Eir gryphons that you brought to the academy."

Aunt Rachel sat up a little straighter, and so did I. It was always nice to be recognized. Everyone else at the table nodded at us, acknowledging our contributions as well, except for Ian, who rolled his eyes. What was his problem? I didn't even know the guy, and he already hated me. Well, the feeling was quickly becoming mutual.

"Unfortunately," Linus continued, "what we didn't realize at the time was that not all of the Reapers were killed or captured."

He hit some more buttons, and several security-camera images appeared on the monitors. Each one showed Reapers sprinting across the grounds, climbing over the wall that ringed the academy, and running away.

I frowned. "I had heard that some of the Reapers had escaped, but I thought the Protectorate was working to round them up and put them in prison."

Linus nodded. "That's true. After Loki was defeated, the Protectorate knew there was still work to do, still Reapers to apprehend. But we wanted everyone to get on with their lives as best they could, so we've downplayed the danger as much as possible. Ever since the battle, we've been quietly hunting down the rest of the Reapers. But I'm afraid we've had our work cut out for us."

"What do you mean?" Aunt Rachel asked.

"The Reapers all obeyed Agrona and her lieutenants, but now that she's dead and the others are in prison, there's no one left to keep the remaining Reapers in check." Linus rubbed his head, as though it were suddenly aching. "Many of the Reapers have become bolder and more violent than ever before. Slaughtering mythological creatures to sell their fur, teeth, and talons on the black market. Kidnapping wealthy mythological citizens and holding them for ransom. Murdering Protectorate guards. Some Reapers have even been stealing from regular mortals, robbing banks, jewelry stores, and the like." He sniffed, indicating how low-class he thought that was.

What he was saying made sense, but it certainly didn't make me feel any better. Then again, I imagined that Linus felt worse and had more guilt about the Reapers than anyone else, since Agrona, his former wife, had only married him so she could spy on the Protectorate. Linus had finally discovered the horrible truth about Agrona but not before she had almost turned Logan, his son, into her Reaper puppet.

"But I thought that things would be better once Loki was gone," I said. "That the Reapers would collapse without him. That we would all finally be *safe*."

Linus shook his head. "I had hoped that as well, but it hasn't turned out that way. In fact, things have gotten far worse than we ever imagined they would."

"Worse how?" I asked.

"From what we've learned over the past few months, a secret group has existed within the Reapers for years, people who were never really interested in freeing Loki but just used the other Reapers as a way to hide their own evil actions," Linus said. "These Reapers didn't participate in the final battle against the god, even though they were at the North Carolina academy."

"So what did they do?" Aunt Rachel asked.

"Their goal was something far more sinister: stealing as many artifacts from the Library of Antiquities as they could while everyone else was busy fighting."

Linus hit some more buttons, and yet more security-camera photos popped up, this time showing Reapers smashing into glass display cases in the library, grabbing the weapons, armor, and other objects inside, and leaving with them.

"Given the overall destruction at the academy, we didn't uncover the thefts for several days," he continued. "By that point, this secret group of Reapers had completely vanished and had gone back underground to resume their normal lives in the mythological world the way they would after any battle. Only this time with the bonus of powerful magical artifacts."

Images of weapons, armor, and more appeared on the screens, flashing by one after another. The Reapers hadn't just stolen a few trinkets—they'd swiped dozens of artifacts from the library. A shiver slid down my spine. A single artifact could cause plenty of damage in the wrong hands. I didn't even want to think about all the people and creatures the Reapers could hurt and kill with this many artifacts.

"Now, this secret faction of Reapers does have a leader, someone who has been pulling everyone else's strings and slowly taking control of all the remaining Reapers," Linus said. "We haven't been able to identify the leader yet, but we know that it's a man and that he goes by the code name Sisyphus."

I frowned. Sisyphus was a name from my myth-history class, that of a mortal man doomed to keep pushing a rock up a hill, only to have it roll back down, forcing him to start all over again. Strange name for the leader of the Reapers. Or perhaps Sisyphus had chosen that name because he knew what an enormous task it would be to resurrect the group after Gwen had decimated them.

"So what does all this have to do with the warrior band here?" I sniped, gesturing at Ian and the other kids. "What were they doing on campus today? And what was that other girl, Amanda, doing in the library earlier?"

"Over the last few months, Sisyphus has been building

his group, mostly by recruiting Mythos students to join his new band of Reapers," Linus said.

I rolled my eyes. "Seriously? Who would be stupid enough to want to join the Reapers?"

"Kids whose Reaper parents died during the battle at the North Carolina academy," Linus said in a soft, serious voice.

He fell silent, and everyone looked at me, the girl with the dead Reaper parents. That familiar mix of guilt, shame, and embarrassment churned in my stomach, and I dropped my hands to my lap so that no one would see them tighten into fists. Even here, in this strange place, I couldn't escape what my parents had done.

I would *never* escape it.

Linus cleared his throat. "Many of these kids are mixed up and hurting. They want revenge for their parents' deaths, and Sisyphus is taking advantage of them, using them to further his own ends. But other students, well, they were already Reapers, or at least on the path to becoming Reapers, thanks to their parents and their own anger and greed. Those kids are all too happy to do whatever Sisyphus asks, no matter who they have to hurt and betray."

"And?" Aunt Rachel asked.

"And a couple of weeks ago, we got a tip that one of those Reaper students was going to try to steal an artifact from the Library of Antiquities when the Colorado academy opened for the new school year. We didn't know which artifact the student was targeting, but we now realize that it was Typhon's Scepter."

Linus hit another button, and new photos appeared on the screens, each showing a gold stick that was about as long as my forearm. Several figures were etched into the gold, and it took me a moment to realize that they were Nemean prowlers, rams, and scorpions, all curled together. A single figure, also made of gold, crouched on the top of the scepter. That figure was a combination of all the other creatures, with a prowler's body, ram's horns on its head, and a scorpion's stinger on its tail. It was an ugly, monstrous thing, made even more so by the two glittering blood-red rubies that made up its eyes. I shivered. The creature was the same as the monsters I'd fought in the library earlier: a Typhon chimera.

I stared at the photos of the scepter and thought back to that glimmer of gold that I'd seen in the display case. "So that's what the Reaper stole from the library."

"Typhon was a Greek giant with several creatures sprouting out of his body—prowlers, rams, scorpions, and more. Typhon pulled bits and pieces of the creatures off his own body and fused them together to create one new being, the chimera." Linus pointed at the images on the monitors. "The scepter is thought to be made of one of Typhon's bones, which was encased in gold. All someone has to do is wave the scepter in a specific pattern, and chimeras spew forth from the end of it in clouds of dense black smoke. Chimeras cannot be reasoned with, and they are extremely dangerous. But they can be killed like any other creature, and a mortal wound makes them dissipate into a cloud of smoke."

"Amanda would know that better than anyone," Ian muttered.

Linus looked at the Viking, sympathy flashing in his eyes. "Yes, she would."

We all fell silent again, thinking about the poor girl who'd lost her life tonight. And for what? So a Reaper could steal an artifact? I shook my head. What a sad, tragic waste.

"As I said before, we got a tip that a Reaper was going to try to steal an artifact," Linus continued. "So Takeda and the others came to the academy a few days ago when the students starting moving into the dorms to see if they could figure out who the Reaper was. Our plan was to identify the student, let him steal the artifact, follow him back to his friends, and arrest all the Reapers at the same time, including Sisyphus. But, regrettably, that didn't happen."

"We were watching the library, and we saw the student approaching, but we lost track of him. So Amanda decided to go into the library ahead of everyone else," Mateo said in a soft, sad voice. "I was on comms with her the whole time. I tried to talk her out of it, but she wouldn't listen to me. Then, when she got into the library, she couldn't find the Reaper."

"You wouldn't know anything about that, would you?" Ian glared at me, and I realized what he was really saying.

I glared right back at him. "You think that *I'm* somehow working with the Reapers? Viking, you are seriously off your rocker. I would never, *ever* work for the Reapers."

"Really? Just like your parents couldn't have possibly been Reaper assassins?" he shot right back at me.

This time, my hands curled into fists on top of the table where everyone could see them. "You should shut your mouth—unless you want me to shut it for you."

Ian's eyes narrowed. "Bring it on, cupcake. Bring it on."

I shoved my chair back so I could get up and lunge across the table at him, but Linus stepped forward and laid a hand on my shoulder.

"Enough," he said. "That's enough. From both of you. We need to work together, not fight among ourselves."

I glared at him too, but Linus raised his eyebrows, and I shrugged his hand away and sat back down in my seat.

"Fine," I muttered. "The Viking can keep his teeth. For now."

"Wow. Thanks." Ian's voice dripped with sarcasm.

Linus might have said that I was a hero, but it was obvious that Ian didn't believe him. Either that, or Ian hated me for some other reason. Whatever it was, I was tired of the Viking's attitude problem.

Linus cleared his throat, wanting us to get back on track, so I looked at the monitors again, staring at the chimera scepter until I got my anger under control.

"So Sisyphus and his Reapers are stealing artifacts," Aunt Rachel said. "But you still haven't explained what all of *this* is."

She waved her hand around at the room, with all of its high-tech monitors, tools, weapons, and shelves full of artifacts.

"Not many people know this, but every single Library of Antiquities has a basement level deep underground," Linus said. "Most of them are used to store artifacts, books, and the like from the library's collection. The Colorado library is unique in that it has two basement levels, the second of which is not listed on any of the library schematics. Several months ago, after Loki was freed, I had this second, secret level converted into a fallback headquarters and stocked it with the Protectorate's most powerful artifacts in case things didn't go our way. It was going to be our last resort, our last base of resistance and operations, if we weren't able to defeat the god."

Now that he mentioned it, I realized that the shape and size of this room was an exact match for the main space around the checkout counter and the fireplace on the first floor. I had thought I knew every single inch of the library, but apparently not.

"And them?" Aunt Rachel asked, waving her hand at Takeda and the others.

"Sisyphus is recruiting kids and turning them into Reapers," Linus said. "Kids who won't talk to adults wandering around campus in Protectorate robes, much less gossip around them or share any sort of information. So I put together a group of people those kids *will* talk to—other students. This is Team Midgard."

Midgard was another name I recognized from myth-history class. The term often referred to the mortal realm, but it was also the name of an enormous wall that the gods had once built to protect people from monsters and other threats.

I eyed the other kids sitting at the table. "Doesn't look like much of a team to me. Or a guard."

This time, Ian, Zoe, and Mateo all glared at me.

Linus ignored my snide remark and gestured at Takeda. "Hiro Takeda is the team leader. A Samurai with impressive fighting and tactical skills, as well as healing magic. Takeda has been a member of the Protectorate for more than ten years, joining as soon as he graduated from the Tokyo branch of Mythos Academy."

Takeda was already sitting perfectly straight, but he seemed to grow even straighter at his boss's praise. Ten years out of the academy would put him in his early thirties, a few years older than Aunt Rachel. Takeda's dark brown gaze dropped to my arm. He must have been the one who had healed me. I tipped my head, silently thanking him. He nodded back at me.

"Mateo Solis," Linus continued. "A Roman with remarkable quickness and even more remarkable computer skills. If it's electronic, Mateo can hack it."

A blush stained Mateo's cheeks, but he too sat up a little straighter.

"Zoe Wayland," Linus said. "A Valkyrie with an affinity for creating all sorts of interesting gadgets and weapons."

Zoe lifted her chin and waved her hand toward her desk covered with tools. "In other words, I make all the awesome stuff around here."

"And Ian Hunter," Linus finished. "A Viking warrior whose family has a long history of Protectorate service."

I expected Ian to sit up straighter too, just like Takeda and Mateo had, but he grimaced instead, as though Linus's praise bothered him. Weird. I would think he would be chomping at the bit for Linus to tell everyone how awesome he was.

"So you guys are basically the mythological equivalent of supersecret, black-ops spies," I said.

Linus nodded. "Something like that."

"Well, superspies, do you know who the Reaper was in the library? The one who stole the scepter and unleashed those chimeras? Because all I could see was his black cloak."

Linus hit another button on his remote. "We believe it was this student."

A familiar face popped up onto the screen. Black hair, blue eyes, tan skin, great smile, perfect dimples.

Surprise shot through my body. "But...that's Lance Fuller."

"The guy you were getting cozy with earlier today," Ian sniped. "I saw your little meet-cute in the dining hall."

I wanted to point out that Ian and I'd had the same sort of *meet-cute* on the quad earlier today, but I bit back my snarky words. I didn't want Ian to realize how gorgeous I had thought he was—at least until he'd opened his mouth and started insulting me.

"Lance and I weren't getting cozy," I muttered. "We just

bumped into each other. That's all. He was actually nice enough to apologize for running into me. But that's not surprising, since he's practically the only person at this stupid school who will even talk to me now."

Aunt Rachel glanced at me. She knew all about my crush on Lance, since I had pretty much gushed to her every single time he'd smiled at me or laughed at one of my stupid jokes last year.

"According to our intel, Lance is one of Sisyphus's new recruits," Linus said. "He joined the Reapers over the summer."

I shook my head. "You've got the wrong guy. Lance's family is totally rich and connected. His dad works for the Protectorate."

"His father *used* to work for the Protectorate," Linus said in a cold voice. "James Fuller was caught stealing weapons and armor from the Protectorate warehouse where he worked in New York. In addition to stealing the weapons, he sold many of them on the black market to Reapers. Mr. Fuller and several Reapers were killed during a Protectorate raid on that warehouse a few months ago."

I hadn't heard a whisper about Lance's dad dying, much less that he'd been selling weapons to Reapers. Then again, the Protectorate would have wanted to keep it quiet that one of their own had betrayed them. Lance would have wanted to keep it quiet too. He had seen what happened to me at school last year, and he wouldn't have wanted the same thing to happen to him. He wouldn't have wanted to lose his golden-boy status, especially since he was so much more popular than I had ever been and had so much farther to fall.

"So you think that Lance joined up with the Reapers so he can get revenge on the Protectorate for his dad's death," I said.

Linus and Takeda both nodded.

"Just because Lance's dad was a Reaper doesn't mean that he's one too!" I snapped.

My voice boomed out far louder and angrier than I had intended. A tense, awkward silence fell over the room, and everyone looked at me again. This time, I glared right back at all of them, including Ian. After a moment, he dropped his gaze from mine and shifted in his seat, as though he were suddenly uncomfortable.

"We understand what you're saying, Miss Forseti," Linus said. "But the Midgard has been tracking Lance for several days now."

"So you actually saw him put on a Reaper cloak and break into the library."

"No." This time, Takeda answered me. "We spotted Lance approaching the library, but he wasn't wearing a Reaper cloak. We tried to follow him, but he vanished."

"So you don't know for sure that he's the Reaper," I said. "He could have been sneaking around campus for some other reason."

"It was him," Ian muttered. "It had to be. No one else was around."

Takeda tipped his head, agreeing with the Viking, then looked at me again. "We were expecting Lance to steal a sword or a piece of armor, since that's what the Reapers have been targeting so far. Something far less dangerous than the scepter. That's why we were going to let him leave the library with the artifact and then follow him back to the other Reapers. But Lance slipped away in the confusion of the battle with the chimeras." Takeda's voice remained calm, but anger sparked in his dark eyes. He wanted to catch Lance and make him pay for Amanda's death. Couldn't blame him for that.

"So you're going to track down Lance and arrest him, right?" Aunt Rachel asked. "Before he can hurt anyone else with the scepter."

"We don't have to track down Lance," Linus said. "He's in his dorm room right now."

Understanding filled Aunt Rachel's face. "You're not going to arrest him. Not yet, anyway. You're going to let him keep the scepter and see if he'll lead you back to the other Reapers like you originally planned."

Linus nodded. "We think that Lance stole the scepter, but he was wearing a cloak, so we have no real proof that it was him. No security footage or anything like that, which means that we have no grounds to arrest him. But don't worry. We have Protectorate guards discreetly watching his dorm right now to keep all the other students safe. If Lance does try to use the artifact, the Protectorate will move in and arrest him immediately."

"And if he doesn't use it?" I asked. "What then?"

"Letting him keep the scepter is a calculated risk, but our intel suggests that Lance will meet up with Sisyphus—or one of his trusted lieutenants—sometime in the next few days to hand over the scepter," Linus said. "We need to find out when and where the handoff will take place, recover the scepter, and capture and arrest all the Reapers."

He paused and looked at Takeda, who nodded. Linus turned back to me, and I knew what he was going to say next.

"And we want you to help us do it, Miss Forseti."

CHAPTER EIGHT

Linus's words echoed from one side of the briefing room to the other and back again.

For a moment, I sat there, wondering if I'd heard him right. But Linus's and Takeda's steady stares told me that they were very, very serious.

"You want me to join your team and spy on Lance," I said.

The two men both nodded again.

"You're a student here, so you know the campus and all the other kids much better than we do," Takeda said. "You would be on the team in a temporary capacity, until we figure out what Lance and the other Reapers are planning."

"And now that Lance has the scepter, we need another fighter on our side," Linus added. "Chimeras are extremely dangerous. Just one is an enormous challenge for even the most skilled warrior. You killed two of them tonight with relative ease."

I thought of the chimera's burning red eyes and jagged teeth and the deep, bloody gashes it had clawed into my arm. Please. Nothing about that fight had been *easy*.

"I've seen you in action, Miss Forseti. You're one of the

best fighters I've ever had the pleasure of watching." Linus paused. "Except for Logan, of course."

So much warm pride filled his face that I merely nodded, instead of saying that I was a better warrior than Logan Quinn. Or at least admitting that we were equal when it came to our fighting skills.

"So you want me to watch everyone's backs while they try to stop Lance, Sisyphus, and this new army of Reapers," I said. "Is that about right?"

"It is," Linus said.

Aunt Rachel shook her head. "Absolutely not. Rory did her part at the Eir Ruins when Agrona and all those Reapers attacked us trying to get the Chloris ambrosia flowers. Not to mention how hard she fought during the final battle against Loki. She doesn't have to do anything else. You can't *make* her do anything else."

"No," Linus said. "I can't make Rory do anything. And you're absolutely right, Ms. Maddox. The two of you have done more than your fair share of fighting against the Reapers."

Aunt Rachel sighed. "But?"

"But if Lance, Sisyphus, and the Reapers aren't stopped now, then more people will die. People at this academy and beyond. The situation is critical."

"Does Gwen know about this?" I asked. "Why isn't she here? Why isn't she part of Team Midgard?"

Linus hesitated a moment before answering. "Miss Frost did her job as Nike's Champion. She imprisoned Loki, even though it almost cost Gwen her own life in the process. I can't ask any more of her. No one can, nor should they. She deserves a little peace and quiet after everything she's been through. She's happy now, rebuilding the North Carolina academy. Besides, the threat is here, not there."

I'd thought it would be something like that, and he was right. Gwen had done enough—*more* than enough. She had never told me exactly what had happened when she'd faced off against Loki, when she'd gone to that other place, that realm between this world and the one where the gods lived, but the experience clearly haunted her. Gwen might have defeated Loki, but he'd left a deep scar on her heart, one that she would carry for as long as she lived.

"And what happens if I say no?" I asked.

Linus shrugged. "We will proceed with the mission as planned, Miss Forseti. With or without you."

Silence fell over the room, and once again, all eyes turned to me, but I didn't automatically say yes. Linus and Takeda might want me on their team, but Aunt Rachel didn't, and she was the one I listened to, the one I trusted. Besides, the three kids hadn't exactly been friendly to me so far, especially Ian, who had been downright hostile. Their mission might be noble, but I had zero desire to spend time with kids who obviously disliked me. I got enough of that during regular school hours.

The silence stretched on, and everyone kept staring at me. Linus and Takeda looked at me with hope. Aunt Rachel shook her head again, obviously wanting me to tell them no. Zoe and Mateo stared at me with curiosity, wondering what my answer would be.

And then there was Ian, whose eyes darkened to a thundercloud gray. "We don't *need* her," he growled again. "We can spy on Lance ourselves and figure out when and where he's going to hand Typhon's Scepter over to Sisyphus. I know we can."

"Just like Amanda thought that she would be fine going into the library all by herself?" Zoe muttered.

Ian jerked back as though she'd slapped him. Regret

filled Zoe's face, and she bit her lip, knowing that it was too late to take back her snarky words. Ian shoved his chair away from the table, whipped around, and stormed out of the room. His footsteps slapped against the stone, growing fainter and fainter. Several seconds later, a door slammed shut in the distance.

The others winced. For a moment, no one said anything, but then Linus looked at me again.

"The choice is yours, Rory," he said. "I hope you make the right one—for everyone's sake."

Zoe and Mateo got to their feet, left the briefing room, and disappeared into the same hallway that Ian had stormed down. I wondered if they were going to check on the Viking or leave him alone. I would leave him alone, given how angry he'd been. And heartsick too, over Amanda's death. I felt sorry for him. Angry and heartsick were emotions that I knew all too well, especially how hard they were to get rid of.

Takeda nodded at Aunt Rachel and me, then murmured an excuse to Linus and left the room as well. Linus sighed, turned off the monitors, and ran his hand through his hair, lost in his own thoughts. After a moment, he jerked his head toward another hallway.

"Come on," he said. "I'll walk you out."

Aunt Rachel and I got up from the table and followed him.

We walked down a long hallway with several glass windows set into the stone walls. I peered through the glass, staring into all the rooms we passed. An armory filled with metal lockers, wooden benches, and rows of weapons hanging on the walls. A training area populated by plastic practice dummies. A computer room bristling with laptops, wires, and servers. A library with shelves of books. A kitchen with stainless-steel appliances.

Aunt Rachel noticed the kitchen too, and she eyed the pots, pans, and other equipment with professional interest. Once a chef, always a chef.

"We call this entire level the Bunker," Linus said as we walked along. "It contains everything you would need to survive a war with the Reapers or anyone else. Weapons, artifacts, communication equipment, food. Very few people in the Protectorate know of its existence, which is why Takeda and his team decided to use it as their base of operations. They're going to protect all the items down here, as well as increase security in the regular library upstairs so that the Reapers can't steal any more artifacts. At least, while they're in Colorado."

"What do you mean, while they're here? Where are they going?" I asked.

"Once the scepter is recovered and Lance, Sisyphus, and the other Reapers are taken into custody, the team will move on to a new mission," Linus said. "They'll most likely head back to the New York academy, since that's where they all came from."

We reached the end of the hallway, which opened up into a small square room that reminded me of a coat closet, given the gray Protectorate cloaks hanging on hooks on the walls. I eyed the cloaks, and a sharp knife of longing sliced through my heart. I wondered what it would be like to wear one of those and be seen as one of the good guys for a change, instead of the daughter of dead Reaper assassins.

Aunt Rachel stared at the cloaks too, as if she were thinking the same thing.

Linus walked over to the far side of the room, where an elevator was embedded in the wall. The three of us stepped into the open car, and the door shut behind us. Linus pressed his thumb on a slot in the metal panel, and a green light shot out, scanning his print. Something chirped, and that panel slid back, revealing another one with floor numbers on it, like in a regular elevator. This area was marked *Level B*, and Linus hit the button for *Level 2*.

"Biometric keypad," he explained. "The elevator only works for people Mateo programs into our security system."

The elevator floated up and stopped a few seconds later, but the door didn't open right away. Instead, that first panel slid back out, covering up the one with the floor numbers, and a monitor appeared on it, showing a familiar view of a balcony ringed with statues.

"That's the second floor of the library," Aunt Rachel said.

"Yes," Linus replied. "Mateo has set up several scanners to make sure that no one is on this level of the library to see us coming and going. The elevator won't open until the scanners tell it the coast is clear."

A few seconds later, a light on the top of the panel flashed green, and the door swung outward. We stepped out of the elevator car and back onto the second floor. Behind us, a bookcase creaked shut, hiding the elevator from sight.

"A secret entrance," I said. "Cool."

I would have said more about how awesome I thought it was, and the Bunker too, but it wasn't the right time.

Not when a girl was dead.

Linus gave me a faint smile, then moved over to the balcony railing and stared down at the first floor.

We were only a few feet away from Sigyn's statue and

the spot where I had battled the chimera. To my surprise, someone had already cleaned up the broken remains of the display case that Babs had been sitting in. I wondered if it had been one of the Protectorate members or Sigyn masquerading as Raven again.

I would put my money on Sigyn. The regular librarians didn't come up to the second floor all that often, so I was betting that no one had even realized she had put the sword on display in the first place, much less disposed of the broken case afterward. For some reason, it seemed the goddess didn't want anyone to know that I had Babs. Maybe she thought that a secret mission like battling the Reapers required a secret weapon.

"I see you have a new sword," Aunt Rachel said in a low voice that only I could hear. "A talking sword."

My hand dropped to Babs's hilt. Of course Aunt Rachel would notice that I was wearing a sword. She knew me better than anyone, and she had the same Spartan skills and instincts that I had when it came to weapons.

"Her name is Babs. She was sitting in a display case up here. The chimera destroyed the case, and I needed a weapon to kill it, so I grabbed her."

Aunt Rachel raised her eyebrows. "Is that all that happened?"

I shrugged. I wasn't ready to tell her about seeing Sigyn in the Eir Ruins, especially since I was still trying to make sense of everything the goddess had said to me.

"More or less. But I'd like to keep her, if that's okay with you."

Aunt Rachel studied Babs again. "I'm okay with it. You should have a weapon of your own, at least until this business with the Reapers is resolved. Besides, she looks like a fine sword."

I flashed her a grateful smile. "I think she's a fine sword too."

Aunt Rachel smiled back at me, and then the two of us walked over to where Linus was standing by the balcony.

Down below, several men and women wearing gray cloaks were picking up pieces of broken chairs and righting overturned tables from the fight with the chimeras. One man sporting black coveralls was down on his hands and knees, with a bucket of water beside him, vigorously scrubbing a brush over a large red stain on the floor. He was trying to get blood off the stone—Amanda's blood.

My chest tightened with a mixture of guilt, sadness, and relief. I might be a great fighter, but the chimeras had been the most dangerous creatures I'd ever encountered, and I hadn't been prepared for them. I had gotten lucky tonight. That could just as easily have been my blood on the floor. It *was* Amanda's blood, and it could still be the blood of Ian, Zoe, Mateo, and Takeda, given their dangerous mission.

Linus sighed. His shoulders slumped, and his eyes dulled with grief and weary resignation. In an instant, he looked ten years older. "It never ends," he murmured. "It just never *ends*."

He stared at the man scrubbing the floor for another second, then shook his head, as if rousing himself out of his own dark thoughts. Linus turned and pointed at the bookcase behind us.

"There's a small silver button on the side of the bookcase," he said. "Press in on it, and the scanner will read your thumbprint, open the case, and unlock the elevator for you. I've already had Mateo program both of you into the security system."

My eyebrows drew together in confusion. How had the

Protectorate gotten my thumbprint? Probably while I was unconscious after the chimera attack. Linus must have scanned Aunt Rachel's thumb when he brought her down to the Bunker to see me.

"I know this is a lot to take in," Linus said. "Sisyphus, the Reapers, the Midgard. But I meant what I said before. The others...they need someone like you, Miss Forseti. Someone who's lost just as much as they have."

My eyes narrowed. "What do you mean?"

"Their secrets aren't mine to tell, but we've all been betrayed. We've all had friends and family members killed by Reapers."

I winced, and so did Aunt Rachel. Linus hadn't meant it as an insult, but his words were another reminder of my parents and all the evil things they'd done—all the innocent people they'd killed.

Linus stared at me, his blue eyes blazing with conviction. "But this is a chance for us to stop the Reapers before they get started again. This is a chance for us to save lives. I can't make you do anything, but you truly are one of the best warriors I've ever seen. You could make a difference in this battle, Rory, just as you did against Loki."

"We almost died in the battle with Loki," I pointed out. "And Amanda *did* die here tonight. I might be a Spartan, but even I get tired of fighting."

"I know, and I feel the same way." Linus smiled, but it was a sad, tired expression. "But Spartans are meant for fighting. Like it or not, it's the thing we do best. Besides, if we don't battle the Reapers now, then nobody will get to have a safe, normal life. Just promise me that you'll at least think about it. If you decide that you want to be part of the Midgard, go down to the Bunker tomorrow after school, and Takeda will help you get started. The choice is yours."

"Okay. I'll think about." It was the least I could do after Linus and the others had healed me.

Linus nodded at Aunt Rachel and me, then turned and strode away. A minute later, he was back downstairs with the other members of the Protectorate, overseeing the cleanup.

Aunt Rachel and I stood by the railing, watching as Linus moved from one guard to the next, speaking to them each in turn. Once again, my gaze focused on that bloodstain on the floor. The bright red color reminded me of the chimeras' burning eyes and sharp claws. I shivered.

"Come on, Rory," Aunt Rachel whispered, putting her arm around my shoulder. "Let's go home."

I let her lead me away from the railing. On the way toward the stairs, we passed Sigyn's statue, and I thought of my conversation with the goddess in the Eir Ruins.

But unfortunately, evil never quite dies, no matter how hard you try to kill it. Her voice whispered in my mind.

She was certainly right about that.

Well, at least one of my questions had been answered. I knew exactly what threat Sigyn had been talking about in the Eir Ruins: this new group of Reapers who were stealing artifacts. But I still didn't understand why the goddess thought that I was the only one who could stop them. Sure, the chimera scepter had been stolen, but Linus, Takeda, and the other kids seemed capable enough. They could probably recover the artifact without my help, but I couldn't help wondering how many more of them might get hurt—or killed—in the process.

I glanced back over the railing, my gaze focusing on Amanda's blood still on the floor, slowly dulling from red to pink as the man scrubbed and scrubbed at the stain. If only I could erase her death from my mind the same way.

I shivered again and looked away, not sure what I was supposed to do now. Not sure whether to accept Sigyn's mission and Linus's offer. Not sure about anything except how lucky I had been to live through the night.

Aunt Rachel and I left the library and went home.

Babs had closed her eye and stayed completely silent through the meeting with Linus and the others, and she seemed to be sleeping now, given her steady, even breathing. The fight with the chimeras must have exhausted her. The sword was still belted to my waist, and I wrapped my hand around her hilt as we walked across campus, ready to pull her free from her scabbard at the first sign of danger.

I carefully scanned all the shadows, but I didn't see anyone. Still, I felt like they were out there, Reapers and chimeras, just waiting to leap out of the darkness and tear us to pieces. I gripped Babs's hilt a little tighter and hurried on, ready to go to bed and try to forget that tonight had ever happened.

Aunt Rachel was right. The battle at the North Carolina academy had been horrific enough. So had watching Amanda die tonight. Did I really want to put myself in danger again? Did I really want to take on more Reapers? Especially when I was trying so hard to leave all of that behind?

I didn't know—I just didn't know the answer to anything anymore.

We made it to the cottage safely. An hour later, after taking a long, hot shower, I was sitting at the vanity table in my bedroom, brushing out my wet hair, my mind still churning with everything that had happened.

Babs was propped up in a chair in the corner. Her eye was still shut, and soft, breathy snores rumbled out of her mouth. Every once in a while, she would smack her lips together and mutter something, although I couldn't make out her exact words.

A knock sounded, and Aunt Rachel cracked open my door. "May I come in?"

I nodded and laid down my brush. Aunt Rachel stepped into my bedroom, her hands clasped behind her back.

"How are you holding up?" she asked.

"Fine, I guess." I shrugged. "Tonight wasn't the first fight I've been in."

She opened her mouth, then hesitated, as if she was having trouble getting out her words. After a moment, she spoke again. "I have something for you."

She walked over and held out her hand. A small black velvet box rested in her palm.

My heart dropped, my stomach flipped over, and my entire body tensed. "Is that—is that what I think it is?"

"Yes. I've been meaning to give it back to you for a while now. After everything that happened tonight, it seemed like the right time."

"Why?" I whispered, my voice cracking. "I told you that I didn't want it. That I *never* wanted to see it again."

"I know, sweetheart, and I understand why you feel that way," Aunt Rachel said, pain rasping through her words. "I'm still so angry at Rebecca that I can't even think straight sometimes."

I kept staring at the box. "But?"

"But there are still Reapers out there, and people are still in danger." She sighed. "And as much as I hate to admit it, as much as I want to keep you safe, you are a Spartan warrior through and through. You would be a great asset to the Midgard. You could help them stop the Reapers."

I stared at her. "But in the Bunker, you said that you didn't want me to help them, that you didn't want me to join their team."

"No, I didn't. I was so worried when you texted me that there were Reapers in the library, and I would be even more worried if you actually joined the Midgard. I don't want to see you get hurt—or worse." Aunt Rachel's voice dropped to a whisper. "I don't want to lose you too, Rory."

Her green gaze fell to the black velvet box in her hand, and I knew she was thinking of her sister, my mom. Aunt Rachel's fingers curled around the box for a moment, and then she stepped forward and set it down on the edge of the vanity table.

"But I also don't want to hold you back. Linus was right. We're Spartans, and like it or not, fighting is one of the things we do best."

"I don't want you to worry about me," I replied. "And if that means not joining the Midgard, then I'm okay with that. You're more important to me than this is."

"I'm always going to worry about you, no matter how old you are. Being on the Midgard might not be safe, but if it makes you happy, then I'll just have to learn to live with my worry." Aunt Rachel gave me a grim smile. "Linus was right about something else: it's your choice. We've both been at the mercy of your parents and what they did for far too long. It's time for you to choose what you want. But know this—no matter what you decide, I'll always support you."

She leaned over and pressed a kiss to my forehead.

"Thank you," I whispered.

She drew back and stroked my wet hair. Then she smiled and left my bedroom, shutting the door behind her.

My gaze zoomed over to the black velvet box. Anger roared through my body, and I thought about shoving it off the side of the table and into the trash can below. But the anger burned out in an instant, leaving behind the familiar heartache. Sighing, I grabbed the box and slowly cracked open the top.

A bracelet lay inside, with a single charm dangling from its links—a silver locket shaped like a heart.

I hesitated, then picked up the bracelet and opened the locket. The photo inside looked exactly the same as I remembered it. My dad, Tyson, was in one half of the heart, a rare smile on his face, while my mom, Rebecca, was in the other half. I was also on my mom's side of the locket, standing between my parents, my arms wrapped around both their shoulders, grinning like a fool.

I couldn't remember the last time I'd been that happy.

My parents had given me the bracelet, locket, and photo for my sixteenth birthday last year, a few weeks before they'd been murdered. I had loved the gift, especially the locket, and I'd jokingly said that I was wearing my Spartan heart on my sleeve for everyone to see.

The day of their funerals, I had torn off the bracelet and thrown it down on top of their graves, but Aunt Rachel had picked it up, saying that I might want it back someday. I had told her I never wanted to see it again and had stormed off. But here I was, holding the bracelet in my hands again roughly a year later.

I traced my fingers over the simple, delicate links, which were ice-cold against my skin. The small locket felt as heavy as a lead weight in my hand, and the heart's sharp point pricked my thumb like a needle, drawing a drop of blood and making me hiss. I concentrated on that icy chill, on that heavy weight, and especially on that tiny sting of pain, letting the sensations ground me, steady me.

Holding the locket reminded me of all the times my mom had told me to focus on my sword during a fight, to really *feel* the hilt in my hand, to *notice* the blade dangling from my fingers, to *listen* to the whisper of the sharp edge slicing through the air, until the sword was a part of me, and I was a part of it. That was what having a Spartan heart had meant to her, and my dad too.

In that moment, I made my decision.

Maybe I had already made it back during the Battle of Mythos Academy, when I'd seen all the blood, bodies, death, and destruction. Maybe I had made it weeks before then, the day I first met Gwen when she'd come to Colorado searching for a cure for a poisoned Nickamedes. Maybe I had even made it long before then, in the instant I found out that my parents were Reapers.

Either way, I knew what I had to do now.

I was joining the Midgard, and I was going to get justice for Amanda and help Takeda and the others stop the Reapers from hurting anyone else. The bracelet and locket were both symbols of my parents and their mistakes— mistakes that I didn't want to make. So as much as it hurt me, I wrapped the chain around my wrist and snapped the clasp shut.

The metal still felt cold and heavy against my skin but not unpleasantly so. I hoped it would remind me that I wasn't my parents and that I didn't have to follow the same dark path they had taken.

Time would tell.

I stared at the bracelet and heart locket glimmering around my wrist a moment longer, then closed the black velvet box, pushed it aside, and went to bed.

CHAPTER NINE

I told Aunt Rachel my decision at breakfast the next morning.

She was standing in front of the stove, making cheesy scrambled eggs, and she opened her mouth like she was going to try to talk me out of it. Then she shook her head, remembering her promise from last night.

"I knew it. I knew you were going to join the team." Her gaze dropped to the bracelet around my wrist, and she brandished her spatula at me. "But I want you to remember something. What your parents did is what *they* did. It doesn't have anything to do with you or me or anyone else. They made their own choices. You don't have to try to make up for their mistakes."

I let out a tense breath. "I know that, and I'm not doing it for them."

Aunt Rachel gave me a sharp, knowing look.

I held up my hands in mock surrender. "Okay, okay, so I'm not doing it entirely for them. I'm doing it for me too. Because this is the kind of person that *I* want to be. I'm a Spartan, and Spartans protect people, right?"

She nodded. Then she turned off the stove, dished the

eggs onto two plates, and brought everything over to the kitchen table.

Aunt Rachel pushed a plate of eggs over to me. "That's right. We protect people. It's who we are, and it's what we do—both of us."

"Wait a second. What are you saying?" My eyes narrowed. "You've decided to join the Midgard too. Haven't you?"

"Well, I wouldn't say that I'm *joining*, exactly, but someone needs to watch your back." She winked at me. "Besides, I'm a Spartan too, remember?"

I got up from my seat, walked around the table, and hugged her tight. "Yes, yes, you are."

Aunt Rachel laughed and hugged me back. Then she picked up her fork and stabbed it at my plate. "Now, sit down and eat your eggs. I imagine that spying is hard work, and you'll need a good breakfast to help you get through the day."

I sat back down, picked up my own fork, and saluted her with it. "Yes, ma'am."

I wolfed down the scrambled eggs, along with some country-fried ham and whole-wheat toast slathered with Aunt Rachel's sweet, delicious homemade strawberry preserves. Then I grabbed my messenger bag, left the cottage, and walked across campus to the main quad.

Once again, all the kids turned to stare at me the second I stepped onto the quad, but I ignored them. Aunt Rachel was right. My parents' mistakes were their mistakes, not mine, and if the other kids couldn't understand that and accept me for who I was, then that was their problem, not mine.

At least, that's what I told myself. But it got harder and harder to ignore the mocking stares and snarky whispers that chased me across the quad, and I was grinding my teeth by the time I reached the English-history building for my first class. I was about to go up the steps when someone called out my name.

"Rory! Hey, Rory! Wait up!"

I froze, wondering if I'd imagined the sound. No one ever spoke to me on the quad, much less called out my name like they wanted to talk to me. But I stopped and turned around, and Lance Fuller jogged up to me.

Lance's black hair gleamed in the early-morning sun, which also brought out his amazing blue eyes. He wore a black leather jacket over his polo shirt and jeans, and a black backpack dangled off his shoulder.

Despite his friendly wave, my stomach still clenched with worry. Linus Quinn and Takeda thought that Lance had stolen Typhon's Scepter and summoned those chimeras in the library last night. I didn't know if they were right about Lance secretly being a Reaper, but I couldn't take a chance that they were wrong either.

So I casually dropped my hand to Babs's hilt, since I was wearing the sword again today. I didn't think Lance would be stupid enough to attack me, especially not in the middle of the quad, but stranger things had happened at Mythos Academy. I also glanced around, but I didn't see any sign of the Protectorate guards who were supposed to be watching Lance. They must have been keeping to the edges of the quad and staying out of sight so as not to spook him.

Lance flashed me a smile. "Hey! You're a hard person to catch up to."

"Hey, yourself," I said, trying to make my voice sound as normal as possible. "What's up, Lance?"

He grinned and stepped a little closer to me. "Can't a guy just come over and say hi?"

I snorted. "In case you haven't noticed, I'm not exactly popular these days. Not ever, actually."

He glanced around at the other kids, who were staring at him and glaring at me. "Ah, don't mind them. They're just jealous of how cute you are."

A hot blush flooded my cheeks. No guy had ever told me I was cute, especially not someone as handsome as Lance.

He stepped even closer to me and glanced around again, as though he wanted to be sure that no one was eavesdropping on us. "Listen," he said in a low voice. "I heard that some girl got attacked in the Library of Antiquities last night."

And just like that, my brief spark of happiness was snuffed out.

According to Linus, the only people who should even know about the chimera attack were the members of the Protectorate. Of course, some kid sneaking around campus last night could have seen the Protectorate guards coming out of the library or maybe even overheard them talking about the attack. But *Lance* was the one asking me about it—the alleged Reaper who might be responsible for everything, including Amanda's death. Was this just a bizarre coincidence? Or something much, much worse?

"You didn't get attacked, did you, Rory?" Lance asked, his blue gaze steady on mine. "I mean, you look fine, you look great, but I wanted to make sure that you were okay. I know you spend a lot of time in the library, especially given…everything that happened last year."

"You mean everyone finding out that my parents were Reaper assassins," I said in a cold, flat voice.

He winced. "Well…yeah."

I studied him, but his face was a perfect mask of concern and sympathy. If Linus and Takeda hadn't told me their suspicions, I would have totally believed that Lance was worried about me. More than that, I would have been absolutely thrilled that he was talking to me, that he had braved everyone else's scorn to come over and check on me, and my crush on him would have grown to epic proportions. But now…now I wasn't sure what to believe about Lance. My judgment when it came to detecting Reapers and their lies wasn't exactly great—more like nonexistent.

"So, the library," Lance continued. "Do you know what happened? I heard that some serious monsters just appeared out of thin air. How freaky is that?"

My mind raced, trying to figure out how to respond. He was obviously fishing for information, but I couldn't tell if he wanted some juicy gossip to spread around campus or if he really was the Reaper who'd stolen the chimera scepter and wanted to see how much I knew. Either way, I decided to play dumb. At least until I could figure out whose side he was really on.

I shook my head. "I was in the library studying last night, but I left right before closing. I didn't see anything, and I haven't heard anything about any monsters. Sorry, Lance."

Disappointment flashed in his eyes, but he smiled at me again. "No worries. It was probably just a crazy rumor. I'm just glad you're okay."

He hesitated, then reached out and gently squeezed my shoulder, as if he were truly concerned about me. All around us, I could hear the collective gasps of the other students, followed by a sudden surge of whispers. Lance talking to me was noteworthy enough, but actually touching my shoulder? In front of everyone? That would send the rumor mill into a frenzy. I didn't have to glance around to know that the other girls were shooting daggers at me with their eyes, especially Kylie, who was no doubt wondering why Lance was paying so much attention to me instead of her.

I looked at Lance, but I wasn't really seeing him anymore. Instead, the image of Amanda's bloody body crumpled on the library floor filled my mind. My hand curled around Babs's hilt, and I thought about pulling the sword, pointing it at Lance, and demanding that he tell me if he was the Reaper who was responsible for Amanda's death.

But I couldn't do that. Not here in the middle of the quad with everyone watching us. The other kids would grab their own weapons and attack me, thinking that I had finally shown my true Reaper colors.

"Rory?" Lance asked. "Are you okay? You have a strange look on your face."

I forced myself to smile at him. "Yeah, I'm fine. Just thinking about what you said. I hope it's not true. I'm tired of monsters in the library."

He squeezed my shoulder again. "Yeah. Me too."

Lance dropped his hand from my shoulder and shifted on his feet, as though he was thinking about what to say next.

After a few seconds, he looked at me again. "I'm having a few friends over to my dad's house tonight. Sort of a back-to-school bash. I did it last year, remember? You should come."

I blinked. "Me? You want *me* to come to your party?"

He grinned, showing off his two perfect dimples. "Well,

yeah. I was hoping you would be back at the academy this year. And now that you are, of course I want you to come to my party."

I blinked again, totally surprised. Pumping me for information about the chimera attack was one thing. But actually inviting me to his party? Even after I had told him I didn't know anything? What was up with that? Was Lance a Reaper or not? My head ached. I couldn't tell. I just couldn't tell anymore, and I couldn't trust my own instincts one way or the other.

"Let me see your phone." He held out his hand.

I was so confused that I did exactly what he wanted, digging my phone out of my jacket pocket and handing it over to him. Lance texted me a message, then handed the phone back to me.

"There. I sent you all the details. Party starts at eight tonight and goes until whenever. I hope you can make it, Rory."

"Yeah. Sure. Thanks," I replied, still in a daze.

Lance kept smiling at me, his eyes crinkling at the corners. I stared back at him, still trying to figure out what he was really up to—

"Hey, Rory," a cool, familiar voice sounded. "Who's your friend?"

Ian walked up to me, along with Zoe and Mateo. The three of them clutched their phones in one hand and their bags in the other like everyone else on the quad, as though they were regular students instead of Protectorate spies. They were taking this whole undercover gig very seriously.

And they weren't very happy about my talking to Lance. At least, Ian wasn't. He dropped his bag on the ground, making the battle axes attached to the sides *clank-clank-*

clank together, almost in warning. Then he crossed his arms over his chest and alternated between glowering at me and at Lance. Maybe Ian wasn't as good at this undercover spy thing as I'd thought.

"Aren't you going to introduce us, Rory?" Lance asked.

"Um...sure." As if I had any choice in the matter now. "This is Lance. Lance, this is Ian, and that's Zoe and Mateo. They're, um, well..."

Zoe stepped up and flashed Lance a smile. "We're some new transfer students from the New York academy. Nice to meet you." She looked him up and down, and her smile widened. "I have to say that so far, the guys here are a *lot* more interesting than the ones back home."

He grinned at Zoe. Of course he did. The petite Valkyrie was as cute as cute could be and twice as charming.

Lance shook Zoe's hand, then Mateo's, and finally Ian's. Lance started to drop the other guy's hand, but instead of letting go, Ian tightened his grip, making Lance wince. I rolled my eyes. Vikings. Always thinking their superstrength made them *so* special.

Zoe cleared her throat in warning, and Ian finally dropped Lance's hand.

"So what's this party I heard you talking about?" Zoe asked in a fun, flirty voice.

She batted her eyelashes at Lance, which made her look even more adorable. A bit of jealousy spiked through me. If I'd tried to do that, I would have seemed like a complete idiot. And probably made myself dizzy.

"I'm throwing a little back-to-school party tonight," Lance said. "You guys should come."

"Oh! That sounds like so much fun!" Zoe squealed. "Tell me more."

She drew him off to the side, and he took her phone and

texted her the details like he had done with me. Mateo started fiddling with his own phone, while Ian crossed his arms over his chest and glared at me again.

I glared right back at him. He hadn't wanted me on his precious Midgard last night, not even on a temporary basis, but now he thought he could barge in and interrupt my conversation with another guy? Okay, okay, so the guy in question might be a Reaper, but Ian didn't have to be a grade A jerk about it. What was his problem with me?

"Great! Thanks so much!" Zoe said, favoring Lance with another dazzling smile. "We'll totally be there tonight, won't we, Rory?"

"Yeah. Sure." My voice was far less enthusiastic than hers.

Lance grinned at Zoe, then turned to me. "Great. I'll see you guys tonight. I'm looking forward to it. Hope you are too, Rory."

He winked at me, still working his smooth charm, then hoisted his backpack a little higher on his shoulder and headed across the quad.

The four of us watched him go in silence. Ian opened his mouth, probably to make some snide remark, but I was all too aware of the other students still watching us, intensely interested in me and these three new kids. Lance had a lot of friends at the academy, and if he was a Reaper, then some of his friends might be Reapers too.

So I nudged Ian in the side with my elbow, hard enough to make him wince and cut off whatever he'd been about to say. Served him right for being so rude.

"Gotta go, guys. I have class, and so do you. We'll talk more about the party at lunch, okay? Save me a seat, Viking." I emphasized the last few words so he would realize that it wasn't a request.

Ian gave me a stiff nod. "Sure, cupcake. We can talk all about the party and your new boyfriend then."

"Yeah. Whatever."

I glared at him one more time, then whipped around, trudged up the steps, and marched into the English-history building to get to my first class. A sour thought filled my mind.

So far, the second day of school wasn't going any better than the first one had.

CHAPTER TEN

My morning classes dragged by, especially since all I could think about was my conversation with Lance. I replayed it over and over again in my mind, trying to figure out if he was a regular guy asking about a juicy rumor or a Reaper wanting to cover his tracks. The black-cloaked figure I'd seen in the library last night could have been Lance...or any other guy at the academy.

I didn't know—I just didn't know *anything* anymore.

Every minute of my morning classes seemed slower than the one before, but the bell finally rang, signaling that it was time for lunch, and I headed over to the dining hall. Aunt Rachel was once again working the dessert station at the end of the lunch line, and I stopped and talked to her.

"How are things going today?" she asked.

"Better, I think." I glanced around the dining hall. "I'm supposed to meet up with my new friends so we can talk about...things."

"Ah, sounds like fun. Don't forget your dessert." Aunt Rachel winked at me and placed a couple of items on my tray.

I stared down at the two jumbo chocolate-frosted chocolate cupcakes. Cupcakes were my absolute favorite dessert. Cake, filling, frosting. It all came together in one perfect package, whether it was some gourmet flavor or the classic chocolate ones on my tray now. Still, I grimaced.

"Is something wrong?" Aunt Rachel asked. "You love cupcakes."

"Yeah," I muttered. "And I know who's going to remind me of that."

She frowned, but I forced myself to smile at her.

"I'll see you later."

She nodded, winked at me again, and served the next person in line.

I paid for my food, grabbed my tray, and glanced around the dining hall, searching for my temporary teammates...or whatever they were. I spotted them sitting at the same table in the corner where Ian had been with Amanda yesterday. Sadness filled my heart, but I walked over to them anyway. They had actually saved me a seat, so I plopped my tray down on the table and joined them. Ian, Zoe, and Mateo all gave me blank looks, as if they were surprised that I'd shown up after all.

"Cheer up, guys," I drawled. "You all look like you're about to face down a bunch of Reapers or something."

Zoe snorted out a laugh, while Ian huffed at my sarcasm. Mateo grinned, but he focused on his phone again, his fingers flying over the screen. I looked around the dining hall, searching for Takeda, but I didn't see him sitting with any of the other coaches or professors.

"Where's the team leader?" I asked. "Why isn't he around to keep an eye on you guys?"

"Takeda has his own cover to maintain," Ian said. "Not that it's any of your business."

"Oh, I think you made it my business with that little scene on the quad this morning," I said. "What were you thinking, coming up and acting like you were my new best friends? All the other kids hate me. You guys should too."

"Who says we don't?" Ian muttered.

I sighed. "You know what I mean. It looks suspicious."

Zoe waved her hand, making blue sparks of magic flicker in the air all over the table. "You worry too much. Trust me, everyone else is busy thinking about their own problems. If their hair looks okay, if anyone realizes that their purse is a designer knockoff instead of the real thing, if they have a shot at hooking up with that cute guy or girl at the party tonight. Nobody cares about you, Spartan. Not really. So chill."

I eyed her, but her tone was more matter-of-fact than snarky. Zoe shrugged, telling me that it was just the way things were.

"Well, I'm guessing that Lance cares," I said. "Especially since he asked me about some girl getting attacked by a monster in the library last night."

Ian's hand tightened around his fork, and he glared at Lance, who was sitting in the middle of the dining hall, surrounded by his adoring friends and fans like usual. Lance threw his hands out wide, telling some story, and everyone around him howled with laughter, particularly the girls, who giggled like he'd just said the funniest thing ever.

"I should break his face," Ian muttered. "He's the one who summoned those chimeras. He's the one who killed Amanda."

"Relax, Viking," I said. "You'll have your chance to avenge Amanda. But Takeda wants to get Sisyphus and all the other Reapers at the same time. So you'll have to wait until tonight and see if any of them show up at Lance's party."

"Are you finally ready to admit that your boyfriend is a Reaper?" Ian asked.

I stared at Lance, who was grinning at the girl sitting next to him the same way he'd grinned at me on the quad this morning. A tiny blade of jealousy stabbed my heart. "My judgment isn't the best when it comes to Reapers. I don't know what he is, but I want to find out."

I looked at Ian. Grudging respect filled his eyes, and he nodded at me. Then his gaze dropped to my tray and the two desserts sitting there.

Ian arched an eyebrow. "Cupcakes, huh? I never would have guessed that you liked those...cupcake."

For once, his tone was more teasing than taunting, and I decided to play along. I grabbed one of the cupcakes, stripped off the paper wrapper, and sank my teeth into all the delicious layers of cake, filling, and frosting.

"I don't just like cupcakes—I *love* cupcakes," I mumbled through a mouthful of chocolate.

Ian snorted, but his lips twitched, like he was holding back a smile. I'd definitely won that round. I grinned and took another bite.

"Whether Lance is a Reaper or not, he's invited pretty much the whole academy to his party," Mateo chimed in, still staring at his phone. "Right before lunch, he sent out an email to everyone who's on the official academy roll."

"How do you know that?" I asked.

Mateo looked up, a satisfied smile creasing his face. "I hacked his phone while you were talking to him on the quad earlier. Now I have access to all his calls, texts, emails, everything."

Zoe leaned over and punched him in the shoulder,

making blue sparks of magic fly out of her fingertips. "You mean while *I* was flirting with him and distracting him from what you were really doing."

Mateo grinned at her. "That too."

"All those kids packed into one place..." Ian's voice trailed off. "That would make for great cover for Lance to meet with Sisyphus and the other Reapers. That might even be why he's throwing the party. So the Reapers can blend into the crowd and the Protectorate has a harder time tracking who comes and goes."

I polished off my first cupcake and started unwrapping the second one. "Then we'll have to keep an eye on Lance and see who he talks to. If he is a Reaper, he'll have to meet with the others sooner or later."

"We?" Ian shook his head. "There is no *we*. This doesn't concern you."

I waggled my cupcake at him. "Ah, ah, but that's where you're wrong. I've decided to take Takeda up on his offer to join your merry little band of misfit toys. Temporarily, of course."

Ian's eyes narrowed. "Like I've said all along, we don't need you, and we certainly don't want you."

"Well, that's too bad, because I'm in this thing now, and nothing you do or say is going to change my mind. So you might as well lose the attitude and start being civil to me. Before something bad happens."

"Like what?"

I gave him a razor-thin smile and gestured at the items on my lunch tray. "Like me accidentally-on-purpose stabbing you with my fork. Or braining you with my plate. Or breaking your nose with my water glass. You know. All the usual Spartan tricks."

Anger flashed like lightning in his gaze, which darkened

to that storm-cloud gray. As much as I hated to admit it, the intense, moody glare worked for Ian, and he looked totally hot right now. Not that I cared how gorgeous he was. Not at all. Not when he was so determined to hate me for some mysterious reason.

Ian's eyes narrowed to slits, but I smiled in the face of his anger. If I didn't get anything else out of being on Team Midgard, at least I would get to annoy the Viking. It was quickly becoming my favorite new hobby.

"Great," Zoe drawled. "Just what we need. Another alpha on the team. Can't we all just get along?"

"No," Ian and I both snapped in unison.

We glared at each other for a few more seconds before Ian crossed his arms over his chest and leaned back in his chair.

"Fine," he muttered. "Come to the Bunker this evening, and we'll talk about how we're going to handle Lance's party. If you think you're up for it, cupcake."

"Oh, I'm up for it."

I was still holding my second cupcake, and I saluted him with it before sinking my teeth into the chocolate dessert. Ian's eyes glittered with fresh anger, but I smirked at him and took another bite of my cupcake.

This was going to be fun.

To my surprise, my afternoon classes went by much quicker than the morning ones had.

Zoe was right. The other kids might have been shocked that I'd come back to the academy this year, but they were rapidly going back to their own lives and getting caught up in their own little dramas. For the most part, the other students ignored me, and I did the same to them. I didn't necessarily like being ignored, but it was certainly better than everyone gossiping about me.

And Ian was right too. Takeda was once again acting as the gym coach, although now I knew better than to mouth off to him, and I avoided having to run any laps. After gym, I went to the cottage, did my homework, took a shower, and put on a fresh pair of jeans, along with a clean T-shirt and my green leather jacket. Then I headed over to the library.

I walked down the main aisle, my steps slow, staring at the space in front of the checkout counter where the chimera had been. The study tables and chairs were in their usual positions, and so were all the couches around the fireplace. Not a trace of last night's attack remained, not so much as a scorch mark from the chimera's smoking paws on the floor. My gaze moved over to the spot where Amanda had taken her last breath. Even her blood was gone, scrubbed away like she hadn't died here last night, with only the faint lemony scent of cleaner left behind to mark her passing.

It made me sad.

Sad that a girl's life could be cut so tragically short. Sad that no one even noticed that Amanda was gone. Sad that no one would *ever* notice that she was gone. But Linus Quinn had made it this way so that the other students wouldn't panic. I couldn't blame him for wanting to spare everyone this fresh new fear about the Reapers. I just wondered if anyone would notice if I vanished one day and never came back. Probably not.

And that made me even sadder than before.

I pushed my depressing thoughts away and headed deeper into the library. The Protectorate might think that

Lance was a Reaper, but that didn't mean there weren't others here at the academy. And if any of the Reapers knew I'd been in the library last night, they might try to keep tabs on me to see if I did anything interesting.

So I wandered around the library for thirty minutes to make sure no one was following me. I also used the time to check out the reference books I'd dropped during my fight with the chimeras last night. Midgard or not, I still had a myth-history paper to do.

No one paid any attention to me, so I headed up to the second floor to the bookcase that doubled as the secret entrance to the Bunker. Just like Linus had said, a small silver button was embedded in the side of the wood. I stared at the button, then slowly pressed in on it. A green light flashed under my thumb, scanning it, and a second later, a soft *click* sounded as the bookcase detached itself from the stone wall and swung outward, revealing the elevator. I stepped inside the car.

A few minutes later, I was in the briefing room down in the Bunker. No one was sitting at the table, and the surrounding desks were empty as well. Since I was the first and only person here, I decided to give myself the grand tour.

I roamed up and down the hallways, making sure that I knew where everything was, from the armory to the computer room to the kitchen. I even opened the refrigerators and all the drawers and cabinets in the kitchen to see what kind of food was in here. Mostly canned and prepackaged stuff that wouldn't spoil. Even worse, it was all health food, like granola, brown rice, and energy bars that looked like they were made of cardboard. Blech. No cookies, no cupcakes, no sugary desserts of any sort. No fun, in other words. My stomach grumbled in disappointment.

I did find a door marked *Stairs*, which was another exit that led back up to the main part of the library, as well as some air vents that looked like they were attached to the rest of the building's temperature-control system. I made a special note of the door and the vents. The Midgard's supersecret spy headquarters was cool, but I didn't want to be trapped down here if the power to the elevator ever went out. Or if Reapers somehow discovered the location and decided to attack.

My grand tour didn't take long, and I wound up back in the briefing room a few minutes later. Part of me wanted to search through the desks to discover what secrets Ian, Zoe, and Mateo might be hiding. I especially wanted to go through Mateo's desk to see if he might have some more candy bars stashed in one of the drawers. But that would have been totally rude, so instead, I headed toward the back half of the room and started wandering through the shelves full of books and artifacts.

I did a slow, methodical circuit, going up and down each aisle twice, looking at all the objects lined up on the shelves. I recognized many of the items, especially the books, since they were the original first editions of various research tomes I'd read through or used information out of for myth-history papers and other class projects. But I had never heard of many of the artifacts, not so much as a whisper, and with good reason.

They were all extremely dangerous.

Linus had said the Bunker would have been the last holdout against Loki and the Reapers, and the Protectorate had packed the area with powerful, deadly artifacts that they couldn't afford to let anyone get their hands on—*ever*—especially not the Reapers.

Things like the Hammer of Hephaestus, named for the

Greek god of fire, which burned with red-hot flames whenever it was wielded. Or the Gauntlets of Serket, an Egyptian goddess associated with poisons, which were coated with a magical acid that would eat right through your enemy's skin and bones if he so much as brushed up against the gold gauntlets.

And on and on the artifacts went, each one more terrible and deadly than the last. Daggers and spears and staffs that would let you inflict cuts that wouldn't stop bleeding or shoot lightning at your enemies or even let you break their bones without ever even touching them. Every single shelf held those sorts of horrors and dozens more.

And those were just the weapons. Far more insidious artifacts lined the shelves, things that would mess with your mind and heart without your even realizing it. Like the Tears of Venus, the Roman goddess of love. Venus had once cried over a lost love, and her tears had hardened to opals, which had later been fashioned into a beautiful necklace. As long as you were wearing Venus's Necklace, you had the power to make anyone fall in love with you and do whatever you wanted.

I shivered, thinking about Logan Quinn and how he had almost killed Gwen when he was under the influence of the Apate jewels. I had always thought that losing control, losing your own free will, losing *yourself*, would be the worst thing in the entire world. Like being a mindless doll acting out someone else's whims and desires.

I reached the end of the last shelf and had started to head back to the center of the room when a glimmer of silver caught my eye. A small glass box was sitting behind Venus's Necklace, and I pulled it out to the edge of the shelf where I could see it. A silver bracelet lay inside, along with an identification card:

The Bracelet of Freya, the Norse goddess of love. When her husband, Odin, sacrificed one of his eyes for knowledge, he almost died from the grievous wound he inflicted upon himself. In order to save him, Freya cut her hand and used her own blood to help heal Odin. Blood from that cut also dripped down Freya's wrist, solidifying into this bracelet. Legend has it that whoever wears this bracelet will be protected by Freya's love, just as Odin was, along with the love of the person(s) who bestows the bracelet upon the wearer. However, what real power the bracelet has, if any, has never been conclusively proven...

I looked at the bracelet. Venus's Necklace and most of the other jewelry were large, ornate pieces made of dazzling jewels and gleaming gold, but Freya's Bracelet was a plain silver chain. I liked its simplicity. It looked a lot like the charm bracelet my parents had given me, the one I was still wearing—

"You might as well put me on one of these shelves," a sad, mournful voice muttered.

Startled, I looked around, wondering where the voice had come from. Then I realized it was Babs, who was belted to my waist. I slid the sword out of her scabbard and propped her up on one of the shelves so that I could talk to her face to face. The sword had been surprisingly quiet today, just like she had been last night after the fight with the chimeras. But now her green eye was open, although her metal features were twisted into a miserable expression.

"What do you mean?" I asked. "Why would you want to stay down here?"

Babs sighed. "I don't *want* to stay down here. But it

would be better for everyone if I was locked away in a glass case, collecting dust on one of these shelves, never to see the light of day ever again."

"Why would you say that? You're a perfectly nice sword, as far as talking swords go. Not that I've had much experience with talking swords, mind you. I only know Vic, but you're much nicer than he is. He's all the time crowing about how many Reapers he wants to kill."

I didn't mention Babs's own tendency to babble on and on whenever she got riled up. Sure, the sword's chatter could be a bit annoying, but it was also part of her unique charm.

Instead of cheering her up like I'd hoped, my words only made Babs look more miserable. "As well he should. Vic might be a blowhard, but he can at least be helpful, useful, to his warrior. Me? I'm nothing but an albatross, dragging you down, down, down." She let out a long, loud sigh, but for some reason, I didn't think she was being overly dramatic.

"What do you mean? You're a sword too. Of course you're useful." Another thought occurred to me. "Wait a second. Does this have something to do with the chimera attack? You didn't even want me to pick you up last night, much less actually wield you in battle. Did I do something wrong?"

"Oh, no! You didn't do anything wrong. It's me—it's *always* me."

"What do you mean?"

Babs sighed again, but she rolled her eye around to look at me. "I mean that I'm cursed."

I frowned. "Cursed? What curse?"

She sighed for a third time. "*My* curse. The one that Macha, an Irish war goddess, placed on me long ago."

Shock zinged through me. My muscles tensed, and I

wanted to lurch away from the sword. But I knew that would hurt Babs's feelings, so I forced myself to stand still.

For a moment, I thought she was going to stay silent, but Babs looked at me again.

"I used to be Macha's sword, and for centuries, she proudly wielded me in battle. Even among the gods, Macha is a very strong, fierce warrior, and she never lost a fight with me in her hand."

"So what happened?"

An embarrassed blush colored her metal cheek. "I got a little…arrogant. I started bragging about how I was the best sword in all the realms, how no one could ever defeat me, and I started challenging other beings to fights. Gods, goddesses, warriors, even creatures." Babs winced. "If there's one thing that you don't do around the gods, it's talk about how awesome you think you are."

I nodded. Myth-history was full of people who claimed they could do things better than the gods, and most of them got punished as a result of their boasting. Like Arachne, the mortal woman who was turned into a spider after she'd claimed she could weave better than Athena, the Greek goddess of wisdom.

"So what happened?" I asked.

"Macha got tired of my constant bragging and all the fights that went along with it. We were in the middle of a sparring contest with some of the other Irish gods one day, and my boasting distracted her. Another goddess managed to slice her arm, making her lose the contest. Macha was furious." Babs's voice dropped to a whisper. "Absolutely furious. Trust me. You do not want to see a war goddess when she's angry."

I nodded again. I had seen Loki's rage during the academy battle, so I could well imagine Macha's wrath.

"Anyway, since I'd made her lose the contest and embarrass herself, Macha decided to curse me," Babs continued. "And any warrior who dares to wield me."

"Curse you how?"

"Everything's fine for the first two battles that any warrior fights with me. But during the third battle..." Her voice trailed off, and she dropped her gaze from mine, as if she couldn't stand to look at me right now.

"What happens?" I asked. "What's so important about the third battle that someone fights with you?"

The sword focused on me again. A tear shimmered in her eye, but she still didn't answer me.

Dread curled up in the pit of my stomach. "Babs, what happens during the third battle? You need to tell me. Please."

She cleared her throat several times, as if she was having trouble getting the words out, but she finally spoke. "My warrior dies."

Her voice came out as a low, raspy whisper, and that tear welled up in her green eye, streaked down her cheek, and fell off her chin. The tear spattered onto my hand, which was resting on the shelf next to her. The drop felt as cold as a snowflake stinging my skin. More dread filled me.

"You're kidding, right?" I said. "How is that even possible? Surely some warrior can win a third battle with you."

Babs's entire hilt quivered, as though she were trying to shake her half of a head. "No, no, they can't. No matter how weak their opponent is or how good a fighter my warrior is, they can never, ever win the third battle. They might be able to kill their opponent, but something always happens to my warrior, and they die as well. Like their opponent cutting my warrior with a poisoned blade or getting in one final lucky strike. Trust me. I've seen it all, and the curse never fails."

Another tear slipped down her face and hit my hand, adding to the cold sensation there.

"You have no idea how *horrible* it is," she rasped. "Knowing that as soon as someone picks me up, they've been cursed to die, all because I couldn't keep my stupid mouth shut. It's the worst thing that Macha could have possibly done to me."

"But surely there must be some way around the curse." I thought about it for a moment, then snapped my fingers. "I know. I'll just use a different sword. No big deal."

Babs's hilt quivered, as though she were trying to shake her half of a head again. "That doesn't work. As soon as you touched me, you bound yourself to me. You can't get rid of me, Rory. Even if you locked me away down here, as soon as you started fighting, I would magically appear in your hand, even if you were miles away and holding another sword or weapon at the time."

A chill slithered down my spine. I'd heard of such things before, of weapons that you couldn't get rid of no matter how hard you tried. Daphne Cruz, Gwen's friend, had a bow like that, one that had kept reappearing in her dorm room, no matter how many times she tried to give it back to the museum it had come from.

Babs stared at me with a sad, weary, resigned expression, as if she knew exactly what I was thinking. No doubt she did, since she'd probably had this same conversation with dozens of other warriors over the years.

"The only thing I can tell you to do is not to get into any fights," Babs said. "Sometimes that works. For a while, anyway. A nice Amazon once kept me for almost a year before her third and final battle."

I shook my head. "I can't do that. You know I can't do that. Not now, when I just joined the Midgard to track down these new Reapers. Besides, I'm a Spartan. Fighting is what we do, and being warriors is what we are."

She gave me another miserable look. "I know. And Spartans always die the fastest because of that. I'm sorry, Rory. So very, very sorry. I was so happy when that nice old lady took me out of storage. I thought that being up on the second floor meant I could be out in the world a little bit and everyone would still be safe from me. But that's not the case. That's *never* the case." Her mouth quivered, as though she were fighting back a sob.

Part of me wanted to leave her on the shelf, walk away, and never look back, just like she'd suggested. I had enough problems already without adding a cursed sword to the mix. And I couldn't help but wonder why Sigyn had done this to me. She had told me that she had put Babs out in the library for me to use in the battles to come. So why would she give me a cursed sword?

Perhaps Sigyn hadn't known about the curse, since Babs had belonged to another goddess. Or perhaps she thought I could help give Babs that fresh start she said the sword needed. Either way, it seemed as though I was stuck with the sword now, whether I liked it or not.

Babs looked so utterly miserable that I found myself stepping closer to her. I knew what it was like to have something forced on you, something that was completely out of your control, something that ruined your life no matter how hard you tried to fight it.

I leaned forward so that I was at eye level with the sword. "Listen, don't worry about this whole curse thing. There has to be some book in the Library of Antiquities that can tell us how to break it. Or maybe even one of the artifacts down here in the Bunker can help. Besides, if anyone can survive having a cursed sword, it's a Spartan, especially this Spartan. Trust me. Okay?"

"Okay," she whispered, although I could tell she didn't really believe me.

I didn't believe me either. Despite all my comforting words, we were still talking about a curse enacted by a vengeful goddess. How could I possibly beat that without getting killed myself? But then again, this was why I'd agreed to be on the Midgard—to protect everyone else. Maybe that included Babs too. Maybe the sword just needed someone to help her fight her curse, instead of trying to get rid of her.

A third tear welled up in Babs's eye, this time sliding all the way down her chin and onto her blade below. I reached out and gently wiped it off, even though it made my own hand even colder than before. As my finger slid down the blade, I felt some faint markings in the metal. I leaned forward again and squinted. At first, I thought they were just scratches, but then I realized that the marks almost looked like...letters.

I squinted at the blade again, tilting my head this way and that, trying to find the right angle so I could make out the letters, but I couldn't quite bring them into focus. I almost thought they spelled out the word *devotion*, but I wasn't sure.

"What's wrong?" Babs said. "Why are you staring at me like that?"

"Nothing." I straightened up and forced myself to smile at her. "Nothing at all. Now, come on. Let's get you cleaned up before the others get here."

CHAPTER ELEVEN

I grabbed Babs, left the shelves behind, and sat down at the main table in the center of the briefing room. I'd just finished wiping away the sword's tears and polishing up her face when the others trooped into the Bunker.

Zoe and Mateo both nodded at me, and Zoe even came around the table to sit next to me, but Ian scowled as he dropped into the chair across from mine. I ignored him. I was here, whether he liked it or not, and I didn't have anything to prove to him. Not one thing. That's what I kept telling myself, anyway.

A moment later, Takeda strolled into the Bunker wearing the same dark gray tracksuit that he'd had on in gym class earlier. He looked at the four of us gathered around the table. If he was surprised that I was here, he didn't show it or comment. Then again, I imagined it took quite a lot to crack the Samurai's ever-calm attitude.

"Okay, team," he said. "Where are we at? Report."

Mateo grabbed the remote from the center of the table and passed it over to Ian, who hit some buttons on the device. Images of a large mansion appeared on the monitors on the wall.

"Our suspect, Lance Fuller, is throwing a party tonight. All of the academy kids have been invited, including the four of us," Ian said. "We think that Lance might use the party as a cover to meet with the other Reapers. He might be planning to hand the chimera scepter over to them, maybe even Sisyphus himself, if the Reaper leader shows up. But the party will also give us a chance to snoop around the mansion. If we're lucky, we might be able to find the scepter before Lance meets with any Reapers."

Ian hit some buttons, and more photos of the mansion appeared on the monitors, showing the spacious rooms inside, as well as the pools, tennis courts, and landscaped grounds that surrounded the sprawling structure.

Each image brought back memories. I had gone to Lance's back-to-school party last year, and I had even flirted with him a little when we'd both been getting sodas in the kitchen. It had been one of the best nights of my life. Then, a few days later, my parents had been killed, and everything had changed.

I shifted in my seat, suddenly uncomfortable, and my charm bracelet clattered against the table. I winced at the harsh jangling sound.

"Something wrong, cupcake?" Ian asked.

"Just wondering when you're going to get to the point."

Ian opened his mouth to snipe at me, but Takeda crossed his arms over his chest, silently telling the Viking to focus on the briefing.

"We'll do our usual operation," Ian said. "Zoe and I will infiltrate the mansion, while Takeda and Mateo stay in the van. Mateo will hack the security system so the two of them can see and track our progress through the mansion. Zoe will use her gadgets on any locks or alarms that we encounter, and I'll watch her back in case we run into any Reapers while we're searching for the chimera scepter. Once we have the scepter, we'll remove it from the premises, then wait for the Reapers to arrive. Depending on how many of them show up, we'll either capture them ourselves or call for Protectorate backup."

As much as I hated to admit it, Ian had come up with a solid plan. Takeda nodded, along with Zoe and Mateo, but I raised my hand as though we were in class.

"And what do I get to do, professor?" I asked.

Ian rolled his eyes, as though the answer should have been obvious. "You get to flirt with Lance like you did on the quad this morning."

I frowned. Not the assignment I'd expected. "Why me? Zoe is way cuter."

The petite Valkyrie perked up and blew me a kiss, making blue sparks of magic shimmer in the air around the two of us. I grinned back at her. It was true. She was way cuter than me.

"Because you're the one Lance personally invited to his party," Ian said. "You're the one he knows, so you can keep tabs on him while Zoe and I search the mansion. Do you think you can handle that?"

"Yes, I can handle being the distraction. Why don't you give me something more challenging to do?"

"Because I don't trust you," Ian snapped.

He didn't trust me? He didn't even know me, but he'd already condemned me for what my parents had been, just like everyone else at this stupid school. Well, I'd had enough of his attitude and insults. Anger roared through me, and I shot to my feet, my hands balling into tight fists.

"You don't trust me?" I snarled. "Well, I don't trust you either. How about I make you eat your own teeth? How would you like that, Viking?"

Ian shot to his feet as well. "Bring it on, cupcake—"

A sharp whistle cut through the air, making us all wince. Takeda blew on his silver gym whistle two more times before letting it drop back down around his neck.

"That's enough," Takeda said, his voice as calm as ever. "We have work to do. The two of you need to get over your petty dislike of each other. Now, gear up. We leave for the party in thirty minutes."

Ian and I kept glaring at each other, our hands still clenched into fists.

"That's an order," Takeda said, a little bite in his voice this time. "Don't make me repeat myself."

"Fine," Ian muttered. "But when this goes sideways, remember that you're the one who wanted her on the team."

He gave me one more hostile glare before he marched out of the briefing room.

Mateo started talking to Takeda about some computer equipment that he needed for the mission. Zoe got to her feet, grabbed her purse from the table, and crooked her finger at me.

"Come on," she said. "I'll help you get ready."

I followed her out of the briefing room, down one of the hallways, and into the armory. Gray metal lockers hugged one of the walls, while swords, daggers, and other weapons lined another wall.

I eyed the weapons, wondering if I should take one of them with me instead of the cursed Babs. But Babs had said that she would reappear in my hand no matter what I did or where I left her, and I didn't want to hurt the sword's feelings by choosing another weapon, especially if it wouldn't keep me safe from her curse anyway. Besides, we were going to steal the scepter from Lance, not fight him for it. I should be fine taking Babs with me tonight.

Zoe moved past the weapons to the far end of the wall, where some shelves held several oddly shaped items. At first glance, the items looked like ordinary swords, daggers, and spears. But on closer inspection, I noticed that all sorts of buttons, wires, and battery packs were attached to the weapons, making them anything but ordinary.

Zoe crouched down, then stood up on her tiptoes, scanning the items on each shelf and humming to herself all the while. She finally grabbed something that looked like a small gun with three long metal prongs sticking out of the barrel.

She noticed my curious stare and struck a pose with the item. "A lockpick gun. Put this in just about any lock, pull the trigger, and it's open sesame. The gun does all the work of jimmying the lock instead of someone wasting precious seconds actually picking it open. I made it myself."

"You invent things?"

Zoe nodded and dropped the lockpick gun into her purse. "Yep. Mateo does all the computer stuff, but I like messing around with tools and weapons and seeing what I can come up with. Like this little beauty." She grabbed a dagger off one of the shelves and held it out where I could see it. "This one's my favorite. I call it my electrodagger."

It looked like an ordinary silver dagger—until Zoe pressed her thumb against the blue stone set into the hilt. Blue-white sparks of electricity sizzled up and down the blade, making me jerk back in surprise.

"It's a dagger *and* a stun gun." She beamed at me, pride filling her face. "Why carry two weapons when you can have them all in one?"

I grinned back at her. "Now, *that* is cool."

Zoe shoved the electrodagger into her purse, along with a few more gizmos, then grabbed a small glass case that contained several wireless earbuds. She stuck one of them into her own ear, then handed one to me and gestured that I should do the same. The device slid easily into my ear, and I could barely tell it was there.

"Check, check," Zoe said.

Her voice echoed in my ear, and I flashed her a thumbs-up, telling her that I could hear her loud and clear.

"All you have to do is talk in your normal voice, or even whisper, depending on the situation, and we'll be able to hear you through your earbud," she said. "And you can hear the rest of us too. This is how we communicate with each other during missions."

I nodded. "Got it."

We both removed our earbuds. Zoe put them back into that glass case, then slid the whole thing into her bag. The sides of her blue-plaid purse were already bulging, as if the enormous bag were going to explode from all the spy gear she had crammed inside, but Zoe looked over the shelves again, debating whether she needed anything else.

I didn't know the Valkyrie—didn't know her at all—but she seemed nice enough. Or at least willing to give me the benefit of the doubt when it came to my parents. It was one thing to trade insults with Ian while we were in the safety of the Bunker. But now that we were getting ready to leave the academy, anything could happen, and I wanted to know what kind of people were going to be watching my back.

"Can I ask you something?" I said. "About…Ian?"

Zoe kept staring at the gadgets. "You mean why he's been so snarky to you?"

"Yeah. What's his problem? He doesn't even know me, and he already hates me."

"Maybe that's because you remind him of himself."

I frowned. "What do you mean?"

Zoe glanced around the armory, as if making sure that we were still alone, then looked at me again. "Ian's family, the Hunters, are a big deal in the Protectorate. Like almost as big a deal as the Quinns. His entire family, they've all been members of the Protectorate going back I don't know how many generations, including his mom and dad. His parents...well, let's just say they aren't the best. All they do, all they really care about, is traveling all over the world on Protectorate missions. So it was pretty much just Ian and his older brother, Drake, growing up together."

"So?" I asked. "What does that have to do with me?"

"So Ian absolutely adored Drake. Loved and looked up to his big brother more than anyone else. We're talking some serious hero worship here, especially when Drake graduated with honors from the New York academy and went to work for the Protectorate."

I sighed. "Let me guess. A group of Reapers killed Drake, and now Ian hates all Reapers as a result."

"If only it were that simple." Zoe glanced around again, making sure that we were still alone. "It turned out that Drake was secretly a Reaper—and that he had been a Reaper for *years*."

My eyes widened. "No way."

"Oh, yeah."

"So what happened?" I asked, totally caught up in her story.

"Well, since Drake was a rookie member of the Protectorate, he was assigned to guard some weapons, armor, and artifacts that were being stored at a warehouse near the New York academy. But after the battle in North Carolina, stuff started disappearing from the warehouse. Takeda got suspicious, since no one but Protectorate members are supposed to know where the warehouse is. I don't know how, but he realized that Drake was the one leaking information to the Reapers, so he set a trap for him. Takeda told Drake about a shipment of artifacts coming to the warehouse, then sat back and waited for Drake and the other Reapers to try to steal the artifacts. Takeda wanted to catch and arrest all the Reapers at the same time, including Drake." Zoe bit her lip, stopping her story.

"What happened?" I asked. "What went wrong?"

"Drake bought Ian along to the warehouse the night of the Protectorate raid. Ian didn't realize that they were meeting a bunch of Reapers, but Drake finally told Ian that he was a Reaper and he wanted Ian to join them. As you can imagine, Ian didn't take that well."

No, that wasn't the kind of thing you took well. That was something that shattered your heart in an instant and made you question everything you thought you knew about the people you loved.

Zoe shook her head. "Ian was absolutely devastated. But that's not even the worst part."

"What was that?"

"Drake told Ian to either join the Reapers or die," she said. "Of course Ian refused, but Drake attacked him. Ian didn't have a choice. He defended himself, and he stabbed Drake in the chest."

I sucked in a horrified breath. So that was why Ian hated Reapers and everything to do with them—he had been forced to fight his own Reaper brother. I had thought that finding out about my parents was bad, but this was worse— so much *worse*. At least my parents had never tried to force me to join the Reapers. They had never attacked me, and they had never made me choose between my life and theirs.

"Ian left to get help for Drake, but one of the Reapers set off some sort of bomb," Zoe continued in a sad voice. "The warehouse exploded. Ian got out, but Drake didn't. He's still buried somewhere in the rubble."

"Poor Ian," I whispered.

"Yeah. You can say that again."

We fell silent, each of us lost in our own thoughts.

"Look," Zoe said. "Ian is a really great guy. Ian, Mateo, and me—we've all been friends for years. Ian and I lived next door to each other in New York. When he wasn't with Drake, Ian was hanging out at my house. He's like the brother I never had, and he's always watched out for me."

"But?"

She let out a breath. "But finding out the truth about Drake almost destroyed him. So when Linus Quinn and Takeda put together the Midgard, Ian was the first one to volunteer. Ian thinks that if he stops Sisyphus and these new Reapers, he can somehow make up for not seeing the truth about Drake."

I shifted on my feet. Just like I wanted to make up for my parents' evil actions. Ian Hunter and I were far more alike than I would have thought possible.

"Mateo and I just joined the team to keep Ian from doing something stupid, like getting himself killed." Zoe sighed. "But Amanda was the one who died instead."

Guilt and grief flashed in her hazel eyes, and blue sparks of magic fizzed in the air around her before slowly winking out one by one.

"Amanda's death wasn't your fault," I said. "If it was anyone's fault, then it was mine for not confronting the Reaper as soon as I spotted him in the library. But none of us realized that the Reaper was going to summon those chimeras. And you said yourself that Amanda went into the library without waiting for backup."

"I know that, but I still feel guilty." Her face twisted with regret. "Although it's not like I could have helped Amanda against the chimeras."

I felt guilty too, but I wondered at her words. "What do you mean? You're a Valkyrie."

Zoe let out a bitter laugh. "And Valkyries are supposed to be these great, amazing, superstrong fighters, right? Well, guess what? That particular magic skipped right over me."

She waved her hand, causing more blue sparks to streak out of her fingertips. "I'm not any stronger than you are, Rory. In fact, I'm probably not as strong, given how short I am. I'm not a great fighter either. Not like you are. The only reason I'm here is to watch Ian's and Mateo's backs."

She sighed and waggled her fingers again, watching the shower of sparks. Zoe glared at the flashing lights, then snapped her hand into a tight fist, snuffing them all out.

"Anyway, we need to get going. The others are probably waiting on us."

She gave me a grim smile, then left the armory. But I stayed where I was, thinking about everything she'd said.

My hand crept to my charm bracelet, and I opened the heart locket, staring at the photo of me with my parents. That was the last happy moment I remembered having with them before they were killed. I wondered what Ian's last happy moment with his brother had been.

Sympathy surged through me, softening my anger and annoyance at the Viking. Ian didn't hate me because my parents had been Reapers—he hated himself for what he'd been forced to do to his brother. Because Drake had died and he had lived. I was a reminder of his own guilt, grief, and heartache.

Still, just because I felt sorry for the Viking didn't mean I was going to let him take his emotions out on me. I hadn't done anything wrong, and tonight I was going to show him that. I was going to show Ian and the others that I could be a part of the team and help them stop the Reapers—for good.

Chapter Twelve

I left the armory and went back to the briefing room, where the others were waiting. Takeda nodded at me, while Zoe and Mateo both gave me encouraging smiles. Ian ignored me, and I did the same to him.

"Let's move," Takeda said. "We need to get to the party before the Reapers show up."

Takeda led us to the back of the Bunker to the door marked *Stairs* that I'd noticed on my tour earlier. But instead of opening the door and climbing up the stairs, he went over to a bookcase along the wall and pressed a button on the side of it. A green light flashed, scanning his thumb, and the wooden case creaked back, revealing a stone passageway.

"Another secret entrance? One that's really a secret tunnel that leads to yet another secret entrance on the other end?" I brightened. "Awesome!"

Gwen had her comic books, but there was nothing I loved more than a good mystery. Agatha Christie, Nancy Drew, Sherlock Holmes. I devoured those kinds of books, along with all the movies and TV shows. And you couldn't have a proper mystery without secret passageways, hidden compartments, and the like.

Mateo grinned, picking up on my excitement. "No spy lair is complete without one, right?"

I grinned back at him. "Right."

We stepped into the tunnel, and the bookcase swung shut behind us. Lights clicked on in the stone ceiling, and then we started walking, walking, walking.

About fifty feet in, a tunnel branched off to our right. Then, fifty feet later, another tunnel branched off to our left. Given their placement, I was guessing that those tunnels led to the student dorms and some of the other outbuildings.

Eventually, we reached what looked like the heart of the underground labyrinth, with tunnels branching off in five different directions. Unless I was mistaken, these passageways led to the other buildings on the main quad. I eagerly peered down each of them, trying to figure out which one went where, but the other corridors remained dark. I would have to come back down here one day and explore all the secret entrances and exits for myself.

We kept going. We weren't in the tunnel for more than a few minutes, but it seemed much longer than that before we reached another door at the far end. Takeda opened it with his thumbprint, and we stepped into a basement office crammed full of free weights, exercise balls, yoga mats, and other fitness equipment. *Coach Takeda* glimmered on a gold nameplate on the desk in the corner.

"No wonder you're the new gym coach," I said.

Takeda gave me a small smile and led us through his office, up some steps, and out a side door that opened up into the parking lot on the back side of the gym. A single van was sitting in the lot, with the words *Pork Pit Catering* on the side. Not very incognito as far as spy vehicles went, but I supposed it was a little less conspicuous than something that had *Property of the Protectorate* painted on it. Takeda slid into the driver's seat, while Ian, Zoe, Mateo, and I climbed into the back.

This wasn't any old van. A large desk was bolted to one wall, along with several monitors, laptops, and other computer equipment. A shelf clung to the opposite wall, crammed full of swords, staffs, hammers, pliers, walkie-talkies, and other odds and ends. Mateo plopped down in a chair in front of the desk. Zoe sat in the chair next to him, and Ian and I took seats across from each other in the very back of the van.

No one spoke on the ride over to Lance Fuller's house, although Takeda tuned the radio to a classical station and started humming along with the music. Thirty minutes later, he steered the van into a ritzy subdivision and pulled over to the curb.

"We're down the street from the Fuller mansion." Takeda twisted around in his seat. "Mateo, you're up."

Mateo rubbed his hands together in anticipation, then grinned, leaned over one of the laptops, and got to work. "Come to Papa."

Mateo had impressive speed, even for a Roman, and his fingers flew over the keyboard in a quick, staccato rhythm, as though he were playing an elaborate piano concerto. Less than a minute later, images popped up on the monitors, showing different views of the mansion. The party was already going strong, with dozens of kids talking, laughing, drinking, and dancing inside the mansion and around one of the heated outdoor pools.

Mateo kept typing, his gaze locked on the monitors. "I'm in the security system. I can see and track you guys through most of the mansion, although it looks like several rooms don't have cameras covering them."

Takeda nodded. "Zoe, time for comms."

Zoe pulled the glass case out of her purse and passed out an earbud to everyone. We all wiggled the devices into our ears. Mateo hit some more buttons on his laptop, then leaned forward and spoke into a microphone on the desk.

"Wakey-wakey, guys." His voice echoed in my ear, along with his gleeful snicker.

"Yeah, yeah, we're awake," Zoe muttered. "Why do you have to say the same stupid thing every single time we use comms?"

Mateo grinned at her. "Just to drive you crazy."

She rolled her eyes, leaned over, and punched him in the arm, causing blue sparks to flicker around both of them. Mateo snickered again.

"Everyone good on weapons?" Takeda asked.

Zoe patted her blue bag. "Electrodagger in my purse."

"I've got a dagger tucked into the side of my boot," Ian said.

I tapped my finger on Babs's hilt, since the sword was still belted to my waist. "I'm good too."

Takeda nodded. He slid out of the driver's seat, came around, and opened the back door, and Ian, Zoe, and I got out of the van.

"Be careful," Takeda said, looking at each of us in turn. "A couple of Protectorate guards who have been following Lance around campus are stationed outside the mansion, and a full team of guards will be here soon in case we need backup, but we don't know how many Reapers might show up tonight or might already be inside the mansion. Remember, they could be regular kids, just like you guys. So get in, find the chimera scepter, and get out. Good luck."

We all nodded back to him. Takeda climbed inside the van with Mateo and shut the door behind them. That left me standing in the street with Ian and Zoe. We all looked at each other.

"Let's get this over with," Ian said.

For once, I didn't argue with him. Together, the three of us stepped onto the sidewalk and headed toward the Fuller mansion.

Lance's party was definitely the place to be tonight. Luxury cars and SUVs lined both sides of the street in front of the mansion, and every single light in the house seemed to be on. It wasn't even eight o'clock yet, the party's official start time, but the Mythos kids had kicked things off early, given the loud, thumping music that reverberated up and down the street.

We left the sidewalk and hiked up the cobblestone driveway to the mansion. The front door was standing wide open, so we stepped inside.

People were already packed inside the large living room that took up the front of the mansion, talking, laughing, and dancing. Kids stood two and three deep in front of a glass table along the wall, passing soda and beer bottles back and forth and pouring the fizzing and foaming liquids into their plastic cups. Still more kids trailed along behind a couple of guys who were rolling an enormous beer keg along the floor, heading toward the kitchen so they could tap it. Some folks had even started smoking, and the harsh stench of cigarettes made me want to sneeze.

"Come on," Ian said over the din. "Let's find Lance."

Zoe and I nodded, and together the three of us moved deeper into the mansion.

It was a massive house, three stories tall, with room after

spacious room. At least, the rooms would have been spacious if so many people weren't crammed inside. Mateo had been right. It looked like Lance had invited every single kid at Mythos to his party, and they were all determined to kick off the school year with a loud, drunken bang.

Zoe grinned and started shimmying to the music, but Ian winced, looking as pained, uncomfortable, and out of place as I felt. Something else we had in common. He caught me staring at him and shrugged. I shrugged back. I had never understood why people thought that the louder you turned up your music, the better time you would have. I actually liked to *listen* to music, not have it burst my eardrums.

"Where do we start?" I asked, almost having to yell at Ian to get him to hear me, even though I was standing right beside him.

"In the kitchen!" he yelled back. "That's where Mateo says Lance is."

I hadn't heard Mateo say anything through my earbud, but that wasn't surprising, given how insanely loud it was in here. I gave Ian a thumbs-up, telling him I understood, and pointed toward the kitchen. The three of us fell into step behind the kids following the beer keg. It was slow going, but we finally made it into the kitchen. It was actually a little less crowded in here, since the room had a set of double doors that opened onto a stone patio. Outside, kids shrieked and splashed in one of the heated swimming pools.

Ian, Zoe, and I moved over to the corner of the room, out of the way of the crowd gathering around the beer keg.

"Now what?" Zoe said.

Ian glanced around. "Now we find Lance—"

"Rory! Hey, Rory! Over here!" Someone shouted my name over the music.

I turned around. From the opposite side of the kitchen, Lance waved at me.

Ian leaned down. "You keep him distracted. Zoe and I will start searching for the chimera scepter. As soon as we find it, we'll let you know, and then the three of us will get out of here."

"I'll do my best."

Ian nodded at me, for once completely serious and without a trace of his usual hostility. I nodded back. He and Zoe disappeared into the crowd, and I plastered a smile on my face and started threading my way over to Lance.

"Hey! Great party!" I called out when I reached him.

Lance grinned. "Thanks!" He pointed at the guys tapping the beer keg in the kitchen sink. "You want some?"

I shook my head. "Nah. I don't drink."

I never drank. Alcohol dulled the senses, something that could be fatal for warriors. Especially in a place like this, where I didn't know who was a friend—and who might secretly be a Reaper.

Lance put down his plastic cup and pointed to a set of stairs at the far end of the kitchen. "You want to go somewhere a little quieter and talk?"

"Sure! That would be great!"

At this point, I didn't care if Lance was a Reaper and might be luring me into a trap. I just wanted to get away from the crowds and the thumping music that was rapidly giving me a migraine.

Lance and I went up the stairs to the third and top floor of the mansion. It was much quieter up here, and I could finally hear myself think again, as well as the others murmuring updates in my ear.

"That's it, Rory," Takeda said. "Keep Lance busy. Ian and Zoe have found a wall safe in a library on the second floor. We think that's where the chimera scepter is. Zoe is working on opening the safe right now."

Takeda stopped talking, but Zoe's voice sounded. She was muttering to Ian, telling him what tools to pull out of her purse. I blocked her out and focused on Lance again.

He led me to a pair of open double doors at the end of the hallway, and we stepped into an enormous office. Floor-to-ceiling bookcases took up one wall, filled with the same sorts of old, thick, leather-bound books that were in the Library of Antiquities. Gold-framed paintings of famous mythological battles hung on another wall, along with more than two dozen swords, daggers, and other weapons. A wet bar stood in the corner, while an antique desk sat in the back of the room. Behind the desk, a couple of glass doors led out to another stone patio that overlooked the pool.

"This is my dad's office, but he won't mind us borrowing it," Lance said. "He's on a trip, of sorts."

His calm, matter-of-fact tone made a cold finger of unease slide down my spine, especially since I knew that his dad had been killed by the Protectorate. What kind of game was Lance playing? I didn't know, but I was getting a sinking feeling that the others were right about him being a Reaper.

Lance shut the office doors, then walked over to the bar, grabbed a bottle of Scotch, and held it out to me. "You want some?"

"I told you already—I don't drink."

"Afraid it might interfere with your Spartan killer instincts?" A faint sneering note crept into his voice.

"Something like that."

He shrugged. "Suit yourself."

Lance put the bottle down and leaned back against the bar. I wandered around the room, looking at the weapons on the walls. No identification cards hung next to the swords, but they were all finely made, with fancy jeweled hilts and sharp, polished blades. I wondered if any of them were the weapons Lance's dad had stolen from the Protectorate warehouse, but there was no way to tell.

"Rory," Takeda murmured through my earbud again. "There aren't any cameras in that office, so we can't see you. Say something and let me know that you're okay."

I stopped in front of a bronze sword and pretended to admire it. "Your dad has a really cool weapons collection."

"I guess. I'm not into weapons myself," Lance said. "I like artifacts much better. What about you, Rory? Do you like artifacts?"

My back was to him, so he didn't see my eyes widen. I blinked away my surprise, schooled my face into a neutral expression, and turned to face him.

"Artifacts?" I shrugged. "They're okay, I guess. I've never really had much to do with them."

Lance's gaze sharpened, as though he'd caught me in a lie. "Really? I find that hard to believe, since your parents were such bigtime Reaper assassins. Surely they must have stolen some artifacts too."

Shock rippled through me. Why was he talking about my parents? Especially about them stealing artifacts? Once again, I got the feeling that Lance was fishing for information. That sinking feeling in my stomach intensified. The only reason he would be doing that, the only reason he would be asking these kinds of questions, was if he was a Reaper himself.

I wasn't surprised. Not really. Not after everything Takeda and the others had told me about Lance wanting revenge for his dad's death. But disappointment filled me all the same. I had liked him *so much* last year, but now he was a bad guy. Or maybe he had always been a bad guy, and I had been crushing on him too hard to see the truth until now. Either way, I was sick and tired of Reapers and all their stupid mind games.

"Well, Rory?" Lance asked again. "Do you think your parents ever stole any artifacts?"

His snide tone burned away my disappointment and made anger sizzle through me instead. I crossed my arms over my chest. "I didn't know anything about my parents being Reapers. Not that that's any of *your* business."

Lance held up his hands in apology. "You're taking this the wrong way. I didn't mean it as an insult. Just the opposite. I think it's really interesting that your parents were Reapers."

"And why is that?"

"Haven't you ever thought about what it would be like? To be a Reaper?"

I frowned. "Of course not. Why would I think about something like that?"

"Why *wouldn't* you think about something like that?" His blue eyes glittered with a strange, bright light. "I mean, surely there were hints that your parents were Reapers. Didn't you ever suspect them?"

I shifted on my feet. "No. I never suspected them. I never had a clue."

And I really hadn't. Rebecca and Tyson Forseti had been my mom and dad, the parents I loved, the warriors I had strived so hard to be like. I had never suspected they were anything else, and I had never dreamed in my darkest nightmares that they were Reapers. But apparently, being Reapers had been more important to my parents than anything else, including me, since they'd never told me anything about it. Not one single word.

And what had being Reapers gotten them in the end? Nothing but dead, dead, dead, and me with a broken heart, desperately trying to understand why they'd done so many terrible things. That made me angrier than anything else— that I would never get the chance to ask them *why*.

More and more anger surged through my body, like matches flaring to life, but they burned out just as quickly, replaced by that familiar combination of guilt, shame, and embarrassment. Once again, that icy frost coated my heart, numbing me from the inside out. This time, I welcomed the chill. I didn't want to feel the sharp sting of my parents' betrayal. Not again. And especially not now, when I was facing a dangerous enemy.

Lance pushed away from the bar, walked over, and stopped right in front of me. "Ever since I found out about your parents, I've been thinking a lot about you, Rory."

As far as pickup lines went, that was the worst one ever. What kind of sick game was Lance playing? Was he trying to upset me so that he could attack me by surprise? He didn't seem to be carrying any weapons, but I still dropped my hand to Babs's hilt.

"Really? Why? Have you been planning how you can mock me like all the other academy kids?" I snarked. "Well, don't bother. They all did a bang-up job of it last school year, and they're doing the exact same thing again this year. They've made an art form out of it."

He shook his head. "No, nothing like that. In fact, I admire your parents for being Reapers."

Of course he did, since he was a Reaper himself. As much as I would have liked to punch Lance in the face for talking about my parents, I forced myself to focus on the others murmuring updates through our earbuds. Zoe and Ian were still trying to open that safe to get the chimera scepter, which meant that I needed to keep Lance busy for at least a few more minutes.

So I decided to play dumb. "Why would you admire my parents? Reapers are *evil*. They hurt and kill other people. Reapers used to do those things in service to Loki, but now I suppose they do them just because they can, just because they want to, just because they like hurting other people."

Excitement sparked in Lance's gaze, and he snapped his fingers. "Exactly! That's exactly what I'm talking about. I always thought it was stupid that the Reapers worked so long and hard to serve an exiled god. I was actually glad when Gwen Frost and her friends defeated Loki and locked him away for good. Who is Loki to tell us what to do? Why should he rule us? Why shouldn't *we* be the ones to rule this world and everyone in it, including the regular mortals?"

"What are you talking about?" I wasn't playing dumb anymore. Now I was genuinely confused by all the riddles and nonsense that he kept spouting.

"I'm talking about the Reapers doing what they should have done all along, taking control of things, not for Loki or some other god but for themselves."

Lance grinned at me and stepped forward. I wrapped my fingers around Babs's hilt and moved to the side, thinking that he was going to attack me, but he walked past me, went to the desk in the back of the office, and opened one of the drawers. Lance started digging through the junk inside, tossing pens, pencils, paper clips, and more onto the top of the desk.

I listened to the others, but Zoe and Ian were still trying to get inside that safe. I opened my mouth to ask Takeda and Mateo if they were seeing Lance's sudden freak-out, but then I remembered that the office didn't have any security cameras. So I focused on Lance again, ready to yank Babs free from her scabbard if he pulled a dagger or some other weapon out of that drawer. But he only yanked out a wad of papers, tossed them on top of the desk with the rest of the mess, and kept digging.

Several long, slender pieces of paper slipped off the side of the desk and landed on the floor. I frowned. Those looked like...tickets.

I sidled a little closer and squinted at the black type. They were tickets—more than half a dozen tickets to the Fall Costume Ball this weekend. The annual ball always kicked off the academy's school year and social events. But why would Lance have so many tickets to it? Weird.

He didn't notice that the tickets had fallen to the floor, and he kept right on digging through that desk drawer.

"What are you doing?" I asked. "What are looking for?"

"There's something I want to show you," Lance said. "Something that will explain everything. Ah, there it is."

He grabbed a final item from the drawer and straightened up. He smiled at me, came around the desk, and raised his hand. A gold stick topped by a familiar creature glimmered in his fingers.

Lance was holding the chimera scepter—and he was pointing it straight at me.

CHAPTER THIRTEEN

I froze, my hand still curled around Babs's hilt, but I didn't dare draw my sword. I hadn't seen Lance unleash the chimeras in the library last night, so I didn't know exactly how the scepter worked. But I was betting that he could summon the monsters before I could wrest that scepter out of his hand.

"Lance?" I asked, still playing dumb. "What are you doing? What's that weird golden stick?"

I said that last part for the others' benefit. For a moment, I didn't hear anything through my earbud. Then Takeda let out a low curse.

"Lance has the scepter," he muttered. "Ian, Zoe, forget about the safe. Go help Rory. Right now."

"On it," Ian replied. "We're leaving the library."

He and Zoe started talking to each other, and several loud *clank-clank-clanks* sounded, as though Zoe was stuffing her tools back into her purse. Since they were on their way, I tuned them out and focused on Lance again.

He started flipping the chimera scepter end over end in his hand, like it was a golden baton instead of a powerful artifact. "Oh, Rory. I expected more from you. A better performance, at the very least."

"I don't know what you mean."

He flipped the scepter up into the air one more time, then caught it and stabbed it at me. "You know *exactly* what I mean. I saw you in the library last night, fighting my chimeras. I had forgotten what a fantastic warrior you are. So strong, so graceful, so deadly."

Lance smiled, but his lips slowly twisted into more of a sneer. His condescending expression and compliments made me sick to my stomach.

"Let's be honest. You know that I'm a Reaper, that I'm the one who stole Typhon's Scepter from the library." He shrugged. "I'm sure your new Protectorate friends told you all about it. After all, you're Gwen Frost's cousin. They have an interest in you. In making sure that you're on their side for the upcoming war."

"And what's your interest in me?" I asked. "Because I don't think that you asked me up here just because you think I'm cute."

He let out a low laugh. The sound made my skin crawl. "I wasn't lying when I said that you were cute earlier today. Then again, I've always been attracted to strong women."

My hand clenched a little tighter around Babs's hilt. I would show him exactly how strong I was when I took that scepter away from him. Lance smirked at me, as if he knew exactly what I was thinking. I hoped he did, and I hoped he realized how badly this was going to end for him.

"But cute or not, you're right. That's not why I asked you up here. I wanted you out of the way so that my friends could capture your friends." He pulled his phone out of his jeans pocket and brought the device up to his mouth. "Take them. Now."

For a moment, nothing happened. Then, through my earbud, I heard Ian let out a vicious curse. He shouted at Zoe to get behind him, and then a series of crashes and bangs sounded, so loud that they made me wince. Mateo started yelling too, telling Ian that the security cameras were down and that he couldn't see anything on his monitors. I could also hear Takeda barking out orders to someone, demanding to know where the Protectorate reinforcements were and how long it would take them to get to the mansion.

I stepped back, ready to run out the office to go help Ian and Zoe, but Lance slashed the chimera scepter through the air in a warning motion. I froze again.

"Ah, ah, ah," he said. "You're going to stay right here where I can keep an eye on you, Rory."

"What do you want, Lance?" I snapped. "What's the point of all this?"

A smug, satisfied grin filled his face. It made me want to punch him even more than before.

"The point is that my friends and I have finally found a way for the Reapers to take control, not only of all the Mythos Academies and the Protectorate but of *everything*, of the entire world." He waggled the chimera scepter at me. "And guess how we're going to do that?"

My stomach twisted at the obvious answer. "Artifacts. You're going to use artifacts."

"Ding, ding, we have a winner." He waved the scepter around again, pointing it at the swords on the wall. "As you can see, my dad loved to collect weapons. He never saw a rusty old sword or dagger that he didn't want, and he spent all the Fuller family fortune buying every single weapon he could get his hands on."

"Why are you telling me this?" I asked, still playing dumb. "What happened to your dad?"

"He was desperate for money, so he started stealing weapons and armor from the Protectorate warehouse where he worked in New York and selling them to the Reapers." Lance's face darkened. "And the Protectorate killed him for it. Slaughtered him in a raid."

That matched what Linus Quinn had said—and it also sounded like the story Zoe had told me about Ian and his brother, Drake. Could Lance's father have worked with Ian's brother? I didn't know, and it wasn't important right now. All that mattered was getting that scepter away from Lance before he conjured up any chimeras. Then I could go help Ian and Zoe.

I moved forward a couple of steps, trying to get into position to lunge at Lance and grab the scepter. "Is that why you stole the scepter? Is that why you're planning to give it to Sisyphus? Because the Protectorate killed your dad and you want revenge on them?"

Lance barked out a harsh laugh. "Well, it's certainly a bonus, but no, I didn't join the Reapers only for revenge."

I crept forward another step. "Then why?"

"Because Sisyphus is right. For centuries, Reapers hid in the shadows, sneaking around and waiting for Loki to return. Well, Loki is gone for good now, but we're still here. And you know what? I'm tired of playing by the Protectorate's rules. I'm tired of being a good little warrior and pretending to blend in with the regular humans when I'm so much better than they are." That bright, fanatical light burned in his eyes again. "We're warriors. We're the ones with magic and artifacts and fighting skills. We're the ones with the real *power*, and we should act like it. We should be in charge, not these weak, inferior mortals who wouldn't know the sharp end of a sword if you stabbed them in the gut with it."

I shook my head. "Wow, this Sisyphus guy really did a number on you. He's totally brainwashed you."

Lance barked out another laugh. "Sisyphus didn't do anything but show me the truth about how the world should work. How the world *will* work, once we're through with it."

I took another step forward, adjusting my grip on Babs's hilt and getting ready to pull the sword free of her scabbard. I would only have one shot to get that scepter away from Lance, and I had to make it count.

"Well, here's a news flash for you. I don't care what your evil master plan is, because it's *never going to happen*," I snapped. "The Protectorate will stop you and Sisyphus and all the other Reapers."

"No, they won't. The Protectorate won't be able to stand against us—not with *you* on our side, Rory."

"Me? Join the Reapers?" I let out a harsh, mocking laugh. "Now I know you're crazy."

Lance tilted his head to the side and gave me a knowing look. "We'll see about that."

My heart squeezed with worry. What was he talking about? Why did he think that I would join the Reapers? I would never do that—*never*. But Lance was talking about it like it was a foregone conclusion. What did he know that I didn't?

I stepped forward to demand some answers, but the office doors burst open, and Ian and Zoe staggered into the room. My heart lifted, thinking that they were here to help me, but they weren't the only ones who came into the office.

Half a dozen Reapers stormed in behind them.

I drew my sword and whirled around, ready to battle the

Reapers, but Lance pointed the gold scepter at me again.

"Stop," he commanded. "Unless you want to fight some more chimeras."

Six Reapers was bad enough, but add chimeras to the mix, and they could easily kill us, along with all the other kids partying downstairs. So I bit back a curse and held my position, with Babs still clutched in my hand.

The Reapers brandished their swords at Ian and Zoe and shoved them to the middle of the office, several feet away from where I was standing. I had been so focused on Lance that I hadn't paid attention to the noises echoing through my earbud, but the fight had not gone Ian and Zoe's way.

Blood dripped out of Ian's broken nose, and his knuckles were red and swollen from where he'd hit the Reapers. Zoe had a nasty bruise on her right cheek, and a long bloody gash sliced along her right arm from where a Reaper had cut her with a sword.

Ian stood absolutely still, his hands clenched into fists, the muscles in his neck and shoulders stiff with anger and tension. Zoe winced and cradled her injured arm up against her chest, along with her purse, as if the enormous bag would shield her from further harm. Pain glimmered in her hazel eyes, and blue sparks of magic oozed out of her fingertips and spattered like raindrops onto the thick rugs underfoot.

The two of them were battered but still breathing, so I turned my attention to the Reapers. Like every other Reaper I had ever seen, all six of them were wearing long black cloaks with the hoods pulled up. But to my surprise, they weren't wearing the usual rubber masks of Loki's melted face. Instead, these Reapers sported black harlequin masks with large blood-red diamond shapes over their eyes. New masks for a new group of evil. Terrific. Just terrific.

"Good," Lance drawled. "I'm so glad that Ian and Zoe could join our party."

Ian drew back his fist and surged forward like he was going to hit Lance, but one of the Reapers grabbed Ian's shoulder and pressed a dagger up against his throat, making him stop short. The Reaper dug the blade into Ian's neck, breaking the skin and causing blood to trickle down his throat. The message was clear: quit fighting or get your throat cut. Ian didn't have a choice, so he quit fighting. For now.

"Good," Lance repeated. "Now that the Viking has decided to be reasonable, we can continue our conversation."

"I don't have anything to say to you," Ian snarled.

Lance smirked. "Oh, I think you'll be very interested in what I have to say. Especially since it involves your beloved big brother."

Ian jerked back, as though he'd been punched in the gut. "What do you mean? What do you know about Drake?"

Lance smirked at him again and started pacing back and forth from one side of the office to the other. He was still clutching the chimera scepter, and he slashed it through the air in time to his movements. I held my breath, wondering if he might accidentally summon a chimera, but nothing happened.

"Guys," Takeda whispered in an urgent voice through my earbud. "The Protectorate reinforcements will be here in five minutes. Mateo and I are calling in the guards around the mansion and leaving the van right now. Just stay alive until we can get there and help you."

I kept my face blank, not giving any indication that I'd heard him, but Zoe shifted on her feet, and more blue sparks of magic dripped out of her fingertips. She gave me a worried look. She had heard Takeda too, but she knew as well as I did that it would take him, Mateo, and the guards several minutes to shove their way through all the kids in the mansion and make it up to the office. We could be dead long before they reached us.

Ian didn't show any sign that he had heard Takeda. Instead, he glared at Lance, still focused on what the other boy had said.

"What do you know about Drake?" Ian demanded again.

Lance stopped pacing, leaned back against the desk, and crossed his arms over his chest. The gold chimera scepter glimmered in his left hand—the hand that was closest to me. Once again, I thought about lunging forward and snatching the scepter away from Lance, but I couldn't do that. Not while that Reaper still had a dagger at Ian's throat.

"Drake? Why, he and my dad both worked at the same Protectorate warehouse in New York. My dad got transferred there earlier this year after the battle at the North Carolina academy." Lance grinned. "My dad and Drake really hit it off. Did you know that it was Drake's idea to start stealing weapons and artifacts from the warehouse and sell them to Sisyphus and the rest of Drake's Reaper friends?"

Ian's hands balled into fists again, and a muscle ticked in his jaw. Zoe winced in sympathy. Yeah, me too. It was one thing to know that your brother was a Reaper. It was another to have someone rub your face in it the way Lance was doing.

"But of course the Protectorate found out what they were doing, and my dad was killed in that raid." Lance's face darkened again. "But they say that when one door closes, a window opens. In this case, my dad died, but I made a new friend."

"What do you mean?" Ian snapped.

Instead of answering him, Lance gestured at the Reaper who was still holding that dagger on Ian. The Reaper lowered the dagger, slid the weapon into a holster on his belt, and strode over to where Lance was leaning against the desk.

The Reaper turned to face everyone. He pulled off his black gloves and threw them on top of the desk, then reached up and pushed back the hood of his black cloak, revealing his golden hair.

"Oh, no," Zoe whispered.

I glanced at her, wondering what she meant, but her horrified gaze was focused on the Reaper. So was Ian's.

The Reaper grabbed his black harlequin mask and drew it up and over his head, revealing his face. He was in his early twenties, a couple of years older than the rest of us. His eyes were a sharp, piercing blue, but the rest of his handsome features were shockingly familiar. Great cheekbones, straight nose, strong jaw. Even though I had never seen him before, I still knew exactly who he was.

Drake Hunter—Ian's older brother.

CHAPTER FOURTEEN

Contrary to what the Protectorate and everyone else thought, Drake Hunter was very much alive.

At the sight of his older brother, all the color drained from Ian's face, and he swayed on his feet, as though he were about to topple over and pass out from the complete and utter shock.

I glanced at Zoe, but she was still staring at Drake with wide eyes, so I concentrated on what I could hear through my earbud. Takeda and Mateo had made it from the van up to the mansion, although they were stuck somewhere downstairs, yelling at the kids to get out of their way. They didn't realize what was happening yet.

Well, I didn't know Drake, and I wasn't as shocked as Ian and Zoe, so I did the smart thing and started sizing him up as a warrior. As a Viking, he would be strong, probably even stronger than Ian, given that he was two inches taller and much more heavily muscled than his younger brother. A long sword was belted to his waist, along with that dagger he'd brandished at Ian.

A large ruby flashed in the sword's hilt, catching my eye, and I noticed a blood-red spark in the center of the gem. The longer I stared at that spark, the brighter it burned, like it was about to ignite into a raging fire. I didn't know what that ruby was, but it was obvious that it was much more than a pretty decoration. I shivered and looked away from it.

"You—you—you're here. How did you get here?" Ian sputtered, his face still white with shock. "I saw you die, Drake. I—I *killed* you."

Drake raised his golden eyebrows. "You mean when you stabbed me in the chest and left me to be buried under tons of falling rubble when the warehouse exploded?"

Ian grimaced.

"Well, lucky for me, Sisyphus was there. He pulled me to safety, which is more than I can say for you," Drake said. "You know, I never thought my own brother would leave me for dead. But you did, Ian. Just like that."

He snapped his fingers. Ian flinched at the harsh sound and swayed on his feet again. Two of the Reapers stepped up beside him and latched onto his arms. Not so much to guard him as simply to hold him upright.

Drake walked over and stopped right in front of his brother. "You could have been a part of this. You could have been a part of our victory against the Protectorate. You could have fought alongside me the way you always did before. But you chose the Protectorate over me, your own brother. You're a fool, Ian. Such a sad, stupid, shortsighted *fool*."

That last insult roused Ian out of his shocked daze. His face hardened, his chin lifted, and his entire body straightened. Once again, he was the proud Viking warrior I'd come to know.

"You're a *Reaper*, Drake," Ian snarled. "You didn't give me a choice. You told me to either join the Reapers or die.

And then, when I refused, *you* attacked *me*. You say that I stabbed you in the chest? Well, at least I did it to your face. You killed Protectorate guards—innocent men and women you'd fought alongside. Who *believed* in you. Who *trusted* you. And how did you repay their trust? By stabbing them in the back in cold-blooded murder. And for what? A few lousy artifacts?"

"More than a few artifacts," Drake replied. "As you'll soon see for yourself."

Ian glared at his brother again, but Drake smiled back at him.

"Although I have to admit that I was touched by how much you cried at my funeral. I stood in the shadows at the cemetery and watched the whole thing. I didn't expect so many tears from you, but I supposed you felt guilty about leaving me to die." Drake shook his head. "You always were a sentimental fool that way."

Anger and embarrassment stained Ian's cheeks a dark red, but it didn't hide the deep, agonizing hurt that filled his eyes at his brother's cruel words. My heart ached for the Viking. At this moment, Ian's pain was even greater than my own. At least I'd never had to confront my parents about their being Reapers the way he was hearing his own brother gloat about it right now.

Drake kept smirking at Ian, who raised his fists and surged forward again. But the two Reapers held him in place and lifted their swords in warning, stopping Ian from attacking his brother.

Lance cleared his throat. "As touching as this little reunion is, we do have a schedule to keep. You know as well as I do that Sisyphus doesn't like to be kept waiting. We need to get what he wants and get out of here."

Drake opened his mouth like he was going to snipe at

the younger guy, but he closed his lips, apparently thinking better of it. After a moment, he nodded his agreement.

My eyes narrowed. So Lance and Drake were both working for the mysterious Sisyphus, and Lance had stolen the chimera scepter on Sisyphus's orders. Lance and Drake had to realize that Protectorate warriors were on their way to the mansion right now, so why didn't they go ahead, kill us, and leave? What were they waiting for? What else did Sisyphus want besides the chimera scepter?

"You're not going to get away with this." Ian spat out the words. "Neither one of you. I'll make sure of it."

Lance laughed. "Get away with it? We've already gotten away with it." He looked at Drake. "You didn't tell me that your brother was such a clueless idiot."

Drake shrugged.

Ian's hands clenched into fists again, and this time, he surged toward Lance. The two Reapers tightened their grips and brandished their swords, stopping him. Ian glared at the Reapers, then at Lance, who laughed again, amused by his struggles.

"Temper, temper," Lance said in a mocking tone. "That's going to get you into trouble someday."

Ian growled, but he couldn't attack Lance, not without those two Reapers cutting him to pieces with their swords.

Lance looked at Ian another moment, making sure that he was going to stay put. Then he winked at Zoe, who glared back at him.

"And now," he murmured. "To bring Sisyphus what he really wants."

Lance turned to face me, his lips curving up into another wide grin. "That would be you, Rory."

This time, I was the one who staggered back and swayed on my feet. I couldn't have been more shocked if Lance had whipped out a sword and stabbed me in the heart with it.

"What?" I asked. "What are you talking about? I don't even know Sisyphus. What could he possibly want with me?"

"Plenty. Let's talk facts. Vikings, Romans, Valkyries, Amazons. They're all good warriors. But Spartans? Spartans are *great* warriors, the *best* warriors." Lance pointed at me. "Spartans like *you*, Rory. That's why I threw this party tonight. So I could get you away from the academy, bring you here, and tell you how great a warrior you are—and how much you're going to help Sisyphus and the rest of us."

Ian and Zoe both stared at me, surprise flashing in their eyes. A sick, sick feeling filled my stomach. This whole thing—Lance coming up to me on the quad, flirting with me, asking me to his party—I had thought it might be a trap. I had just never expected it to be a trap for *me*.

"What do you mean?" My voice dropped to a hoarse whisper. "What are you talking about?"

"Your parents were legends among the Reapers," Lance said. "Did you know that?"

I shook my head. "No. I told you that I didn't know anything about them being Reapers. Not until Covington murdered them in the Library of Antiquities."

"It's too bad they never told you anything," Drake chimed in. "All the people they killed, all the members of the Protectorate they eliminated, all the artifacts they stole. Rebecca and Tyson Forseti were truly two of the best Reapers ever."

That sick, sick feeling spread through my entire body, and I had to swallow down the hot, sour bile rising in my throat. But now was not the time to give in to my feelings about my parents. Otherwise, I would start screaming with rage and guilt and grief and never, ever stop. So I pushed those feelings down—deep, deep down—into the bottom of my broken heart and coated them with that cold frost, freezing them out the way I had been doing for months now, ever since I'd found out the awful truth.

"I know what my parents did." I ground out the words. "You don't have to keep reminding me how horrible they were."

Lance frowned. "Horrible? They weren't horrible. They were amazing warriors. And you're just like them. Why, you're an even better warrior than they were. Your dad used to brag about you all the time to my dad. About how you were the best Spartan he'd ever seen and how you were going to be one of the greatest warriors of your generation, maybe even better than Logan Quinn."

"So?"

"So we're asking you to put those skills to good use," he said.

"What do you mean?" I snapped, tired of all his word and mind games.

"I mean join me—join me and Drake and Sisyphus. Forget about the Protectorate and whatever deal you've made with them. Come with me, and fight for us, fight for the Reapers. Be the warrior your parents always wanted you to be." Lance flashed me a smile. "Become a Reaper."

His words bounced around inside my head, but I couldn't make sense of them. It was like he was speaking some foreign language that I didn't understand—one that I didn't *want* to understand.

"Come on, Rory," Lance crooned. "You know you want to say yes. Why should you fight for the Protectorate? For all the kids at the academy who hate you? Why should you do *anything* for them? No matter what you do, you'll always be the girl with the Reaper parents, and the other kids will always hate you for it. So you might as well give in and become what they all already think you are."

As much as I hated to admit it, he had a point. Everyone at Mythos Academy thought I was a bad guy, and they all went out of their way to let me know how much they despised me. I told myself over and over again that it didn't matter, that I didn't care what the other kids thought of me, but every angry look, harsh whisper, and mocking laugh cut into my heart like a razor-sharp sword.

Now all that was left behind were the thin ribbons of myself that I had tried to braid together into some sort of armor. But that armor was thin, weak, and flimsy, and it didn't protect me from anything. Not the other kids' taunts, not my parents' betrayal, and especially not my own pain. I had never done anything wrong—not one single *thing*—but I was still paying for all the sins of my parents, and I was still suffering for all the hurt they'd caused. And there was nothing I could do to stop it, nothing I could do to escape it.

"Don't listen to him, Rory," Ian said. "Your parents might have been Reapers, but that doesn't mean you have to be one too."

"Says the guy with the Reaper brother," Drake replied in a snide tone.

Ian ignored him and looked at me. "Don't listen to them," he repeated. "Do what you want to do. Be what you want to be—not what someone else wants you to be."

"Ian's right," Zoe said. "You're a good person, Rory. Don't let anyone tell you otherwise."

"Shut them up," Drake growled.

This time, all five of the Reapers pointed their swords at

Ian and Zoe. They both opened their mouths like they were going to keep talking to me, but one of the Reapers shoved his sword up against Zoe's side in a clear warning to keep quiet—or else.

Zoe bit back her words, and so did Ian.

Lance stepped in front of me, blocking my view of Ian and Zoe. "Forget about your parents and everything else. Think about us."

I blinked. "Us?"

He nodded. "Us. You and me, Rory. I could tell that you had a crush on me last year. The way you looked at me, the way you smiled at me, the way you laughed at all my jokes."

A hot, embarrassed blush scalded my cheeks. I hadn't realized that I'd been so obvious, and now everyone knew my secret. Could this night get any worse?

Lance gave me a sly look. "And I liked you too. I really did. I was even going to ask you out, but I never got the chance to before your parents were killed. But now…"

"Now what?" I muttered.

"Now I can," he said. "All you have to do is come with me, and we can finally be together, Rory. Wouldn't you like that?"

Lance smiled, showing off his perfect dimples and being supersmooth, suave, and charming. But the sight of his smug face made white-hot rage roar through me. First he threw my parents in my face, then my crush on him. Now he was promising to be my boyfriend if only I would be a good little girl and join the Reapers like he wanted me to.

Did he really think I would do something that stupid? Especially for him? Lance Fuller wasn't cute and charming. Not to me. Not anymore. Now I saw him for what he truly was: a conniving con artist who used his good looks to get whatever he wanted.

Well, he wasn't getting me. Not now, not ever.

In that moment, I wanted to surge forward and attack him with every fiber of my being. I wanted to use all my Spartan skills and instincts to cut Lance to pieces for daring to think that he could smooth-talk me into doing whatever he wanted.

But that would only get Ian and Zoe killed, given the Reapers still watching them. I had to get Lance, Drake, and the other Reapers to lower their guard, at least for a few seconds, so that Ian and Zoe would have a fighting chance.

So I wet my lips and stared at Lance, as though I were actually considering his offer. "You...you like me?" I said in a breathy voice. "You *really* like me?"

Lance grinned again. "Of course I like you, Rory. I've always liked you. We'll be great together, you'll see."

I gave him a small, faint smile, as though his lies made me happy. All the while, though, I kept clutching Babs's hilt, focusing on the feel of my sword in my hand and getting ready for the fight to come.

Lance walked toward me. "Just think of all the fun we'll have, doing whatever we want, whenever we want. Why, if you like, we can even go back to the academy and show all those snotty kids what a real fight looks like. Just think, Rory. You could hurt them all the same way they've been hurting you for months now, ever since they found out about your parents."

I nodded. "You're right. If I were a Reaper, I could do all those things."

"And more," Lance promised. "So much more."

He stopped right in front of me and held out his hand. "So what do you say, Rory? Are you ready to embrace your destiny? Are you ready to become one of us? Are you ready to finally be with me?"

"You're cute, Lance." I smiled at him. "But you're not *that* cute."

I whipped up my sword, lunged forward, and attacked him.

CHAPTER FIFTEEN

Lance's mouth dropped open in surprise. He had really thought I'd agree to become a Reaper, just like that, just because he asked me to. Arrogant idiot.

Lance was still holding the chimera scepter, so I chopped my sword at his hand, hoping to make him drop the artifact, but he used his Roman speed to duck out of the way. But Lance didn't watch where he was going, and he hit the side of the desk hard. His feet slid out from under him, making him curse and fall to his knees.

I'd thought he might be able to dodge me, but that was okay, because I had a plan B. Lance lurching back gave me a clear path all the way across the office, so I charged over and swung my sword at one of the Reapers guarding Ian and Zoe. The Reaper wasn't expecting the attack, and I sliced my sword across his stomach, making him scream and drop to the ground.

"Yeah!" Babs called out, her mouth moving under my hand. "Show him what's what, Rory!"

I grinned. The sword might have been quiet through my confrontation with Lance, but she was in the fight now, and I knew I could count on her.

The other four Reapers snapped up their weapons and started toward me, and Ian and Zoe took advantage of their distraction. Ian reached out, grabbed the shoulder of the closest Reaper, and slammed his fist into the man's masked face. The Reaper's nose crunched, and he grunted with pain, but Ian wasn't done yet. In an instant, he had plucked the other man's sword out of his hand, whirled the weapon around, and stabbed the Reaper in the chest with it. That Reaper screamed and crumpled to the ground, but Ian was already turning to battle the next enemy.

Zoe snapped up her hand, spread her fingers wide, and blasted blue sparks of magic into the face of the Reaper who'd been guarding her. The Valkyrie sparks didn't do any real damage, since they were just flashes of light, but they still made the Reaper yelp in surprise and turn away from her. Zoe yanked her electrodagger out of her purse and pressed it up against the Reaper's side, jolting him with electricity. The Reaper yelped again and staggered back, his entire body twitching. He tripped over a rug, and his head cracked into one of the end tables. He dropped to the floor without another sound.

Ian sliced his sword across the stomach of the second Reaper he'd been battling, so that left one warrior standing for me to attack. The Reaper raised his weapon, ready to block my blow, but I was expecting the move, so I went low, slashing my sword across his thigh instead. His knee buckled, and I surged forward, grabbed his black mask, and slammed his head back against the wall, knocking him out.

The five Reapers were all down, moaning, groaning, and bleeding out from their wounds. I glanced at Ian, then Zoe, who both nodded, telling me they were okay.

Together, the three of us turned to Lance, who had finally gotten back up onto his feet. Drake shoved Lance behind him, then raised his sword into an attack position. A tense, heavy silence fell over the office as the five of us sized each other up, each one waiting for someone to break the standoff and attack.

Lance, I thought. He would be the first one to move. I could tell by the nervous twitch of his eyes and how he kept rubbing his thumb over the gold scepter in his hand. We had to get the artifact away from him before he summoned a room full of chimeras, but we'd have to go through Drake first. I studied Drake, but the Viking was cool, calm, and in control. His posture never shifted from his strong attack stance, and his sword never dipped, not even for a second.

"Ian! Zoe! Rory! Talk to me!" Mateo's voice sounded in my ear. "What's going on? What's happening? Are you guys okay? Takeda and I are still downstairs with the guards! We're coming to help you!"

Nobody answered him. Ian, Zoe, and I were all still focused on Lance and Drake.

"You—you turned me down," Lance sputtered. "No one's ever done that before."

"Did you really think I was going to join the Reapers just because you smiled and told me I was cute?" I rolled my eyes. "Please. You need to rein in your ego, dude."

Lance's face twisted, and anger flashed in his eyes. "So be it," he hissed. "I gave you a chance, Rory. If you won't join us, then you can die, just like all the other members of the Protectorate!"

Thanks to my Spartan instincts, I knew exactly what was going to happen next. I could see it all unfolding in my mind. Only this time, I wasn't three steps ahead of everyone else—I was three steps behind, thanks to Lance and his Roman speed.

Before I could move, much less try to stop him, Lance

waved the gold scepter in the air three times in a sharp figure-eight motion.

Ian and I both surged forward, but three clouds of thick, black smoke boiled out from the end of the scepter, driving us back. I coughed and coughed, trying to clear the sulfur stench out of my lungs. But instead of dissipating the way normal smoke would, these clouds drew in on themselves. In an instant, they solidified into familiar, distinctive shapes.

Three chimeras now stood in the middle of the office, snarling and spewing smoke everywhere.

"Kill her!" Lance ordered the creatures. "Kill the Spartan girl! Kill them all!"

I was a step ahead of Ian, front and center, and all three chimeras sprang at me at once.

"Get back!" I screamed at Ian and Zoe. "Back! Back! Back!"

Ian cursed and pushed Zoe behind him. And that was all I saw before the creatures were on me.

I ducked one chimera, making it slam into the second one, but the third one had a straight shot at me—and me at it. I whirled around, already snapping up Babs for the attack that I knew was coming next.

Crash!

The chimera's paws caught me square on the shoulders and knocked me to the floor. I landed on my back, and the creature fell right on top of me, driving the air out of my lungs, but I wrapped both hands around Babs's hilt and shoved the sword straight up into its heart. The chimera threw back its head and screamed at the mortal wound, making me wince, then disintegrated into a cloud of smoke. I ignored the burning sensation of the smoke slithering across my skin and scrambled back up onto my feet.

Lance growled with frustration that I was still alive, but Drake shoved him toward the glass patio doors at the back of the office.

"Move!" Drake yelled. "Get out of here! Now!"

Lance yanked open one of the doors and sprinted outside. I started after him, but the other two chimeras jumped to their feet and cut me off, so I attacked the creatures.

I swung my sword left and right, spinning, dodging, ducking, and twirling, letting my Spartan killer instincts take over and guide me through the fight. Everything else disappeared except for the feel of Babs's hilt in my hand, the whisper of her blade slicing through the air, the bunch and flex of my muscles stopping the chimeras' attacks, then the quick counterstrikes of my own sword cutting into their bodies.

The creatures screamed, and their blood splattered all over me, but I kept moving, fighting, attacking. Determination raged through me to cut down the chimeras and then do the same thing to Lance.

I battled first one chimera, then the other. Zoe brandished her electrodagger at the creatures and looked for an opening, but she couldn't get into the fight for fear of hitting me, and she couldn't move past me to help Ian either.

The Viking was battling his brother.

Ian and Drake moved back and forth through the office, knocking over chairs, tables, and lamps, snarling and slashing their swords at each other over and over again. Their Viking strength was so great that sparks shot off their blades where the weapons crashed together time and time again. Add those to the blue sparks spitting out of Zoe's fingertips, and I felt like I was standing in the middle of a giant fireworks show.

I sliced my sword across the stomach of the second chimera, making it disappear in a cloud of smoke, then whirled around and stabbed the third creature in the throat. It too vanished, and I finally had a clear path to the patio doors that Lance had gone through. I headed in that direction—

"Ian!" Zoe screamed. "Look out!"

I whirled around.

Drake lashed out with a vicious blow, forcing Ian back. Ian didn't see the Reaper sword lying on the ground behind him, and he stumbled over it and fell down. His head clipped the corner of the desk, stunning him, and his sword slipped from his hand and dropped to the floor.

"Ian!" Zoe screamed again. "Ian!"

She raised her dagger and ran forward, but Drake stepped up and punched her in the stomach. His Viking strength threw her all the way across the room. Zoe hit the wall, rattling the weapons there, and fell to the floor. The hard, bruising impact made blue sparks explode in the air all around her, but they winked out an instant later. Zoe didn't move after that, and I could tell that she was unconscious.

"And now, little brother," Drake hissed, "I'm going to show you what it feels like to die for real."

Drake slashed his sword down, and Ian threw his hand up in a desperate attempt to block the blow.

I rammed my body into Drake's, knocking him away from Ian and sending us both tumbling to the floor. Drake snarled and lashed out with his sword, trying to gut me, but I rolled out of the way. I started to get back up, but I hit one of the unconscious Reapers. My feet got tangled in his long black cloak, and I floundered around on the floor.

"Die, Spartan!" Drake hissed again, lifting his sword high.

Just like Ian, I raised my hand, trying to ward off the deathblow that I knew was coming.

Ian surged forward and threw himself at his brother. He hit Drake around the knees, driving him back against the desk. Drake lashed out with his sword, slicing it all the way across Ian's arm, shoulder, and back. Ian yelled with pain and fell to the floor.

I finally managed to kick free of the Reaper cloak and get back up onto my feet. I swung my own sword out in a wide, reckless arc. Not because I had any chance of hitting Drake but to make him lurch away from Ian and keep him from killing the other Viking.

It worked.

Drake snarled, turned around, and ran out the same patio door Lance had gone through.

I rushed over to Ian. "Are you okay?"

He waved his hand, blood dripping off his fingers. "I'm fine! Go! Get him! Don't let him get away!"

I hesitated, my gaze flicking over to Zoe's still form.

"Go!" Ian shouted again. "Go! I'll take care of Zoe! Get Lance and Drake!"

I nodded at him, then turned and ran through the open patio door, chasing after my enemies.

CHAPTER SIXTEEN

The door led out to a stone patio that overlooked a large heated pool. Dozens of kids splashed in the water, while others lounged around on chairs all around the pool, laughing, talking, texting, and drinking.

I ran over to the iron railing and scanned the crowd below, trying to figure out where Lance and Drake had gone.

There they were.

I spotted Lance on the far side of the pool, his phone against his ear, trying to worm his way through the crowd. He got stuck behind a group of giggling girls and glanced up at the patio, checking to see if anyone was following him. His eyes widened when he saw me standing there. No doubt Lance had been hoping that the chimeras had killed me and the others. He should have known better. I was a Spartan. It was going to take more than a few monsters to murder me.

"Hey! Watch where you're going!" a voice called out down below.

I looked in that direction and spotted Drake shoving another guy out of his way. The other guy flew through the air and landed in the pool with a loud *splat!* Water sprayed everywhere, making the other kids shriek with laughter.

"Run, you idiot!" Drake yelled at Lance. "Run! Now!"

Lance kept staring at me, his face twisting with rage at the fact that I was still alive. The feeling was definitely mutual. I moved toward the steps to chase after him, but Lance lifted his hand, the gold scepter glimmering in his fingers. I froze. Lance gave me an evil grin and drew back the scepter, like he was going to summon more chimeras, but Drake broke free of the crowd, ran over to him, and shoved his hand down.

"Forget about her!" Drake yelled. "There's no time! The Protectorate's here! We have to leave! Now!"

He pushed Lance forward, and the two of them shoved their way through the crowd, heading toward the lawn on the far side of the pool. From there, they could easily vanish into the woods beyond.

More and more shouts rose up, and several men and women wearing long gray cloaks streamed out of the mansion and into the pool area. Through my earbud, I could hear Takeda barking out orders, trying to coordinate with the Protectorate warriors, but I ignored his shouts. The warriors were on the opposite end of the pool from Lance and Drake, and they wouldn't reach the Reapers in time.

But I could.

I tightened my grip on Babs, pounded down the stairs, and chased after Lance and Drake. Pushing past the other kids was almost like being in a fight, and I let my Spartan instincts take over and show me which way to move, when to sprint ahead, when to fall back, and when to dart around.

None of the other kids batted an eye at my running past them, a sword in my hand and blood covering my clothes. A few kids glanced at me as I rushed by, but no one called out or followed me to see what was going on. Of course not. They were all too busy partying to pay any attention to the danger they were in.

I skirted around tables, leaped over lounge chairs, and plowed through groups of kids, trying to catch up to Lance and Drake. I even knocked a couple of guys into the pool, although they howled with delight, thinking it was all part of the fun. Warm water cascaded all over me, soaking me to the bone, but I shoved my wet hair out of my eyes and kept going.

Up ahead, Lance and Drake had already reached the lawn, and they crossed it and sprinted into the dark woods beyond. I finally broke free of the kids around the pool and followed them.

It took me less than a minute to reach the woods. The trees crowded together, and the dense tangle of leaves and branches blocked out most of the light from the pool area and the mansion. Unlike many of the Mythos kids, I didn't have enhanced senses, so I had to slow down for fear of tripping over a tree root or a loose rock in the darkness. I might be a Spartan, but even I couldn't fight on a broken ankle. Still, I moved as quickly and quietly as possible, peering into the shadows and searching for the telltale glint of a sword or the faint glitter of someone's eyes—

Crack!

A tree branch slammed into my back, making me grunt with pain and fall down on my hands and knees. I lost my grip on Babs, and the sword tumbled away, smacked up against a nearby tree trunk, and clattered to the ground.

"Rory!" Babs cried out, her eye widening. "Behind you!"

I rolled to the side, and a sword bit into the dirt where my body had been a moment ago. I looked up. The Reapers loomed over me, Lance clutching the tree branch that he had hit me with and Drake raising his sword for another strike. I snapped up one hand, desperate to ward off the brutal blow, even as I kicked myself backward on the ground and clawed my other hand through the dirt and dead leaves, trying to find a loose stick or a rock or something—anything—that I could use to defend myself.

"Die, Spartan!" Drake brought his sword down.

Clang!

A silver katana banged into Drake's weapon, stopping it from cutting into me. Suddenly, Takeda was there, along with Mateo, who was also holding a sword. Lance and Drake turned and ran off deeper into the woods, with Takeda and Mateo charging after them. In an instant, all four of them had vanished.

I scrambled to my feet, grabbed Babs, and whirled around, ready to get back into the fight. I could hear Takeda and Mateo yelling through my earbud, but I couldn't see them, so I didn't know which way to go. Shadows cloaked everything around me, and I couldn't pick out any movements or trails in the darkness.

Clash-clash-bang!

Clash-clash-bang!

Swords crashed together in a loud, violent chorus, but I couldn't pinpoint which direction the noises were coming from. After a few seconds, the sounds vanished. In the distance, I thought I heard a car engine rumble to life, along with the squeal of tires. If Lance and Drake had gotten into a vehicle, they were gone. But I didn't know for sure, so I held my position in case the sound was some kind of trick and the Reapers decided to double back this way.

Footsteps scuffed through the fallen leaves, heading in my direction, and I raised my sword into an attack position. A few seconds later, Takeda appeared, with Mateo following him.

I let out a tense breath and lowered my weapon. "What happened?"

Takeda shook his head. "They had a car waiting at the edge of the woods. We lost them. I'm sorry, Rory."

"It's okay," I said, even though it wasn't. "We need to get back to the mansion. Ian and Zoe are hurt."

Takeda nodded and headed in that direction. Mateo stopped and squeezed my shoulder, letting me know that he was glad I was okay, then followed the older man. I sighed, slid Babs back into her scabbard, and headed after them.

By the time we made it back to the mansion, the kids around the pool had finally realized that something was wrong. So had everyone in the house. Someone had cut off the insanely loud music, and the students huddled in groups, being questioned by the Protectorate members.

The party was definitely over.

I pointed out the steps I'd raced down earlier, and Takeda, Mateo, and I climbed up to the third-floor office where Ian and Zoe were.

Zoe was awake and sitting up against the wall, although her hazel eyes were distant and unfocused, as if she wasn't really seeing what was in front of her. She kept blinking and peering at the dagger in her hand like she didn't know if it belonged to her. I'd seen that dazed look before, and I knew she had a concussion.

Ian crouched down beside her, making sure she was all right, even though he was hurt just as badly as she was. His shirt was torn, and blood oozed out of the deep gash that Drake had sliced all the way across his arm, shoulder, and back.

Takeda looked them over, making sure they were okay for now, then pulled his phone out of his pants pocket, hit some buttons, and started talking to someone. I yanked out my earbud and stuffed it into my jeans pocket so I wouldn't have to listen to his conversation. Mateo did the same, and the two of us headed over to the others.

"Are you guys all right?" Mateo asked, his face creasing with worry.

"Just fine and dandy," Zoe said, her words slurring a bit.

Ian grimaced and slowly straightened up. Every movement made more blood trickle out of his wound, and he swayed on his feet again, as though he might pass out from the pain. "We'll live," he rasped. "That's what matters, right?"

Mateo helped Zoe to her feet, while I went over and put my arm under Ian's good shoulder. He stepped forward, trying to shrug me off, and almost fell on his face, but I grabbed him around the waist and steadied him.

"You need to lean on me, Viking," I said. "Whether you like it or not."

Ian opened his mouth like he was going to argue, but he clamped his lips shut. That alone told me how much he was hurting.

"Tell me that you got them," he rasped again.

I shook my head. "I'm sorry. We lost them in the woods."

Ian's gaze locked onto the black and red Reaper mask that Drake had left behind on the desk. Fresh pain glimmered in his gray eyes, and I knew it wasn't caused by his wounds. Once again, my heart ached for him and this new, shocking betrayal he'd suffered.

"C'mon," I said in a gentle voice. "There's nothing else we can do tonight. Let's get out of here."

Ian stared at the Reaper mask a second longer. Then he nodded and let me guide him out of the ruined office.

CHAPTER SEVENTEEN

Two hours later, we were back in the Bunker. Takeda had used his magic to heal everyone's wounds, including my bumps and bruises, and we had all showered and put on clean, blood-free clothes. Now we were gathered around the briefing table, along with Aunt Rachel.

Thanks to the security cameras and our earbuds, Takeda had seen and heard most of what had happened in the mansion, but Ian, Zoe, and I still recapped everything for him, including Lance trying to get me to become a Reaper and join him, Drake, and the mysterious Sisyphus.

"And you have no idea who Sisyphus could be?" Takeda asked. "Or what he wants with you?"

I shook my head. "I've never heard of anyone by that name before, except for the guy in the classic myth."

"You're absolutely sure?" he asked again. "No one comes to mind? Not even someone your parents might have mentioned to you?"

"Rory said she didn't know anything," Aunt Rachel said. "She would tell you if she did."

"I know she would," Takeda replied.

Aunt Rachel crossed her arms over her chest, annoyed by his ever-calm tone.

Takeda eyed her a moment, then looked at the rest of us again. "So we don't know who Sisyphus is, and we still don't know what the Reapers are planning. Lance Fuller was our best lead—our only lead. Now he's gone, and we have no idea where the Reapers might be. Or more important, where they might strike next." Takeda rubbed his forehead, as though he had a migraine, in a rare sign of frustration.

We all slumped in our chairs as the cold, hard reality of the situation set in. My first mission with Team Midgard had not been a rousing success. More like a complete and utter failure. The others looked as sick and exhausted as I felt, and a sense of defeat hung over the room like a dark cloud.

"What about Drake?" Ian asked.

Takeda quit massaging his forehead. "What about Drake?"

"You haven't said anything about Drake. I told you that he was alive. That he had survived the warehouse explosion. My brother. I told you that he was alive and here in Colorado, and you haven't said one word about him. Not one single *word*."

Takeda shrugged, but an emotion flared in his eyes, ruining his calm façade. It almost looked like…guilt.

Ian picked up on it too, and he leaned forward. "Wait a second. You're not surprised that Drake is alive. Not at all. Did you—did you *know* that he was alive?"

Takeda paused a moment before answering. "I had my suspicions."

Ian shot to his feet, making his chair topple to the floor with a loud bang. "Your suspicions? What does that mean?"

"You know as well as I do that the Protectorate never found Drake's body in the rubble. Officially, he was declared dead, but the possibility always existed that he had somehow survived."

Ian's hands clenched into fists. "You never told me that."

Takeda's face softened. "You were having a hard enough time coming to terms with the fact that Drake was a Reaper. I didn't want to say anything about him possibly being alive. Not until I knew for certain that he was."

"And when did you know?" Ian snapped. "Because I'm guessing it was before tonight."

Takeda sighed, the soft sound laced with heavy regret. "I always suspected that Drake might still be alive, but it seemed far more likely when we put the Midgard together and discovered that a Reaper student was planning to steal an artifact. Once we realized that student was Lance, I grew even more suspicious. I knew that Lance's dad and Drake had worked together at the New York warehouse, and it seemed likely that Drake was the one who'd recruited Lance to become a Reaper."

"But I signed up for the Midgard weeks ago…" Ian's voice trailed off, and fresh anger sparked in his eyes as a new thought occurred to him. "The Midgard. This whole mission. It's all been about finding Drake, hasn't it?"

Takeda nodded. "Part of it, yes. I knew that Drake was Sisyphus's top lieutenant. I thought that if we could find Drake, then he would lead us to Sisyphus and all the artifacts the Reapers have stolen."

Instead of appeasing him, Takeda's confession only made Ian angrier. "All this time, you knew that my brother was alive, and you let me think that he was dead—that I had *killed* him," Ian snarled in a loud, angry voice. "How could you do that to me?"

"Because I didn't have any way of actually proving it, and I didn't want to get your hopes up in case I was wrong." Takeda shook his head. "Drake's betrayal hurt you so much. I didn't want you to get hurt again by realizing that your brother was still alive. That Drake could be cruel enough to let you think you'd killed him. You had done enough already—sacrificed enough already. I didn't want to ruin whatever love you might have left for your brother on top of everything else."

A tense, heavy silence fell over the room. Everyone else glanced back and forth between Takeda and Ian, but I stared at the Viking. For once, his guard was down, and his hurt was written all over his face for everyone to see. For the third time tonight, my heart ached for him. The two of us were far more alike than different. Both of us had been lied to and betrayed by the people we'd loved the most.

"But I *trusted* you. After everything that happened with Drake, you and Zoe and Mateo were the only ones I trusted. How could you do this to me?" Ian asked, his voice dropping to a ragged whisper. "How *could* you?"

Takeda winced, guilt creasing his features. He opened his mouth to explain, but Ian snapped up his hand, cutting him off.

"Forget it," he growled. "I don't want to hear it right now."

Ian whirled around, kicked his chair out of the way, and stormed out of the briefing room.

Once again, that tense, heavy silence fell over the room.

Takeda reached down, picked up some papers, and started shuffling them from one side of the table to the other. He didn't look at anyone, but his lips pinched into a tight line, and his fingers curled around the papers like he wanted to rip them all to shreds. It was the most emotion I had seen him show so far.

He hadn't liked lying to Ian, but he had done it anyway because he'd thought it was the best thing for the Viking. Just like my parents had lied to me about being Reapers. I could understand Takeda's reasoning—and my parents' too—but that didn't lessen the sting of what they'd done. I didn't know which betrayal was worse, Takeda wanting to protect Ian from his brother or my parents wanting to protect me from their secret lives as Reapers.

"Well," Zoe drawled. "That went well. *Not.*"

She started to get to her feet, but I got up instead and waved my hand. "Don't worry. I'll go talk to him. Unfortunately, I have experience with this sort of thing." I looked at Aunt Rachel. "I'll see you at home later tonight. Okay?"

She nodded.

I left the briefing room and started searching the Bunker for Ian. It didn't take me long to find him. All I had to do was follow the loud crashing, clanging, and banging of a weapon slamming into a target over and over again.

I found Ian in the training room, whacking at a plastic dummy and hacking it to pieces with his battle ax. I stood in the doorway and watched him. After about two minutes, he got tired of cutting up the poor dummy, dropped his ax on the mat, and stalked over to one of the boxing bags dangling from the ceiling. Ian didn't bother taping up his hands. Instead, he started punching the bag over and over again, even though his knuckles quickly bruised from the vicious repeated blows.

"You know that's not going help anything, right?" I

called out. "Busting up your hands hurts you a lot more than it hurts the bag. Trust me, I know."

Ian ignored me and kept right on hitting the heavy bag, his blows even harder than before. I wasn't lying. I did know what he was going through. Okay, okay, so the brother I thought I'd killed in self-defense hadn't suddenly come back from the dead. But when I'd learned the truth about my parents, I had felt the same guilt, rage, and disgust that Ian was experiencing right now. I also knew that he didn't want to talk about it any more than I had wanted to talk about my feelings back then. Or wanted to talk about them right now. But one thing had helped me, and I thought it might help him too.

So I went over and grabbed the bag, stopping its sharp swings. Ian glared at me for interrupting, but I stared right back at him. I had faced down far scarier things than an angry Viking, including Loki and an entire academy full of Reapers. This was nothing compared with that. At least, that's what I kept telling myself, even as I tried not to notice Ian's broad shoulders and muscled chest and how his biceps bulged and flexed with every breath he took.

"What are you looking at?" he muttered, and lowered his fists to his sides.

I shook my head and dropped my eyes from his chest. Now was not the time to think about how gorgeous he was. "Instead of busting yourself up and having to get healed again, why don't you do something a little more productive?"

"Like what?" he growled.

"Like get out of here. Go somewhere calm and quiet and clear your head for a little while. I can help you with that, if you want."

"And why would you want to help me?" he growled again. "I haven't exactly been nice to you these past couple of days."

I shrugged. "We're part of a team now, and teammates help each other, right?"

Ian looked at me, his anger warring with his curiosity. Finally, though, his curiosity won out. "What do you have in mind?"

I grinned. "You'll see."

Chapter Eighteen

"This is a bad idea," Ian said. "A really, really bad idea."

"Why, Viking, I had no idea that you were afraid of heights," I said, a teasing note creeping into my voice.

"I'm not afraid of heights," he protested. "Just of falling off them."

I turned away so he wouldn't see my smile.

Fifteen minutes ago, we'd snuck out of the Bunker and ridden the secret elevator back up to the second floor. Then I had used a paper clip to open the door to the stairs that led all the way up to the library roof, where we were now standing.

The roof was an enormous square, just like the library tower itself. A gray stone walkway wrapped around the area, while a matching stone balcony cordoned off the roof from the open air and a five-story drop below.

Golden light from inside the library streamed up through the stained-glass mosaic in the center of the roof, making it glimmer like a carpet of sparkling jewels. The glass was probably thick and strong enough to hold my weight, but

I'd never walked across it. I hadn't wanted my boots to dirty the colorful patterns. Looking down at the gleaming glass from this angle made me feel like I was standing in one of the wildflower fields at the Eir Ruins, and I didn't want to do anything to spoil that illusion.

It was almost midnight, and the moon hung big and bright in the sky, surrounded by thousands of silver stars. Down below, lights burned in the other buildings on the quad, as well as in the student dorms in the distance, but no one moved or stirred, and the campus was still and quiet. A cool, crisp breeze gusted over the roof, and I drew in a deep breath, letting the fresh mountain air sweep away all the horrible things that had happened tonight.

I had discovered the library roof last year, on a day when I'd been particularly desperate to escape from everyone and everything that was bothering me. From what I could tell, nobody ever came up here but me, and it had quickly become my secret hiding spot, the one place where I could always find a little peace and quiet, no matter how bad things got. Up here, the memory of finding my parents' bodies didn't bother me quite as much as it did when I was down in the main part of the library. Plus, I liked looking down through the stained glass and catching glimpses of the various library levels below. I imagined that was what the gods did, up on Mount Olympus or wherever they were.

Well, except for Sigyn, of course. She seemed to be the rare goddess who walked among us mortals. I had looked for her—as Raven—on campus today, but I hadn't spotted her anywhere. Maybe she had already gone back to the North Carolina academy. Or maybe Sigyn could be in two places at once. She was a goddess, after all.

Ian glanced over the stone balcony and down at the quad. He blanched a little and stepped back from the ledge. "Tell me again what we're doing up here in the middle of the night?"

"Well, right now, we're enjoying the peace and quiet. But if we're lucky, we might get to go for a ride."

He frowned. "What do you mean?"

Instead of answering him, I moved over to a corner of the roof. Over the past year, I had spent a lot of time here, and I had decided to make myself as comfortable as possible. So I'd snuck some supplies up here, including a couple of lawn chairs, a cooler full of bottled water and snacks, and, most important, three lanterns.

I dragged the lanterns out from the corner, arranged them in a tight circle, and turned them on. Together, they formed a bright beam of light that shot up into the night sky. It was my version of a superhero beacon, but what it summoned was much, much cooler than any costumed crusader.

"What are you doing?" Ian asked. "What's that for?"

"You'll see."

I went over and rested my elbows on the balcony railing. Ian glanced at the lanterns again, still wondering what they were for, then came over and joined me. We stood there, side by side, soaking up the silence. I was perfectly content to stare out over the silent, empty quad below, but Ian kept tapping his fingers on the railing, shifting on his feet, and sneaking glances at me. This went on for about five minutes before he finally opened his mouth to say something—

Two shadows suddenly fell over us, blocking out the moon and starlight. Gusts of air whistled down from the sky, tangling my hair. Ian's head snapped up. He gasped and staggered back, and I hid another grin.

The gryphons always loved making a dramatic entrance.

Two Eir gryphons hovered above the library roof. Each one had the head of an eagle and the body of a lion, and strong, powerful wings were attached to their backs. Their fur and wings were both a beautiful bronze that gleamed in the lantern light, as though the creatures were made of polished metal instead of flesh and blood. Their eyes were also a warm, burnished bronze, while their beaks and claws were as black and shiny as ebony. In many ways, the gryphons were a lot like the chimeras, but I thought their combination of bronze fur and wings made the gryphons uniquely beautiful, unlike the chimeras with their grotesque black prowler heads, ram's horns, and scorpion-stinger tails.

The two gryphons flapped their wings a final time and dropped down to the roof. One of them was enormous, a strong, fully grown male more than twice my size. I had named him Balder, after the Norse god of light. The other gryphon, his baby, was much smaller but still a force to be reckoned with. I had dubbed him Brono, after the god Balder's son. The names felt appropriate to me, and the gryphons seemed to like them.

"Hey, fellas," I said. "Thanks for coming."

I looked at Ian, who was standing ramrod straight, shocked into stillness by the sight of the gryphons. I rolled my eyes and turned off the lanterns. Then I went over to the creatures and hugged both their necks. Their bronze fur and wings felt soft and smooth under my fingertips, and they smelled crisp and clean, like the mountain air they soared through with such ease. Brono, the baby, gently head-butted me when I drew back, and I laughed and scratched his head again.

"You've gotten even bigger since the last time I saw you a couple of weeks ago," I said. "Pretty soon you're going to be as strong as your dad."

Brono lifted his head and twitched his wings with pride. So did Balder.

I petted both gryphons a final time, then turned to Ian. "Want to go for a ride?"

He shook his head and opened his mouth like he was going to say no. So I raised my eyebrows and crossed my arms over my chest in an obvious silent challenge.

Ian scowled, realizing that I would never let him live it down if he chickened out. "Sure. Sounds like fun," he muttered, although his tone indicated that he thought it was going to be anything but fun.

Balder hunkered down, and I climbed up onto the gryphon's broad back and held my hand out to Ian. He stared at me, then at the gryphon. I thought he was going to back out, but he swallowed, stepped forward, took my hand, and climbed up behind me.

"What do I do with my hands?" Ian asked.

"If I were you, I would hold on to me."

He sighed, his warm breath kissing the back of my neck, but he placed his hands on my waist. I dug my own hands and legs into the gryphon's fur and body, getting a good grip on the creature so we wouldn't fall off. Behind me, Ian did the same with his legs. When I was sure we were both firmly anchored in place, I stroked Balder's head, telling him we were ready.

"And away we go," I whispered, although I doubted that Ian heard me.

Whoosh!

We left the ground in a rush of air and wings. Behind me, Ian sucked in a surprised breath, and his hands tightened around my waist. Balder had also felt the Viking's shock. The gryphon glanced over his shoulder at me, and I could see the laughter shining in his bronze eyes.

Balder would never let us fall. Ian would figure that out sooner or later.

Balder and Brono climbed higher and higher, their wings pumping faster and faster, streaking up through the sky like rockets. In seconds, it seemed we were close enough to touch the moon and stars themselves. I laughed, but the wind tore away the happy sound.

"Isn't this great?" I yelled.

I didn't know if Ian heard me, but he tightened his grip on my waist. I was going to take that as a yes. Either way, it was too late for him to get off now.

We soared through the night sky. A few lights glimmered far, far below in the town of Snowline Ridge, but we quickly zoomed past them and climbed up the mountain. The evergreen forests and rocky crevices passed by in a blur, although the sharp, tangy scent of the pine trees tickled my nose, even at this height.

I closed my eyes and focused on the wind whistling in my ears, the cool, crisp air tangling my hair, the brush of Balder's powerful wings rising and falling against my body, making me feel as light and weightless as a feather. Riding on the gryphons always gave me a sense of peace, of freedom, that I had never experienced anywhere else.

Our ride ended all too soon.

In minutes, the gryphons had flown us all the way from the academy up the mountain to the Eir Ruins. Balder and Brono landed in the main courtyard, which was full of wildflowers, herbs, and even a few small trees. The moon and starlight bathed the plants and surrounding stones in a soft silver sheen, making the area look even lovelier than it had when I'd been here in my dream—or whatever that had been—with Sigyn last night.

I swung my legs over the side of Balder's back and slid down off the gryphon. Ian did the same, at a much slower speed, and he wobbled when his boots hit the ground. I laughed, and he scowled at me, but his expression quickly melted into a sheepish smile, and I could tell that he'd enjoyed the ride as much as I had.

Ian hesitated, then gave Balder's side a soft pat. The gryphon snorted his amusement, then wandered away and started snatching up wildflowers with his beak and eating the delicate petals and stems.

Ian glanced from one side of the courtyard to the other. "Are these the Eir Ruins? After Takeda told us that we were coming to the Colorado academy, I read up on them, but they're even more beautiful than the pictures in my history books."

"I love them," I said in a soft voice. "And the gryphons too."

He nodded. "I can see why."

"C'mon. I'll show you around."

On an impulse, I reached out and grabbed Ian's hand. He jerked back, as startled by the motion as I was, but he didn't let go.

And neither did I.

We stood there, frozen in place, staring into each other's eyes. Like the ruins, Ian was even more handsome in the moonlight, his face looking as though it had been carved out of marble, and his gray eyes seeming to be the exact color of the silver tint that coated everything around us—

Brono head-butted me again, jealous that I wasn't paying any attention to him, and my hand slipped free of Ian's. I laughed, but it was a high, nervous sound, and I quickly turned to the baby gryphon and started petting him to hide how much I had enjoyed the feel of Ian's warm hand in mine, his strong body close to mine, his soft breath kissing my cheeks.

Ian cleared his throat, as determined to ignore the moment as I was. "You said something about a tour?"

"Yep. This way."

I petted Brono a final time, and the gryphon joined his father. While the gryphons grazed, I led Ian all around the ruins, pointing out the different types of wildflowers and herbs, the gurgling stream, the fountain in the center of the courtyard, and the animal carvings that covered many of the broken, crumbling stones.

We ended up sitting on a pair of round, smooth boulders at the edge of the ruins, which offered an incredible view. The rocky ruins ended in a wide canyon that was so deep I couldn't see the bottom of it this late at night. On the far side, the forest took over and rolled like a dark carpet all the way down to the valley below. In the distance, the lights of Snowline Ridge burned bright and steady, along with those of the academy.

Ian peered down at the steep drop below and scooted a little farther back on his rock. "What is it with you and heights? I'm starting to think you're dragging me around to all these high places just to torture me." His words might be grumpy, but his tone was light and teasing, and he seemed more relaxed than at any other time since I'd met him.

"Well, if it makes you feel any better, Aunt Rachel isn't crazy about heights either. So you're not the only scaredy-cat around here."

Ian straightened up. "I am a Viking. I am most certainly *not* a scaredy-cat."

I gave him a look.

He winced. "Except when it comes to heights."

"Glad to know that's the only chink in your armor."

He shrugged, but his face crinkled into a smile.

We sat there, enjoying the view. The gryphons moved back and forth in the courtyard, still eating wildflowers. The wind whistled around us, and I pulled my knees up to my chest and wrapped my arms around them, hugging myself into a tight ball to help keep warm. The motion made my jacket sleeve ride up, and my silver charm bracelet and heart locket glimmered in the moonlight.

"That's pretty," Ian said. "Did your aunt give that to you?"

I grimaced. "Sort of. Aunt Rachel gave it back to me. It was originally a gift from my parents on my birthday last year. I used to wear it all the time. Until, well, you know."

Ian looked at me. "How did it feel? To realize that they were Reapers?"

"You mean that they were the bad guys and they'd been lying to me my whole life about who and what they really were?"

He nodded.

I let out a harsh, bitter laugh that echoed out from this side of the canyon, hit the far side of the rocks, and bounced right back to me, like a slap in the face. "It was the worst moment of my life."

"What happened?" Ian asked in a soft, sympathetic voice.

I fiddled with my bracelet and locket instead of looking at him. "I was in class, and everybody started getting these text alerts on their phones. The next thing I knew, everyone was staring at me and whispering about me. Then a couple of the academy administrators showed up, took me out of class, and told me what was going on. They tried to be nice and vague about it, saying that my parents had been in an accident, but I didn't believe them. I ran off and went straight to the library. People tried to stop me, but I shoved past them. That's when I saw my parents lying on the library floor, dead and bloody, with their black Reaper robes billowing out all around them." My voice dropped to a whisper. "That's when I realized what they really were."

"I'm sorry," Ian said. "I know what that's like. I couldn't believe it when Drake turned his sword on me. When he told me that he was a Reaper, that he had been a Reaper for years, and that I was going to join him—or else."

I nodded, and we both fell silent again, lost in our own thoughts, memories, and heartache. But these feelings bubbled up inside me, shaping themselves into words— words that I'd never told anyone before, words that I couldn't hold back any longer.

"Do you know what the worst part is?" I said.

"What?"

I let out another bitter laugh. "I was actually *happy* that they were gone. At least, at first. Once all the other kids learned that my parents were Reaper assassins, everything in my life imploded. The few friends I had pretended they didn't know me anymore, and all the other kids treated me like I had the plague, like they were going to catch being a Reaper just by sitting next to me at lunch. Everybody gossiped about me, but no one would actually talk to me. I blamed my parents for that—for *all* of that—and for a long time, I was happy that they were dead. I was so *angry* at them for so many things. For being Reapers, for never telling me, for making me the most hated person at the academy."

"And now?" Ian asked.

I sighed. "And now I just miss them. More than anything else, I wish I could talk to my parents one final time and ask them *why*. Why they were Reapers. Why they did the horrible things they did. Why they didn't tell me what they really were."

"Maybe they were trying to protect you," he suggested. "Maybe they didn't want you to become a Reaper. I read the Protectorate reports. According to what Gwen Frost saw with her psychometry magic, your parents were trying to get out. They were trying to leave the Reapers for good."

"And Covington killed them for it." I spat out the words.

Covington had been the head librarian and the person in charge of giving my parents all their Reaper assignments. He was the one who'd told them where to go, what to steal, and whom to kill. When my parents tried to leave the Reapers, Covington stabbed them both in the back and then made it look like my parents had attacked him, killed several students, and tried to steal artifacts from the Library of Antiquities.

Thanks to Gwen, the truth had eventually come out, and she and her friends had helped me capture Covington here at the Eir Ruins. The librarian was in prison now, locked away where he couldn't hurt anybody else. At least, not physically. But Covington was still hurting me every single day, whether he realized it or not. He had taken my parents away from me, and nothing would ever change that.

"Maybe you're right about them wanting me to take a different path, to be a good person, a good warrior, a good Spartan." My voice rasped with emotion. "But I'll never know for sure, will I? That hurts more than anything else. That I'll never know what they really wanted for me."

Ian nodded, and once again, we lapsed into silence for a long time. Another breeze gusted over the rocks, making us both shiver, but we stayed still. Neither one of us wanted to move and break the fragile truce, the tenuous peace, between us.

"At least your parents tried to get out." Ian's voice was as rough and raspy as mine had been. "Drake never did that. He never wanted out. He *likes* being a Reaper. He likes stealing and betraying and killing anyone who stands in his way. He proved that again tonight at Lance's mansion. He's the same as he always was."

"And how was that?"

Ian sighed. "He was the older brother, and he was always so much cooler and stronger and smarter than me. I looked up to him, you know? He was my bloody *hero*, right up until the moment I found out that he was a Reaper."

"What about your parents? Where are they? Zoe told me they travel a lot, working for the Protectorate."

Ian sighed again. "Yeah, they're always gone, collecting artifacts and fighting Reapers in different parts of the world. They were on a mission when everything happened with Drake. They didn't even come home for his funeral. They said they couldn't leave before their mission was finished, but I think they were embarrassed and didn't want to hear all their Protectorate friends gossiping about how their son had turned out to be a Reaper. How Drake had ruined the Hunter family name and legacy."

He picked up a jagged rock and started turning it over and over in his hand.

I winced. It sounded like Ian's parents didn't care much about him or Drake, if they had stayed away to avoid hearing people gossip about them. My parents might have been Reapers, but at least they had always been there for me, and I knew they had loved me.

"After Drake supposedly died, I was a mess," Ian confessed. "But Zoe and Mateo helped me through it. The three of us have always been best friends, ever since we were little. Zoe's parents pretty much took me in, and Zoe was always there, making sure I was eating and sleeping and not wearing myself out training too hard. Mateo too. He was always trying to cheer me up by letting me beat him at soccer or tennis or video games."

"And what about Takeda? It seems like the two of you are also pretty close."

Ian nodded. "We are. Takeda was the one who kept Drake and me updated about where our parents were and what they were doing, and he always checked in on us while they were gone. Takeda trained both of us, and he was always there whenever I had a problem or needed to talk to an adult. He's been more like a father to me than my own dad ever has been."

"So Takeda's probably hurting too," I pointed out. "Over Drake's betrayal and everything else that's happened."

"Yeah," Ian admitted. "But that didn't give him the right to lie about Drake still being alive. And it doesn't change what Drake is now, what he's *always* been. Or the fact that I was too blind to see it."

His hand tightened around the rock, and he reared back his arm and threw it as hard as he could. The rock disappeared into the canyon below, and several seconds passed before I heard it hit bottom. Even then, it was a soft sound, little more than a whisper, but Ian still flinched, as if it were as loud as a clap of thunder roaring out all of his mistakes.

He looked at me, regret filling his face. "I'm sorry that I've been such a jackass to you, Rory. It's just...when Takeda told me that your parents were Reapers, I thought that you might be like Drake. That you might fool me the same way he had. And I couldn't stand that. Not again. Especially not from you."

"What's so special about me? I'm just a Spartan girl, going to Mythos Academy like all the other warrior kids."

He shook his head. "No, you're not just another warrior. You're so much more, so much *better* than that. I saw how all the other kids treated you when you stepped onto the quad the first day of school. But you walked right through the gauntlet of them anyway. You were—are—so strong, so brave. I was jealous of you."

"Why?"

"Because I couldn't have done that. I couldn't have walked past all those kids. Not without screaming, going crazy, and punching everyone in sight. That's another reason I joined the Midgard. So I wouldn't have to go back to school in New York right now and deal with the fact that everyone knows my brother is a Reaper."

"What are you going to do now that you know Drake is alive?" I asked in a soft voice. "That he's here in Colorado and working with Sisyphus."

Ian's face hardened, and determination blazed in his eyes. "I'm going to stop him—no matter what." He hesitated. "I'll even…kill him, if I have to. I don't want to. But if it comes down to him or me or one of you guys on the team, then I will take him out."

I gave him a sad smile. "Then that makes you stronger than me. If my parents were still alive, I don't think I could do the same to them."

"It doesn't make me stronger," Ian replied in a low voice. "It just makes me sadder."

I couldn't argue with that. Then again, I supposed we were both pretty sad, caught in the bad choices our loved ones had made, and struggling to make things right, even though we weren't the ones who'd caused the pain and problems in the first place. Still, I liked sitting here and talking with Ian. Much more than I'd thought I would. I'd brought him up here to clear his head and heart, but he'd helped me clear mine as well.

Ian leaned down and picked a stray wildflower that had somehow managed to bloom in a group of rocks. In the time we'd been sitting here, a pale frost had coated the ground all around us, making everything look encased in ice, including the flower. Still, despite the icy sheen, the delicate white petals gleamed and curled up, protecting a smaller, dark green, heart-shaped blossom in the center of the flower, which glimmered almost like an emerald.

"That's a winterbloom," I said, seeing his puzzled look. "They only blossom when the ground is covered with frost or snow. I think they're some of the prettiest flowers up here."

Ian studied the wildflower. "Me too. The heart in the center reminds me of your locket. Here. You should have it, Rory."

He grinned and held the flower out to me. My breath caught in my throat. No one had ever given me a flower before. At least, no one like Ian.

He frowned, as if realizing what he'd done. I thought he might take back his words, make a joke, and toss the flower away. But then he pressed his lips together and looked at me, his gaze steady on mine. I stared into Ian's eyes and reached for the winterbloom—

Bzzt. Bzzt. Bzzt.

His phone buzzed, startling us both and breaking the spell.

Ian lowered the flower down to his side, pulled his phone out of his jeans pocket, and stared at the message on the screen. "Takeda wants to know where we are. He says it's hours past curfew."

I rolled my eyes. "He's the one who recruited us to be

supersecret spies. And now he's talking about curfew? Kind of ironic, don't you think? That we're old enough to fight Reapers and chimeras but not old enough to know when to go to bed?"

Ian grinned. "Yeah. But you were right before. Takeda would never admit it, but he's hurting over Drake just as much as I am. This is him trying to make peace and watching out for me. I'll tell him we're on our way back to the academy."

Ian texted Takeda, and I let out a soft whistle and waved my hand, summoning the still-grazing gryphons back to our sides. I started to climb onto Balder's back, but Ian reached out and grabbed my hand.

"Thank you," he said. "For bringing me up here. For listening. It was really nice of you, especially given how awful I was to you before."

I smiled and squeezed his hand back. "You're welcome."

He stared at me, and I found myself swaying closer to him and falling, falling, falling into his stormy gray eyes...

Ian cleared his throat, dropped my hand, and stepped back. I curled my fingers into a fist, trying to capture the warmth of his skin against mine, but the sensation quickly faded away, although not the light, dizzy feeling in my heart.

I turned away from him and climbed on top of Balder's back. Ian settled himself behind me, his hands gently curving around my waist. When I was sure he was ready, I scratched the gryphon's head.

"And away we go," I whispered.

A second later, we were airborne and flying back to the academy, but all I could think about was the feel of Ian's body against mine, his warm breath kissing the back of my neck, and how the touch of his hands made my heart soar even higher and faster than the gryphons were flying.

CHAPTER NINETEEN

The gryphons flew us back to the library roof.

I scratched their heads again and thanked them for the ride, and then Balder and Brono sailed up, up, up, and away into the night sky. It was late, and we had classes in a few hours, so Ian and I went our separate ways for the rest of the night. He headed to his dorm, while I walked home to the cottage.

Aunt Rachel was already in bed, but she'd left me a note on the kitchen table saying that a lasagna was warming in the oven. My stomach rumbled, reminding me how long it had been since I'd eaten. So I used some oven mitts to grab the lasagna and dished myself up a generous serving, along with a couple of garlic breadsticks and a garden salad with homemade Italian dressing.

Everything Aunt Rachel cooked was wonderful, and the lasagna was no exception. Layers of pasta sheets, melted mozzarella, rich tomato sauce, and crumbled bits of spicy Italian sausage. The breadsticks had just the right amount of tangy garlic butter slathered on them, while the salad was full of crisp, crunchy vegetables. Best of all, Aunt Rachel had made dark-chocolate fudge with dried cherries for dessert. The rich, decadent treat was the perfect way to finish off my meal.

By the time I'd cleaned up the kitchen and taken a shower, it was after two in the morning, and I was more than ready to go to sleep. I crawled into bed and started to pull the covers up to my chin, but my charm bracelet snagged on the sheets, and I had to stop and work it free.

The moonlight streaming in through my bedroom window made the delicate links gleam like a ring of snow around my wrist, with the locket glimmering like an icy heart in the center of the chain. My fingers stroked over the locket, but for the first time since I had thrown it down on my parents' graves, the sight of the silver charm didn't fill me with anger.

Ian was right. At least my mom and dad had tried to leave the Reapers. I might never know the answers to my questions about my parents, but in the end, they had wanted out of the evil group. That had to count for something. That *did* count for something. Even if I had been too angry, upset, and stubborn to realize it until tonight.

Still thinking of my parents, I put my head down on my pillow, curled my fingers around the heart locket, and drifted off to sleep.

My alarm went off way too early, given how late I'd gone to bed, but I got up, got dressed, and trudged to my classes. And just like usual, none of the other kids talked to me as I walked across the quad. They were all too busy gossiping about Lance's party last night.

"It was great!"

"I had, like, *so* much fun!"

"Yeah, it was terrific! Except for the part where I puked my guts out."

And the conversations went on and on, although another concern quickly crept into the gossip.

"Hey, where's Lance?"

"I haven't seen him this morning."

"Do you think the Protectorate arrested him because we brought a keg to his party?"

So the Protectorate guards hadn't told the other kids what had really happened last night. No surprise there, since Linus Quinn wanted to keep everyone in the dark about the new group of Reapers.

I wondered how long it would take the other students to realize that Lance wasn't coming back to Mythos Academy—ever. One week? Two weeks? Or maybe he would end up like Amanda, here one day, then gone the next, with no one batting an eye at his sudden, unexplained disappearance. It would serve Lance right if no one remembered him, since he'd ordered those chimeras to murder Amanda in the library—and me too last night at the mansion. He was going to pay for that—all of it—and so were Drake and the mysterious Sisyphus.

But the good thing about Lance's party was that everyone was too busy talking about it to hassle me. I actually got through the morning without one single person giving me a dirty look.

By the time lunch rolled around, I was actually in a good mood. We might have lost Lance, Drake, and the chimera scepter last night, but Takeda would use his Protectorate resources to find them again. Once we figured out where they were hiding, we would get the scepter and put them in prison, where they belonged, along with Sisyphus and all the other Reapers.

In the lunch line, I grabbed a burrito stuffed with spicy grilled chicken, black beans, rice, cheese, sour cream, and pico de gallo, along with a couple of chocolate chip cookies, then went over to the corner table where Ian, Zoe, and Mateo were already sitting.

Ian looked up at me and smiled. My heart did a funny little flutter, and I smiled back at him. Then he realized that Zoe was staring at us, and he quickly scowled at me like usual.

"Hey." Ian ducked his head and concentrated on his food.

"Hey," I replied, trying to play it cool.

Mateo had a candy bar in one hand and his phone in the other, so he didn't notice the sudden awkward silence between Ian and me. But Zoe did. She waggled her eyebrows and gave me a knowing look, which I did my best to ignore. I set my tray on the table, plopped down in a chair, and started eating.

Slowly, the awkward silence faded away, and the four of us started talking about our classes, our professors, and more. Even Mateo put down his phone and joined in the conversation. It was all so…*normal.*

After being alone at school for so long, it was nice to hang out with other people. To sit and eat and laugh and talk and not worry about my parents being Reapers or the other kids whispering about me or all the other drama that made up my life.

It was nice having friends again.

I had missed it more than I'd realized, more than I'd thought possible—and I would soon miss it again. When this was all over, Ian, Zoe, and Mateo would go back to the New York academy like they'd planned, and I would be all alone again, except for Aunt Rachel and the gryphons.

The thought jarred me out of my happy bubble. My

hands froze, and I stopped breaking apart the last cookie on my plate.

"Rory?" Mateo asked. "Are you okay? You look like you're about to be sick."

I put the cookie down and pushed my tray away. "I'm fine. Just full, I guess."

I tried to make my tone light and breezy, but it didn't quite come out that way. Ian glanced at me, then at the uneaten cookie, and back again. His gray eyes narrowed. He'd only known me for a few days, but he could still tell that something was wrong, especially since I hadn't finished my dessert. But he didn't say anything, and I was glad for that.

Eventually, the four of us bent our heads together and started talking about what had happened last night, keeping our voices soft so that we wouldn't be overheard.

"As far as I can tell, no one on campus has seen Lance this morning," Ian said.

Mateo held up his phone. "None of the security cameras has caught him coming or going either. Not at his dorm or any of the other buildings. He's definitely not at the academy. I even plugged Lance's picture into the Protectorate facial-recognition database this morning, but he hasn't been spotted on any cameras anywhere in Snowline Ridge or the surrounding area."

"Wouldn't you be hiding out if a bunch of Protectorate spies crashed your party and tried to arrest you last night?" Zoe snarked. "I certainly would."

"Sure," I chimed in. "And I would tell the rest of my Reaper friends who were still at the academy to keep an eye on those spies and let me know what they were up to."

Ian frowned. "You think that Lance told his friends to watch us?"

I shrugged. "I would have. Besides, that's how Reapers work. They never come right out and attack you head-on. Not until they absolutely have to. No, they stay in the shadows and play games and keep their true selves hidden until they're ready to strike."

Ian noticed the bitter tone in my voice. He stared at me, and I knew he was thinking about our talk last night and all the feelings we'd shared about our Reaper relatives. But I didn't want to think about that right now. I'd already obsessed about my parents' betrayal long enough. So I looked out over the dining hall. Ian, Zoe, and Mateo all did the same thing, staring at first one student, then another.

All around us, the other kids laughed and talked and wolfed down their food, since lunch was almost over. No one pointed at our table, no one whispered about us, and no one snuck a sly glance at us and then started texting on their phone. Everything seemed normal, but at Mythos Academy, that was usually when things got the most dangerous.

"If there's one thing I've learned, it's that you need to be careful who you trust," I said. "Lance has a lot of friends. He tried to recruit me to become a Reaper, so maybe he did the same thing to some of the other kids. Everyone needs to watch their backs. At least until we know where Lance is and what he and Drake are planning. We might think Lance is gone, but he could always come back to the academy and surprise us."

Ian nodded. "Rory's right. Everyone needs to be careful. Takeda wants us all down in the Bunker after classes today. Maybe by then, he'll have found out something about Lance and Drake and where they are. See you guys later."

We all murmured our good-byes. Ian and Mateo got to their feet, grabbed their trays, and walked away from the table, leaving me alone with Zoe. She sat back in her chair, crossed her arms over her chest, and gave me another one of those knowing looks.

"So you and Ian, huh?" she asked.

I stiffened. "I don't know what you're talking about."

"Ri-i-ight." She drawled out the word. "You go off and talk to him last night, and now the two of you are being totally awkward and adorable with each other."

"I don't know what you're talking about," I repeated, although I could feel the hot, guilty blush staining my cheeks.

Zoe laughed and waggled her fingers, shooting blue bursts of magic all over the table. "Oh, please. You guys are giving off more sparks than I do."

My face kept getting hotter and hotter, and I started fidgeting in my seat. Zoe kept smirking at me, and I knew she wouldn't stop until I spilled my guts to her. At least, some of them.

I sighed. "Okay, so maybe Ian isn't a complete jackass like I thought he was. But that doesn't mean the two of us are going steady or anything. We just hate each other slightly less than before."

"Ri-i-ight," Zoe drawled again. "Keep telling yourself that."

I sighed again and slumped down in my seat. "Even if I did...like Ian, or whatever, it wouldn't matter anyway. As soon as we find and arrest Lance, Drake, and Sisyphus, you guys will go back to the New York academy and get ready for your next mission."

Zoe picked up her phone from the table and waggled it at me the same way she had waggled her fingers. "Guess what? There are these things called *phones*. And there's this other thing called the *internet*. You might not be familiar with them, but they are both perfect for long-distance relationships."

I rolled my eyes. "Whatever. It still doesn't matter, because Ian and I are not having any relationship, much less a long-distance one."

"We'll see about that. But I'll tell you one thing."

"What?"

Zoe's face turned serious, and she leaned forward and stabbed her finger at me, causing blue sparks of magic to shoot out all over the table again. "Ian's a good guy, and he's been through a lot. I might not be a great fighter, but if you hurt him, then I will run you through with your own sword. Got it?"

I held up my hands in mock surrender. "Got it. I know what it's like to be hurt by the people you care about. I'm not going to do that to Ian. I promise."

Zoe stared at me, but whatever she saw in my face must have satisfied her, because she dropped her hand and sat back in her chair. "Good. Then we won't have a problem, Spartan."

"No, we won't, Valkyrie."

We stared at each other, our expressions serious, but we couldn't stay that way for long. Zoe's lips started twitching, and so did mine. A second later, we were both smiling and laughing, knowing we'd just cemented our new friendship.

I made it through my afternoon classes, then went to the library, snuck through the secret bookcase entrance, and rode the elevator down to the Bunker. The others were already here, and I stood in the doorway watching them.

Takeda sat at the head of the briefing table, flipping

through stacks of papers and photos, while Ian was over at his desk, sharpening his Viking battle ax and other weapons. Mateo pounded away on his laptop, while Zoe was soldering bits of metal onto a broken shield, repairing it.

Nobody was talking, although Takeda's classical music was playing in the background. Everyone was focused on their own projects, and the mood was far less tense than it had been last night. Team Midgard might have had a setback in losing Lance, Drake, and the chimera scepter, but we weren't defeated. Not yet. Not by a long shot.

Takeda sensed my presence and looked up from his reports. "Ah, Rory. There you are. Please come in, and we'll get started."

Takeda picked up the remote and turned off the music. I pulled out a chair at the briefing table and sat down. Ian and Mateo took the seats across from me, while Zoe plopped down in the chair next to mine. Once we were all settled at the table, Takeda got to his feet.

"As you all know, our mission last night was not a success." His voice was as calm as ever, as though he were talking about the weather instead of the fact that the Reapers had gotten away. "While we did take some of the Reapers into custody, Lance and Drake escaped with the chimera scepter. Mateo, where are we in tracking them down?"

Mateo shook his head. "Nowhere. I've double-checked all the security footage from campus today, and Lance and Drake haven't shown up on any of the cameras. I've also checked the footage from the shops in Snowline Ridge. There's no trace of them anywhere near the academy. Lance also turned off his phone, so I can't track him that way."

Takeda nodded. "No doubt Lance and Drake are in hiding

and planning their next move. I've reached out to my Protectorate sources, but so far, no one's spotted them. Which means that we have to find them ourselves—before they strike again. Lance stole that chimera scepter for a reason, and I want to know what Sisyphus plans to do with it."

"And how are we supposed to find them?" Zoe asked.

"I don't know," Takeda admitted. "But we have to try. Let's start by reviewing everything from the mansion last night. Maybe Lance, Drake, or one of the other Reapers left behind something that will lead us to them."

He passed each of us a thick stack of papers and photos, and we all started looking through the files. Much of the information focused on the Reapers from the office fight, who they really were, where they were from, and all their known associates. I didn't recognize any of their names or mug shots, so I moved past those reports and started studying the photos the Protectorate had taken of the mansion and the surrounding area.

The empty cups, cans, and other trash the kids had left behind in the living room. The library safe Ian and Zoe had tried to break into. The overturned furniture, bloody rugs, and other destruction from the office fight. Several footprints in the mud in the woods outside the mansion. Even a set of tire tracks from where Lance and Drake had peeled away in their getaway car.

The photos tracked the mission from beginning to end, but I found myself going back to the shots that showed the office. One picture of the desk caught my eye, showing all the items Lance had pulled out of the drawer. Pens, pencils, and paper clips were strewn all over the top of the desk, and papers littered the floor all around it. Nothing out of the ordinary, except for Drake's black Reaper mask, with those large, creepy red diamond shapes over the eyes. But even that was just a simple harlequin mask, the kind you could buy in any costume shop.

Still, something about the photo bothered me, like there was an obvious clue in the jumble of objects that I should be picking up on. I kept scanning the photo, studying every single part of it, just like I would go back and reread certain passages two or three times whenever I was reading a really good mystery and trying to figure out whodunit. But this was far more important than the satisfaction of figuring out who the villain was before the end of a book.

"What is it?" Zoe asked, nudging me with her elbow. "You've been staring at that same photo for the last five minutes."

"I'm not sure. Hey, Mateo. Can you put this up on one of the monitors?"

I slid the photo across the table to him. Mateo glanced at the reference number stamped on the back and hit some keys on his laptop. A second later, the photo popped up on the center wall monitor. I got up, walked around the table, and stopped in front of the screen so I could have an even better look at the photo.

"What do you see, Rory?" Ian asked.

I shook my head. "I don't know yet."

I stalked back and forth in front of the monitor, examining the photo from top to bottom and side to side. The wooden desk. The pens and pencils strewn across the glossy surface. Drake's Reaper mask perched next to a wad of paper clips. The long, slender papers lying on the floor beside the desk—

My eyes narrowed, and I stopped in front of that part of the photo. Papers...something about those papers...

I remembered Lance reaching into the drawer, pulling

out a handful of papers, and tossing them on top of the desk. The papers had slipped off and landed on the floor, and I'd snuck a glance at them. But they hadn't been papers at all—they'd been *tickets*.

And just like that, I knew the clue that solved the mystery.

I stabbed my finger at the monitor. "Those are tickets to the Fall Costume Ball. Lance pulled them out while he was rooting around inside the desk for the chimera scepter."

Zoe frowned. "So what?"

"So Lance had more than half a dozen tickets. Not just one or two for himself and a date. Why would he have so many tickets printed out? Especially when they get emailed to people's phones too? Unless…"

"Unless he was going to invite all his Reaper friends to crash the costume ball." Ian finished my thought.

"Exactly."

Takeda looked at Mateo. "Where's the costume ball going to be this year?"

Mateo's fingers flew across his laptop. "Looks like the ball is being held this weekend at…the Cormac Museum."

He kept typing, and photos of the museum appeared on the monitors one after another. The more pictures appeared, the more certain I was that Lance, Drake, and Sisyphus were targeting the museum.

Because it was filled with artifacts.

Weapons, armor, jewelry, clothing, paintings, statues, and more flashed by on the screens, almost too fast for me to follow. I waved my hand at the monitors.

"That's what makes this place so special," I said. "Lance and Drake must be planning to use the costume ball as a cover so they can sneak into the museum and steal whatever artifact Sisyphus wants. Maybe even multiple artifacts, given how many are there."

"And the chimera scepter?" Mateo asked. "What are the Reapers planning to do with that?"

Takeda stared at the monitors. "The same thing they did at Lance Fuller's mansion: use it to cover their escape. The Reapers were probably hoping they could slip into the museum during the ball, steal the artifacts, and vanish before anyone realized what was happening, just like they did during the battle at the North Carolina academy. But Sisyphus is smart. He knew the Protectorate might figure out what he was up to, so that's why he had Lance steal the chimera scepter—as insurance. So Lance can summon more monsters and stop anyone who tries to get in the Reapers' way."

I thought of how easily Lance had waved the scepter and made those chimeras appear in the office last night. Facing down those monsters would be a tall task for anyone, even Protectorate guards, making it that much easier for the Reapers to escape in the chaos and confusion.

"Do you think Sisyphus will be there?" Zoe asked.

"He'll be there," I said. "He's gone to a lot of trouble to set things up. Working with Drake, having Lance steal the chimera scepter from the library, trying to kill us at the mansion last night. He won't want to miss the grand finale of his evil plan."

I couldn't explain how I knew the Reaper leader would be there, but I did. I could *feel* it deep down in my bones.

"Rory's right," Takeda said. "Sisyphus will most likely be there to oversee the operation, which means that this is our chance to finally take him down. Now that we know what the Reapers are up to, let's see if we can figure out which artifacts they might be after."

Mateo hacked into the Cormac Museum's computer system and printed out a master list of all the artifacts on display, along with photos and the location of each object. He split the list and the photos into five stacks, and we all sat at the table and studied the information.

The museum housed dozens of swords, daggers, spears, axes, and other weapons, along with a fair share of armor, everything from helmets to breastplates to gauntlets. Still, I couldn't help but feel those items were way too obvious. Swords and armor could be found at myth-history museums all across the country, places the Reapers could break into at any time. So what artifact was so special, so powerful, so one-of-a-kind that Sisyphus was willing to risk being caught by the Protectorate to get his greedy hands on it? And what did he plan to do with the artifact once he had it? Those were the most important questions, but try as I might, I couldn't puzzle out the answers.

And neither could the others. An hour passed, then two, and none of us could pinpoint which artifacts the Reapers might want or why.

"All right," Takeda finally said, scrubbing his hands over his face. "That's enough for tonight. We'll come back at this tomorrow with fresh eyes."

We gathered up our things and left the Bunker. The others headed back to their dorm rooms for the night, but I was too restless to go home, so I stayed behind in the library, and I wound up at Sigyn's statue on the second floor.

I sat on the floor across from the statue and stared at the goddess, but her stone face remained still and frozen. Ever since she'd first appeared to me in that dream realm at the Eir Ruins, I had been on the lookout for Sigyn, expecting the goddess to be lurking somewhere in the library, either as herself or as the old woman Raven, but the only glimpse of Sigyn that I'd seen had been her statue. I wondered if I was doing what the goddess wanted by joining the Midgard and hunting down Lance, Drake, and Sisyphus or if she had some other job in mind for me, some task that I hadn't even considered yet. No way to know for sure.

"What are you thinking about, Rory?" A familiar voice cut into my thoughts.

I looked over at Babs, whom I'd propped up against the wall beside me. Once again, the sword had been quiet all day, as if she'd been utterly exhausted by the fight with the Reapers and chimeras last night. She hadn't said a single word during my classes, lunch, or even the briefing. But now her green eye was open and fixed on mine.

"Did you hear us talking in the Bunker?" I asked.

Babs rolled her eye. "Of course I did. Just because my eye's closed doesn't mean I'm not listening."

"Well, I was thinking about the mission and the artifacts the Reapers might be after."

"But that's not what's really bothering you, is it?"

I shook my head. "I keep thinking about everything Lance said last night and how he tried to recruit me to become a Reaper."

"So?"

"So Lance isn't the one giving the orders—Sisyphus is. That means that Sisyphus told Lance to recruit me. But why? I've never even met this Sisyphus person, so why would he want me to become a Reaper? It doesn't make any sense. I don't know anything about Sisyphus, but he seems to know everything about me."

"Maybe Sisyphus has heard what a great warrior you are," Babs suggested. "Everyone knows that you fought at the Battle of Mythos Academy. You know that Reapers covet power more than anything else. Sisyphus probably thinks he can defeat the Protectorate if he has a strong warrior like you on his side."

"Maybe. But I still feel like I'm missing something important about this whole situation."

Sympathy flashed in Babs's gaze. She opened her mouth, then abruptly closed it again.

"What?" I asked. "What were you going to say?"

"Well, I hate to bring this up, especially since you're already feeling a little down…"

"Bring what up?"

The sword winced. "Sisyphus isn't the only thing you need to worry about."

"What else is there?"

Her wince deepened. "My curse."

With everything that had happened over the past day, I had forgotten about Babs's curse and how it affected every warrior who wielded her.

"Last night, when I fought Lance, Drake, and the chimeras, that was my second time using you in battle," I said.

I hadn't even thought about the curse, much less not using Babs during the fight. The only things I had been worried about were protecting Ian and Zoe and taking down the Reapers before they hurt anyone else. But I had used Babs in the fight, which made me one step closer to being the next victim of her curse.

"Yes, that was the second battle. That means you only have one battle left before…before you die." The sword's voice dropped to an anguished whisper, and a tear gleamed in her eye.

My stomach twisted with dread. And I had just made plans to be part of a third battle by agreeing to take down Lance, Drake, and Sisyphus during the Fall Costume Ball. Even if we managed to corner the Reapers, they wouldn't go down without a fight.

Maybe it was morbid, but I wondered exactly how the curse would kill me. Would Lance get in a lucky strike with a sword? Would Drake wound me with a poisoned weapon? Or would I fall victim to some weird, random bout of extremely bad luck, like tripping, plunging down a flight of stairs, and breaking my neck seconds after the battle was finished?

More dread swirled through me, along with a touch of fear. I might be a warrior, but I didn't want to die. Not like this. Not because of some curse that I had no idea how to fight.

"I'm sorry, Rory," Babs whispered, a tear streaking down her face. "So sorry. I never meant for any of this to happen to you."

Seeing how upset she was reminded me that I wasn't the only one affected by the curse. Babs had been through this with other warriors before me, and she had watched them all die just because they had picked her up. Determination surged through me, drowning out my dread. Well, she wasn't going to suffer through that guilt and heartbreak again. Not if I could help it.

Spartans never, ever gave up.

"Don't worry," I said, gently wiping the tear off her blade. "I still have time to figure this out. We're in the Library of Antiquities, remember? There has to be something here that can help us break your curse."

"Do you really think so?" Babs's voice quavered with a faint bit of hope.

"Yes, and we're going to get started right now."

I got to my feet, buckled Babs's scabbard to my belt, and grabbed my messenger bag from the floor. Then I looked at Sigyn's statue.

Once again, I wondered why the goddess had arranged

for my path to cross Babs's, and I stared at her marble face, hoping she might give me some small clue or sign that I was on the right track, that there was some way to help Babs and myself. But Sigyn's features remained as still and remote as before. No help there. At least, not right now. So I hoisted my bag onto my shoulder, turned, and left the goddess behind.

I had a curse to break.

CHAPTER TWENTY

I stayed in the library until closing time, searching through the computer databases, but I didn't find any books or artifacts about breaking curses.

I would have stayed even later, but the librarians rounded up all the students and made us leave before locking the doors behind us. Frustration filled me, even though I knew that the improved security measures were Takeda's doing and that they were for the best to protect everything inside the library. But I had no choice but to go home for the night.

Despite everything that had happened with Lance, Drake, and the Reapers, the next few days were surprisingly normal. Well, as normal as they could be considering the fact that I kept wondering if everyone around me was a Reaper and spying on me for the mysterious Sisyphus. But that was just life at Mythos Academy.

I went about my routine as though everything was fine. Morning classes, lunch with the others in the dining hall, afternoon classes, then prepping for the mission with everyone in the Bunker. As the days passed, I realized that everything really *was* fine. Well, except for Babs's curse, which I spent every night researching in the library, although I didn't have any luck finding anything to help the sword or keep me from dying. But that was the only black spot in my days.

I'd had more fun hanging out with Ian, Zoe, and Mateo this past week than I'd had since my parents were exposed as Reapers. Even Takeda, with his annoyingly calm demeanor and love of classical music, was slowly growing on me. Plus, being on the Midgard gave me a sense of purpose, like I was making a difference, like my actions would protect people. But most of all, being on the team made me feel like I was my own person—and not just the despised daughter of murdered Reaper assassins.

I was going to be so sad when we finished the mission and they all went back to their regular lives in New York. But I tried not to think about it too much, and before I knew it, it was the day of the Fall Costume Ball.

Takeda had told Linus Quinn what we thought the Reapers were up to, and Linus had decided to let the ball take place as planned, since it was the Protectorate's best chance to capture Sisyphus and put a stop to this new brewing war with the Reapers. So on Saturday afternoon, I was in the Bunker, going over our final strategy to catch Lance, Drake, and Sisyphus at the museum tonight.

Mateo hit some buttons on his laptop, and photos of the inside of the Cormac Museum popped up on the wall monitors. I stifled a groan. They were the exact same photos we'd been studying for days now, and I had stared at them for so long that I'd started seeing them in my sleep.

Takeda stood in his usual spot at the head of the briefing table. "As you know, the safety of the Mythos students is our top priority tonight, even above capturing Lance,

Drake, and any other Reapers who might be there. Dozens of Protectorate guards will be hidden throughout the grounds, and others will be patrolling inside the museum, dressed in costumes like all the other regular academy chaperones."

Photos flashed by of all the Protectorate guards. I knew their faces as well as I knew the inside of the museum now.

"I will be attending the ball as a chaperone, while the four of you go in as regular students," Takeda continued. "Your job is to mix and mingle and keep an eye out for Lance, Drake, or anyone you think might be Sisyphus. The second you spot one of them, you will let me know on comms, and the Protectorate guards will move in. The four of you can observe the Reapers, but you are not to engage them unless absolutely necessary. Let the guards do their jobs. Okay?"

"Okay," we all murmured back to him, although Ian's response was a little slow and surly.

I looked at Ian, who was staring at the monitor. His face was calm, but a muscle ticked in his jaw, and his hand slowly curled into a fist on top of the table. We hadn't talked much since that night at the Eir Ruins, but it was obvious that Ian wanted to confront Drake at the museum. I would have felt the same way if my parents were going to be there. I wondered if the Viking would be able to stop himself from charging after his brother.

I'd find out tonight.

We reviewed a few final details, then split up and went our separate ways to get ready. Like it or not, this was a costume ball, and we would be far too obvious if we didn't dress up. Ian, Mateo, and Takeda had gotten their costumes from a shop in Snowline Ridge, but Zoe was creating her own. The Valkyrie liked making clothes as much as she liked inventing gadgets, and she'd spent the last few days designing and sewing.

I had been planning to wear an old green party dress, along with a cheap plastic tiara, for a quick and easy princess costume, but Zoe was horrified by my lack of imagination, and she insisted on giving my costume a serious upgrade. I told her I was fine being a generic princess and that she shouldn't go to so much trouble, but she was determined to work her creative magic on me. I'd tried to sneak into her dorm room to see what she was doing, but Zoe wouldn't let me in, saying she wanted our costumes to be a surprise.

An hour later, a knock sounded on my bedroom door, and Aunt Rachel stepped inside. She was attending the ball tonight as a chaperone, although she was really going to help Takeda and keep an eye out for the Reapers.

Aunt Rachel was wearing a long dark blue dress with a poofy tulle skirt and silver heels. Tiny silver sequins sparkled all over her dress, and she was carrying a long silver wand with a large star on the end. Her black hair was pulled back into an elegant bun, and a small silver tiara perched on her head.

I got up from the bed, went over, and hugged her. "You look like the perfect fairy godmother."

"Thanks, Rory." Aunt Rachel hugged me back. "Now it's your turn to get ready. Zoe's here."

She stepped aside, and the Valkyrie sashayed into my bedroom.

Zoe had gone all out, transforming herself into a beautiful mermaid. Her strapless dress had a tight-fitted bodice made of bright teal-blue sequined leather panels that had been draped over each other and stitched together to look like fish scales. More of those scalelike panels dotted the long, flowing skirt, which curled up and tapered to two points, just like a mermaid's tail.

The teal-blue scales brought out the Valkyrie's lovely mocha skin, along with her wavy black hair. Teal shadow and liner emphasized her hazel eyes, and she'd painted her lips a deep, dark fuchsia. A pearl choker ringed her throat, while stacks of pearl bracelets shimmered on her wrists. Her electrodagger was holstered to her thin silver belt, which was also studded with pearls.

"You look amazing," I said.

Zoe grinned, glanced at herself in the mirror in the corner, and fluffed out her hair. "Yeah, I totally do. Now, Cinderella, it's your turn."

"That almost sounds frightening, when you say it like that," I joked.

Her grin widened. "You have no idea, Spartan. No idea at all. Now, sit down, and let's get started."

Thirty minutes later, I was wishing I'd gone with my original princess costume, but there was no denying the will of Zoe Wayland. I fidgeted in my chair, but Zoe put her hand on my shoulder and yanked me back into place, dabbing a little more gloss on my lips. She was a bit of a perfectionist.

"Are you done yet?" I groused. "If you keep messing with my makeup, we're going to miss the entire ball."

Zoe rolled her eyes. "Yeah, yeah. I know you're all eager to get to the museum so you can capture the bad guys, but there's nothing that says you can't look fabulous while you're kicking ass. Now, is there?"

I opened my mouth to snark back at her, but Zoe used

the opportunity to dab even more gloss on my lips.

Two minutes and tons of lip gloss later, Zoe finally nodded with satisfaction, capped the tube, and tossed it on top of my vanity table. Then she grabbed my hands and pulled me to my feet.

"I'm finished, and I have once again outdone myself. Voilà!"

She grabbed my shoulders and spun me around so I could look at myself in the full-length mirror. I gasped. Zoe had kept her promise to completely transform me. I wasn't plain old Rory Forseti anymore. I was something more than that—Cinderella and then some.

Zoe had taken my light green satin party dress, cut it into pieces, and braided it together with a beautiful emerald-green leather, creating a tight-fitted bodice with cute cap sleeves and a sweetheart neckline. Zoe rapped her knuckles on the tough but flexible leather covering my chest and stomach, then on her own mermaid scales. The solid *thwacks* rang out through my bedroom.

"My version of armor." She grinned. "Just what every warrior girl needs for a night out hunting Reapers."

I grinned back at her. "Absolutely."

Zoe had also stitched long strips of the leather together with more pieces of my satin dress, then draped everything over a layer of black crinoline to create the gown's poofy ballerina skirt, which fluttered down to my knees. A wide black leather belt studded with dark green heart-shaped stones circled my waist, so I could carry Babs with me to the ball, while a pair of sparkly black sandals covered my feet.

"The flowing skirt gives you great range of motion, you've got your sword on your belt, and you can actually run and fight in those shoes," Zoe continued.

I smoothed down the skirt. "And my hair and makeup? Anything special about that?"

She grinned again. "Fun and functional like everything else."

Zoe had pulled my black hair up into a high ponytail and fastened it with a clip that featured the same heart-shaped stones as my belt. She'd painted my green eyes with a dark, smoky shadow and added a scarlet gloss to my lips. My only jewelry was my silver charm bracelet and heart locket, which dangled from my right wrist like usual.

"All put together, I call this look *Spartan Princess*," Zoe said, a smug tone in her voice.

I stared at myself in the mirror again. She was right. I did look like a Spartan princess, a fierce warrior straight from the pages of some old myth-history book. More than that, I felt strong, like an ordinary person turned into someone extraordinary.

"I agree," Babs called out from her perch in a nearby chair. "You look fantastic, Rory. Absolutely fantastic. You too, Zoe."

I smiled at the sword and stared at myself in the mirror again. So many emotions welled up in my chest. Surprise, pleasure, pride, gratitude. But the strongest one was happiness—pure, genuine happiness that Zoe was my friend and that she'd taken the time to make me such an amazing costume.

"I don't know how or when, but one day, I will find a way to pay you back for this," I said. "Thank you. Thank you so much!"

I turned around and hugged her tight. Zoe seemed startled by my show of affection, but her arms crept up, and she hugged me back just as tightly, making blue sparks of magic crackle in the air all around us.

"You're welcome," she said, drawing back. "Now, what do you say we go meet up with the others and catch some Reapers?"

I grinned back at her. "I'd say that sounds like the perfect night."

Zoe left my bedroom to text Takeda and tell him we were heading to the gym parking lot. I looked at myself in the mirror again, still amazed by the terrific costume, then went over to grab Babs from her chair. To my surprise, a tear welled up in the sword's green eye before slowly streaking down her metal cheek.

"Babs? What's wrong?"

I grabbed a tissue from a box on the vanity table and dabbed the tear off her blade, but the sword sniffled, and another tear streaked down her half of a face.

"You look so wonderful, Rory. I can't stand it! I just can't stand it!" She let out a loud wail.

"Shh, shh. There's no reason to cry."

"There is *every* reason to cry." Babs's voice trembled with grief. "You're such a brave, strong, lovely girl. You're the best warrior I've ever had. And I'm going to ruin everything, just like I always do."

"What do you mean?"

She stared at me, her face completely serious. "Tonight will be the third and final battle you carry me into."

"I know. Believe me, I know."

With every day that passed, I had become a little more worried and a whole lot more desperate, especially since I hadn't been able to find a single book or artifact in the library to help me break the curse. Now it was the night of the ball, and the battle with the Reapers was looming, which meant that I was out of time.

And that I was most likely going to die tonight.

Babs must have seen the dread on my face, because she sniffled again. "I'm so sorry. You don't deserve such a gruesome fate. You didn't ask to be saddled with my curse, but it's going to kill you anyway. Unless…"

"Unless what?"

She gave me a hopeful look. "Unless you forget about the costume ball and stay here tonight. The Reapers won't be content with just stealing artifacts. They'll attack sooner or later. You know they will. Your only chance to survive is to stay here, Rory. Stay here where it's safe. Please. *Please* do that for yourself. And for me too. I couldn't stand it if you died the way all my other warriors have."

I wiped the second tear off her blade, giving myself time to think. I didn't want to die, and fear, worry, and dread filled my heart at the thought that Babs was right. That her curse would get me killed tonight, no matter what I did or how well I fought against the Reapers. I'd trained for years to become a warrior, and it wasn't fair that all my hard work had been for nothing. It just wasn't *fair* that the battle was rigged and that the outcome—my death—had already been predetermined.

Did I really want to go through with this? Did I really want to die trying to stop Reapers from stealing artifacts and hurting a bunch of kids who all hated me? The other Mythos students wouldn't care about any sacrifice I might make for them, and they certainly wouldn't miss me if I was killed tonight. No doubt the other kids would think that justice had finally been served and that I was finally paying for all the terrible things my parents had done.

Maybe they were right about that.

I thought about staying here, safe and sound in my bedroom, like Babs wanted. It would be so *easy* to do that. I hadn't wanted the others to worry, so I hadn't told anyone else about Babs's curse, but no one would blame me for not going on the mission if I told them about the danger. Aunt Rachel would demand that I stay here and would probably lock me in my room to make sure that happened. Yes, it would be so simple, easy, and safe to stay home and pretend nothing was going on.

I had opened my mouth to tell Babs that I would do as she asked, that I would stay here, when my gaze fell to the charm bracelet on my wrist. The silver heart locket brushed against my skin, and I thought of my parents.

Ever since I'd learned the truth about them, I had been searching for a way to make up for their past mistakes, to right some of the wrongs they'd committed as Reapers, to make things better for everyone. And I *had* made a difference. I'd helped Gwen find the Chloris ambrosia flowers that had saved Nickamedes, and I'd fought alongside her and her friends during the Battle of Mythos Academy. I hadn't been the ultimate hero like Gwen that day, but I'd fought and raged and bled right alongside everyone else.

Those things had given me a sense of purpose that I'd been lacking ever since I learned about my parents. More than that, they had made me *happy*—happy that I was finally using my Spartan fighting skills to help and protect people the way I'd always dreamed of doing.

In that moment, I realized that if I gave in to Babs's wishes, if I stayed here where it was safe, I would regret it. I would regret not fighting against the Reapers. But even more than that, I didn't *want* to be the girl who stayed safe at home while other people risked their lives. Especially not when those people were my friends.

My parents had made their choice, and now I was making mine—even if it might result in my death.

I shook my head. "I'm sorry, Babs. But curse or not, this is something I have to do. I want justice for Amanda. She would still be alive if Lance hadn't sicced that chimera on her in the library. Plus, I want to know why Lance tried to recruit me to become a Reaper and especially why Sisyphus is so interested in me. I have to go to the ball tonight, no matter what might happen to me. I hope you understand."

She stared at me, misery filling her eye, and a third and final tear slowly streaked down her face. I gently wiped it away like I had the others.

"Besides," I said, trying to make my voice strong and confident. "I'm not just *any* old warrior. I'm a Spartan, remember? We're the best warriors around. I'll be fine. You'll see."

"I hope you're right, Rory," Babs whispered. "I really hope you're right."

Her voice sounded soft, small, and depressingly sad, and I could tell she didn't believe me. Truth be told, I didn't believe myself either. I could take down Reapers with ease, but I had no idea how to fight a curse.

But it was my choice, and I was going to see this thing through—even if tonight might be the end of me.

CHAPTER TWENTY-ONE

I snapped Babs's black leather scabbard onto my belt and left my bedroom. Aunt Rachel and Zoe were hanging out in the kitchen, and the three of us left the cottage and walked across campus to the parking lot behind the gym where Takeda, Mateo, and Ian were waiting.

Takeda was dressed like the Samurai he was, in a long red robe topped by a black armored breastplate, and a katana hung from the black belt around his lean waist. He looked quite handsome, something Aunt Rachel noticed as well, given the way she stopped and blinked at him. Takeda eyed her poofy blue fairy godmother costume, and his lips twitched up into a small smile.

Mateo wore a pirate costume, with a white shirt and a black leather vest patterned with tiny white skulls and crossbones. A red bandanna hid most of his dark brown hair from sight, and black leather pants and boots finished off his outfit. Instead of the traditional cutlass, a large crossbow dangled from his belt, and the weapon's metal bolts glimmered in slots all around the black leather.

Mateo saw me eyeing his costume, grinned, and patted his crossbow. "Wearing this seemed like the best and easiest way to bring my crossbow into the ball. Besides, I always wanted to be a pirate. Yargh!"

I grinned back at him, then turned my attention to Ian. Like Takeda and me, he had dressed up as the warrior he was, a Viking.

He wore a black leather shirt, pants, and boots, and a silver chain-mail vest covered his muscled chest. His Viking battle ax dangled from his black leather belt, along with several small daggers. His dark honey-blond hair had been slicked back, and his gray eyes gleamed with anticipation. He was looking forward to taking down the Reapers. Me too.

"No horned helmet?" I asked, deciding to make a joke instead of telling him how great he looked.

Ian rolled his eyes, but a smile crept over his face. "Are you kidding? I would look ridiculous in one of those things. Besides, Vikings didn't really wear that kind of helmet."

Takeda cleared his throat. "Now that we're all here, we need to get to the museum. I want to make sure that we're all set up on comms and that the Protectorate guards are in place. So let's move out."

He gestured at the waiting van, and we all headed in that direction.

Somehow I found myself walking side by side with Ian at the back of our pack of friends. I could see him staring at me out of the corner of my eye, because I was doing the exact same thing to him.

Ian leaned down. "You look nice, Rory," he murmured in my ear, before straightening up and getting into the van with the others.

I ducked my head so no one would see the pleased blush staining my cheeks and climbed into the vehicle after him.

Thirty minutes later, Takeda steered the van up to the side of the Cormac Museum. Through the windshield, I could see a long line of limos crawling up the hill and dropping off kids at the main entrance.

We got out of the van and walked over to the side door. Two Protectorate guards dressed like medieval knights in suits of shiny armor were stationed by the entrance, and they both snapped to attention at the sight of Takeda striding toward them.

"Any sign of the Reapers yet?" Takeda asked.

The guards shook their heads.

"No, sir," one of them said. "We have costumed guards posted at all the entrances, as well as patrolling inside the museum, but so far, there are no signs of anyone or anything suspicious."

Takeda nodded and led us inside. We walked down a long hallway and stopped at a wide archway that opened up into an enormous rotunda in the center of the museum. The floor and walls were made of a beautiful white marble streaked with pale blue, while the ceiling was a round dome that featured white, blue, and black panels of stained glass fitted together to form several giant stars. Four sets of stairs were spaced around the room, all of which led up to a second-floor balcony that wrapped around the entire rotunda. On both floors, hallways led from the main space to other rooms, where the artifacts were on display.

The Fall Costume Ball didn't officially start until eight o'clock, fifteen minutes from now, but Mythos students had already packed into the museum. Guys and girls streamed into the rotunda, all of them dressed in fancy costumes that represented everything from princesses to superheroes to zombies. I even spotted a couple of guys wearing giant wolf heads, as though they were real Fenrir wolves.

Music thumped through the air, and dozens of couples had already started grooving on the wooden dance floor set up on one side the rotunda. Still more couples were hitting the buffet tables, nibbling on gourmet snacks and dipping strawberries, marshmallows, and other goodies into the white-, milk-, and dark-chocolate fountains lined up along one wall.

"We need to split up so we can cover more ground, but I want everyone to stay in teams of two," Takeda said. "Rory and Ian, Zoe and Mateo. You guys spread out and search the rotunda for Lance and Drake. Rachel and I will start checking the hallways and exhibit rooms on this level. Got it?"

We all nodded at him.

"Keep your eyes open, and stay in contact on comms," Takeda said. "If you see anything suspicious—anything at all—let everyone know. And watch each other's backs. We don't know how many Reapers might be here tonight or what kind of costumes they might be wearing as disguises."

We all nodded again. Takeda and Aunt Rachel headed for the nearest hallway. Zoe hooked her arm through Mateo's, and the two of them wandered over to the dance floor.

"You ready for this?" Ian asked.

I stroked my fingers over Babs's hilt. Now that I was here, I wasn't feeling nearly as confident as I had earlier. I still hadn't told anyone about the curse and Babs's prediction that I would die tonight, and it was too late to bring it up now. It would just be one more thing for everyone to worry about, so I decided to keep the information to myself.

I dropped my hand from the sword. "Yeah, I'm ready. Are you?"

"Let's do this." He looked at me. "For Amanda."

"For Amanda," I echoed. "And for us too."

Ian held his arm out to me, and I slipped mine through his. We stared at each other, and I saw the same determination shining in the Viking's eyes that I felt deep down in my own heart. Curse or not, we were in this thing together, and there was no turning back now. Ian nodded at me, and I nodded back. Together we left the archway behind and stepped out into the rotunda.

It was time to find Lance, Drake, and the mysterious Sisyphus and end this.

Ian and I moved around the perimeter of the ballroom, skirting around one group of students after another.

I'd thought the costumes had looked fancy from a distance, but up close, they were positively stunning, gleaming with gold, silver, and sparkling jewels. The Mythos kids had embraced the costume theme, and they'd spared no expense to bring their favorite characters to life.

Still, I noticed a weird pattern to many of the costumes, at least among the girls. Several of them wore long, flowing, togalike gowns in various shades of purple, with enormous silver wings attached to their backs. They also carried swords and had crowns of spray-painted silver laurels on their heads. Some of them were also wearing snowflake necklaces. But the strangest thing of all was that each of them sported a pair of contact lenses that turned their eyes a bright, eerie purple.

Ian frowned, also noticing the similar costumes. "Who are they supposed to be? Some goddess?"

I studied the girl closest to me. She was cradling her sword in the crook of her elbow, and I realized that she'd used a black marker to draw a crude face on the hilt. Purple gowns, purple contacts, swords with faces. Suddenly, I knew exactly who that girl and all the other similarly dressed ones were supposed to be.

Gwen Frost.

More than three dozen girls had dressed up like Gwen— or at least how they thought she would dress. I knew that Gwen preferred her sneakers, jeans, hoodies, and T-shirts to glittering gowns and sparkly wings, but of course there was no telling the other girls that. They wouldn't have listened to me anyway.

"They're supposed to be Gwen," I said.

Ian looked at the other girls, then back at me. "Does that make you jealous? That they're dressed like her?"

"You mean that they all think she's this wonderful hero, while I'm Reaper trash?"

He winced. "I didn't mean it like that. Not at all."

"I know you didn't." I shrugged. "And yeah, maybe I am a little jealous. I was at the battle too. But Gwen went through a lot, and she was the one who figured out how to defeat Loki. She's the one who trapped him forever. She's definitely earned the hero title. Plus, she's too nice not to like."

"Kind of like her cousin Rory, huh?" Ian winked at me, and I smiled back at him.

We made it over to the buffet tables, walked past the chocolate fountains, and moved around the rest of the rotunda, but I didn't see any sign of Lance, Drake, or anyone else who looked like they might be a Reaper. All the kids were focused on eating, laughing, dancing, and gossiping, and it seemed like everyone was here to have a good time.

"You guys got anything?" Ian asked, talking to Mateo and Zoe through our earbuds.

The two of them were in the middle of the dance floor, grooving to the music, although they kept glancing at the kids around them.

Mateo's voice crackled in my ear a second later. "Nothing. We're going to finish this dance and then help Takeda and Rachel search the exhibit rooms on this floor."

"Roger that," Ian said. "Rory and I will check out the exhibit rooms upstairs."

Ian led me over to a set of stairs, and we climbed up to the second floor. Some of the kids had migrated up here, talking, leaning against the balcony railing, and staring down at the rotunda below. More than a few couples had already retreated to the darkest corners they could find, eager to kiss the night away. The music shifted into a slow song, and everyone on this floor started coupling up to dance, mirroring the kids downstairs.

Ian cleared his throat. "Maybe when this is all over and we find the Reapers, we can come back and enjoy the rest of the ball. Maybe even…dance?"

I stared at him, but he shifted on his feet and stared down at the floor instead of looking at me. Was he actually nervous? About asking me to dance? My heart did that funny little flutter.

"I'd like that," I said in a soft voice. "I'd like that a lot."

Ian nodded, still not looking at me, and moved away from the railing. I followed him.

The main rotunda was only one part of the Cormac Museum, and we walked down a long hallway and into another wing where the exhibit rooms were located. The music, conversations, and laughter faded away, and the only sounds were our footsteps on the floor, but I didn't mind the quiet.

Ian and I moved from room to room, staring at the

weapons, armor, clothing, and other objects on display. All the items were housed in protective glass cases, and every single case was plugged into the museum's security system, according to what Takeda had told us during our briefings. If Lance, Drake, or any other Reaper so much as scratched the glass on one of the cases, alarms would start blaring in the museum's security office, and the Protectorate guards would come running. But everything remained quiet, so Ian and I walked on.

I didn't mind strolling from room to room and checking on things. This was way more fun than the dance downstairs, especially since Ian was with me and seemed to enjoy studying the artifacts as much as I did.

"Hey, Rory," he said. "Come check this out. It's really cool."

He was standing in front of a glass case. A tiny silver whistle lay inside, so small that it looked like a toy or a charm that would go on my bracelet instead of something you could actually use.

"*Pan's Whistle.*" Ian read the identification card inside the case. "*This whistle can be used to summon mythological creatures, including Nemean prowlers, Fenrir wolves, and more. It can be used over great distances, especially if you know the particular creature or creatures that you wish to summon. As its name suggests, the whistle was used by Pan, the Greek god of music, the wild, and more.*"

He looked at me, excitement shining in his eyes. "I bet you could use that to summon your gryphons. All you would have to do is think about them, blow on the whistle, and *bam!* They would fly right to you. No more turning on lanterns on the library roof and hoping the gryphons see them and show up."

I smiled back at him. "Probably. Although I doubt

Takeda would appreciate me swiping an artifact when we're supposed to stop the Reapers from stealing them."

Ian laughed. "You're probably right about that. Let's keep looking. Maybe we can at least figure out which artifact the Reapers are after."

He gave the whistle one more longing glance, and then we both moved on.

Ian and I went from case to case. Everything was interesting and cool in its own right, but I didn't see anything that seemed powerful enough to appeal to the Reapers. They could get weapons and armor at other museums that weren't crawling with Mythos students and Protectorate guards. So what was here that was so special?

And even more worrisome, what were the Reapers planning to do with the artifact once they had it?

I didn't know, and I wasn't sure I wanted to find out.

We were running out of time and options. Ian and I were down to the final set of rooms on the second floor, and we stepped into another large rotunda.

This part of the museum had been fashioned after a medieval dungeon, and heavy iron gates with sharp metal spikes hung in the two archways that marked the entrance and exit. Both gates were held up by thick, heavy ropes tied off to iron posts embedded in the walls, and the light fixtures were shaped like torches that continuously flickered. I glanced up, expecting the ceiling to be made of some dark stone, but clear glass panes glimmered overhead.

"Nothing," Ian growled. "There's absolutely nothing in here that the Reapers would want. You got anything, Rory?"

I shook my head. "Nothing out of the ordinary and nothing that seems superpowerful."

Ian lifted his hand and adjusted his earbud. "What about you guys? Mateo, Zoe, you got anything downstairs?"

A second later, Mateo's voice crackled in my ear. "Nope. We checked all the exhibit rooms down here, but they're all full of kids dancing and partying."

"There's no sign of Lance, Drake, or any Reapers," Zoe added. "We're at the front of the museum, but we'll work our way back to the main rotunda, then come upstairs and help you guys look through the artifacts on the second floor. Maybe we'll see something you missed."

"Roger that," Ian said.

We continued our search. I scanned all the display cases on my side of the rotunda again, but everything was the same as before, and nothing stuck out to me. I was about to walk over to Ian when a gleam of red caught my eye.

Curious, I headed toward a display case I hadn't noticed before. I glanced around the rotunda, comparing where the case was with what I remembered from the surveillance photos, but this case hadn't been in any of the pictures. Maybe it was part of the new exhibit Takeda had said the museum was going to open after the costume ball. We had found a few cases like that in the other rooms, but why the case was in here wasn't important right now, only what it contained.

A box.

The case held a long rectangular box made of polished jet. Silver vines curled across the top of the box, wrapping around glittering rubies that formed small flowers. If I had to guess, I would say it was a jewelry box, although it was large enough to hold a dagger or some other weapon.

I'd seen a lot of artifacts, but something about this box made me shiver. Maybe it was the way the midnight-black stone absorbed the light instead of reflecting it back. Or how the silver vines looked more like thorns, pinning the rubies in place like they were bloody hearts. Either way, this box radiated power.

I looked inside the glass case, searching for the identification card that would tell me who the box had belonged to and what magic it supposedly had. But it didn't have a card, and I didn't see one lying on the floor anywhere around the case. A sinking feeling filled my stomach. An unidentified artifact that gave me the creeps? This had to be what the Reapers were after.

"Ian!" I called out. "Come look at this!"

He hurried over to me. "Did you find something?"

I pointed at the case, and he leaned forward and studied the box.

Ian frowned. "What would Reapers want with a jewelry box? Or whatever that really is?"

I shook my head. "I don't know, but this is what they're after. I'm sure of it."

"And you're absolutely right, Rory," a familiar voice sneered behind us. "How nice to see that you have brains as well as Spartan brawn."

Ian and I whirled around.

Lance stood behind us, along with Drake and half a dozen Reapers.

Chapter Twenty-Two

Lance and Drake were both dressed like vampires, in black tuxedos topped with long black cloaks lined with red satin. White makeup coated their faces, black circles ringed their eyes, and fake blood covered their lips, as though they'd taken a bite out of someone.

The other six Reapers sported black bodysuits outlined with white bones, making them look like skeletons, and the same eerie white, black, and red paint scheme covered their faces. Swords hung off all the Reapers' belts, and Lance and Drake were armed too.

Between the costumes and the face paint, Lance and Drake looked like completely different people, which must be how they'd slipped past the Protectorate guards manning the entrances. I wouldn't have recognized them either if Lance hadn't called out to me.

At the sight of the Reapers, Ian and I both drew our weapons. So did Lance, Drake, and their six skeleton friends, and we all stood there facing off, with Ian and me standing in front of the display case. I looked at the Viking, and he nodded back at me. Whatever happened, we both knew we couldn't let the Reapers get their hands on the jewelry box…or whatever it really was.

"Takeda," Ian murmured in a low, urgent voice. "The Reapers are here. Repeat. The Reapers are here—"

Drake held up a small black box. "Don't bother, little brother. I was part of the Protectorate too, remember? I know exactly how Takeda and the rest of the guards operate. We've jammed all of your communication devices. The earbuds, the security cameras, the alarms. They're all down, and Takeda and the guards are completely blind. They have no idea where we are or what we're doing, which means that no one's coming to save you."

"We don't need anyone to save us," I growled. "We can deal with you."

Drake shoved the black box into his pants pocket. "Keep telling yourself that." He sneered. "I've killed Spartans before. You're not nearly as tough as you think you are."

I twirled Babs around in my hand, moving the sword into an attack position. "Big talk for someone all the way across the room. Why don't you come over here and say that again?"

He grinned. "I'd be happy to, especially since you're standing right in front of what we came here for. But do you know what the good thing is about being at the top of the Reaper food chain?"

"What?" I snapped.

Drake's grin widened. "Ordering other people to do your dirty work for you." He waved his hand at the six skeleton-clad men. "Kill them. Now."

The Reapers raised their swords and charged at us, and Ian and I surged forward to meet them.

"Back to back!" I yelled at the Viking. "Now!"

We skidded to a stop in the open area in the middle of the rotunda, and Ian whipped around so his back pressed up against mine. And then the Reapers were on us.

Clash-clash-bang!

Clash-clash-bang!

I whipped Babs back and forth, back and forth, parrying the hard, vicious blows dished out by the three Reapers in front of me. Behind me, Ian was fighting the other three Reapers, and I could hear his ax slamming into the men's swords over and over again. I kept my back pressed up against his, and he did the same thing to me so that our enemies couldn't overwhelm and attack both of us at once.

Adrenaline surged through my body, my Spartan instincts kicked in, and I started cataloging all the Reapers' weaknesses. One raised his sword two inches too high, allowing me to knock his weapon aside, surge forward, and stab him in the heart with Babs. He screamed and tumbled to the floor. He rammed into his buddy on the way down, making the second Reaper curse and stumble forward, suddenly off balance.

I took advantage and swiped my sword all the way across his stomach. That Reaper screamed as well and landed right on top of his friend, both of them bleeding out from their wounds.

That left one Reaper standing in front of me. He'd hung back so far, but I could tell by the way he struggled to keep his sword up that the weapon was too big and heavy for his short, thin frame. The extra weight would make him a second slower than me, which was all the time I needed. I feinted like I was going to stab him in the chest, but at the last moment, I changed direction and went low, swiping my sword across his leg instead. Babs's blade dug into the meaty part of his thigh, making him yelp with pain.

"That's it!" Babs cried out, her mouth moving underneath my palm. "Cut him down to size, Rory!"

I yanked my sword out of his thigh, making his leg

buckle. He also crashed to the floor. Desperate, he lashed out with his weapon so hard that the sword flew right out of his hand. I dodged the weapon, stepped up, and drove my sword into his chest, ending his struggles.

Killing the last Reaper had separated me from Ian, and his warm, strong back was no longer pressed up against mine. I whipped around to help him, but Ian had already killed two of the Reapers, and he rammed his ax into the chest of the final man, dropping him as well.

With the six Reapers dead, Ian glanced at me. I nodded back. Then, together, we faced Lance and Drake again.

"What were you saying about getting other people to do your dirty work for you?" I called out, a mocking note in my voice. "That's not working out so well for you so far."

Drake shrugged and looked at Lance. "I'll let you handle this."

"You really think he can beat me in a fight?" I snorted. "You obviously haven't been paying attention."

"Ah, ah, but you forgot about my secret weapon," Lance said.

Even though I knew exactly what he was going to do next, I was still too slow to stop it, given Lance's Roman speed. I'd only taken three steps forward when he yanked the gold chimera scepter out of his pants pocket, snapped it up, and slashed it through the air in a series of sharp figure-eight motions.

Two thick, choking clouds of smoke exploded out of the end of the scepter and immediately solidified into two very large, angry chimeras. The creatures snarled, their lips drawing back to reveal their jagged teeth, and started pacing back and forth, their paws leaving black scorch marks on the floor. With every step they took, the chimeras scraped their claws against the stone, as if they weren't sharp enough already. I winced at the harsh, loud *screech-screech-screeches*. Worse than fingernails on a chalkboard—and much, much deadlier.

"What's wrong?" Lance called out from his position behind the monsters. "Chimeras got your tongue, Rory?"

He and Drake both snickered at the stupid joke.

"I'm going to enjoy punching that smirk off his face," Ian muttered.

"Not if I beat you to him," I said.

Lance finally stopped laughing and stared at me, a smug expression on his face. "You wanted a fight, Rory. Let's see how well you do against my chimeras this time."

He raised the gold scepter again, like he was going to order the creatures to attack. I tensed and snapped up my sword. So did Ian, and we braced ourselves for the upcoming fight—

"Enough!" another voice called out. "That's enough. I told you to let the others wear her down so we could capture her. I want the Spartan girl alive."

A man strode into the rotunda. He was wearing a red cloak trimmed with black, along with a red harlequin mask with black diamond shapes over the eyes. For a moment, I thought he was in some bizarre court jester's costume, but then I realized that his outfit was like the ones the Reapers had worn at Lance's mansion, only with the colors reversed. All the other Reapers had sported black cloaks and masks, and only one person would wear blood-red from head to toe like that: their leader.

Lance and Drake both bowed their heads to the other man, further confirming my suspicion about who he was.

"Sisyphus." I spat out the name.

The mystery man tilted his head in agreement. Then he did the last thing I expected. He reached up, pushed the red hood off his head, and removed his mask, revealing his true identity.

He was on the short side, and his billowing cloak swallowed up much of his thin frame. His hair and eyes were both a light hazel-brown, although the goatee that clung to his chin was a few shades darker. His skin was a bit paler than I remembered, but he still had the ruddy look of someone who'd spent years in the sun and now had a permanent tan as a result.

I recognized him at once, this horrible, horrible man who had caused me so much pain. Cold shock flooded my body, as though I were drowning in an icy tidal wave. For a moment, everything inside me felt numb and frozen, and I struggled to breathe. But in the next instant, the cold shock burned away, replaced by sizzling anger, and my heart started beating so hard and fast that I thought it might explode right out of my chest.

Sisyphus wasn't some anonymous bad guy. I knew *exactly* who he was, and the sight of his smug face made me sick to my stomach.

Covington, the former head librarian at the academy and the Reaper who'd murdered my parents.

CHAPTER TWENTY-THREE

I staggered back and clutched my chest, sucking down breath after breath and trying to get my pounding heart under control.

"You—you—you're supposed to be in *prison*," I sputtered. "How did you get out?"

Covington tossed his mask down onto the floor and let out a low, amused laugh. The sound made my skin crawl. "Did you really think I was going to let myself rot in some silly Protectorate prison? You should know me better than that, Rory." He shook his head, as though he were disappointed in me. "Despite Loki's defeat, Reapers are still everywhere, even right under their family's noses in the precious Protectorate. Ask your friend. He would know."

He smirked at Ian, who glared back at him.

"I never thought I'd say this, but Gwen Frost actually did me a favor," Covington said. "When Loki attacked the North Carolina academy, many of the Protectorate members dropped everything and rushed to campus to join the battle. That made it so much easier for the Reapers working at my prison to free me. They snuck me out of my cell just like that."

He snapped his fingers, making me flinch. Out of all the bad things that had happened with my parents, I'd thought that I had at least captured their killer. That the evil librarian was locked away in some dark cell where he could never hurt anyone ever again.

But I'd been wrong about that—so very, very *wrong*.

"Who is this guy?" Ian asked.

Covington arched an eyebrow. "Rory hasn't told you about me? About how I worked with her parents all the years they were Reapers?"

"You *murdered* my parents," I snarled. "Cut them down from behind like the coward you are. You knew you could never beat them in a fair fight, so you stabbed them both in the back."

Sympathy flashed in Ian's eyes, and he stepped up so that he was standing right beside me in a silent show of support. Knowing that he was here calmed me, and I finally felt like I could breathe again.

Covington shrugged. "Fighting fair is overrated. You heroes never seem to understand that. It's why you always lose."

I opened my mouth to snap that he was the only one who was losing tonight, but Covington started pacing back and forth, and the loud *tap-tap-tap-tap* of his wing tips on the marble drowned me out before I could get started. The sharp motions made his red cloak billow out around him as though he were wrapped in a cloud of blood.

Lance and Drake moved back out of their boss's way, while the two chimeras sat down on their haunches, waiting for someone to give the order to attack.

Finally, Covington stopped pacing. His hazel gaze flicked past me to the jewelry box still sitting in its case. Then he focused on me again.

"In addition to making it easier for me to escape from prison, your dear cousin Gwen actually did all of us a huge service, especially the Reapers."

I frowned. "Why would you say that?"

"For centuries, the Reapers tried to bring Loki back. Generation upon generation worked so hard and fought so long to make it happen." Covington shook his head. "They were grand fools. All of them."

"And why is that?" Ian asked.

"We didn't need a god to come here and rule us. We didn't need a god to help us defeat the Protectorate. We were doing just fine on our own."

"Really?" I snarked. "Living in the shadows? Lying to everyone? Worried that you'd be discovered as an evil monster and put in prison at any moment? Yeah, you Reapers have really been living the high life."

Covington ignored my mocking tone. "I tried to convince Agrona and the other Reaper leaders that they were being fools. That Loki wouldn't care about us and all our hard work to free him. That he was a god and would expect us to bow down to him, just like he'd wanted the entire world to bow down to him when he first tried to conquer it. But Agrona and the others didn't listen to me, and now they're all either dead or in prison." He shrugged again. "Their loss was my gain. I always was smarter than Agrona. I realized something a long time ago that she never did."

"And what's that?" I asked, even though part of me didn't want to know the answer.

Covington's face twisted into a sneer, and a bright, fanatical light burned in his hazel eyes. "Why should people bow down to Loki when they can just as easily bow down to me?"

My heart dropped like a stone in my chest. Takeda had told me that Sisyphus—Covington—was the leader of the Reapers. That was bad enough, but that wasn't all the evil librarian wanted. Not even close. No, he wanted to rule the world, just like Loki had, and he would do whatever it took in order to make that happen—hurt, lie, cheat, steal, kill.

"What are you up to?" Ian demanded. "What do you plan to do with the artifacts you've stolen?"

Covington let out a soft laugh. "I could tell you, but it's none of your concern. Besides, you'll soon be too dead to care."

Drake stepped up beside the librarian and stared at his brother. "This is your last chance, Ian. Join us, and be on the winning side."

"Never," Ian snarled, raising his battle ax. "I will *never* join the Reapers, and I will never join *you*."

Drake shook his head. "You always were more stubborn than smart. You just don't get it, do you?"

"Get what?" Ian snarled again. "The fact that you don't even care about your own brother? Oh, I think I've gotten that message loud and clear."

"You don't get how the world really works, little brother. The only things that truly matter are magic, power, and money. Love? Family? Friends? Honor? Those are *distractions*." Drake sneered. "They make you weak. They make you vulnerable."

Ian stared at his brother like he was a stranger he'd never seen before. I knew that horrified look and all the turbulent feelings that went along with it. "If family makes you weak, then why do you want me to join you?"

"Because you're a great warrior and would be a valuable asset to the Reapers," Drake said. "Nothing more, nothing less. This is your last chance, Ian. Join us—or die."

Ian looked at his brother, then at Lance and Covington, and finally at the two chimeras sitting on the floor waiting to attack. His face hardened, and anger sparked in his eyes, turning them that beautiful storm-cloud gray.

"I'll take my chances with my friends," Ian said. "With Rory."

Drake shrugged. "Suit yourself."

He looked at Covington, who nodded and stepped forward again.

"Well, just because the Viking has turned down our generous offer doesn't mean you have to, Rory," Covington said.

That was the last thing I'd expected him to say. "What are you talking about?"

"Your parents and I did great things together, so naturally, I took an interest in their daughter. I've been watching you ever since you first started attending the academy last year. And of course I heard the reports about how well you fought during the battle in North Carolina." Covington smiled at me. "You're an even better warrior than your parents were. Smarter, stronger, faster, more cunning and vicious. With you at my side, the Protectorate doesn't stand a chance. So join us, Rory. Join me, and become a Reaper. Become the Reaper you were always *meant* to be, the Reaper your parents always *wanted* you to be."

I opened my mouth to tell him to forget it, that I would never join him, the man who'd murdered my parents. But then the strangest thing happened. Covington's words echoed from one side of the rotunda to the other, reverberating back to me time and time again, until they were all I could hear, blocking out everything else.

Ian shifting on his feet beside me, Lance and Drake

sneering at me, the chimeras idly scraping their claws against the floor. All of that faded away, and all I could see was Covington, and all I could hear was his sly voice whispering to me.

Become a Reaper... Become a Reaper... Become a Reaper...

My vision clouded over, and a dull roar filled my ears, as though I were underwater. But Covington's voice remained sharp and clear, like a knife digging deeper and deeper into my brain. I blinked, and my vision cleared, although the librarian's words continued to echo in my mind. There was something almost...*hypnotic* about Covington's voice, and I actually found myself wanting to say yes to him, even though I knew how wrong it was.

Become a Reaper? Could I really do that? Turn my back on the Protectorate? On Gwen and everything she stood for? On everything *I* stood for?

I'd never wanted to be a Reaper, I'd never wanted to be like my parents, and I'd especially never wanted to do all the horrible things they had done. At least, not until right now...

"Come on, Rory," Covington said, his voice stabbing into my brain again. "Think about it. Think about how things really are. Why should you fight for the Protectorate? Linus Quinn and Hiro Takeda are just using you for your fighting skills. And once they're done with you, once you've died for them like a good Spartan, they'll find someone to replace you without a second thought. Just like that."

He snapped his fingers, making me flinch again, although this time, I nodded in agreement. It was more or less the same thing Lance had said to me in his mansion a few days ago, but for some reason, it made so much more *sense* coming from Covington. The Protectorate would replace me like I'd replaced Amanda. It was the way of the warrior.

"Don't do it, Rory!" Ian said. "Don't listen to him!"

Ian stepped forward and reached out, like he was going to grab my shoulder, but Lance waved the gold scepter, and the two chimeras surged to their feet and snarled at the Viking. Ian froze, looking back and forth between me and the creatures. I stared at Ian, but he seemed far away, as though he were under the same water I was and slipping farther and farther away with every breath I took.

Covington walked forward, slowly moving past the chimeras, and stretched his arm out to me. And I found myself shuffling toward him and this amazing new future that he was offering me. One where I would be accepted and appreciated for who and what I truly was—a fierce Spartan warrior—instead of constantly being ridiculed for trying to do the right thing, for trying to be a good person, for trying to be a better person than my parents had been.

Covington was right. Why should I fight so hard for people who didn't appreciate it? Who thought I was a bad guy? Who automatically condemned me for being the daughter of Reaper assassins? And those were just the other students at the academy.

He was right about Linus and Takeda too. The members of the Protectorate would be happy to let me fight for them, and they wouldn't bat an eye at my death, whenever it might happen. In a way, that was worse. At least the Mythos kids were honest about hating me. I would much rather be hated than used.

But I could escape it. I could escape all the angry glares, rude remarks, and muttered accusations. All I had to do was quit fighting. All I had to do was give in. All I had to do was become the thing I'd always hated and feared: a Reaper assassin, just like my parents before me.

"Well, Rory?" Covington asked, moving even closer to me. "What do you say? Are you finally ready to embrace your destiny?"

"I—" I wasn't sure what I was going to say, but I never got the chance to finish my sentence.

"Don't listen to him, Rory," another voice cut in. "Don't you *dare* listen to him. You aren't your parents, and you certainly aren't a Reaper. You're a good person, one of the kindest, strongest souls I've ever met. Don't you *dare* sully yourself and throw away all that goodness by listening to this—this smooth-talking *fool*."

I blinked and looked around for the source of the sharp, biting voice. Covington stopped and glared at my hand, and I finally realized who was talking.

Babs.

I was still holding Babs in my right hand, and I glanced down. The motion made my charm bracelet slide down my wrist, and the heart locket clinked softly against Babs's blade. The sword looked the same as always, but my bracelet and locket were glowing with a pure, bright silver light. I changed my grip on the sword, holding Babs's blade in my hand, and slowly raised her up so I could see her face. She was also glowing, although not nearly as brightly as my bracelet.

I glanced around, but no one seemed to notice the strange glowing but me, so I looked back at the bracelet. The silver glow intensified, and that's when I realized that everything else in my entire field of vision was tinged with red.

Reaper red.

"Rory," Covington crooned again. "Don't listen to that

silly piece of metal. Listen to me. Just listen to me, and everything will be fine."

The red haze intensified, making my head swim, and I stared at the librarian. Covington clenched his hand into a fist, making a large gold signet ring flash on his right index finger. A square ruby was set in the center of the ring, burning with the same blood-red haze that was clouding my vision.

And that's when I remembered Gwen telling me how the Reapers had snapped a gold collar studded with Apate jewels around Logan Quinn's neck to control him. Covington was trying to do the same thing to me now. That ring was more than just a ring—it was some artifact that let you bend other people to your will. Lance hadn't been able to recruit me, and now Covington was using an artifact on me, trying to force me to become a Reaper whether I wanted to or not.

White-hot rage roared through me, searing through the thick fog that had crept into my mind. The red haze vanished from my vision, and everything snapped back into focus. Suddenly, I could think clearly again. More rage roared through me, and in an instant, I'd flipped Babs over in midair so that I was holding the sword by her hilt again. More than anything, I wanted to surge forward and attack, to cut Covington to pieces for daring to think he could control me and make me his Reaper puppet.

But such a reckless move would only get Ian and me killed, especially since those two chimeras were still standing by, waiting to attack. No, I had to be smart about this. So I kept my face blank and swayed on my feet, as though I were still under Covington's spell, even though I was actually studying everyone and everything in the rotunda, getting ready for what was to come next.

Babs kept babbling at me to fight, fight, fight, but I didn't need her to tell me that anymore, so I curled my hand around her hilt, muffling the sound of her voice, although I could still feel her lips moving frantically underneath my palm as she continued to shout her warnings. I clenched the sword as tightly as possible, letting the feel of the cold metal in my hand ground me. I also focused on my charm bracelet sliding along my skin and the heart locket swaying back and forth and kissing the inside of my wrist. The cool, soft touch of the jewelry further centered me.

"Come on, Rory." Covington clenched his hand into an even tighter fist, which made the ruby in his ring burn an even brighter, bloodier red. "You know you want to join us."

I plastered a smile on my face and nodded, as though I were actually agreeing with him. Then I shuffled toward him again, as though I were still drifting along in that sickening red Reaper fog and was willing to do whatever he told me to. It was the same trick I'd used on Lance when he'd tried to recruit me, and I was betting that Covington would fall for it too, especially since he thought he was controlling me with his creepy ring.

"Wow," Drake said in a snide voice. "Given everything I've heard about her, I didn't think that artifact would actually work on her. Lance made her out to be a lot tougher than she really is."

Covington shrugged. "No one can resist this kind of magic, this kind of power."

The librarian glanced down at his gold signet ring and the embedded ruby, which was still glowing an eerie, sickening blood-red.

He smiled, then looked up, focusing all of his twisted attention on me again. "That's it. Come here. All you have to do is say yes, and you'll be a Reaper for the rest of your life. Don't you want that, Rory? Don't you want that more than anything?"

I smiled at him again, as though the thought made me happy. All the while, though, I kept clutching Babs's hilt, focusing on the feel of her in my hand, along with my charm bracelet around my wrist. That was what was *real*, not the red Reaper fog that Covington wanted to drown me in forever.

I wasn't a Reaper, and I never, ever would be—no matter what. Aunt Rachel was right. My parents had made their own choices, their own decisions, their own mistakes. But I was my own person, and I made *my* own decisions. And I knew exactly what I was going to do next: wipe that smug smirk off Covington's face.

"You're right," I said in a soft, dreamy voice, easing closer and closer to him. "I should become a Reaper. Everyone hates me anyway. I might as well give them a good reason for it. Don't you think?"

Covington nodded. "Exactly my point."

I nodded back. "Not to mention all the fun I could have, doing whatever I wanted. Taking whatever I wanted. Hurting whomever I wanted. Hurting all those kids at the academy the way they've been hurting me ever since they found out about my parents."

Covington smiled. "That's the spirit."

"Don't do it, Rory," Ian said again, despite the chimeras still snarling at him. "Don't listen to him! He's just using you the way Reapers use everyone—"

Lance waved the scepter, and the two chimeras stalked toward Ian. But the Viking kept right on talking, despite the fact that the creatures could attack him at any moment.

"Don't listen to him, Rory!" Ian said. "Don't—"

I raised my hand, cutting him off before he got himself killed. I appreciated Ian trying to save me, but I had already saved myself—and I was going to save him too.

"It's all right, Ian," I said in that same soft, dreamy voice, pretending I was still under the artifact's spell. "I know what I have to do now."

I stopped right in front of Covington. Sly satisfaction filled the librarian's face.

"And what's that, Rory?" he asked. "What do you have to do now?"

This time, when I smiled at him, it was a genuine expression. "This."

I tightened my grip on Babs, then snapped up the sword and brought it down on his hand as hard as I could.

CHAPTER TWENTY-FOUR

Covington's eyes widened as he realized I wasn't under his spell anymore. He started to jerk his hand away, but I was quicker.

Besides, I was a Spartan—and I didn't miss.

The sword slammed into his hand. The second Babs's blade touched the signet ring, a searing red light filled the entire rotunda, making everyone yell and avert their eyes from the harsh glare, even the chimeras.

Crack!

The blood-red stone shattered under Babs's blade, and a second later, the intense light snuffed out. I blinked and blinked until my vision cleared. The stone had vanished, although fire had taken its place—a literal ring of fire around Covington's hand.

The librarian screamed, yanked the burning ring off his finger, and tossed it onto the floor, where the gold started to melt. But the flames continued to scorch Covington's hand, and he snarled and slapped his fingers up against his red cloak, trying to smother the fire.

"Yeah! Take that, Reaper scum!" Babs called out, proud of the destruction she'd caused.

I grinned. I was proud of her too.

While I dealt with Covington, Ian took care of the chimeras, which were rearing back on their haunches, getting ready to strike. Ian plucked a dagger off his belt, drew his arm back, and threw the weapon at one of the creatures. The blade sank deep into the chimera's throat, and the monster screamed and vanished in a cloud of smoke at the mortal wound.

The second chimera hissed and sprang at him, but Ian was expecting the attack, and he went down on one knee and sliced his ax all the way across the creature's chest. That chimera also screamed in pain, and then it too vanished in a cloud of smoke.

With the monsters out of the way, Ian charged forward and ran up beside me.

"Get them!" Covington screamed, finally snuffing out the fire on his hand. "Kill them, you fools!"

Lance and Drake raised their weapons and charged at us, and Ian and I stepped up to meet them.

Clash-clash-clang!
Clash-clash-clang!

The sound of our weapons crashing together rang out through the rotunda. I battled Lance, while Ian took on Drake.

Lance was a good fighter, but he was no match for me, and he knew it. Almost immediately, he started swinging his sword in wider and more reckless arcs, trying to take me by surprise, but I anticipated everything he was going to do, and I easily avoided his clumsy blows. His Roman speed was the only thing that was saving him right now, and he'd get tired and slow down soon enough.

Lance realized it too, and he decided to fight dirty. He snapped up the gold scepter to conjure more chimeras, but I slashed out with my sword, making him drop his hand before he could complete the summoning motion.

Out of the corner of my eye, I saw Ian swing his ax, trying to bury the weapon in his brother's shoulder, instead of straight into his heart like he should have. Drake dodged the blow, stepped up, and punched Ian in the face. His massive Viking strength made Ian stagger back.

Ian wasn't trying to kill his brother. Wound him, yes. But kill him, no. Despite everything that had happened between them, Ian was still trying to save his brother. At least from dying. Because that's the kind of good guy he was.

The same couldn't be said for Drake, who seemed determined to run his brother through with his sword the first chance he got. I just hoped that Ian would realize that it was him or Drake and that Drake wasn't giving him a choice. That he wouldn't be captured and put in prison and that there was only one way to end that kind of fight.

But for right now, I had my hands full with Lance. The other warrior's speed was quickly deserting him, and he kept trying to raise the scepter to conjure more chimeras. Every time he lifted the scepter, I lashed out with my sword and forced him to drop his hand back down to his side or risk my chopping it off completely.

"What's wrong, Lance?" I mocked. "You're looking slow and weak. I thought Romans were faster than that. You've spent too much time partying and not enough time training. Your endurance sucks."

"Shut up, Spartan," Lance growled back. "I've still got plenty of energy left to kill you!"

He swung his sword at me again, but I ducked under the blow, came up, spun around, and sliced my blade across his back. Lance screamed and staggered forward. He managed to hang on to his sword, but the gold chimera scepter flew out of his hands, hit the floor, and rolled away. I charged after the artifact—

"Rory!" Babs's hand moved under my mouth. "Over there!"

I stopped and looked to my right. While Ian and I had been fighting Drake and Lance, Covington had made a beeline for the display case. With everything that had been going on, I'd forgotten that he was a Roman and how fast he could move. He shoved his elbow into the glass, shattering it, then reached inside and grabbed the black jewelry box.

"Forget about them!" Covington screamed. "We got what we came for! Let's go!"

Drake ducked Ian's latest attack, put his shoulder down, and barreled into his brother. The move took Ian by surprise, and his legs flew out from under him. He hit the floor hard, and his head snapped back against the stone. Ian let out a low groan, and I could tell he was dazed. But instead of attacking him again, Drake kept right on going, running past his brother and scooping up the gold chimera scepter from the floor.

"Lance!" Drake yelled. "Let's go!"

Covington was already sprinting toward the closest archway, and Drake fell into step behind him. Lance darted forward as well, but he didn't follow the other Reapers. Instead, he veered off to the left, where Ian was still groaning and trying to shake off his hard fall. My breath caught in my throat, and I raced in that direction, moving faster than I ever had before.

Lance stopped right in front of Ian and raised his sword high. "Die, Viking!" he snarled.

"No!" I screamed.

Lance raised his sword even higher, then started to bring his weapon down on top of Ian's head. I leaped forward, closing the distance between us, and thrust out with my own sword—shoving it straight into Lance's heart.

His eyes bulged, and he screamed with pain. I yanked Babs free of his chest, making him scream again. Lance stood there, wobbling on his feet. He stared down at all the blood staining his chest, as though he couldn't believe I'd actually gotten the best of him. Then his sword slipped from his hand, and he toppled to the floor—dead.

"Ian!" I turned to him. "Are you okay?"

He shook off the rest of his daze, took my outstretched arm, and let me pull him to his feet. "I'm fine! We can't let them get away!"

My head snapped around just in time for me to see Covington and Drake vanish through the open archway. Ian and I headed after them, but we hadn't taken three steps in that direction before Covington and Drake rushed right back into the rotunda. A second later, I realized why they'd changed course.

Zoe and Mateo were here.

The Amazon and the Roman stormed into the rotunda. Zoe was brandishing her electrodagger, while Mateo had his crossbow in his hand. The two of them charged after Covington and Drake, and Ian and I did the same thing.

"Give it up!" I yelled. "You've got nowhere to go!"

The Reapers didn't pay any attention to me. Instead, Covington and Drake raced for the other archway on the far side of the rotunda.

"We can't let them get away!" Ian yelled again.

The four of us chased after the two Reapers. Mateo pulled ahead of the rest of us, since his Roman speed made him the fastest. He snapped up his crossbow and fired off a bolt.

Thunk!

The bolt clipped Covington's arm and slammed into the wall. The librarian yelped, and the sharp, stinging blow made him lose his grip on the jewelry box. The artifact clattered to the floor. Covington slowed down, like he was going to double back for it, but Drake shoved him forward. Covington cursed and kept running. So did Drake.

Ian stopped long enough to snatch the jewelry box up off the floor, and we all ran on.

The Reapers sprinted from one room to another, with us chasing after them. Covington's Roman speed easily kept him in the lead, and Drake lagged a few feet behind him. Around and around we all went, from one exhibit area to another, until I almost felt like we were running laps of the dungeon section of the museum.

My gaze darted left and right, and I hoped that Takeda, Aunt Rachel, and the Protectorate guards would show up, but they didn't appear. They must still be searching the exhibit rooms on the first floor. With our comms jammed, they probably had no idea what was going on up here, which meant it was up to me and my friends to stop the Reapers.

I was okay with that.

Covington and Drake darted into a room up ahead of us and disappeared from sight. We charged after them, and I realized that we were right back where we'd started, in the rotunda with the smashed display case and dead Reapers littering the floor.

I expected Covington and Drake to already be gone from this area, but to my surprise, the librarian was standing in the archway on the far side of the rotunda, bent over double, his hands on his knees, as if he'd run out of energy and couldn't take another step. I didn't believe that for one second.

Mateo was still ahead of Ian, Zoe, and me, and he increased his pace, determined to get to Covington before he escaped.

"Stop!" I yelled. "It's a trap!"

Mateo charged ahead anyway, and Covington stepped back into the other room. Drake was in there as well, and he slashed his sword through the air at something I couldn't see. A loud *screech* of metal rang out, and the spiked iron gate at the top of the archway dropped down. Drake must have hacked through the rope that was holding up the gate.

"Mateo! Watch out!" Ian shouted.

Mateo's head snapped up, and he realized he was about to get skewered by the gate's sharp daggerlike points. He stopped running, but one of his boots slipped on the floor, and he stumbled forward, right into the center of the archway. He also lost his grip on his crossbow, which hit the floor and skittered away.

Zoe reached out, grabbed Mateo's shirt, and yanked him back as hard as she could. Blue sparks of magic exploded in the air all around them. The Valkyrie must have been stronger than she realized, because Mateo lurched back, and the two of them fell to the floor on this side of the archway. And not a second too soon.

Bang!

The spikes slammed into their slots in the marble floor inches away from Mateo's boots.

Ian and I rushed over to our friends and helped them to their feet.

"Are you guys okay?" I asked.

"Yeah," Mateo said. "I'm fine, thanks to Zoe."

He flashed her a grateful smile, and she winked back at him.

"And don't you forget it," Zoe said.

Together, the four of us turned toward the archway. The gate was still down, blocking the opening, and we didn't have any way to lift it from this side. Something that Covington and Drake both realized, since they were standing right on the other side of the iron bars, smirking at us.

"This isn't over," I growled. "You won't get away with this."

Covington gave me an evil grin. "I already have, Rory. You just don't realize it yet."

I opened my mouth to growl at him again, but Covington lifted his hand, and I realized that he was holding the gold chimera scepter. Drake must have given it to him sometime during the chase.

"Good-bye, Rory." Covington saluted me with the scepter, then snapped it around in those sharp, familiar figure-eight motions.

Thick, choking clouds of smoke exploded out of the end of the scepter, driving us away from the iron bars. The clouds of smoke vanished in an instant, but something far, far worse stood in their places.

Seven chimeras, all slowly advancing on me and my friends.

CHAPTER TWENTY-FIVE

"**B**ack! Back! Back!" I yelled.

Mateo and Zoe were standing in front of Ian and me. Mateo shoved Zoe behind him and backpedaled after her, but for once, he wasn't quite quick enough, and the closest chimera swiped at him with one of its massive paws. The creature's claws ripped deep into Mateo's shoulder, making him scream and tumble to the floor. Blood spattered all over the white marble, and I couldn't tell how seriously he was injured.

Zoe lashed out with her electrodagger, driving the chimera back. Ian dropped his ax and the jewelry box he'd been holding, darted forward, and used his Viking strength to grab Mateo and haul him to his feet. Ian put his arm under Mateo's, getting blood all over his own clothes. Mateo grimaced, his mouth pinched tight with pain, but he shuffled back out of the way with Ian's help.

"We have to get out of here!" Ian yelled.

He started dragging Mateo back toward the other archway, which was still open. Zoe and I covered their retreat, brandishing our weapons at the chimeras, but the creatures didn't want to attack us. Not yet.

They wanted to play with us first.

The chimeras paced back and forth in front of the closed iron gate, arching their backs the way regular house cats would. They were working out the kinks, as though they'd been cooped up in that scepter and needed to stretch before they attacked us. I wondered if the creatures would eat us after they killed us, the way cats would dine on the mice they caught.

Because they *were* going to kill us.

Mateo couldn't fight now, and Ian couldn't set him down, or the chimeras would pounce on the injured guy first. Or worse, the chimeras would go ahead and pounce on both of them at the same time. Zoe was an okay fighter, but she was no match for the chimeras, not even with her electrodagger. She would go down next, and then I would be left all alone to face the creatures.

I might have taken out two chimeras in the Library of Antiquities and three more at Lance's mansion, but I couldn't fight seven of them at once. Sooner or later, one of the creatures would wound me, and then they would all move in for the kill at the same time.

I was a Spartan, so I knew the odds better than anyone else. We weren't going to win this fight. The chimeras would make short work of us, and then they would head into the main part of the museum, leap over the second-floor balcony, and attack all the Mythos kids partying below—kids who had no idea how much danger they were in. Eventually, Takeda, Aunt Rachel, and the Protectorate guards would take down the chimeras but not before the creatures killed dozens of students.

It would be a massacre.

I couldn't let that happen, but I didn't know how to stop it either. My gaze darted around the rotunda, searching for something that would help us, but no weapons or armor were displayed in here, only paintings, carvings, jewelry, and small statues.

The chimeras finished their stretching and stalked toward Zoe and me. I risked a quick glance over my shoulder. Ian and Mateo were almost to the open archway, but they were moving slowly, and the chimeras could easily leap over Zoe and me and go after them at any moment.

Desperate, I looked around again, but I only saw the same things as before. Paintings, carvings, jewelry, statues, the iron gate hanging in the archway—

Wait a second. My head snapped back in that direction. *The gate.*

Maybe I didn't have to fight the chimeras. Maybe all I had to do was trap them in the rotunda. Even the chimeras couldn't force their way through those heavy iron bars. The more I thought about it, the more sense it made. It would work. I knew it would work.

Until Mateo stumbled.

He must have been weak from the blood loss, because his legs sagged, and he would have crumpled to the floor if Ian hadn't been holding on to him. Zoe looked back and forth between the two guys and the chimeras that were slowly creeping up on us. She didn't know whether to stay here and fight with me or rush over and help Ian get Mateo out of the rotunda.

I knew what would happen next. I could see it all unspooling in my mind. If Zoe stayed here with me, we would both get mauled to death by the chimeras. If she helped Ian and Mateo, the three of them could get out of the rotunda to safety.

The only problem was that someone had to stay in here

with the chimeras and slash through the rope in order to lower the gate and trap the creatures.

And that someone was going to be me.

"Go!" I yelled. "Help Ian and Mateo! I've got this!"

"But—" Zoe started.

"Go!" I yelled again, cutting her off. "I'll be right behind you!"

I would be right behind her—I just wouldn't be getting out of the rotunda alive.

Zoe nodded, whirled around, and rushed over to Ian with Mateo. She put her arm under Mateo's other shoulder, and together she and Ian dragged the injured Roman toward the archway.

And not a moment too soon.

Two of the chimeras realized that their dinner was getting away, and they sprinted around me and went after my friends.

"Faster!" Ian called out, still dragging Mateo toward the archway. "Faster!"

With one hand, Zoe held on to Mateo, and with the other, she brandished her electrodagger at the creatures again. The electricity crackling on the blade made the chimeras stop short, but Zoe's threat wouldn't keep them at bay for long.

That left five chimeras standing in front of me. Once again, the creatures paced back and forth, their paws scorching the floor, noxious clouds of black smoke spewing out of their mouths. They were enjoying playing with me, so I decided to give them something to chase.

I lashed out with my sword, momentarily driving them back, then turned and ran in the other direction, heading toward the archway as fast as I could.

Mateo stumbled again, but this time, Ian and Zoe

managed to backpedal completely out of the room. The three of them fell in a heap on the floor outside the rotunda.

The two chimeras in front of me growled and surged forward. Desperate to distract them, I stopped running, snatched a statue off its pedestal, and threw it at them. The statue hit one of the chimeras square in the back and broke apart into a hundred pieces.

"Hey!" I yelled, waving my hand in the air to get their attention. "Over here!"

The creature snarled and whipped around to face me. So did the second chimera right next to it. Out of the corner of my eye, I could see the five other monsters creeping up on me as well. One chimera stepped on another's paw, and they all started hissing at and jostling each other. They were jockeying for position, trying to decide which one was the alpha and would get to pounce on me first.

Since they weren't going to attack me immediately, I slowly started backing away, trying to put as much distance as possible between myself and the creatures without them noticing. I also turned my sword around, so that I was holding Babs by her blade.

"Rory!" Babs yelled. "What are you doing?"

"Do you really think you're cursed?"

She frowned. "What? Why are you asking me about that right now? You should be running, not talking!"

I brought her face up to mine so I could look her in the eye. "Do you really think you're cursed? And that I'm destined to die here tonight?"

Babs blinked, and her face twisted into a miserable expression. For a moment, I thought she wasn't going to answer me, but she finally did.

"Yes," she whispered. "I do. I really do. I'm so sorry, Rory."

I grinned back at her. "Well, then, if I'm going to die anyway, I might as well make it count, right?"

Her green eye narrowed, and I thought she would have nodded her half of a head if she could have. "Aye. A warrior's death should always count for something."

My grin widened. "I was hoping you would say that. Here we go."

"What are you doing?"

Babs started to ask what my plan was, but I'd already turned the sword back around and grabbed her by the hilt again. I would need her sharp blade for this. The chimeras got tired of snapping at each other, and they all stalked toward me again, but I ignored them and sprinted forward, straight toward the archway.

Outside, Ian scrambled to his feet. "Rory! Look out! Behind you!"

I heard the *scrape-scrape-scrape-scrape* of claws on stone, and I knew that one of the chimeras was pouncing at me. But I kept going, still running toward the archway.

At the very last second, I lurched to the side, slamming into the wall instead of going through the opening. The chimera barely missed punching its claws into my back. It passed by so close that I felt its black fur brush along my arm.

The creature landed in a heap, right in the middle of the archway, and shook its head, dazed by the hard, unexpected fall. I didn't hesitate. I slashed out with Babs, using the blade to cut through the rope that held up the iron gate.

Bang!

The gate dropped down, and all those iron spikes slammed right into the chimera's body. The creature screamed in pain and disappeared in a cloud of smoke.

I coughed and waved my hand in front of my face, and

the burning smoke dissipated, revealing exactly how dire my situation was.

I was trapped in the rotunda with six chimeras and no way out.

The chimeras blinked and blinked, staring at the doorway where the other creature had died and then disappeared. The creatures looked confused, and it didn't seem they were going to attack me right away.

Their confusion wouldn't last long, though.

"Rory! Rory, where are you?" Ian called out.

I kept one eye on the chimeras and hurried over to the closed gate, peering through the bars at Ian, who was standing on the other side.

"Get out of there!" he said. "Open the gate! Hurry!"

I shook my head. "I cut the rope. I can't get out."

Ian's gray gaze flicked past me to the chimeras, which had started pacing back and forth again, getting ready to attack me. Fear and horror filled his eyes, but those emotions quickly solidified into stubborn determination. The Viking wrapped his hands around the iron bars and braced himself.

"What are you doing?" I asked.

"Getting you out of there!" he yelled back. "Stand back!"

Ian strained and heaved and pushed up with all his might. He was strong, even for a Viking, and he actually managed to lift the gate one inch, then two, then three. Every muscle in his body clenched with the effort, his face went tomato-red, and all the veins stood out in his neck. But the gate was too heavy, even for him. A second later, his hands slipped off the iron bars, and the gate crashed back down to the floor.

I risked another glance over my shoulder. The chimeras had quit their pacing, and they were licking their chops. I had less than a minute before they all attacked me at once.

I straightened up to my full height. "You need to leave me. Go find Drake and stop him and Covington from getting away. Please, please do that for me."

Ian shook his head. "No! I'm not leaving you, Rory. I have to find a way to get you out of there."

I smiled at him. "It's not your fault. This was my choice. I did what I had to in order to save you guys. I don't regret that. Not for one second, and you shouldn't either."

Ian stared at me, anguish glimmering in his eyes. His gaze flicked past me to the chimeras, and his mouth hardened into a stubborn line. "I'm getting you out of there," he repeated. "You are *not* going to die tonight, cupcake."

I smiled at him again, then stepped forward and put my fingers on the gate. He wrapped his hand around mine, and the two of us stood there, holding hands despite the iron bars that separated us. I stared into his gray, gray eyes, marveling at the emotions sweeping through his gaze like storm clouds. Guilt. Grief. Concern. And a spark of something that made my heart do that funny little flutter in my chest.

"Good-bye, Ian." I dropped my hand from his and stepped away from the gate.

"Rory!" he called out. "Rory!"

As much as I wanted to look back at him, I made myself turn toward the chimeras instead. I gripped Babs by her blade and held the sword up where I could see her face again.

"So this is my grand plan. Sacrifice myself so my friends can live. An oldie but a goodie. At least, I think it is. I hope you agree."

This was what having a Spartan heart really meant to me, even if it had taken me a while to figure it out.

"I'm so proud of you, Rory," Babs said, a tear streaking down her cheek, her green eye glowing as bright as an emerald in her silver hilt. "So very, very proud. It's been an honor to serve you."

"Just as it's been an honor to wield you." I bowed my head to her. "Now, let's show these chimeras what a real fight looks like. What do you say?"

Babs's mouth split into a wide grin. "Bring on the beasties! We'll slay them all! Victory will be ours!"

She kept right on talking, each statement getting bolder and more outrageous than the last. I grinned the whole time, letting her words wash over me and fill me with confidence. I wasn't going to survive the fight, but I was going to give the chimeras all they could handle—and then some.

With one thought, the chimeras licked their chops a final time and headed straight for me.

I grabbed Babs by the hilt, raised the sword high, and rushed forward to meet the monsters.

CHAPTER TWENTY-SIX

I plunged into the pack of chimeras.

The creatures must have been used to people running away from them, because my full-frontal attack surprised them and slowed their reactions for one precious second. One of the creatures swiped its paw out, trying to lay my stomach open with its sharp claws, but I dropped to my knees. Even as I slid forward across the slick floor, I snapped up my sword, slicing it all the way down the creature's side. Smoke and blood boiled out of the mortal wound. The chimera snarled a final time, then vanished.

Two down, five to go.

Too many to go.

I slid all the way over to the opposite side of the rotunda, but I didn't stop moving. Not even for an instant. I kicked out with my left foot, stopping myself right before I hit the wall. Then I surged to my feet and whirled back around.

"Rory! Rory!" Multiple voices screamed my name.

Across the room, Zoe stood on the other side of the gate, her hands wrapped around the iron bars, trying to lift it so she could come in here and help me. Aunt Rachel was there too, straining to lift the gate with her, along with Takeda. Mateo was lying on the floor behind them, still bleeding from his injuries.

To my surprise, Ian wasn't there. I frowned. Where had he gone? Why wasn't he trying to help me like the others were? Maybe he'd already realized that it was a lost cause and didn't want to stick around to see my death. Couldn't blame him for that.

"Guards! Guards!" Takeda barked out. "All guards converge on my position at once!"

He was trying to summon enough men to lift the gate, but it would take them precious minutes to get here—minutes I didn't have.

The five remaining chimeras whipped around, and they all leaped at me at once. I threw myself to the right, trying to get out of the way, but I couldn't avoid them all.

I managed to dodge four of the creatures, but the fifth swiped its claws down my left arm, making me scream with pain. I staggered forward and hit one of the display cases hard enough to rattle the glass in its frame. The blow stunned me, and my knees hit the floor. One of the chimeras used the opportunity to leap across the rotunda, charging right at me, and I knew I wouldn't be able to get out of the way of its sharp claws and jagged teeth—

Thunk!

A dagger zipped across the rotunda and lodged itself in the chimera's right eye. The creature screamed and exploded in a shower of smoke, and the dagger clattered to the floor. I coughed and looked across the room. Aunt Rachel was pressed up against the gate, her arm stuck through one of the openings. She'd thrown the dagger, and her Spartan aim had been true.

"Get me a bow and some arrows!" she screamed. "Now!"

Zoe darted away from the door, but it would take her time to find a ranged weapon that Aunt Rachel could use. Her Spartan killer instincts were the only reason she'd been able to throw that dagger and hit her mark.

"Rory!" Babs's mouth moved under my hand. "Get up! Get up!"

I shook off my daze and staggered to my feet. I glanced down at my injury and wished I hadn't, given the blood that covered my arm from my shoulder all the way down to my fingertips. More and more pain pulsed through my body, the red-hot intensity of it threatening to block out everything else, but I forced myself to take slow, deep breaths, push the agony away, and tighten my grip on Babs's hilt. I couldn't afford to let myself feel the pain right now. Not with the chimeras advancing on me again.

Another one pounced, and I lurched to the side, barely avoiding the scorpion's stinger on the end of its tail. The chimera slammed into the display case, breaking the glass and crushing the wooden stand to bits. The hard blow stunned the creature, and I charged forward and stabbed it in the side, shoving my sword deep into its body. The creature screamed and vanished in a puff of smoke.

Four down, three to go.

Still too many to go.

The other chimeras were tired of playing with me, and they moved so that they were all standing in a loose circle around me. Then they slowly started closing in. I drew in a deep breath and raised Babs, getting ready for the multiple attacks that were coming next.

And then there was no more time to think.

There was only fighting.

The three chimeras all pounced at me at the same time, swiping out with their claws and snapping at me with their jagged teeth. For once, I was glad Takeda had spent so much time on agility drills in gym class this past week. I ducked and dodged and spun this way and that, avoiding as many of the blows as I could.

But I couldn't avoid them all.

One of the chimeras lashed out with its paw, catching me square in the chest, but its claws skidded off the tough leather that Zoe had woven into my dress. I had never been so grateful for armor before.

But it wasn't going to be enough to save me.

My chest might be protected by Zoe's braided leather armor, but the rest of my body wasn't, and the creatures quickly took advantage.

The first chimera swiped its claws across my right arm. The second creature nicked my left thigh, while the third caught me across the back of my right calf. In an instant, I was the one on the defensive, trying to ward off all their attacks and failing miserably. The chimeras realized that they had me trapped and beaten, and they were going to kill me, one swipe of their claws at a time. Even if Aunt Rachel somehow got her hands on a bow and some arrows, she couldn't help me now. Not with the chimeras all around me. She couldn't risk shooting at the creatures for fear that she would hit me instead.

I gritted my teeth, pushed the pain of my many injuries away, and kept fighting, just like any Spartan would, just like any true warrior would.

Even if I hadn't been injured, the chimeras were far bigger and stronger than I was. One of them lashed out with its long tail and knocked my legs out from under me. I hit the floor hard and slid back ten feet, slamming into another display case and losing my grip on Babs.

The sword landed a few feet away, and I slowly crawled

across the floor and grabbed her blade with my bloody fingers. But my entire body felt cold, heavy, and numb from where the chimeras had clawed me, and I simply didn't have the strength to pick up the weapon, much less wield her.

"Looks like you were right about that curse after all," I mumbled.

"I'm sorry, Rory," Babs whispered, staring up at me, tears streaming out of her green eye. "So sorry."

I tried to smile, but I didn't have the strength for that either. "It's not your fault," I mumbled again. "This was my decision, my choice."

Babs kept staring at me, more and more tears streaming down her half of a face. The drops were as cold as snowflakes stinging my skin.

I looked over at the archway, but I was in the front corner of the room, and I couldn't see anyone from this angle, although I could hear my friends shouting, along with Aunt Rachel and Takeda. They were still trying to save me, even though it was already too late.

A series of low, pleased growls sounded. The three remaining chimeras all grinned, showing me their teeth, and started advancing on me for the final time. In seconds, they would leap on me and rip me to pieces. I just hoped it wouldn't hurt too much—before the end.

I stared at the chimeras, too injured and exhausted to do anything but watch them come for me. At least I'd saved Ian, Zoe, and Mateo. I took comfort in that.

The chimeras got down on their haunches and crept forward, one foot at a time, their paws scorching the floor. They rocked back, all readying themselves to leap at me...

And then they stopped.

They just *stopped*.

The chimeras' heads snapped up, and they all stared at

the glass ceiling. I craned my neck up too, wondering what they were looking at, since all I saw were the moon and stars twinkling in the night sky far, far above...

I frowned. Wait a second. Maybe it was my imagination or the blood loss, but it seemed there were several patches of sky that were darker than the rest and rapidly dropping down toward the museum...

The ceiling exploded with a roar.

Glass fell down all over me, *tink-tink-tinking* against the floor like drops of crystal rain. I put my arms up over my head, protecting my face as best I could, but the sharp shards still sliced into my skin, making me hiss with even more pain.

The roaring shower of glass stopped, but a series of loud *screech-screech-screeches* rose up to take its place. My heart lifted with hope. I knew those screeches.

I dropped my arms, raised my head again, and blinked, trying to focus on the scene in front of me. Sure enough, one after another, Eir gryphons dropped down through the shattered ceiling and landed right in front of me. Balder, the leader, along with Brono, his son, and a third adult gryphon. But what were they doing here? How had they found me?

For a moment, I wondered if I was imagining things. If maybe I was already dead and just dreaming that this was all happening.

But I wasn't.

The gryphons were here, and they launched themselves at the chimeras. The two sets of creatures went around and around the rotunda, scratching, biting, and attacking each other with their claws, teeth, and beaks. They whirled around in a tangled mass of bronze wings and black fur, so fast and vicious that I couldn't tell where the gryphons began and the chimeras ended.

But slowly, the gryphons began to get the best of the chimeras. One of the chimeras exploded in a puff of smoke, then the second one. The three gryphons cornered the last chimera, then pounced on the creature all at the same time. A second later, the final chimera also disintegrated into a cloud of smoke...

After that, I must have passed out for a minute, because the gryphons were suddenly standing next to me, with Brono, the baby, hunkered down on the floor right beside me. I smiled and tried to lift my hand to pet him, but I was too weak, and I couldn't even move my fingers right now...

I must have drifted off again, because the next thing I knew, someone was shouting my name.

"Rory!" Ian's face appeared above mine. "Rory!"

He fell to his knees, picked me up, and cradled me against his chest. My head dropped down. Maybe it was the pain of all my injuries, but I could have sworn that Ian was holding a tiny whistle in his hand. I frowned. What was he doing with a whistle?

"Rory! Rory! Stay with me!" Ian kept shouting at me, but his voice got fainter and farther away with every passing second.

Then his voice cut off altogether, and the world faded to black.

CHAPTER TWENTY-SEVEN

I woke up in the Eir Ruins.

I must have fallen asleep, since I was sitting on the ground, slumped against the stone fountain in the center of the main courtyard. The sun was setting behind the mountain, and a lovely purple twilight was creeping over the landscape. I rubbed the grit out of my eyes and got to my feet. Something brushed against my bare legs, and I realized it was the skirt from the Spartan princess outfit Zoe had made me for the costume ball.

I frowned. Weird. Why was I wearing this?

A gleam of silver caught my eye. I looked down to find Babs lying on the wide rim that circled the fountain, her green eye closed as though she was sleeping. How had she gotten here? How had *I* gotten here? The last thing I remembered was battling the chimeras at the museum. My stomach dropped. The only way Babs and I could have gotten from the museum all the way up here was…if I…

If I were *dead*.

I'd thought the chimeras would kill me, but to realize that it had actually *happened*…

My heart squeezed tight. Tears pricked my eyes, but I

ruthlessly blinked them away. I wasn't going to break down just because Babs had been right about her curse. Wielding her in battle had been my decision, and now I was facing the consequences. I was a Spartan. Tough, strong, fierce. I wasn't going to cry just because I was dead—

"Hello, Rory," a voice called out.

I whirled around, not sure who or what I would find, but I wasn't too surprised at the familiar figure standing in front of me.

Sigyn.

Black hair and eyes. A long white gown. Old, faded scars crisscrossing her hands and arms. A beautiful face tinged with perpetual sadness. The Norse goddess of devotion looked the same as I remembered from our previous talk here.

The goddess stepped forward, a smile spreading across her face. "Hello, Rory," she repeated.

"Um, hi." I glanced around, but we were all alone in the ruins, except for Babs lying on the stone rim of the fountain and the colorful carpet of wildflowers at our feet. "So… I guess the chimeras killed me after all."

Sigyn let out a laugh. "Why would you think that?"

I shrugged. "Oh, I don't know. All their claws. All my wounds. All the blood dripping out of my body."

She laughed again. "It takes more than that to kill a warrior like you, Rory. You should know that by now."

"So…I'm *not* dead, then?" I asked, totally confused.

Instead of answering me, Sigyn gestured with her hand, asking me to fall into step beside her. I did, and we began walking around the courtyard like we had the first time we'd met here. Once again, all the wildflowers bowed their heads as the goddess brushed past them. I stepped as lightly as I could, trying not to crush any more of the flowers underfoot than necessary, but they all sprang right back up again the second I moved on. Even more unusual, the wildflowers all swiveled in my direction, as though they were tracking me through the courtyard.

I shivered. I wondered if this was how Gwen felt with her psychometry magic. Like flowers and other inanimate objects were watching her all the time. It wasn't as cool as you'd think it would be. In fact, it was downright creepy.

"You're probably wondering why I brought you here to the ruins again," Sigyn said. "You have done well, Rory Forseti. No one could have fought harder than you did against so many chimeras."

"Not well enough," I muttered. "Mateo got hurt, and Covington and Drake got away. Plus, they still have the chimera scepter."

She shrugged. "You can choose to focus on the negative, if you wish. But I choose to focus on the positive."

"And what would that be?"

"Covington used an artifact to try to turn you into a Reaper. A gold signet ring studded with a ruby that once belonged to Apate, the Greek goddess of deception. Have you heard of her jewels and what they can do?"

"That they can control people's minds? Yeah, Gwen told me about them."

"Then you know how powerful they are." Sigyn tilted her head to the side, studying me. "But you resisted the ruby's magic and Covington's commands."

I shook my head. "I have no idea how I did that."

"Don't you?" she murmured.

Her black gaze dropped to my wrist, and I realized that I was fiddling with the heart locket on my charm bracelet. My fingers stilled, and I remembered how the bracelet and locket had glowed with that pure, bright silver light that no one had seemed to notice but me.

"This isn't just a charm bracelet, is it?" I whispered.

"No, it's not," Sigyn said. "But you know that. You've known that for days now."

How could I possibly know that? I started to ask the goddess what she meant, but then I remembered all the artifacts I'd seen in the Bunker, including one that had looked exactly like my charm bracelet.

"The Bracelet of Freya," I whispered. "This is Freya's Bracelet—the *real* bracelet. The one I saw in the Bunker is a fake, isn't it?"

Sigyn nodded.

"But how did I wind up with it…" My voice trailed off as the realization hit me. "My parents. They gave me this bracelet. They…they must have stolen Freya's Bracelet sometime before it was taken to the Bunker. They must have left a fake behind in its place, so they could give me the real artifact without anyone realizing I had it."

I thought of all those times I had searched the library and our old house, looking for a clue from my parents. They had left something behind for me after all, even if I had been too blind to see it until right now.

"But why? Why would they give me the bracelet?"

"What do you know about the artifact?" Sigyn asked.

I fiddled with the heart locket again. "On the identification card, it said that whoever wears the bracelet will be protected by Freya's love. It didn't really say exactly what the bracelet would protect someone from."

"Protected not just by Freya's love but also by the love of your parents," Sigyn said. "Your parents gave you the bracelet out of love, which means that no one can ever take it away from you by force. Remember that."

I stared down at the heart locket. My parents had surprised me with the bracelet on my birthday, and I remembered my mom telling me that it was special, just like I was special to her and my dad, and to always keep it close. I'd absolutely loved the bracelet, and I'd worn it every single day, right up until their funerals. All this time, I had been so angry at my parents, but now I realized that they'd been in an impossible situation, and they'd done what they could to help me. They'd tried to protect me the best way they knew how—and they had.

They had given me a Spartan heart in more ways than one.

"My parents must have known that they might not be able to leave the Reapers," I said. "They must have guessed that Covington would kill them and try to get me to take their place someday. That's why they gave me the bracelet, isn't it? To protect me from Covington and whatever magic or artifact he might try to use on me. So he couldn't force me to become a Reaper. So I could use my own free will and decide for myself what kind of warrior I want to be."

Sigyn nodded. "And that you did, Rory. That you did."

Another thought occurred to me. "But the bracelet wasn't the only thing, the only artifact, that helped me. So did Babs with all her talking. That's why you put the sword out for me to find in the library that first night, isn't it? You knew that Babs would try to talk me out of becoming a Reaper. That she would help me resist Covington and his magic."

A smile curved the goddess's lips, confirming my suspicions. "As I said before, talking swords can be quite useful."

We kept strolling around the courtyard, both of us lost in our own thoughts. My parents were gone, but I still had the bracelet and my memories of them in my heart. Those were the things I would keep close to me, those were the things I would focus on, those were the things I would treasure, just like my mom and dad had wanted me to.

Sigyn and I walked past a crumbling wall at the back of the courtyard. The goddess stopped and trailed her fingers over the gryphon carved into the stone. I knew this spot—it was where Gwen had found the Chloris ambrosia flowers that had healed Nickamedes. But instead of more ambrosia, a small white winterbloom was growing out of the gryphon's beak now. Sigyn plucked the flower out of the stone and rolled the dark green stem back and forth between her fingers.

"Your cousin, Gwendolyn Frost, is a true Champion. She did what no one else could, and she saved countless lives by imprisoning Loki. Nike chose her Champion well." The goddess kept staring at the flower. "I've never had a Champion. Not a single one."

"Never? Why not?"

"It was my fault that Loki escaped his prison, so I thought I should be the one to put him back in it. I didn't want anyone else getting hurt because of me. It was my error, and I wanted to fix it myself."

Sadness filled Sigyn's face, and I knew she was thinking about all the mistakes she'd made with the evil god. About how she'd loved him and how he'd used that love against her. About how Loki had tricked her into freeing him and about all the people who had died as a result. Sigyn sighed, and I could hear all of her heartbreak and regret in that one soft sound.

After a moment, she spoke again. "Loki might be back where he belongs, but unfortunately, a dangerous new threat has risen to take his place."

"Covington," I snarled.

"Yes. And I think it's time for me to have a Champion after all. Now that I've finally found someone worthy." Sigyn looked at me. "I would like that Champion to be you, Rory."

Shock rippled through me. Gwen had told me that she thought Sigyn had plans for me, but I'd never expected *this*. Oh, I had considered the possibility during my first meeting with the goddess here in the dreamscape ruins, but since she hadn't asked me to be her Champion then, I didn't think she ever would.

I should have, though. Finding Babs in the library. Joining the Midgard. Realizing that Covington had escaped from prison. Fighting the chimeras in the museum. It had all been leading up to this moment.

"Why me?" I asked. "Why would you want me to be your Champion? I'm the daughter of Reaper assassins, remember? That doesn't exactly make me Champion material."

Sigyn smiled. "Because we're a lot alike. We both want to make up for the sins of those we loved. Together, I think we can. Covington has dark, dark things planned. If he succeeds, in a way, it will be worse than what Loki tried to do. But I think you can stop him, Rory. And you've already proven yourself worthy of being my Champion."

"How did I do that?"

"By going to the museum tonight, even though Babs asked you not to. By choosing to fight the Reapers, even though you knew about the sword's curse. And most of all, by locking yourself in that room with all those chimeras in order to save your friends, even though you knew the creatures would most likely kill you."

She kept staring at me, and something that Gwen had

said to me popped into my mind, something that Nike, the Greek goddess of victory, had once told her.

"Self-sacrifice is a very powerful thing," I whispered.

Sigyn smiled again. "I see you've been talking to Gwendolyn about quite a lot of things. But she and you are both right. Self-sacrifice *is* a very powerful thing. Perhaps the most powerful thing that exists in all the realms."

The goddess moved away from the wall. I followed her, digesting her words. A minute later, the two of us were back at the fountain in the center of the courtyard.

Sigyn turned to me, a serious expression on her face. "Loki might be gone, but the world still needs protecting. So I would like you to be my Champion, Rory Forseti. I would like you to fight on my behalf, to help me battle Covington and his new band of Reapers. You're the only one who has a chance of stopping him. But it's up to you. Unlike Covington, I won't try to force you into it. You must choose it of your own free will."

I thought about everything that had happened over the past few days, from running into Ian on the quad that first morning to fighting the chimeras in the museum tonight. And I realized something: I'd been happier this past week than in all the months before.

My new friends were a big part of that, but I had been truly happy because I was finally doing what I'd dreamed of all along. Helping people and protecting them from the Reapers and their many schemes. And I knew what my decision was—what it would *always* be.

"I would be honored to be your Champion," I said. "I would love to be your Champion."

"But?"

"But how can I actually *do* that? You know, since I'm dead or whatever? And even if I wasn't dead, I still have a cursed sword. Not exactly a Champion's weapon. Especially since it's one of the reasons I'm dead now."

Sigyn let out another pleased laugh. "You said it yourself. Self-sacrifice is a very powerful thing—powerful enough to break even a goddess's curse."

She stepped forward and held out her hand, gesturing at Babs, who was still lying on the fountain rim, her eye closed. A silver light flashed, searing my eyes with its intensity, and I had to look away from it. But the light faded, and when I looked down at the sword again, Babs's green eye was wide open, and she was staring up at me.

"Babs once belonged to the Irish goddess Macha," Sigyn said. "You knew about the curse, and yet you carried her into battle anyway. Not only that, but you sacrificed yourself in order to save your friends. That was more than enough to break Macha's curse. Now the sword is free of the curse, forever. Babs is yours, Rory. If you want her."

Babs smiled at me, her metal face shining with hope.

"Of course I want Babs," I said. "She's the best sword ever."

"Then pick her up and make her yours," Sigyn said.

I bent over and put one hand under Babs's pointed blade and the other under her hilt. As soon as I picked up the weapon, Babs grew ice-cold in my hand, and the metal started glowing with that silver light again. I had to look away from the brilliant flare, but it faded away a few seconds later.

I looked back down at Babs, and I realized that the symbols on her hilt, the ones I'd noticed when she first told me about her curse in the Bunker, were much more defined now. I traced my finger down the runes. I hadn't been able to read the symbols before, but now they made perfect sense.

Babs rolled her eye down and stared at the runes.

"Finally!" she crowed in a happy voice. "Something good's carved on me!"

I laughed and slid Babs into the black leather scabbard that was still belted to my waist. Then I looked at Sigyn again.

"And I have a gift for you as well," the goddess said.

She was still holding that winterbloom, and she brought it up to her lips and gently kissed it. An icy layer of frost immediately covered the flower. In seconds, the frost solidified, turning the white petals a bright, polished silver, with the heart-shaped blossom glittering like a small emerald in the middle of the flower.

Sigyn stepped forward and gently took hold of my hand. She pressed the winterbloom up against my bracelet, and that intense silver light flashed again. When I looked back down, the flower had hooked itself to my charm bracelet, right next to my heart locket.

"It's beautiful," I whispered. "Thank you."

"Not just beautiful," Sigyn teased. "Useful too. And a part of you now, forever, whether you wear the bracelet or not."

Sigyn bent down and whispered three words into my ear—the same three words that were now carved into Babs's blade. Then she drew back, still smiling at me. "And now it's time for you to use your new gift, your new magic, to return to your friends."

I closed my eyes and concentrated. A strange new power flowed through my body, like the wildflower had taken root in the cold frost that had coated my heart for so long. In my mind's eye, I could see the winterbloom growing and growing, breaking through the hard shell of icy frost, and I could feel the power spreading out to every single part of my body. I sighed, welcoming the cool, soothing rush of power, and suddenly, I was able to breathe easier. Not only that, but I felt better, stronger, like the chimeras hadn't clawed me to shreds.

Like I was whole again.

I opened my eyes and stared at the goddess. "Thank you, Sigyn. For everything."

"No, Rory. Thank you for choosing to fight with me." She smiled at me a final time, then stepped back and bowed her head. "Until we meet again..."

Sigyn's gown started swirling around her, and that intense silver light flared again, separating us. When the light faded, the goddess was gone, and I was alone in the Eir Ruins. But I smiled, knowing that I would see her again, even as my own eyes slid shut and the ruins faded to black...

"If you don't shut up, I'm going to come over there and cleave you in two," a voice with a sharp, biting English accent snapped.

"Heh. I'd like to see you try it, you old codger," a voice with a distinctive Irish accent snapped right back.

The two voices kept sniping at each other, and I slowly realized that one of them was Babs. But who was the other one? The low male voice seemed familiar, but I couldn't quite place it...

I must have drifted off yet again, because the voices faded away. Sometime later, my eyes fluttered open, and I realized I wasn't dead. At least, I didn't think I was dead. Not since I was lying in a hospital bed with a white sheet and a matching blanket draped over me.

"I told you to shut up," that English voice snapped again. "Now look what you've done. You've woken her up when she should be resting."

"*I* woke her up?" Babs sniped back. "Well, I say that *you* woke her up with your incessant chatter."

And the two voices went at it again. This time, I came fully awake, and I pushed myself up into a sitting position.

Babs was propped up in a chair to my right, glaring at the chair next to her. Another sword was also propped up in that second seat, one with a man's face carved into the hilt, complete with a single twilight-colored eye.

Vic, Gwen's sword.

Vic and Babs glared at each other, and I got the impression that if they'd had hands, they both would have put up their fists and duked it out over who was making more noise, even though they were being equally loud.

"Hey, cousin," a third voice called out.

I looked to my left to find a girl sitting in a chair on the other side of the bed. She was a year older than me and quite pretty, with her frizzy brown hair and violet-colored eyes. She was reading a Karma Girl comic book, which she set aside as she leaned forward in her chair.

Gwen Frost grinned at me. "It's about time you woke up."

Chapter Twenty-Eight

I sat up straighter in bed and glanced around. I was in one of the infirmary rooms in the Bunker, wearing a pair of white pajamas. An eerie sense of déjà vu swept over me. This was the same place I'd woken up in the first time after I'd seen Sigyn at the Eir Ruins.

"What happened?" I asked, my voice thick with sleep and dreams. "How did I get here?"

Gwen gestured at the two swords, who were still bickering about who had woken me up. "Well, from what Babs has told me, your friends rushed you out of the museum and down here. They didn't know if you were going to make it, given your serious wounds, but by the time they got you here, your wounds were gone, like they had magically healed all by themselves. Everyone was quite shocked by that."

I glanced down at my left arm, but the blood and claw marks were gone, and my skin was smooth and whole again. My other wounds had vanished as well.

"I was shocked by it too, until I noticed those runes on your sword."

Gwen pointed over at Babs, who had finally fallen silent, along with Vic. Gwen, Vic, and I all stared at Babs, our gazes dropping to the silvery runes that glimmered on her blade. A red tint tinged her cheek, as if she were embarrassed by the sudden attention.

"What do the runes say?" Gwen asked in a soft voice.

Only a Champion could read the words on her specific weapon. To everyone else, even another Champion like Gwen, the runes would just look like gibberish.

I cleared my throat. "*Devotion is strength.*"

"And what does that mean?" Gwen asked.

"You know that Sigyn is the Norse goddess of devotion."

She nodded.

"After I passed out, I woke up in the Eir Ruins, in the main courtyard with all those wildflowers. The two of us talked. It's the second time she's appeared to me in the last few days."

Gwen's eyes narrowed with understanding. "Sigyn made you her Champion." Then she grinned again. "Well, it's about time."

I hadn't known how Gwen would react to the news, but seeing how happy she was put me at ease. I told her everything that had happened, everything Sigyn had said to me about how my sacrifice had broken Babs's curse and how she needed me to be her Champion to stop Covington and his evil plan.

"Every Champion receives some kind of weapon or magic from their goddess. Sometimes both. What did Sigyn give you?" Gwen asked.

I looked down at my charm bracelet. The winterbloom flower that Sigyn had given me was hanging from the silver links, right next to the heart locket containing the photo of me and my parents. I thought of what Gwen had said about my wounds healing themselves.

"I have a theory. Let's see if I'm right."

I reached over and plucked Babs up off the chair. I held the sword in my left hand and sliced the blade across my right palm. I hissed at the wound, and blood welled up out of the deep cut. But that strange, cool, soothing power I'd felt at the ruins flooded my body, and the wound began to seal itself shut. A moment later, the cut was completely gone, like I'd never sliced open my hand.

"Well," I said. "That looks like healing magic to me."

I set Babs back down in her chair.

"I feel different too. Stronger. Not like Viking or Valkyrie strong but more like my endurance is better and I can fight longer and harder."

"You probably can," Gwen said. "And you know what this means."

"What?"

Her grin widened. "A goddess gifted you with magic, so I'd say that officially makes you a Gypsy girl now. Just like me."

"Nah," I said, grinning back at her. "I'm way cooler than you are."

Gwen laughed at my joke, and I joined in with her chuckles. We sat there for a minute, lost in our own thoughts. Even Babs and Vic remained quiet.

I looked at Gwen again. "What you doing here?" I asked. "The last time we talked, you were still at the North Carolina academy, helping with the cleanup and getting ready for the first day of school."

"Oh, I'm still doing that," Gwen said. "But your Aunt Rachel talked to my Grandma Frost and told her about you joining Team Midgard. She told Grandma about the mission tonight, and I thought you guys might need some backup. I would have been here sooner, but my plane got delayed by bad weather."

I frowned. "You know about the Midgard?"

She nodded. "Of course. Linus keeps Logan and me updated about all the major Protectorate missions. As soon as he said that Takeda was tracking some Reapers near the Colorado academy, I told him they should ask you to join the team."

"So it was your idea for Takeda to recruit me?"

I couldn't keep the disappointment and bitterness out of my voice. I'd thought Takeda had wanted me on the team because I was, well, *me*. Not because I was Gwen's cousin and he wanted to do her and Linus Quinn a favor.

"I might have suggested it, but you totally earned it, Rory," Gwen said, picking up on my thoughts. "All on your own. You're a great warrior, and they're lucky to have you."

I sighed. "Yeah, except for the part where Covington and Drake got away."

She shook her head. "You can't think like that. Sure, they might have escaped, but you kept them from getting their hands on that artifact, and you saved your friends from being killed by those chimeras. Not to mention the fact that you stopped Covington from turning you into a Reaper. That's a definite win in my book."

"It doesn't feel like a win," I muttered.

Sympathy filled Gwen's eyes. "I know. But it *is* a win. So enjoy it as much as you can before the next bad thing happens."

I nodded, telling her that I understood. She was right. It was a win. For now.

Gwen got out of her chair and grabbed a stack of clothes from a table by the door. "Rachel brought these over for you. Get dressed. There are a lot of people waiting to see you." She pointed at my white pajamas. "Unless you want to walk around in those for the rest of the night."

"Yes, ma'am." I snapped off a cheeky salute to her.

Gwen grinned back at me and tossed the clothes onto my lap.

I got dressed in sneakers, jeans, and an *I Love Cloudburst Falls* T-shirt. I also slid Babs into her scabbard and hooked it to my belt before leaving the infirmary room and heading into the main briefing area.

Gwen and Vic were already there, along with the rest of my friends. Zoe, Mateo, Aunt Rachel, Takeda, and Ian. They all jumped to their feet, came over, and hugged me, even Ian, although he quickly dropped his arms from me and stepped back.

"I'm so glad you're okay, Rory," he said.

I smiled at him. "Thanks to you. Although how did you get the gryphons to come to the museum? That was your doing, right?"

"Later," he whispered.

I frowned, wondering what he meant, but Aunt Rachel swallowed me up in another hug, and I didn't have time to ask him any more questions. After a few more hugs, Aunt Rachel finally let me go.

We all sat down at the table, and Takeda looked at me. "I've briefed the others, but you should know that so far, we haven't been able to find Drake or Covington," he said. "There's no sign of them on any of the security or traffic cameras anywhere around the museum. It's like they vanished into thin air."

I nodded. I'd expected as much, but disappointment filled me all the same. "When did Covington escape from prison?"

"It looks like he's been free since the day of the battle at the North Carolina academy," Takeda said.

"How is that possible?" Aunt Rachel said. "He was supposed to be locked away for good. And once he got out, why weren't we notified?"

Takeda shook his head. "From what we've been able to piece together so far, several Reapers worked at the Protectorate prison where he was being kept. They helped him escape. Not only that, but they swapped his paperwork and identification numbers with those of another inmate who was in custody to make it look like Covington was still in prison. We didn't even consider the idea that he might be Sisyphus, because we thought he was still locked away. But don't worry. We're looking for him and Drake right now. They won't get far."

Takeda's lips pinched together, as though he were holding back a grimace, and I could tell that he didn't really believe what he was saying. The Protectorate wouldn't find Drake and Covington. Not until the Reapers decided to strike out at us again.

"Despite their escape, we did keep them from getting away with the artifact," Takeda said. "We recovered the box from the rotunda."

Takeda nodded at Ian, who got up from the table and disappeared among the shelves in the back of the room. A moment later, the Viking returned, carrying the box, which he set down in the middle of the briefing table.

It looked the same as it had in the museum—a jewelry box made of polished jet, with that tangle of sharp silver thorns wrapping around those heart-shaped rubies. And once again, just looking at it made me shiver.

"What is it?" I asked. "What does it do? What's inside it? And why does Covington want it so badly?"

Takeda shook his head again. "We don't know. Some museum officials bought the box at an estate sale a while back, but they don't have any other information about it. They were planning to put it on display with some other items from the sale, which is why it was already sitting out in the rotunda. The Protectorate is searching for more information on it right now. As far as we can tell, there's no way to actually open the box, so we have no idea what might be inside. I was hoping Gwen might help us learn more about it."

He looked at my cousin, silently asking her to use her psychometry magic to see what emotions and memories might be tied to the jewelry box. Gwen nodded, let out a breath, and pushed up the sleeves of her purple hoodie. She stared at the box a moment, then closed her eyes, reached out, and wrapped both of her hands around the artifact.

I held my breath, wondering if she might start muttering or even screaming as the thoughts and feelings of everyone who had ever touched the box washed over her.

Nothing happened.

Gwen didn't scream or yell or even mutter to herself. A minute passed, then two, then three, and still, nothing happened.

She frowned, opened her eyes, and stared at the box. She touched it again, and then again, running her hands all over the surface, frowning all the while.

"What's wrong?" Aunt Rachel asked.

Gwen shook her head. "I'm not getting any vibes from it. Nothing at all. Not a single flash of emotion or memory. Not so much as a single image of someone picking up the box, much less putting something inside it. It's like my psychometry magic isn't working on it at all. That's never happened to me before. *Never*."

She looked at me, and I could see the worry filling her violet eyes.

"Well, then, I guess it's a good thing that Covington didn't get away with it," Zoe said.

"Yeah," Mateo added. "That dude is scary enough all by himself."

We all stared at the jewelry box, wondering what secrets it might contain, but we wouldn't get those answers tonight. By this point, it was after midnight, and Takeda told us all to go home, get some sleep, and take the rest of the weekend off.

"You've earned it," he said. "Especially you, Rory."

Takeda bowed his head to me, and I returned the gesture. Everyone got to their feet and started collecting their things. One by one, the others headed out of the briefing room and toward the elevator that would take them back up to the main part of the library. Takeda left the box where it was on the table, and I found myself glancing back over my shoulder at it.

Once again, the black box seemed to absorb all the light in the room, instead of reflecting it back. The silver vines gleamed sharp and bright, and the ruby hearts almost looked like red Reaper eyes, staring at me.

I didn't have Gwen's psychometry magic, but somehow I knew that the box—and whatever was inside—was extremely dangerous. And that sooner or later, Covington would try to take it away and use it against us.

I shivered, turned away from the box, and left the Bunker.

CHAPTER TWENTY-NINE

I rode the elevator up to the second floor of the library. Aunt Rachel and Gwen were standing there waiting for me—and so was Ian.

He pushed away from the wall, straightened up, and walked over to me. "Can I talk to you for a few minutes? There's something I want to show you."

"Sure." I looked over at Aunt Rachel and Gwen. "I'll see you guys at home."

Aunt Rachel nodded, turned around, and headed for the stairs. Gwen glanced back and forth between Ian and me, her lips curving up into a knowing smile. I rolled my eyes and made a small shooing motion with my hand. Her smile widened, but she followed Aunt Rachel down the stairs.

"Come on," Ian said. "This way."

I followed him. To my surprise, he led me over to the stairs, and we climbed them all the way up to the library roof. Ian opened the access door and stepped back.

"There's someone here who wants to see you," he said.

Brono was waiting on the roof.

I rushed over to the baby gryphon, wrapped my arms around his neck, and buried my face in his soft wings.

"Thank you," I whispered. "Thank you so much for saving me."

The baby gryphon head-butted me. I laughed and started scratching his head. Brono let out a snort of pleasure and leaned into my touch. I kept petting the gryphon and looked over at Ian.

"It *was* you, wasn't it?" I asked. "Everyone else thinks it was luck. Or that the gryphons somehow sensed the chimeras and came to help us. But it was you. Somehow you got the gryphons to come to the museum. Didn't you?"

Ian grinned, the expression lighting up his entire face. "Guilty as charged."

"How did you do it?"

"I knew we wouldn't be able to open the gate in time," he said, coming over and stroking Brono's wings. "And I thought about the gryphons. I saw how much you loved them and how much they loved you that night they flew us to the Eir Ruins. I knew that if I could get them to come to the museum, they would save you from the chimeras. That they were the only ones who could save you. And then I remembered that artifact we had seen in another room."

I'd thought Ian had been holding a whistle in the rotunda earlier. "Pan's Whistle. The artifact that lets you summon mythological creatures."

He nodded. "So I ran back to that exhibit room, smashed the case, and grabbed the whistle. Then I thought about the gryphons and started using the whistle. I wasn't sure it would actually work. I blew and blew on it, but I didn't hear anything."

"But it did work, because the gryphons heard it, and they came to the museum."

Ian nodded again, then reached into his jacket pocket and held his hand out to me. Pan's Whistle glimmered in his palm. I stared at the silver whistle, once again marveling at how tiny it was and how something so small could have such great power. But it had saved my life tonight.

Ian had saved my life tonight.

He looked at the whistle, as if he couldn't quite believe that he still had it—or that he'd taken it in the first place.

I arched an eyebrow. "Stealing an artifact from the museum? That's not like you, Viking. Not at all. You're such a straight arrow. Always following the rules. You've probably never stolen anything in your life, especially not an artifact."

He gave me a sheepish grin. "I know. But Drake and Covington have artifacts, and I figured that as long as they have the chimera scepter, it wouldn't hurt for us to have some backup too. Or, rather, you."

I blinked. "Me?"

"You're the one who's best friends with the gryphons," Ian said. "Besides, the whistle is small enough to fit on your charm bracelet. That way, you can carry it with you all the time. I asked Zoe, and she agreed with me. She even made a tiny clasp to hook it to your bracelet. May I?"

I nodded and held out my arm. Ian stepped forward, towering over me. He undid the clasp on the whistle and gently slid it through a link on my bracelet, close to the heart locket with my parents' picture inside. So many emotions surged through me. Admiration that he'd so cleverly used the whistle. Gratitude that he'd saved my life. And that dizzying, dizzying sensation that made me feel like I was falling and flying all at the same time.

His fingers lingered on my wrist. I wondered if he could feel how fast my pulse was racing right now—and I wondered if his was racing in return.

Ian snapped the clasp shut. "There you go," he said, his voice rough with emotion. "Now, anytime you need to summon the gryphons, all you have to do is grab the whistle off your bracelet, and they'll find you, wherever you are."

"Thank you for this," I said in a soft voice.

He shook his head. "No, thank *you*. You saved us all tonight. Zoe, Mateo, me. We all would have been mauled to death by the chimeras if you hadn't sacrificed yourself to save us. I'm sorry that I ever doubted you. You are a true hero, Rory."

"So are you, Ian. So are you."

We stared at each other. Ian dipped his head, as though he might lean forward and kiss me. I swayed closer to him, suddenly wanting that more than anything. But at the last second, he bit his lip and looked away, as though he'd lost his nerve. He stepped back, and the moment passed.

Ian cleared his throat. "I have something else for you. It's over here."

We walked to the corner of the roof, where a green pot sat on the stone railing. A small white flower stood straight and tall in the center of the rich, dark soil.

"That's the winterbloom I picked for you at the Eir Ruins. I found it in my pocket the next day. It seemed like it was still alive, so I put it in this pot. I've been watering it for the past few days, and I think it's going to make it." Ian cleared his throat again. "You told me how pretty you thought the winterbloom was, so I'd like you to have it."

Emotion clogged my throat at his thoughtfulness, and I reached out and stroked one of the soft white petals. The single blossom was one of the most beautiful things I'd ever seen, and I knew I would keep it forever. In a way, it was even more precious than the winterbloom charm Sigyn had given me.

"Thank you," I rasped. "Thank you so much for this. For everything."

"It's nothing."

"It's not nothing—it's *amazing*."

And it truly, truly was. I smiled at Ian, trying to let him see how much this meant to me, how much *he* meant to me. An answering smile spread across his face, and the emotion in his gray gaze took my breath away. He stepped closer to me, and once again, I found myself swaying closer to him. And closer...and closer...

Brono snorted, upset that we'd stopped petting him, and wormed his way between Ian and me. But I didn't mind—too much. I had a feeling there would be other nights, other moments, just like this one.

Ian and I looked at each other, laughed, and started scratching the gryphon's head. And we stayed there on the roof, petting the gryphon and enjoying the quiet of each other's company, for a long, long time.

Despite my new healing magic, the fight with the chimeras had taken a lot out of me, and I slept most of the next day, between hanging out with Gwen and Zoe. Monday morning rolled around all too soon, and I begrudgingly got up, took a shower, and got dressed for school.

By the time I stumbled into the kitchen, Aunt Rachel and Gwen had already eaten, but they sat with me while I inhaled two plates of peach waffles and hash browns, along with loads of bacon. Once again, we talked about everything that had happened at the museum, but none of us had any new ideas about how to open the jewelry box, what was inside it, or why Covington wanted it so badly.

"Takeda texted me," Aunt Rachel said. "He'd like the two of us to meet with him and the others in the library this afternoon after classes."

I nodded. Now that Team Midgard had foiled the Reapers' plot to steal the box, Takeda and the others would be going back to the New York academy like they'd planned. The thought made me sadder than I'd thought possible.

Gwen got to her feet, picked up her gray messenger bag from the floor, and slung it over her shoulder. "I should be going too. Walk me out, Rory?"

Gwen hugged Aunt Rachel good-bye. Then the two of us stepped out onto the front porch. Gwen looked out over the rolling hills, the thickets of pine trees, and the mountain towering above it all. A strange look filled her eyes, as though she were seeing something that was very far away. I wondered what she was thinking about, but I didn't want to be rude and ask.

Finally, she turned to me. "I'm going back to the North Carolina academy."

I'd expected that, but I still tried to talk her out of it. "So soon? Why? You just got here."

"There's still a lot of work to be done cleaning up campus," she said. "And now that we know that Covington and his Reapers are targeting artifacts, I'm sure that Nickamedes will want to increase security at our Library of Antiquities. Just in case the Reapers decide to strike there again and try to steal more artifacts."

I hesitated. "But I thought you might stick around here for a while."

Gwen smiled at me, understanding flashing in her eyes. "I've done my part to stop Loki and the Reapers. I'm ready for a little peace and quiet. But more important, Covington is your enemy, Rory, and this is your fight now. Sigyn picked you to be her Champion because she believes in you, and I do too. You're the best warrior for this battle, and I think you know that, deep down inside."

She was right. I did know that deep down inside. But I was so used to living in the shadow of Gwen Frost, legendary Gypsy girl and warrior supreme, even when she wasn't around, that I wasn't quite sure how to step out into the light. But I knew I would find my way. I'd come this far, and I was eager for the next step—artifacts, Reapers, battles, and all.

"Thank you," I said. "For believing in me."

I held my arms open. Gwen stepped into my embrace, and we hugged for several long moments before breaking apart.

Vic's violet eye snapped open, and he let out a wide yawn from his scabbard on Gwen's belt. "Well, I, for one, am glad all that mushy nonsense is over with. Besides, we need to go home and check on the fuzzball. I bet she's chewed up all of your sneakers by now for being left behind."

I laughed, knowing he was referring to Nyx, the Fenrir wolf pup Gwen was taking care of.

But Babs wasn't to be outdone. Her scabbard was attached to my belt, and her emerald-green eye snapped open as well.

"Oh, sure," she told Vic. "Run away when things are getting interesting, and leave me to fight the Reapers all by myself."

Vic glared at her. "I've killed more Reapers than you've ever dreamed of, you cursed bit of metal."

Babs's eye narrowed. "I most certainly am *not* cursed. At least, not anymore. You take that back, you tarnished piece of tin!"

And so it began, with the two swords trading insults, each claiming that they were the best weapon ever and had killed far more Reapers than the other sword could ever hope to.

Gwen and I looked at each other and laughed.

With all the craziness of Mythos Academy, it was comforting to know that some things—especially talking swords—would never, ever change.

CHAPTER THIRTY

Gwen left to take a cab to the airport, while I went
back inside the cottage, grabbed my messenger bag,
and headed off to my first class of the morning.

I walked across the main quad, listening to the
conversations around me. Of course, all the other kids were
talking about the Fall Costume Ball, who had brought
whom, who had hooked up, and who had broken up. A few
of them mentioned seeing several guys in vampire and
skeleton costumes running around the museum, but they'd
thought those guys were just goofing off. Once again, the
Protectorate had managed to keep everything quiet. As far
as the other kids knew, nothing important had happened at
the ball besides the usual teenage angst and drama. That
was probably for the best.

I slogged through my morning classes and headed to the
dining hall for lunch, but Zoe, Mateo, and Ian never came
in to get something to eat. They were all probably in their
dorm rooms, busy packing up their things to head back to
the New York academy.

More sadness filled me at the thought, but I pushed it
away as best I could and made it through the rest of my

classes. Still, my heart was heavy as I headed over to the Library of Antiquities and rode the secret elevator down to the Bunker. The others had already gathered in the briefing room.

I stood in the doorway and watched them all. Takeda pacing back and forth, murmuring into his cell phone. Aunt Rachel sitting at the briefing table, flipping through one of her recipe books, working on the dining-hall menus. Zoe at her desk, fiddling with different-colored wires and attaching them to some new weapon she was creating. Mateo noshing on potato chips and typing away like mad on his laptop. Ian sharpening his battle ax.

Another wave of sadness washed over me. I was going to miss this. I was going to miss *them.*

But I plastered a smile on my face and stepped into the briefing room, throwing my messenger bag down on the table and propping up Babs in the chair next to mine.

"Hey, guys," I drawled. "What's up?"

"Oh, you know," Zoe said, still working on her project. "Just sitting here being awesome."

"Ditto," Mateo called out, never taking his gaze from his laptop.

"Yep," Ian chimed in, still sharpening his ax.

"Well, count me in on that," I said, sitting down.

My charm bracelet clinked against the table, and the heart locket, the winterbloom, and the whistle tinkled together like tiny wind chimes. Ian looked up at the sound and grinned. I winked back at him. Oh, I knew Takeda would realize that I had Pan's Whistle sooner or later. He might already know. But for now, I liked sharing this little secret with Ian.

It would be the last thing we would share before he and the others left for good.

Takeda finished his call and sat down at the table. The others all stopped what they were doing, moved over, and took their usual seats.

He cleared his throat. "Unfortunately, there haven't been any sightings of Drake or Covington. We still have people out searching, but it looks like they've gone underground. Ian, Rory, I'm sorry I don't have better news for you."

Ian shrugged, and so did I. Drake and Covington were both experienced Reapers. I didn't think it would be easy to catch them. Disappointment rippled through me, but I knew the members of the Protectorate were working as hard as possible to find them.

"I just got off the phone with Linus Quinn, and I do have a bit of good news for everyone," Takeda said. "At least, I hope you will all think it's good news. I certainly do." He paused, looking at each of us in turn.

Zoe rolled her eyes. "What is it? Enough with the dramatic pause, already."

Takeda's lips curved up into a tiny smile. "Well, as you all know, we were going to go back to the New York academy after this mission."

I sat up a little straighter in my chair, and so did everyone else. Even Babs perked up. Well, as much as she could.

"But now?" Ian asked.

"But the mission isn't over. Given the situation with Drake and Covington, especially Covington's interest in Rory, we're staying here," Takeda said. "Linus has given me permission to make this our home base for the foreseeable future. I hope you're okay with that, Miss Forseti."

He raised his eyebrows at me, and I grinned back at him.

"Does this mean I'm officially part of the Midgard?" I asked. "No more temporary status?"

"It does," Takeda said. "If you'll have us."

I looked at Zoe and Mateo and finally at Ian. "I would be honored to fight alongside all of you."

Zoe hooted and hollered, while Mateo gave me a shy smile. I nodded at them both, then turned to Ian. He grinned, his gray eyes glimmering like polished silver in his face.

"Welcome to the team, cupcake," he murmured.

"That's Spartan to you," I replied. "And I'm happy to be here, Viking. Happy to be here."

Takeda looked at all of us, including Aunt Rachel. His gaze lingered on her a moment, and she stared back at him. Takeda cleared his throat and passed out thick folders of papers and photos to everyone.

"We might not have found Drake and Covington yet, but we've started a database of all known artifacts. If we can pinpoint which items they are going after next, we might be able to catch them…"

Takeda ran down what he thought our next steps should be in our search for the Reapers, but I found myself staring at my friends again, then over at Babs. The runes carved into her blade glinted under the lights, and I read the words glimmering there.

Devotion is strength.

And I realized something. Friends were strength too, the best kind of strength there was—not to mention love, hope, and happiness.

Gwen was right. Sigyn had picked me to be her Champion for a reason, and I finally knew what that reason was. To protect my new friends from all the awful things the Reapers were going to throw at us.

This was my battle now, and it was one that I was happy to be a part of. Today, tomorrow, and as long as it took to defeat Drake, Covington, and all the other Reapers.

So I looked at my friends again, then settled in my seat and turned my attention back to Takeda.

I was ready to fight.

Excerpt from

MYTHOS ACADEMY

spinoff book #2 featuring Rory Forseti

COMING SOON

JENNIFER
ESTEP

CHAPTER ONE

"I hate field trips."

I looked at my friend Zoe Wayland. "Why would you say that?"

She shrugged. "Because field trips always end in disaster."

"And why would you say *that*? Field trips are awesome. They're a break from the regular old boring school routine. A chance to leave campus, go somewhere new, and see lots of cool stuff. And best of all, an excuse to miss all the classes we don't like."

Zoe snorted. "Maybe for you, Spartan. But for me, field trips are always a pain."

"Why?"

Instead of answering me, Zoe picked up a pair of pliers from the desk in front of her. She fiddled with the pliers for a few seconds before setting them down and grabbing a hammer instead. Screwdrivers, wrenches, even a small blowtorch. All those tools and more crowded together on one side of her desk, along with swords, daggers, and a couple of arrows. Zoe was a genius when it came to inventions, and she loved creating weapons and gadgets for

Team Midgard to use in our fight against the Reapers of Chaos.

One by one, Zoe picked up the tools and weapons, along with odd bits of metal and piles of twisted wires, as though she were trying to straighten out the jumble, but then she set them right back down where they had been before.

Every time she grabbed something, pale blue sparks of magic streamed out of her fingertips before winking out. Valkyries always gave off more magic when they were upset or emotional. Zoe would tell me what was bothering her when she was ready.

But she wasn't ready yet, and she scooted over and started fiddling with the scissors, ribbons, and bolts of cloth on the other side of her desk, since she loved making clothes and jewelry as much as she did weapons and gadgets. Zoe grabbed a clear plastic box full of red heart-shaped crystals, which she used to embellish some of her designs. She shook the box, making the crystals inside rattle around, before setting the container back down on her desk.

Finally, she sighed and raised her hazel gaze to mine. "I hate field trips because I have an annoying tendency to get carsick whenever I go on one."

I raised my eyebrows. "Carsick?"

She slumped down in her chair. "Well, more like bus sick. I don't know why, but every time I get on a bus to go on some stupid field trip, I always get sick and have to throw up before we get to our destination. Just ask Mateo. I puked all over his boots when we went to the Powder ski resort last year. Everyone on the bus saw me literally lose my lunch. It was *so* embarrassing."

"Well, then it's a good thing that this isn't a field trip and that we aren't taking a bus."

"Oh, no," Zoe said sarcastically. "We're going to explore some creepy old tunnels that run underneath Mythos Academy, the school of warrior kids, mythological monsters, and artifacts that summon mythological monsters. What could possibly go wrong?"

I rolled my eyes. "Oh, come on. Where is your sense of adventure?"

She sighed again and slid even farther down in her chair.

I turned my attention back to my own desk, making sure that I had everything for our so-called field trip. A flashlight, a digital camera, a notebook, several pens, a couple of bottles of water, and some chocolate chip cookies. Okay, okay, it was probably overkill to bring snacks, but Zoe was right. You never knew what might happen at Mythos Academy, and if we did get stuck in the tunnels, I didn't want to starve before someone rescued us.

I wasn't the only one who might be thirsty, so I cracked open one of the bottles and poured a healthy amount of water into a small green pot on my desk that contained a beautiful flower with delicate white petals and a heart-shaped emerald-green blossom in the center. The winterbloom perked up as the water soaked into the soil, and it spread its petals wide, as if it were thanking me.

"There you go," I cooed, and stroked one of its velvety petals. "There's some water for you."

"Have I told you how weird it is that you talk to that flower?" Zoe snarked.

"Don't listen to her," I said, still speaking to the flower. "She's just jealous that she doesn't have anything as pretty as you on her desk."

The winterbloom stood up even taller with pride. I stroked its petals a final time, then capped my water bottle.

Once I had stuffed all my supplies into my green

messenger bag, I glanced around, making sure I hadn't forgotten anything. Zoe and I were in the main briefing room in the Bunker, beneath the Library of Antiquities on the Mythos Academy campus in Snowline Ridge, Colorado. Few people knew of the Bunker's existence, since it was the supersecret headquarters of the Midgard, a team of students and adults who had been tasked with battling a new group of Reapers.

A long rectangular table dominated one side of the room, and all the seats were facing the monitors that took up most of one wall. Zoe's desk was off to one side of the center table, along with mine, while two more desks sat on the opposite side of the table.

One of those desks featured a laptop, along with a couple of keyboards and monitors. Several miniature foam footballs, soccer balls, and tennis balls were stuffed between all the computer equipment. That desk belonged to Mateo Solis, the Roman who was the Midgard's computer guru and another one of our friends.

Battle axes, swords, and other weapons covered the second desk, along with myth-history books with sticky notes on their pages to mark certain passages. That spot belonged to Ian Hunter, the Viking who was the team's warrior muscle, in addition to yours truly.

My gaze moved to the back half of the room, which had several rows of floor-to-ceiling shelves. Books lined many of the shelves, but they weren't your normal paperbacks and hardcovers. No, these volumes were all extremely old, with worn pages, tattered covers, and frayed spines. Many of the books looked like they would disintegrate into dust if you pulled them off the shelves, much less tried to open and read them, but the books—and the knowledge they contained—were far more dangerous than they appeared.

As were all the other artifacts here.

Weapons, armor, jewelry, clothing, and more sat on the shelves next to all those old books. Golden swords, silver shields, diamond rings, bronze sandals. Each artifact was more beautiful than the last and had some magic that made it very, very powerful.

Like the Gauntlets of Maat, named after the Egyptian goddess of truth. Once the gold gauntlets were placed on your arms, you couldn't take them off, and you had to answer truthfully any question you were asked. Oh, you could try to resist the artifact's magic, but for every lie you told, the gauntlets would heat up a little more, until they finally erupted into flames and burned you alive.

And that was just one of dozens of objects that would burn, freeze, or otherwise torture you to death. Not to mention all the artifacts that would make you see monsters that weren't really there or fall in love with someone you hated or otherwise mess with your mind and heart so badly that you lost all your free will.

I leaned to the side and peered down one of the aisles at the shelf along the back wall. My gaze locked on a glass case sitting all by itself. Unlike other warriors, I didn't have enhanced eyesight, so I couldn't see it clearly from here, but I knew exactly what that case contained: a jewelry box made of polished jet, with silver vines running across the top and wrapping around small, heart-shaped ruby flowers.

The Midgard had recovered the jewelry box from the Cormac Museum a few weeks ago. We had kept Covington, the Reaper leader, from stealing the artifact, but we still didn't have any idea what it was, what magic it might have, or what it might contain. Still, something about the box seriously creeped me out. Just looking in its direction made me shiver, and I wondered what was so special about the artifact that Covington had been willing to kill to get it—

"Well, I, for one, am looking forward to our adventure, Rory." A voice with a lilting Irish accent cut into my thoughts.

I looked at the chair to my right. A silver sword sheathed in a black leather scabbard was propped up in the seat, but it wasn't your average weapon. No, this sword had a woman's face inlaid into the hilt, complete with a delicate eyebrow, a round bulge of an eye, a pointed cheekbone, a sharp, hooked nose, heart-shaped lips, and a curved chin. The sword focused on me, and I stared into her deep, dark, emerald-green eye.

"Thank you, Babs," I said. "It's nice to see that someone around here is excited about mapping the tunnels."

Zoe snorted. "Babs is your sword. She goes where you go, so she has to be excited about everything you do, including exploring dusty old tunnels."

Babs sniffed. "Don't listen to her, Rory. It will be grand fun to map the tunnels. Why, it reminds me of a time years ago in Cypress Mountain, when one of my previous warriors was tracking a Fenrir wolf through the forest…"

And she was off, talking about that long-ago adventure. Babs liked to, well, babble. I thought it was an endearing quirk, but Zoe gave me a pointed look, grabbed a silver dagger off her desk, and pressed in on the blue stone set into the hilt, making blue-white sparks of electricity sizzle up and down the blade. Zoe gave me another pointed look, silently telling me that she was going to zap Babs with her electrodagger if the sword didn't pipe down.

"All right," I said, cutting into Babs's story. "I'm ready. How about you guys?"

"Ready!" Babs chirped.

Zoe sighed again, but she got to her feet. She grabbed a glittery blue headband from the mess on her desk and used it to push her wavy black hair back from her face. Then she grabbed a compact from the jumble of items and dabbed a bit of powder on her nose, even though her lovely mocha skin was already flawless. For a final touch, she zipped up the blue coveralls she was wearing over her regular clothes. Red crystal hearts spelled out the words *Valkyrie Power* on the left side.

"Ready," she muttered.

I eyed her heavy-duty coveralls. "We're walking through the tunnels and mapping them. Not digging through the walls."

Zoe slapped her hands on her hips, and more blue sparks of magic streamed out of her fingertips. "And I am not taking a chance on getting my new cashmere sweater dirty or getting cobwebs all over my jeans. Got it, Spartan?"

"Got it, Valkyrie." I grinned. "Now, let's get on with our field trip."

She groaned. "You just had to call it that, didn't you? Now you've jinxed us."

"Just don't puke on my boots, and we'll be fine," I teased.

Zoe gave me a dark look and brandished her electrodagger at me, but her lips curved up into a sheepish smile. I grinned back at her.

Whatever happened, she would always be my friend.

I slung my bag of supplies over my shoulder and hooked Babs's scabbard to my belt, while Zoe stuffed her electrodagger into her pocket. Then the two of us left the briefing room and walked through a long hallway until we reached the back of the Bunker.

A door was marked with a sign that read *Stairs*, but instead of opening the door and going up the stairs, I went over to a bookcase along the wall and pressed a small silver button on the side of it. A green light flashed, scanning my thumbprint. A few seconds later, the light vanished, and the bookcase creaked back, revealing a stone passageway.

Excitement surged through me. I had always loved all kinds of mysteries, like the Nancy Drew books, the Sherlock Holmes adventures, and the old Scooby-Doo cartoons, but my absolute favorites were stories that featured things like secret passages and hidden compartments. Ever since I found out about the tunnels that ran underneath the academy, I had been itching to explore them. Today I'd finally roped Zoe into coming with me.

Zoe peered into the tunnel. "I still can't believe you want to waste a perfectly good Sunday afternoon tromping through these creepy tunnels. I could be taking a nap. Inventing a new weapon. Binge-watching a fantasy show. You know, something *fun*."

"This will be plenty of fun. Besides, it's not only about exploring the tunnels." I pulled a pen and a notebook out of my bag. "It's also about mapping them. I want to know where every single tunnel goes and where all the secret entrances are all over campus."

"Why? It's not like the other Mythos kids know about the tunnels. The Midgard—we—are the only ones who know they exist."

"Covington probably knows about them," I said in a sharp voice. "Which means that I need to know about them too."

Zoe winced at my harsh tone, but sympathy and understanding filled her face.

Covington used to be the head librarian at the Colorado academy, until he had revealed himself to be a Reaper of Chaos. As if that wasn't bad enough, Covington had also murdered my parents, Rebecca and Tyson Forseti, when they had tried to leave the Reapers.

I had been so angry at my parents for hiding their involvement in the evil group, for never telling me that they were Reaper assassins, and especially for not being the noble, honest Spartan warriors I'd always thought they were. But finding out that Covington had killed my parents and blamed them for his crimes was a hundred times worse. He had taken them away from me before I'd had chance to ask them why they had been Reapers and why they had done all those horrible things.

I had thought that Covington was locked away in prison until a few weeks ago, when I discovered that he was the mysterious Sisyphus, the leader of a new group of Reapers who were determined to take over the mythological world. Covington had tried to get me to join him, to become a Reaper. He had claimed it was my destiny as a Spartan warrior. When I had refused, he had used an artifact—a jeweled Apate ring—to try to turn me into a Reaper against my will. With Babs's help, I had managed to fight off the artifact's magic. But the most surprising thing was that my parents had helped me too, even though they were dead and buried.

I shook my arm, and a silver charm bracelet slid down my right wrist. A silver heart locket dangled from the chain, along with two other charms—a tiny silver whistle and a silver winterbloom with a heart-shaped emerald center.

My parents had given me the bracelet for my sixteenth birthday last year, and the heart locket contained a picture of the three of us. I had loved the gift and had worn the bracelet every single day—until I found out that my parents were Reapers. I had been so angry and heartbroken by their betrayal that I'd torn off the bracelet and thrown it down on their graves, although my Aunt Rachel had eventually given it back to me.

I had started wearing the bracelet again when I joined Team Midgard, as a reminder that I didn't have to be a Reaper and that I had the free will to choose my own path in life. But my parents had had another secret. They hadn't told me that the bracelet was actually Freya's Bracelet, a powerful artifact that protected the wearer from other people's magic. It had saved me from Covington and his foul ring. Covington might have murdered my parents, but they had still protected me from him as best they could. I would always be grateful to them for that.

I closed my eyes and concentrated on the cold feel of the bracelet around my wrist, like a ring of snow kissing my skin. I let that coldness seep into my mind and especially into my heart, until it iced over my hurt and rage that Covington was still out there, plotting against me and Team Midgard. I *would* hunt down the librarian and get my revenge on him, but today wasn't going to be that day, and I had to accept that. When I felt calmer, I opened my eyes and looked at Zoe again.

"Covington was the head librarian here for a long time," I said in a quieter voice. "Linus Quinn and Takeda don't think he knows about the Bunker or the tunnels, but I don't want to take a chance that he does. It would be just like Covington to use the tunnels to try to sneak into the Bunker to steal the jewelry box and other artifacts. I want to be ready for all the twisted things he might dream up, and mapping the tunnels is one way to prepare."

More understanding and sympathy filled Zoe's face, and blue sparks of magic dripped out of her fingertips like tears, almost as if her Valkyrie magic were crying at my obvious pain.

"I agree with Rory," Babs piped up from her spot on my belt. "It wouldn't hurt to map the tunnels and see where they lead. Besides, it will be fun. Why, it reminds me of the time I was in the Ashland sewers, chasing after a nasty Nemean prowler..."

The sword started babbling about another adventure she'd had, but Zoe and I tuned her out.

"Please," I said in a soft voice. "I have to do this. Even if mapping the tunnels seems silly and pointless, I have to do *something* other than sit around and wait for Covington to strike. Otherwise, I'll go crazy."

She nodded. "All you had to do was ask." Zoe zipped up her coveralls a little higher and held out her hand. "Give me your camera. I'll take photos while you do your whole treasure map, X-marks-the-spot thing."

I grinned and passed her the camera. Then, together, we stepped into the tunnel.

The bookcase swung shut behind us, and for a moment, everything was pitch-black. I took a step forward, and lights clicked on in the stone ceiling. The motion-activated lights turned on as we approached and clicked off as we moved past them. We walked about fifty feet before another tunnel branched off to our right. I stopped and made the appropriate X on my map.

One by one, we went down all the tunnels to see where they went. Five main tunnels led to the five major buildings on the Mythos quad aboveground—math-science, English-history, the dining hall, and the gym. And, of course, the tunnel we had started out in led back to the Bunker and the Library of Antiquities, the fifth and final building on the quad.

Each tunnel ended in a door, and I pressed the silver button on each one, using my thumbprint to open them and see where we had ended up. I already knew that the gym tunnel opened up into Takeda's office, since he had brought us that way before, but the other secret entrances surprised me. A supply closet in the math-science building, a study room in the English-history building, a broken freezer in the dining-hall kitchen.

By the time we'd finished with the five main tunnels, all sorts of lines, squiggles, and Xs covered my map, and I found myself humming a happy tune.

"You are having way too much fun with this," Zoe groused.

I grinned. She rolled her eyes, but she raised her camera and snapped a photo of me.

Several more secondary tunnels branched off from the five main ones, leading away from the quad and farther out onto campus. We mapped those as well. The tunnels snaked all over the grounds and opened up in all sorts of places—the girls' dorms, the boys' dorms, storage sheds full of landscaping and other equipment. One tunnel even opened up in a stand of trees not too far away from the cottage where I lived with Aunt Rachel. I felt like we were exploring some cool underground spider's web, and I couldn't wait to see where the next tunnel led.

Two hours later, we had mapped all the tunnels and secret entrances, except for a particularly long passageway that left campus and ran all the way over to the town of Snowline Ridge. I wanted to keep going to see where that tunnel led, but Zoe was grumbling about all the walking we'd done, so we headed back to the Bunker instead.

We stepped into what I considered the center of the spider's web, a large junction with the five main tunnels running out to the different sections of the quad. Zoe was in front of me, and she rounded the corner and stepped into the tunnel that would take us back to the library. She looked over her shoulder and opened her mouth, probably to say how glad she was that we were finally stopping, but she tripped over something, staggered forward, and bounced off one of the walls. Her legs flew out from under her, and she sat down hard.

"Zoe! Are you okay?" I rushed over to her.

"I'm fine," she said. "Nothing bruised but my pride. Help me up, please."

She took my hand, and I hauled her to her feet. Zoe glanced around, and her gaze landed on a pile of loose bricks sitting beside one of the walls.

"Stupid bricks," she muttered.

Zoe lashed out with her boot, and one of the bricks disintegrated into shards. Zoe didn't think she had strength magic like other Valkyries did, but I thought she was far more powerful than she realized.

I crouched down and stared at the pile of bricks. "Looks like someone deliberately chipped these bricks out of the wall. See how the mortar is all scraped away from them?"

"Why would someone pull bricks out of a wall?" Babs asked.

"Maybe because they wanted to hide something behind it," I replied.

"Hidden treasure?" Zoe perked up. "Now, *that* would be cool."

My heart started pounding with excitement. Discovering someone's hidden treasure would be the *perfect* way to end our exploring. I unhooked Babs's scabbard from my belt and propped the sword against the wall so she could see what was going on. I didn't have Zoe's Valkyrie strength, but the bricks weren't all that heavy, and I moved them out of the way, revealing a dark space about the size of a large book. Then I leaned down, shone my flashlight into the hole, and realized...that it was nothing but an empty space.

I moved the light back and forth, but nothing was in the wall. It was an empty, hollow space, with no hidden treasure of any kind. Disappointment rippled through me. I sighed, but I grabbed the bricks and stacked them back into the wall so they would be out of the way and we wouldn't trip over them again.

I had just slid the last brick into place when a loud *creak* sounded in the distance.

In an instant, I was on my feet and standing next to Zoe.

"Did you hear that?" she whispered.

I nodded, and we peered down the tunnels, trying to figure out where the sound had come from.

"Hey!" a low voice called out. "Down there!"

At least that's what I thought the voice said. The weird echoes in the tunnels bounced back on each other and garbled everything together, making it hard to figure out the exact words, much less who the voice belonged to. Still, I couldn't help but think that my dire prediction from earlier had already come true and that Covington was here. That he knew about the tunnels and was going to use them to sneak into the Bunker and steal artifacts, specifically the jewelry box.

A series of loud, steady *thump-thump-thump-thumps* rang out, confirming my suspicions. I might not have been able to make out the garbled words, but I recognized those sounds. Footsteps, and more than one set.

Other people were in the tunnels—and they were coming this way.

About the Author

Jennifer Estep is a *New York Times*, *USA Today*, and international bestselling author, prowling the streets of her imagination in search of her next fantasy idea. She is the author of the following series:

The Mythos Academy spinoff series: The books focus on Rory Forseti, a 17-year-old Spartan girl who attends the Colorado branch of Mythos Academy. Rory's parents were Reapers, which makes her the most hated girl at school. But with a new group of Reapers and mythological monsters on the rise, Rory is the only one who can save her academy.

The Mythos Academy series: The books focus on Gwen Frost, a 17-year-old Gypsy girl who has the gift of psychometry, or the ability to know an object's history just by touching it. After a serious freak-out with her magic, Gwen is shipped off to Mythos Academy, a school for the descendants of ancient warriors like Spartans, Valkyries, Amazons, and more.

The Elemental Assassin series: The books focus on Gin Blanco, an assassin codenamed the Spider who can control the elements of Ice and Stone. When she's not busy battling bad guys and righting wrongs, Gin runs a barbecue restaurant called the Pork Pit in the fictional Southern metropolis of

Ashland. The city is also home to giants, dwarves, vampires, and elementals—Air, Fire, Ice, and Stone.

The Crown of Shards series: The books focus on Everleigh Blair, a member of the royal family who is distantly in line for the throne of Bellona, a kingdom steeped in gladiator tradition. But when the unthinkable happens, Evie finds herself fighting for her life—both inside and outside the gladiator arena.

The Bigtime series: The books take place in Bigtime, New York, a city that's full of heroic superheroes, evil ubervillains, and other fun, zany, larger-than-life characters. Each book focuses on a different heroine as she navigates through the city's heroes and villains and their various battles.

The Black Blade series: The books focus on Lila Merriweather, a 17-year-old thief who lives in Cloudburst Falls, West Virginia, a town dubbed "the most magical place in America." Lila does her best to stay off the grid and avoid the Families—or mobs—who control much of the town. But when she saves a member of the Sinclair Family during an attack, Lila finds herself caught in the middle of a brewing war between the Sinclairs and the Draconis, the two most powerful Families in town.

For more information on Jennifer and her books, visit her website at www.JenniferEstep.com. You can also follow her on Facebook, Goodreads, and Twitter, and sign up for her newsletter on her website.

Happy reading, everyone!

Other Books
by Jennifer Estep

E-novellas
Thread of Death
Parlor Tricks (from the Carniepunk anthology)
Kiss of Venom
Unwanted
Nice Guys Bite

THE CROWN OF SHARDS SERIES

Kill the Queen

THE BIGTIME SERIES

Karma Girl
Hot Mama
Jinx
A Karma Girl Christmas (holiday story)
Nightingale
Fandemic

THE BLACK BLADE SERIES

Cold Burn of Magic
Dark Heart of Magic
Bright Blaze of Magic